LOVING

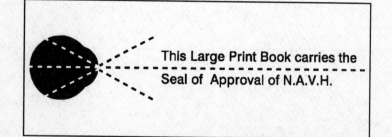

This Large Print Book carries the
Seal of Approval of N.A.V.H.

LOVING

KAREN KINGSBURY

THORNDIKE PRESS

A part of Gale, Cengage Learning

GALE
CENGAGE Learning·

Detroit • New York • San Francisco • New Haven, Conn • Waterville, Maine • London

GALE
CENGAGE Learning

LIBRARY OF CONGRESS CATALOGING-IN-PUBLICATION DATA

Loving / by Karen Kingsbury.
   pages ; cm. — (Thorndike Press large print Christian
fiction) (Bailey Flanigan series ; #4)
   ISBN 978-1-4104-4359-5 (hardcover) — ISBN 1-4104-4359-0 (hardcover)
1. Large type books.
PS3561.I4873L68 2012b
813'.54—dc23   2012000477

Published in 2012 by arrangement with The Zondervan Corporation LLC.

DEDICATION

To Donald, my Prince Charming . . .

Another year behind us, and already Tyler is almost finished with his first year at Liberty University, while Kelsey is just a few months away from getting married. Isn't our Lord so faithful? Not just with our kids, but in leading our family where He wants us to be. Closing in on a year in Nashville, and it's so very clear that God wanted us here. Not just for my writing and to be near Christian movies and music . . . but for our kids, and even for us. I love how you've taken to this new season of being more active in my ministry, and helping our boys bridge the gap between being teenagers and becoming young men. Thank you for being steady and strong and good and kind. Hold my hand and walk with me through the coming seasons . . . the graduations and growing up and getting older. All of it's possible with you by my side. Let's play and laugh and sing and dance. And together we'll watch our children take wing. The ride is breathtakingly wondrous. I pray it lasts far into our twilight years. Until then, I'll enjoy not always knowing where I end and you begin. I love you always and forever.

To Kyle, my newest son . . .

Kyle, you and Kelsey might not be married just yet, but still we see you as our son, as the young man God planned for our daughter, the one we've prayed for and talked to God about and hoped for. Your heart is beautiful in every way, Kyle. How you cherish simple moments and the way you are kind beyond words. You see the good in people and situations and you find a way to give God the glory always. I will never forget you coming to me and Donald at different times and telling us that you wanted to support Kelsey and keep her safe . . . and ultimately that you wanted to love her all the days of your life. All of it is summed up in the way you do one simple action: The way you look at our precious Kelsey. It's a picture that will hang forever on the wall of my heart. You look at Kelsey like nothing and no one else in all the world exists but her. In your eyes at that moment is the picture of what love looks like. Kyle, as God takes you from one stage to another — using that beautiful voice of yours to glorify Him and lead others to love Jesus — I pray that you always look at Kelsey the way you do today. We thank God for you, and we look forward to the beautiful seasons ahead. Love you always!

To Kelsey, my precious daughter . . .

Never in a million years could I have imagined that as I finished the Bailey Flanigan series you would be in your very own season of planning a wedding. You are my inspiration for Bailey Flanigan, and throughout the writing of these four books I've seen life imitate art. You headed off to college after I'd already dreamed up *Leaving,* and as *Learning* hit the shelves you were returning home to pursue acting and finish up at University of Portland. You were *Longing* for God's plan alone when last March you met Kyle. Friendship quickly became a love like nothing you'd ever seen before, the love you have dreamed about from the beginning. In very little time we came to see that Kyle was the guy we've been praying for since you were born. God created him to love you, Kelsey . . . and you to love him. He is perfect for you, an amazing man of God whose walk of faith is marked by

7

kindness, integrity, determination, and passion. We love him like we've known him forever. And so as I finish this series with Bailey's wedding — a wedding I dreamed up years ago — you are planning your very own beautiful wedding day. I'm so grateful we're here in Nashville now, and that we have another front row seat — this time to watch you so very in love and planning your tomorrows as Kyle's wife and best friend. I can't imagine what Dad will feel that day when he walks you down the aisle. Or how the years will swirl together in moments as I take on the role of Mother of the Bride — the most beautiful bride ever. In some ways I guess this means our time raising you is finished. The ride is over far too quickly. But I'm grateful that this is not an ending, but the most glorious beginning. We look forward to sharing it with you. We will be here for you and Kyle, praying for you, believing in you, and supporting you however we best can. With Kyle's ministry of music and yours in acting . . . there are no limits to how God will use you both. I rejoice in what He is doing in your life, Kelsey. He has used your years of struggle to make you into the deeply rooted, faithful girl you are today. Keep trusting God . . . keep putting Him first. I always knew this season would come — and now it is here. Enjoy every minute, sweetheart. So glad that in this season we're close, best friends like you've always said. You will always be the light of our family, the laughter in our hearts . . . the one-in-a-million girl who inspired an entire series. My precious Kelsey, I pray that God will bless you mightily in the years to come, and that you will always know how He used this time in your life to draw you close to Him, and to prepare you for what's ahead. In the meantime, you'll be in my heart every moment. I love you, sweetheart.

To Tyler, my lasting song . . .

Some of my favorite moments since you left for Liberty University are when we gather around the kitchen computer and talk to you on Skype. I love that in those times you slip into your funny self, making us laugh until we cry, and pretending to be every cutup character that comes to your mind. But while you can still make us laugh, the serious truth is you are growing into an amazing godly young man. Your blog, "Ty's Take," is being followed by all my readers who long to know how God is working in your life while you're at college. What's incredible is how you have become such a great writer in the process. I know you're planning to make a ministry-related career out of singing for Jesus on stages sea to sea. But don't be surprised if God puts you at a keyboard where you'll write books for Him too. Oh, and let's not forget your gift of directing. So many exciting times ahead, Ty. I can barely take it all in. I still believe with all my heart that God has you right where He wants you. Learning so much — about performing for Him and becoming the man He wants you to be. You are that rare guy with a most beautiful heart for God and others. Your dad and I are so proud of you, Ty. We're proud of your talent and your compassion for people and your place in our family. And we're proud you earned a scholarship to Liberty University. However your dreams unfold, we'll be in the front row cheering loudest as we watch them happen. Hold on to Jesus, son. I love you.

To Sean, my happy sunshine . . .

It's spring and for the first time you get a whole off-season just to focus on basketball! That's a wonderful thing, but even more wonderful is the way you've improved as a student, Sean. You are growing up and listening to God's lead, and in the process you are taking your studies and your homework so much more seriously. God will bless you for how you're being faithful in the little things. He has such great plans for you, despite the fact that the move to Nashville wasn't altogether easy on you. We all left great friends behind in Washington, and you maybe more than the others. But you are open to communicating about your feelings, and you believe us that the opportunities here are worth pursuing. You've always had the best attitude, and now — even when there are hard days — you've kept that great attitude. Be joyful, God tells us. And so in our family you give us a little better picture of how that looks. On top of that, I love how you've gotten more comfortable talking with me and Dad and Kelsey about your life. Stay that close to us, Sean. Remember, home is where your heart is always safe. Your dream of playing college sports — in soccer or basketball — is alive and real. Keep working . . . keep pushing . . . keep believing. Go to bed every night knowing you did all you could to prepare yourself for the doors God will open in the days ahead. I pray that as you soar for the Lord, He will allow you to be a very bright light indeed. You're a precious gift, son. I love you . . . keep smiling and keep seeking God's best.

■ ■ ■ ■

To Josh, my tenderhearted perfectionist . . .

Soccer was where you started when you first came home from Haiti, and soccer is the game that God seems to be opening up for you — both when we were in Washington and here in Nashville. We prayed about what was next, whether you might continue to shine on the football field and the soccer field, or whether God might narrow your options to show you where He is leading. You still shine on the football field, no question. But in a number of ways God seems to be showing you that more through soccer you can be a very bright light for Him. Now we all need to pray that as you continue to follow the Lord in your sports options, He will continue to lead you so that your steps are in keeping with His. This we know — there remains for you a very real possibility that you'll play competitive sports at the next level. But even with all your athleticism, I'm most proud of your growth this past year. You've grown in heart, maturity, kindness, quiet strength, and the realization that time at home is short. God is going to use you for great things, and I believe He'll put you on a public platform to do it. Stay strong in Him, listen to His quiet whispers so you'll know which direction to turn. I'm so proud of you, son . . . I'll forever be cheering on the sidelines. Keep God first in your life. I love you always.

To EJ, my chosen one . . .

EJ, I wish you could know just how much we love you and how deeply we believe in the great plans God has for you. With new opportunities spread out before you, I know you are a bit uncertain. But I see glimpses of determination and effort that tell me with Christ you can do anything, son. One day not too far off from here, you'll be applying to colleges, thinking about the career choices ahead of you, the path God might be leading you down. Wherever that path takes you, keep your eyes on Jesus and you'll always be as full of possibility as you are today. I expect great things from you, EJ, and I know the Lord expects that too. I'm so glad you're a part of our family . . . always and forever. I'm praying you'll have a strong passion to use your gifts for God as you finish your sophomore year. Thanks for your giving heart, EJ. I love you more than you know.

■ ■ ■ ■

To Austin, my miracle boy . . .

Austin, I can only say I'm blown away by your effort this past school year. Leaving Washington and all your friends was not easy — especially for you, since you were our most social student at King's Way Christian. But rather than grumble and complain or waste time looking back, you simply dove in. From the first day you stepped on the football field, you have given one-hundred percent of your special heart to everything related to your new school. Of course in the process you've made friends and memories because you were willing to pour into this new experience. All of you boys have handled the move so well, but I see you seriously embracing it. Along the way you are becoming such a godly leader, determined to succeed for Him, standing taller — and not just because you've grown several inches lately. Only God would've moved us next door to a family with an indoor gym and a willing heart to let you shoot around every day. Amazing, how faithful our God always is! Austin, I love that you care enough to be and do your best. It shows in your straight As and it shows in the way you treat your classmates. Of course it absolutely shows when you play any sport. Always remember what I've told you about that determination. Let it push you to be better, but never, ever let it discourage you. You're so good at life, Austin. Keep the passion and keep that beautiful faith of yours. Every single one of your dreams are within reach. Keep your eyes on Him . . . and we'll keep our eyes on you . . . our youngest son. There is nothing more sweet than cheering you boys on — and for you that happened from the time you were born, through your heart surgery until now. I thank God for you, for the miracle of your life. I love you, Austin.

And to God Almighty, the Author of Life, who has — for now — blessed me with these.

ACKNOWLEDGMENTS

No book comes together without a great and talented team of people making it happen. For that reason, a special thanks to my friends at Zondervan who combined efforts with a number of people who were passionate about Life-Changing Fiction™ to make *Loving* all it could be. A special thanks to my dedicated editor, Sue Brower, and to Don Gates and Alicia Mey, my marketing team. Thanks also to the creative staff and the sales force at Zondervan who work tirelessly to put this book in your hands.

A special thanks to my amazing agent, Rick Christian, president of Alive Communications. Rick, you've always believed only the best for me. When we talk about the highest possible goals, you see them as doable, reachable. You are a brilliant manager of my career, an incredible agent, and I thank God for you. But even with all you do for my ministry of writing, I am doubly grateful for your encouragement and prayers. Every time I finish a book, you send me a letter worth framing, and when something big happens, yours is the first call I receive. Thank you for that. But even more, the fact that you and Debbie are praying for me and my family keeps me confident every morning that God will continue to breathe life into the stories in my heart. Thank you for being so much more than a brilliant agent.

Also, thanks to my husband, who puts up with me on deadline and doesn't mind driving through Taco Bell after a football game if I've been editing all day. This wild ride wouldn't be possible without you, Donald. Your love keeps me writing; your prayers keep me believing that God is using this ministry of Life-Changing Fiction™. Also thanks for the hours you put in helping me. It's a full-time job, and I am grateful for your concern for my reader friends. Of course, thanks to my daughter and sons, who pull together — bringing me iced green tea and understanding my sometimes crazy schedule. I love that you know you're still first, before any deadline.

Thank you also to my mom, Anne Kingsbury, and to my sisters, Tricia and Sue. Mom, you are amazing as my assistant —

working day and night sorting through the email from my readers. I appreciate you more than you'll ever know. Traveling with you these past years for Extraordinary Women, Women of Joy, and Women of Faith events has given us times together we will always treasure. The journey gets more exciting all the time!

Tricia, you are the best executive assistant I could ever hope to have. I appreciate your loyalty and honesty, the way you include me in every decision and the daily exciting changes. This ministry of Life-Changing Fiction™ has been so much more effective since you stepped in. Along the way, readers have more to help them in their faith, so much more than a story. Please know that I pray for God's blessings on you always, for your dedication to helping me in this season of writing, and for your wonderful son, Andrew. And aren't we having such a good time too? God works all things for good!

Sue, I believe you should've been a counselor! From your home far from mine, you get batches of reader letters every day, and you diligently answer them using God's wisdom and His Word. When readers get a response from "Karen's sister Susan," I hope they know how carefully you've prayed for them and for the responses you give.

Thank you for truly loving what you do, Sue. You're gifted with people, and I'm blessed to have you aboard.

I also want to thank Kyle Kupecky, the newest addition to the LCF staff. Time and again you exceed my expectations with business and financial matters, and in supervising our many donation programs. Thank you for putting your whole heart into your work at LCF. At the same time, I pray your music ministry becomes so widespread and far-reaching that you can one day step down and do only that. In the meantime, just know that I treasure having you as part of the team.

Kelsey, you also are an enormous part of this ministry, and I thank you for truly loving the reader friends God has brought into our lives. What a special season, when you and Kyle can head into marriage knowing that you also work together doing ministry from our home office. God is so creative, so amazing. Keep working hard and believing in your dreams. Along the way, I love that you are a part of all God is doing through this special team. Tyler, a special thanks to you for running the garage warehouse and making sure our storage needs are met, and that we always have books to give away! You're a hard worker — God will always reward that.

Thanks also to my forever friends and family, the ones who have been there and continue to be there. Your love has been a tangible source of comfort, pulling us through the tough times and making us know how very blessed we are to have you in our lives.

And the greatest thanks to God. You put a story in my heart, and have a million other hearts in mind — something I could never do. I'm grateful to be a small part of your plan! The gift is yours. I pray I might use it for years to come in a way that will bring you honor and glory.

FOREVER IN FICTION®

For a number of years now, I've had the privilege of offering Forever in Fiction®* as an auction item at fund-raisers across the country. Many of my more recent books have had Forever in Fiction characters, characters inspired by real-life people.

In *Loving,* I bring you two very special Forever in Fiction characters. The first is Brad Wright, a twenty-two-year-old young man whose life was forever changed in 2006, when the car he was riding in lost control, went off the road, and hit a tree. Brad suffered a severe brain injury and damage to his spinal cord. At the time of his accident, Brad had just finished his junior year in high school. He was an A student, nearly six feet tall and very athletic. He had a big smile that made his eyes

*Forever in Fiction is a registered trademark owned by Karen Kingsbury.

sparkle and he was funny, witty, and very outgoing. People who met him never forgot him, and he dreamed of playing basketball at the University of Alabama. The day of his accident, he took a ride with a friend who had hours earlier bought a new car. The driver was going 55 MPH in a 35 MPH zone when the accident happened. Brad's mother Debbie Harmon won Forever in Fiction™ at the Just Keep Smiling Auction in Mount Olive, Alabama.

In *Loving,* Brad will appear the way he was before the accident. He will be part of a special program that allows kids on movie sets as a prize for their heroic efforts during the year. Brad will have won the right to be on the set of Brandon Paul's movie by raising money for accident victims. Debbie, I pray that you are deeply touched when you see Brad here on the pages of *Loving,* where he will remain forever in fiction.

The second Forever in Fiction™ character is Jade Gilbert, 15, whose parents — Steve and Kathy Gilbert — won the right to have their daughter made into a character at the King's Way Christian School online auction in June 2010. Jade lives in Ontario, Canada, where she sings in choir, volunteers for many organizations, plays the flute and piano, and does ballet and karate. In her spare time Jade also runs marathons with her dad. Her family raises guide dogs, and Jade herself recently raised $1,000 for pediatric oncology in Ontario, Canada. This delightful girl is known for her kindness and patience. She loves the color purple, watermelon, and blueberries. Jade attends youth group and helps with the toddlers at church, and one of her favorite things is watching her younger sister play soccer. In *Loving,* Jade is written as a teenage girl who wins the right to be on the set of a Brandon Paul movie because of her philanthropic efforts. Steve and Kathy, I hope I've captured a glimpse of your amazing daughter, and that you smile when you see her here in the story of *Loving,* where she will always be forever in fiction.

A special thanks to both of my auction winners for supporting your various ministries and for your belief in the power of story. I pray the donations you made to your respective charities will go on to change lives, the way I pray lives will be changed by the impact of the message in *Loving.* May God bless you for your love and generosity.

For those of you who are not familiar with Forever in Fiction, it is my way of involving you, the readers, in my stories, while raising money for charities. The winning bidder of a Forever in Fiction package has the right to have their name or the name of someone they love written into one of my novels.

To date, Forever in Fiction has raised more than $200,000 at charity auctions. Obviously, I am only able to donate a limited number of these each year. For that reason, I have set a fairly high minimum bid on this package so that the maximum funds are raised for charities. All money goes to the charity events. If you are interested in receiving a Forever in Fiction package for your auction, write to *office@Karen Kingsbury.com* and write in the subject line: *Forever in Fiction.*

In His Light,
Karen Kingsbury

ONE

Brandon Paul could almost smell the Montana air. In a month or so he would fly to Butte to film his next movie, two hours out of the city, and lately that was all he could think about. Leaving Los Angeles and clearing his head. Especially since Bailey planned to join him for some of it. But for now thoughts of his April movie shoot outside Butte would have to wait. He stepped into the glass elevator at West Mark Studios and rode it to the twenty-sixth floor — the top of the Century City Plaza building, just outside of Hollywood, California.

Where every day saw the biggest deals in Hollywood go down.

He tugged on his canvas messenger bag, aware of its contents — two copies of the red-lined copy of the West Mark contract and a letter from his attorney. As he did, he caught his reflection on the elevator wall and noticed the slump in his posture. If

Brandon had seen a mountain growing on his shoulders he wouldn't have been surprised. The contract carried that much weight. And today's meeting would only make the burden greater.

A deep sigh rattled from his lungs as he stepped off the elevator and faced the double glass doors at the end of the gold-carpeted hallway. The team at West Mark was expecting that this week or next they would ink their biggest contract ever. A seven-picture deal with Brandon Paul. The announcement, the red carpet event, the after-party — all of it was in the works.

The only detail they'd overlooked was this: Brandon's personal attorney — Luke Baxter.

Brandon opened the heavy door and approached the front desk. The woman taking calls and messages blushed the sort of red usually reserved for apples. She had been midsip into a cup of coffee, and now she coughed a few times and wiped her mouth. Brandon smiled, hoping to put her at ease. "Hi. Jack Randall is expecting me."

The woman was maybe in her midthirties, blonde with a spray tan. The sort of hopeful actress-still-waiting-for-her-break look that came a dime a dozen in Hollywood. "Yes, Mr. Paul, right away. I'll let him know you're here."

Whether it was the influence of Bailey Flanigan or his growing faith, Brandon wasn't sure, but more often lately he was struck by the reaction people had around him. Sure he had filmed a lot of movies. But he'd been born into an average family in a suburban neighborhood. If he'd wound up driving a bus at the airport, no one would clamor for his attention or want his autograph. There would be no blushing at his arrival. So why were movies different?

Brandon leaned against the nearest wall. "What's your name?"

"Mary." The blonde coughed again. "Sorry. Swallowed wrong." She uttered a nervous laugh. "Didn't expect . . ." She shook her head, clearly trying to get a grip. "Sorry. You're on the calendar. It's just . . . yeah. Never mind."

"Hey." He held his hand out and shook hers. "I'm Brandon. Now we're friends, okay?"

The woman visibly exhaled and settled back into her chair. "Okay." She laughed again. "Thanks. I'm new. Everyone says you're like this. So normal."

"Good." He grinned at her. "I like that. 'Normal' is a compliment."

Wasn't that what Bailey wanted most?

Plain old *normal.* It was what she'd told him the last time they walked along the beach. That when she looked ahead she wasn't always sure what she wanted to do or where she wanted to live, but she knew this much: she wanted a normal life. The ability to come and go without wondering whether a posse of paparazzi was lurking in the bushes.

That kind of normal.

Behind her desk, Mary made a few quick calls to alert Jack Randall and his team that Brandon had arrived. As she did, Brandon felt his phone vibrate and he pulled it discreetly from his jeans pocket. A text from Bailey.

Hey, I'm at NTM Studios . . . Can't believe how much I want this part now — thanks to you! Hope all the weird meetings before this amount to nothing. Getting ready to head inside. Pray for me! ILY

Brandon smiled and read the text again and shot a quick answer back. *You'll be amazing. Everything will work out. ILY2*

NTM was where he'd gotten his start starring in half a dozen movies for teens. In the last few years, NTM had produced movies with more drama, more conflict. *Unlocked* — the movie he and Bailey had starred in together — had been one of those. Now Bailey had been cast as the lead in a film

about a young teacher who convinces her gang-member students to care for each other. Her production meeting was set to take place at the same time as his.

She'd had a few strange meetings with the producer of the film, but even so her time today figured to be a whole lot more positive than his.

One of Jack's assistants strode down the back hallway and into sight.

"Mr. Paul," Mary smiled at him. The quietly knowing look in her eyes said she didn't need to feel star struck around him any longer. "Mr. Randall is ready for you."

Brandon winked at her as he walked past. Then he followed the assistant to the back boardroom — where he'd met with the West Mark team a number of times before. Always to discuss the same thing: the pending contract. As they reached the boardroom, Brandon saw he was the last one to the party. His agent, Sid Chandler, and Stephen Chase, his manager, sat together at one end of the table. There had been a time when the two of them were a little at odds, even though they both headed up his team. Power struggle maybe. But since getting word of the big West Mark contract, the two seemed like old college roommates.

Across from them sat Jack Randall; his assistant, Chin Li Hong — a forty-something expert with a doctorate in contracts; two guys from the studio's legal department; and at least four interns, including the suit who'd escorted Brandon to the meeting. A meeting Brandon had requested.

He filled his lungs. Thirty minutes from now they'd all be furious with him. "Gentlemen." He nodded at the men and then at Jack's assistant. "Miss Hong." He gave a more familiar smile to Chandler and Chase. "Thanks for meeting."

"Yes." Jack allowed an uncomfortable chuckle. "We've invested quite a bit in this contract, and of course, in the announcement of the details." He shrugged and looked at the others around the table. "Anytime our top star calls a meeting, we'll find time."

A round of mumbled agreements followed. All eyes were on him.

Brandon cleared his throat. "Thanks. I appreciate that." He pulled his bag up onto his lap and removed a file from inside. No matter how he started, there was no easy way around what he was going to say. "I hired a private attorney . . . Luke Baxter." He worked to keep his tone light. "He's worked with Dayne Matthews and several other actors."

"Dayne's brother, isn't that right?" Jack laced his fingers together and leaned on his forearms. His eyes pierced Brandon's and he didn't wait for an answer. "Was that on counsel from your agent? Your manager?" Jack cast a shadowy look at both men.

"No, Randall." Chandler was the first to cut in. "Neither of us asked Brandon to get another opinion." He smiled with dizzy abandon, like someone about to make fifteen percent of an eight-figure deal. "The contract . . . well, it's perfect."

"Thank you." Jack seemed content to settle in on that for a few beats. After a long moment he looked back at Brandon. "Go on."

Brandon resisted the urge to wipe his brow. He might be sweating, but he couldn't show it. The meeting was bound to be tough, but the tension in the room now was palpable. Not the usual showering of compliments and grandiose statements from the studio brass. This time they were irritated and in a hurry. As if whatever his reason for the meeting, he better hurry and get on with it.

Brandon found another level of resolve. He stared at the file, opened it, then handed a copy of the red-lined contract to Jack. The other one he set on the desk in front of him.

"Luke found some items of concern."

Attorneys handled red-lining differently. Luke Baxter was old school. The thirty-page document was literally marked with red on at least half the pages. Randall took it slowly, the way he might take the report card from a failing son or daughter. He thumbed through a few pages and then allowed a quiet laugh — one without even the slightest hint of humor. He held the contract up and looked at the others again. When his eyes met Brandon's his laughter faded. "Are you kidding me?" He flipped the document to Chin Li. "Look at this."

"Excuse me." It was Brandon's manager. His face seemed to have lost most of its blood supply. He reached out to Brandon. "May I see a copy?"

"Uh . . . we'd like copies also," one of the West Mark attorneys spoke for both of them. At almost the same time Chin Li handed her copy to an assistant. "Make a stack of them."

The assistant took the document and hurried out of the room. Brandon imagined Chandler and Chase were probably quietly trying to grasp this new reality: the fact that Brandon had called a meeting to discuss findings by his private attorney and the reality that the hired gun had used a red pen

to shred the studio's best offer ever. Either way, Brandon was up for the fight. He was protecting himself, and in the process he was protecting someone that mattered more than he did.

Bailey Flanigan.

"Brandon." Chin Li's tone suggested she might've made a wonderful kindergarten teacher. "Maybe you don't understand the scope of the contract." She shot a disdaining glance at his agent and manager. "This is the best deal West Mark has ever offered any actor."

"I realize that." Brandon sat back in his chair and kept his voice pleasant. "But I've said the same thing since the idea of the contract first came up." He looked at Jack Randall again. "I want creative control, or I can't do it."

"Creative control." Jack matched Brandon's posture, easing back and even linking his hands behind his head. The picture of cool confidence. "Explain 'creative control.' I mean, I thought we were very careful to include that."

His attorney, Luke, had told him what to say, and now Brandon didn't hesitate. "The wording in the contract allows for my input, Jack. But not for my final say. If a project compromises my faith or my reputation or my relationships, I can't kill it. I can only comment." He felt his voice rising, and he worked to keep control. "I appreciate the chance to have an opinion. But that's not enough."

"Seems like a lot of red ink for that simple change." Brandon's agent gave a nervous, high-pitched chuckle. He drummed his fingers on the walnut table. "Probably something we can fix this afternoon. I mean, if we all take a look at it."

"I don't know." Brandon angled his head. He could still hear Luke Baxter's advice. "A dozen pages have a line or clause giving the studio power to make final decisions regarding the seven movies." He flipped through the copy in front of him. "That explains all the ink."

Jack Randall's expression went suddenly flat and his eyes turned a sort of slate gray. "Look, Brandon . . . if that's where you're at, we're going to have to rethink this whole deal."

"Now wait." Brandon's manager started to stand and then stopped himself. "Brandon doesn't want a delay in the contract process." His eyes shot lasers at Brandon. "Isn't that right?"

The assistant was back and copies were handed to everyone at the table. After a moment, Brandon spoke up, "Actually . . ." He was undaunted by the intensity in the room, the pressure aimed at him. "Jack's right. Let's take four months and sort through it. Luke wants a final look, but he'll be busy for the next few months. I have a movie to shoot in Montana. Four months gives us time to reschedule the announcement." He shrugged, his calm otherworldly. "West Mark's legal guys can go through it more than once, make the changes." He looked at the lawyers. "Four months enough time, guys? We can announce this around the first of August?"

Their faces fell and they hesitated, the way attorneys often hesitate. As if any wrong word or nuance could result in a lawsuit. Jack didn't wait for them to rebound. "Four months sounds about right." This was personal for the studio executive now. Everyone in the room knew four months was far longer than they needed. But in light of the situation, Jack wasn't about to roll over. He wanted to give the impression that the studio wasn't desperate, that they could even walk away from the contract if Brandon wasn't careful.

"Actually," Jack waved his hand around in front of him, "maybe we take six months. We'll let you know." He checked his watch and pushed back from the table. "Chin Li, you'll cancel plans for the announcement, the red carpet, all of it. We'll give legal plenty of time to think over the contract. We'll need a team meeting before we consider rescheduling."

"Yes, sir." Chin Li cast a sad, disappointed look at Brandon. "I'm very sorry you feel this way, Brandon."

"It's fine." Jack stood and waved his hands at the rest of them. "Meeting's over, guys. We'll revisit this behind closed doors and aim for an announcement four months or so from now."

Across from him, Brandon's agent and manager looked furious with him, torn between releasing a verbal tirade and quitting on the spot. Jack Randall walked around the table and held his hand out to Brandon. "I will say this. West Mark still wants to be your studio. Let's see if we can figure it all out."

"I look forward to it. Thank you, sir." Brandon realized Jack was trying to make him feel like he had lost something here. But Brandon didn't see it that way. He was drawing from every bit of his self-restraint not to start a personal celebration right here in the boardroom. He had bought himself four months and the studio's agreement to

careers. He crossed his arms. "The time away will be good. I mean . . . guys, it's a great contract. I get that."

Chase jabbed his pointer finger at the air in front of him. "Best contract. Not just a great contract, Brandon. Best one West Mark's ever put on the table."

"I believe it's the best any studio's put on any table." Chandler's tone remained understated. "For what it's worth."

The conversation wasn't going anywhere. Brandon breathed in slowly and all he could see were the pine trees of Montana. Maybe Bailey could spend more than a few weeks there, work on the book she'd been talking about writing lately. The time away from LA would be good for both of them. Otherwise he'd fly home each weekend. "Listen." He looked from Chase to Chandler. "You guys are on my side. I know that." He smiled. "Trust me. I'll get creative control, and then we'll throw the biggest party this town has ever seen." He paused. "Okay?"

"Fine." Chase sighed like he had two people standing on his chest. "I'll call you in a few days."

"I'll talk to Randall." Chandler stood first and gathered his things. "Calm him down."

"He'll be fine." Brandon rose to his feet. He wondered how Bailey's meeting at

NTM was going. "Four months is nothing in this business."

Neither of them could argue with that. Brandon shared a cursory couple of hugs with his team. They left West Mark's executive offices and rode the elevator down together in mostly silence. But as Brandon went his own way out of the building and walked to his waiting ride, his steps felt lighter, the air a little sweeter.

Like he was already with Bailey in Montana.

Two

The first hour of the production meeting involved little more than small talk, but the longer Bailey sat at the oversize picnic table on the back lot of NTM Studios, the more uncomfortable she felt. They gathered on a grassy knoll overlooking the set where half a dozen recent movies had been filmed, but Bailey didn't feel excited about any of it. She was homesick and hot and unsure of her commitment to the movie. On top of that the sun had shifted since they first came outside, and despite the trees around them Bailey could feel her forehead getting burned.

At the meeting was producer Mel Kamp, his assistant, the director — a woman Brandon had worked with twice before — and Bailey's two young teenage costars.

". . . Which is why, when I pull a cast together, I expect teamwork." Mel had been droning on for some time. He struggled with charisma, and the past hour was proof. "Teamwork creates synergy and chemistry. We become unbreakable and believable."

In front of the producer sat a stack of scripts — the latest rewrite. A more compelling version, apparently, because he'd already mentioned the fact countless times, both today and at earlier meetings. But either he was afraid of what they'd think or he had no sense of time, because he hadn't made a single move to pass them out.

Bailey shifted and took stock of her co-stars. They'd both been in previous NTM films, and now they would play two of the toughest gang members in what would be Bailey's inner-city classroom. From the beginning, she hadn't been given a full draft of the script, since a rewrite was in progress. But she'd been given the sections that involved her character and she loved what she'd seen. The story was inspired by true events out of Miami and as far as Bailey knew, she would play an idealistic new teacher who believed in compassion and prayer and helping kids care about each other. But not until one of her students is killed in a drive-by shooting does the class begin to turn around.

But at each meeting lately, though Bailey pressed for more information, none was given to her. Not only that, but at the last four meetings, Mel Kamp had said things that concerned Bailey. Even now he was talking about pushing the envelope.

"Finding art sometimes means trying new things, venturing into places other people wouldn't go." He drummed his fingers on the stack of scripts.

Bailey squinted at the man through her sunglasses. What was he trying to say? Why this sense of impending doom? Like God was trying to warn her about something. Whatever was coming, the new script made her uncomfortable.

Finally Mel slowly, almost reverently, began passing out the scripts. "Anyway . . . here you go." His phone sat on the other side of the stack, and as he gave out the last one he checked the time. "I've kept you long enough." He smiled and slapped his palms on the table for emphasis. "Take the scripts home. Give them a read and drop me an email." His look said he was absolutely confident they would like the revisions. "Feedback is important. Garners teamwork."

He stood and checked something else on his phone. "We'll shoot this in New Mexico, the way it looks now. Great tax incentives. You'll have a production schedule well before that."

Her costars stood and thanked the producer, and Bailey did the same. But the two of them looked beyond bored as the trio headed through the back of the building to the parking lot. One of the guys smiled as he rolled his eyes. "There's two hours we can't get back, huh?"

"Exactly." She tried to return his smile, but it fell flat. "I hope the script's more interesting."

"For sure." The other guy looked confident. "They used a team of writers. Some of the best."

"The writers specialize in award-winning films." The first one tucked his copy under his arm and opened the door for the group. "It'll be amazing. I guarantee it."

"I hope so." When they reached the parking lot, Bailey waved. "See you soon."

The taller of the guys returned the wave. "Tell Brandon we said hey."

"I will." Bailey liked the guys. They both dated NTM actresses and had known Brandon for several years. She hoped maybe she and Brandon could hang out with them and their girlfriends during the shoot, if Brandon's schedule allowed for it. Maybe even before the movie while they were all still here in Los Angeles. Other than Katy and

Dayne Matthews, there were no other couples Brandon and Bailey hung out with. She didn't know much about the guys, but they seemed nice. Maybe they'd become lifelong friends.

That would help LA feel more like home.

Bailey walked to the car — she was using Katy's Navigator today. As she pulled out of the parking lot, she headed south to Will Rogers Beach, closer to Santa Monica. At this early hour on a Thursday, the beach would be deserted.

Along the drive she turned on her radio as an old Newsong hit came on, "When God Made You." Bailey felt yesterday rush in like air through the open window of the SUV. She'd been, what, maybe eighteen or nineteen when she first heard the song? And all she could think about then was Cody, how they'd play this song at their wedding someday.

Bailey smiled at the memory. She'd been so young, just a kid, a high school girl who saw Cody Coleman as bigger than life.

She fixed her eyes on the winding turns that made up Pacific Coast Highway, turned up the volume, and sang along. Her voice stayed soft, the memory of the song as much a part of the past as any photo or letter. She loved the lyrics — how they spoke of God's hand in finding true love and the promise of forever. Bailey had never shared the song with Cody. She'd found it when he was little more than a secret crush, and by the time they finally admitted their feelings for each other, they ran out of time before it came up.

Where Cody was concerned there was never enough time.

Tears filled Bailey's eyes and she blinked so she could focus on the road. She could still see herself cleaning her room while the song played from her iPod speakers, still feel what it felt to believe he was the one, to believe God had created Cody for her.

She dabbed at her cheek and let the ocean air dry her face. The tears surprised her, because she didn't love Cody that way anymore, the way she thought she did back then. She knew that now. He was more of a big brother to her, someone she looked up to. The same way she'd been only that for him. But still, she missed those days. Missed the way he'd always been around back then. He made her feel safe and protected and the fact that he adored her family was part of it too. How could it not be?

The two of them hadn't talked since Bloomington, when they took a walk around Lake Monroe a few days after Cody's girlfriend, Cheyenne, died from her brief battle with cancer. He was finishing up the semester teaching at Lyle High School an hour outside of Indianapolis, but then what? Bailey had Brandon now. But since God hadn't made her and Cody for each other, who would Cody find? And without meaning to, Bailey slipped into a silent prayer for her old dear friend.

That God would comfort him in his season of loss, and that in time He would give to Cody what He had so clearly given to Bailey.

A love that had been created for him since the beginning of time.

All night the clock on Andi Ellison's computer seemed to be racing in double-time until finally a few minutes ago she submitted the online test for her business marketing class. She leaned back in her chair and for the first time in two hours she felt herself relax. More than that, she felt great about herself. She was doing something she had doubted she'd ever do: Finishing school.

Despite her rebellious choices back at Indiana University and her wrong relationship with a guy she barely knew. Even after getting pregnant and giving her baby up for adoption to Luke and Reagan Baxter, when the enemy of her soul wanted her to believe her life was tarnished forever, God had done the unthinkable.

He had breathed fresh hope into her soul.

She was taking small parts in Christian films and working as an assistant to her producer father. But now she was also tackling online courses, working to finish her marketing degree. Something she wasn't sure she'd ever do again.

The reality made her feel wonderful, even if it didn't quite take the edge off her loneliness.

She moved her mouse to the Safari browser and opened Facebook. Her life involved very little social interaction, and for a long time Andi could feel God working in the silence: the nine months when she carried her firstborn son, the year of moving to Los Angeles with her family and finding her way back to the heart of God; and now the busyness with acting and working. All of it had left Andi with few chances to meet people.

Her Facebook newsfeed popped up, and she scanned a few status updates from acquaintances she'd met on a handful of sets. But her time with the cast and crew was always too brief to establish real friendships. Whether with guys or girls. Her only real and true friend was Bailey Flanigan. The two of them talked a few times a week, and they planned to see each other more often now that Bailey lived in Los Angeles. But with LA traffic there was still more than an hour's drive between them.

Andi scrolled down the list and stopped cold the way she always did when his face appeared. And like every time, Andi could feel her eyes meet his through the window of the computer screen. She could remember his voice and feel his arms around her the few times they shared a hug. She could see into his soul the way she always could.

The soul of Cody Coleman.

For the longest time Andi hated herself for having any sort of feelings for Cody because he belonged to Bailey. Always and only Bailey. But all that had changed in the last year or so, as Bailey clearly had moved on. Still, her admiration of Cody Coleman wasn't something she shared with anyone — not even Bailey. It was a dream, a figment of her imagination. Something she refused to even entertain except for moments like this. When his face was there before her. Cody in his Lyle High coaching shirt and his hat — the one with the 'W' on it. Bailey had told her Cody wore it in honor of his friend Art. The hat was from the

University of Washington, a school that had recruited Art for its football program. Art chose the Army instead, and when he lost his life on the battlefield, Cody took possession of the hat.

Because that's the sort of guy Cody had always been. Loyal and caring to the depths of his being.

A sigh eased itself up from the unsure places of Andi's heart. Cody had suffered a lot lately. His Facebook posts had been erratic, but Bailey had mentioned that Cody's girlfriend had died of cancer. Maybe that's why Andi found herself thinking about him these days. Because she hated the thought of Cody hurting.

Andi read his status a couple times, mainly because soaking in the words he'd written allowed her for those few seconds to hear his voice again. The post read, "Headed to Liberty University with DeMetri, getting him ready for college. Crazy how fast life goes."

Yes. Andi agreed with that. Even when she thought she'd live forever in the dark shadows she'd created over her life, time moved on. No season — good or bad — lasted forever. All of which made her wish for the sort of loving Bailey had found with Brandon. For a guy who might think the world of her and understand about her past and feel dizzy at the thought of walking alongside through her tomorrows.

Andi drew a slow breath and closed out of Facebook. For a long time she closed her eyes and remembered back. When she first returned to her family and her faith — after she avoided aborting her unborn baby — she had been reading the Bible when a single story changed everything about the way she thought, everything about the way she would love God from that point forward.

It was the story of the rich young ruler.

In the story, a guy who had lived a fairly good life came to Jesus and asked what more he needed to do to have eternal life. Jesus, knowing the guy, looked straight into his soul and told him to sell everything he owned and give the proceeds to the poor. The man went away sad because he had great wealth. Andi had known the story since she was a little girl, but she always had breezed past it.

Her parents were missionaries, after all. They understood the principle of giving. But that day, with her life in disarray, Andi read the story in a new light. The story didn't mean all people should sell their belongings. It meant Jesus had a way of looking deep into the soul and asking people to give up the one thing they wanted more than Him. For Andi, once she returned to the faith she'd been raised with, she absolutely knew the desire God wanted her to give up. The one thing she had sought after more than she'd ever sought after Him.

The desire to be loved.

Her hope for a boyfriend had led her down crazy paths when she was at Indiana University, and after she returned home she determined that she would not pursue guys again. The next time — if God allowed a next time in her life — the guy would pursue her. Like Bailey's mom had said: "Like a dying man goes after water in a desert." Until then, she was content to be lonely.

At least she had been content.

Seeing Cody on Facebook reminded her that she needed to keep praying. Not only that God would give her contentment in her loneliness, but that He might work a miracle in her life.

So that someday, somehow, someone might love her.

THREE

Bailey's doubts burned themselves into her heart and stayed there while the song on her car radio finished. By then she was at the beach, and like she had hoped, the parking lot was empty. She found a spot, grabbed the new script and a towel from the backseat, and walked toward the nearest pale-blue lifeguard station. Staff wasn't on duty at this hour. She walked up the stairs and spread her towel across the platform. Hidden from the world, with her back against the tower wall and the ocean spread out before her, Bailey breathed in deep and stared at the water.

Here it was easy to reflect on the events of the past month. Her uneasy meetings with NTM studios, and a few troubling conversations with Brandon. Assuming West Mark fixed the contract, there was still the issue of Brandon being committed to Los Angeles for the next five years.

Which brought up another frustration that had surfaced lately. Now that she and Brandon were both living in LA, the paparazzi constantly looked for scandalous stories about them. Headlines at supermarket checkout stands regularly questioned whether Bailey was pregnant or Brandon was cheating on her or she was having a secret long-distance affair with someone back in New York. Brandon was used to it, and to some degree Bailey was too. Most people didn't believe the garbage they printed, but still it was wearying.

More days than not she longed for the simplicity of Bloomington, when no one wondered why she was headed into a drugstore or having a phone conversation while she walked down the street. The insanely busy streets and teeming sidewalks of New York City were relaxing compared to paparazzi-crazy Los Angeles. A friend from the *Hairspray* cast had called last week to inform her that a couple shows were auditioning for dancers in the fall. Six months away, but still . . . Could Bailey really commit to LA when her heart was so uneasy? All of it left Bailey confused about her feelings for Brandon, and whether everything between them had maybe happened too fast.

What am I feeling, God? . . . Help me find the peace I felt a month ago.

She exhaled and leaned her head back against the weathered wood. Maybe her whole relationship with Brandon was all a little too easy. The way he'd swept in from the beginning and made her feel loved and cherished and special. Now it was like he took for granted the fact that she'd move to LA permanently or that she could handle the constant throng of photographers capturing their every move. She'd hinted a few times that maybe they should talk, that maybe she'd made the move to LA too quickly. But each time something distracted them. She was beginning to think Brandon simply didn't want to talk about the possibility that her living in LA might not work out.

Because they both loved each other so much. That was the one thing she didn't question.

The ocean was rougher than usual, white caps bouncing in from the distant horizon. Bailey stared at the water but all she could see was Brandon. The time he surprised her and flew to Indiana to help her pack for New York . . . the Empire State Building . . . the carriage rides through the City and seeing him in the front row every night she performed for her last two months on Broadway. The prom on the top of the Kellers' apartment building. Their Skype dates. She smiled, enjoying the bouquet of memories. The ride might've been fast, but it had been beautiful.

So why did she feel so unsettled? Here, on a beautiful windy spring day alone on the beach? It wasn't thoughts of Cody, because he was her past. Really and truly. Whether she missed his camaraderie was irrelevant. Seasons change — if anyone knew that, she did.

The feeling could be the idea of living in LA and committing to the movie and Mel Kamp and . . . and whatever they'd done with the script. Or the uneasiness could be the idea that maybe she'd given up her dream of dancing on Broadway a little too fast.

The sun was overhead but still just behind the lifeguard tower, leaving her place on the platform completely shaded. Like a secret hideaway from the towering glass office buildings of Century City and the relentless traffic of LA and the insidious paparazzi.

A place where she could breathe.

She opened the cover of the script and thumbed through it. The whole thing was a hundred and five pages. She could easily get through it in the next couple hours. She stretched her legs out in front of her, crossed them at the ankles, and began to read.

With the sea breeze swirling around her and the bright blue sky hanging over the ocean, Bailey expected the next hour to be one of the day's best. The first few pages into the script, she felt that way for sure. But there at the top of page six came the first sign that Bailey's uneasiness from earlier was warranted.

At the beginning of that page, her two costars' characters were at a party full of gang members when three girls approached them and offered to sleep with them. The descriptive and graphic scene that followed was both gratuitous and offensive. Bailey stopped halfway down the next page, sick to her stomach. What was this garbage? No one had told her there'd be scenes like this in the movie. Clearly Mel Kamp had been alluding to this in the recent studio meetings. Bailey was angry with herself. She should've asked more questions, pushed more for an explanation about the rewrite. But how could she have guessed this? Not with NTM, the studio known for its clean films.

Panic and disgust filled her mind with

every page of the script. For the next five minutes Bailey flipped through the revised story and found half a dozen scenes she couldn't live with. Even the scene she'd originally read for had a number of cuss words thrown in. And in the director's note on the scene it said: *The teacher is young, but she must dress in a way that turns the heads of the guys in the class. This is how she first gains their attention.*

Bailey closed the script and pulled her knees up to her chest. What was happening? How in the world had the producer thought she'd be okay with this? Surely Brandon's agent had told Kamp how Bailey felt, her absolute determination to only do family-friendly projects, movies with a message or some redeeming value. She brought her hand to her face. What about her costars? How would they feel about the changes?

The sick feeling in her stomach grew. She dropped the script on the wooden floor of the lifeguard tower, stood, and walked to the nearby railing. Leaning on her elbows, she hung her head and closed her eyes. With everything inside her she wanted to be in Bloomington. Spring would be knocking on the door back home, the snow pretty much behind them. On a day like this, Ricky would have a baseball game, or Shawn and

Justin would be tearing up the soccer field. She and her mom could've gone for coffee and talked about life. Not a single person would be lurking in the bushes ready to snap her picture, and she wouldn't be holding a script that made her sick.

Just she and her mom talking like they'd always been able to do.

Her mom would've known what to say, and together they could've discussed what in the world Bailey was doing in LA and where she would wind up if she stayed. Her breathing came faster, and she could hear her heartbeat pounding, almost as if she were being chased.

She lifted her head and stared out at the water. *What am I doing here, God?*

My daughter, I am with you . . . Be still . . . Listen to my voice.

Bailey straightened slowly, her eyes on the horizon. God often spoke to her through quiet certainties in her heart or Scripture verses. But here it was like His voice was in the wind, His eyes directly on her, His hands on her shoulders. She exhaled and felt her heart rate ease a little. *Okay, God . . . what do you want me to hear? What are you saying?*

She waited, but this time there was only the sound of the breeze. Then gradually, thoughts began taking root in her mind. And this time, rather than flitting through her heart, they stayed. Like billboards in her soul. A sudden slew of doubts overwhelming in their intensity.

Maybe after *Hairspray* closed its doors, she should've taken more time. Looked a little longer. Really prayed about God's next move for her. And when she decided to leave, she should've spent more time at home. She didn't need to be with Brandon every spare hour. She needed to seek God's plan for her life, pray longer about her next career move. She and Brandon had handled having a long-distance relationship before. Certainly she could've waited a few months before moving to LA. Then a thought came that seemed more significant than the others: her decision to take the movie role had been rushed. Even though at the time the part had seemed hand-delivered by God.

Bailey leaned into the railing and suddenly she knew, without a doubt, her next move. She pulled her phone from the back pocket of her jeans and called the one person she could share all her doubts and uneasiness with. The one who had known her and guided her and listened to her and loved her all of her life.

Her mom.

She waited while the phone rang, and just before it might've gone to voicemail, her mother picked up. "Hi, honey . . . how are you?" Jenny Flanigan knew about Bailey's meeting that morning, so she sounded upbeat, hopeful.

"Not good." Bailey felt the tears again. The steady ocean breeze made her eyes sting. She swallowed hard, wishing once more that she was home in Bloomington. "They changed the script."

"Hmmm." Bailey's mom sounded surprised, but not overly so. "That's what the meeting was about?"

"Not really. The producer talked around the topic, but then he handed out these completely new scripts." Bailey blinked and two tears rolled down her cheeks. "Not that I ever read the entire script before, but now . . . Mom, the story is awful. Totally different than they told me it would be." She took a shaky breath and launched into a ninety-second explanation of how she'd gone to the beach to read the script and how the story had been changed and the fact that now — combined with so many other moments and meetings — she was doubting everything about the last few months. She wiped at her tears, frustrated. "The whole thing makes me so mad. I

63

mean, I moved here for this part."

Her mom allowed a few seconds of silence. "I'm sorry. I really am." Again she waited, and Bailey knew she was being careful not to hurry into a teaching moment. "I guess I never thought you moved there for that one part."

A group of college-age girls walked along the sand in her direction, five of them laughing and clearly caught up in some story. Bailey took a few steps back and leaned against the wall of the lifeguard station, fading into the shadows. "What do you mean?"

"I mean I thought you moved there for Brandon."

"Well, yeah. Of course. That too." Bailey let the statement shake up her certainties for a few seconds. "I love him. But we were handling having a long-distance relationship."

"I know. I understand that." Her mom sounded kind, as always, her tone warm with patience. "But you've dreamed of dancing on Broadway all your life. And, yes, maybe you had your time and maybe you were ready for something else. But when the show closed, you still had a great setup with the Kellers, right?"

"Yes." Bailey ordered herself not to be defensive about the direction her mom was headed here. "No musicals were auditioning."

"Then maybe that would've been a chance to come home and take a month to see where God was leading. Finish up a couple of your online classes and pray about what might be next." She paused. "Instead Brandon knew of a part, Dayne and Katy had a room, and almost immediately you moved to LA. I know you love Brandon, honey. But have you ever thought maybe it all happened a little fast?"

Bailey stared at the blue sky overhead. "Yes. More than I want to admit." Fresh tears filled her heart, but she refused them. She had to stay controlled so she could focus on her next step. "Right now I don't even know what I'm doing here."

"I haven't sensed you were at peace about it." Her mom's tone remained gentle. "I guess I wanted the realization to come from you."

Bailey used the back of her hand to wipe her cheeks. "Even though I was so sure God had brought me this opportunity." She felt an ache deep in her heart. She'd never experienced something like this. The certainty of believing something was a blessing from God only to see it turn into a mass of confusion.

"You're crying." The compassion in her mom's voice rang strong. "I'm sorry. I wish I could be there."

"Me too." Her words sounded small, buried beneath the hurt in her heart. She pinched the bridge of her nose, the sadness spreading through her. "I wish God would give the answers."

"He will."

The thought of staying in LA made her feel terrible. But the thought of leaving Brandon . . . she squeezed her eyes shut and fought a series of small sobs. "I want to come home, but I'm not sure if that's the right decision." She hesitated. "I should probably try to make it work here. I mean, I chose this — whether that was the right decision or not. Like maybe give it six months at least."

"That makes sense." Her mom's brief silence felt thoughtful. "It's something only you and God can decide, honey."

They talked a few more minutes, and Bailey's tears eased up, though the sting of salt in her eyes and on her cheeks remained. Before the call ended, her mom gave her a Bible verse. "It's from Proverbs 16:9." The sound of pages turning came across the phone line. "Here it is. 'In his heart, a man plans his course, but the Lord determines his steps.' "

The Scripture resonated as if God Himself were speaking to her. Along the beach, the college girls were closer now, their voices loud as they carried on the wind. For a long time Bailey remained quiet, watching the girls and remembering when she'd been at Indiana University. It felt like a lifetime ago, back when she and Andi Ellison first became friends. True friends didn't come easily.

"You're quiet." Her mom's concern filled her tone. "What do you think of the verse?"

"It's confusing." She walked to the railing again and watched the girls head away from her. Her words came slow and measured. Like she was still convincing herself. "I thought God had led me to Los Angeles. But maybe it was just me planning out my course. You know, so I could be with Brandon."

"And maybe in time being there with him is the right place, the right answer."

"I don't know. I have a lot to think about." Bailey let the possibility sway in the early afternoon air, just within reach. "I need to pray." She wiped at a stray tear. "I love Brandon too much to leave. But here . . . this life — it isn't what I really want."

"I understand." Her mom's voice wrapped

around her like the hug she needed. "Hearing God's voice . . . following His lead . . . it's not an exact science."

Bailey agreed, and a strange kind of fear breathed ice-cold against her heart. She still didn't know what she was supposed to do next. Without the film, what would she do in Los Angeles? Was this her chance to write the book she'd been dreaming about lately? The one for teen girls? And wouldn't it be easier to do that from Indiana, where she wouldn't be hounded by paparazzi? But no matter how much of an escape Bloomington might be, how could she even consider leaving Brandon?

She stood a little taller and tried to find a new level of courage, a brand-new sort of resolve. "I love you, Mom. Thanks." She knew what she had to do next. She needed to talk to Brandon. "I don't know what I'd do without you."

"You too." For the first time in the phone call Bailey heard a smile in her mother's tone. "I love you, honey."

The call ended and Bailey didn't hesitate, didn't fight it or second-guess herself. Instead she found a number that had only been in her phone a short while. The number for the producer. This call would be easy. It was the conversation with Brandon she couldn't bear to think about.

After being passed from one secretary to another, the voice of Mel Kamp came on the line. "Hello? Bailey?"

"Yes, sir." She steadied herself. "I'm afraid I have bad news . . ."

Four

Cody Coleman glanced at the sleeping figure of his star running back in the passenger seat beside him and smiled. DeMetri Smith had already committed to a scholarship at Liberty University in Lynchburg, Virginia. But the kid had never been to the campus, ten hours away. When DeMetri asked about making the trip together, Cody didn't hesitate. He couldn't imagine a better way to spend spring break. After all, DeMetri had lived with him for most of the past year. He was the only father figure the boy knew.

So the trip had come together. While most of Cody's players headed to lakes or fishing spots with their dads or grandpas, Cody and his star running back would spend a few days touring campus and meeting administrators and teachers. Class was in session for Liberty, and their visit coincided with CFAW — College for a Weekend — a special event for incoming students.

The winding roads and rolling hills outside Roanoke kept the drive interesting and as of the last road sign they were an hour away from Lynchburg. A hundred miles ago DeMetri had fallen asleep, but Cody didn't mind the break. DeMetri talked almost as fast as he ran the football, and since their predawn departure from Indianapolis, he'd been chockfull of conversation. Now Cody turned up the music and fixed his mind on the drive. His prosthetic lower leg ached the way it did on long road trips, but if he shifted often enough he could handle the pain. Most times he didn't even remember the injury he'd gotten while finishing a tour of duty in Iraq. He rubbed the area beneath his knee and slid a few inches toward the right side of the seat. As he did, the pain let up.

The time passed quickly, and five minutes outside of Liberty, DeMetri woke up. "Coach!" He craned his neck as they blew by a road sign announcing Lynchburg, home of the Liberty Flames. "We're here! We're in Lynchburg!"

"We are." Cody had one hand on the wheel, the other around a cold cup of coffee. A year from now he would miss DeMetri's enthusiasm for sure. "Another couple miles to the campus."

DeMetri sat back hard and stared straight ahead, his smile suddenly gone. "What do you think I should expect, Coach? Do you think the kids will be friendly? You know, like they are back in Lyle?"

"It'll take a while to meet people." Cody chuckled. "But then again . . ." He shot a quick look at DeMetri. "But then again, the way you are, you could probably have a hundred friends in a week."

The kid nodded, like that sounded about right. But then his eyebrows formed a *V.* "You're kidding, right, Coach?"

"Okay, maybe fifty." Cody elbowed his player lightly. "You'll be fine, Smitty. You won't have a problem. I promise."

The conversation fell off as they exited at Candlers Mountain Drive and turned right toward the entrance. They passed East Campus on the left, the newer section of the school where high-end townhouse dorms sat nestled at the base of the mountain. "Those are *not* dorms!" DeMetri's eyes grew wide as he leaned over his knees to see out Cody's window. "Man, remind me again why we didn't sign up for East Campus housing?"

"It was too expensive." Cody laughed again. "Besides, the freshmen are usually in the other dorms." Cody had helped De-Metri through every step of the application process, from his scholarship paperwork to choosing housing. Liberty had offered to pay for everything except books. And Cody had already taken care of that — putting a credit on DeMetri's account for books and whatever extras he might need.

They turned right at the bridge and headed toward the campus Barnes and Noble, where they'd arranged to meet Charles Bigsby. In the days since Smitty's original acceptance, he'd made yet another decision. He would play football for the Flames, but he wanted to study worship, maybe lead music at a church back in Indiana someday. And Bigsby was easily the nation's premier worship leader. He had helped start the worship center at Liberty.

As they parked, Cody saw Mr. Bigsby on the top step of the bookstore. But DeMetri was looking in the opposite direction, toward the football stadium. "Did you get a look at that place, Coach? Looks like a pro stadium!" He paused. "Not that I've seen a pro stadium, but still . . . that has to be better than the usual college fields. The place is beautiful. Can you imagine playing football there, Coach?"

"Smitty."

"Look at the field house! Who has pillars on their field house?"

Cody laughed and managed to sound a little more stern at the same time. "Smitty, Mr. Bigsby's waiting."

That seemed to snap him out of it. "What?" He gasped and grabbed the truck's door handle. "Come on, Coach! What are you doing? We can't keep the man waiting!"

"Yeah, I forgot. I'm holding us up." Cody laughed. He was going to miss DeMetri more than any kid at Lyle. That much was certain.

The campus tour revealed one incredible location after another. DeMetri couldn't stop talking, and Charles seemed to love the kid's enthusiasm. They started at the stadium and made their way to the student union and then to DeMoss Hall. Since it was a school day, class was still in session, and Charles took them to a freshman English class on the first floor. "Go take a seat at the back of the room. The professor knows you'll be observing." He grinned at Cody. "You're in charge after that. Explore. Take a look at the Vine Center and any of the other buildings." He promised to be at the Center for Worship, where they would end up when they were done looking around.

"This is so cool." DeMetri looked over his shoulder at the English room filling up with students. "I can pretend I'm a freshman."

"Absolutely." Charles chuckled. "I think you'll do just fine at Liberty, DeMetri."

Not until they sat down in the back row did Cody look around the room. It held a couple hundred seats, and with the professor already at the lectern up front, the rows were nearly filled. College kids, ready to take the world by storm.

Something caught his attention near the opposite wall. A girl with long brown hair that fell in soft layers around her shoulders and down her back. A girl who, if this were Indiana University three years ago, could've passed for Bailey Flanigan. She sat down next to a tall kid built like a linebacker. Probably played for the Flames.

Cody watched them, the way he angled his head in close to hers, the adoring expression on her face as they shared a few words before the professor began. Why hadn't he treated Bailey like that? He'd been so busy walking the other way that he never stopped to look at her. Really look at her.

He narrowed his eyes, watching the couple. Bailey never would've judged him for having a mother in prison. Never would've pinned his mother's failures on him. And not for a minute would she have believed his past might define him forever. If only he had believed back then the truth about having a new life in Christ. A new life perfectly deserving of a girl like Bailey.

But he hadn't believed it then, and sometimes he struggled to believe it now. Still, for just a minute, he wanted to think he was that guy across the room, that the girl was Bailey, and that he'd figured it out in time. Long before it was too late.

"Coach?" DeMetri whispered in a loud voice. "You in some sort of spacey place or what?"

"Hmm." Cody turned to the kid. "What?"

"Come on, Coach." DeMitri didn't miss much, and this was no exception. He kept the whisper. "That chick looks like your Bailey girl. That what you're thinking?"

"Nah." Cody made a face as if to say DeMetri wasn't even close.

"Coach. Don't mess with me."

"I'm not. She looks nothing like her." Cody looked back at the girl and then at DeMetri. Then he winked at him. "Okay, maybe a little."

The professor took the podium, positioned his ear mic, and launched into a ten-minute discourse on hyperbole. When he came up for air, DeMetri motioned to the door.

Cody nodded and led the way quietly out of the classroom.

Outside the room, DeMetri kept his voice low. "Let's go that way." He pointed to a courtyard behind the building. When they were outside, DeMetri stretched his hands over his head and let loose an exaggerated sound of relief. "I mean, how much can a man talk about hyperbole?"

Cody laughed. "He takes his English seriously."

"Me too, but really?" DeMetri shaded his eyes. "Looks like food in that other building."

They walked past a fountain and several picnic tables of students and headed into the cafeteria. After buying a couple platefuls of tacos, they went back to the courtyard and found a table. As soon as they were seated across from each other, Cody leaned on his forearms. "So what did you think?"

DeMetri opened his taco wrapper and wrinkled his brow. "About how that girl looked like Bailey?"

"About the class."

"Actually, I have a thought about Bailey."

Cody smiled. There was no reigning the kid in. "Okay . . . what's your thought?"

The kid took a big bite of his taco and nodded while he chewed. When he could talk he tapped his finger on the table. "She wasn't the girl for you, Coach. You know that, right?"

Cody waited, his eyes on DeMetri. "Why?"

"Don't get me wrong . . . Bailey's hot." He seemed to dislike his choice of words. "Scratch that. She's very pretty."

"I'm with you so far." Cody could see how seriously Smitty was taking this.

He gave a shake of his head like he was baffled. "I mean, the two of you look good together, and there's all this history stuff between you. Like, anyone could feel it."

A chuckle came from Cody. "Okay."

"But there's this problem in your eyes. Both your eyes." He lifted his gaze to the sky and squinted. "When you were talking to her outside the theater, when we went up to New York, it was like . . . like you both had goodbye in your eyes."

"Hmmm. Goodbye, huh?" Cody liked keeping things light with DeMetri. He struggled to do so now.

"Yeah, you know. The way people look at each other when it's over. When there's nothing left but goodbye."

Cody angled his head, not sure what to say. If a high school kid could see goodbye in their eyes, and if Cheyenne could see it, then no wonder he and Bailey were finally able to see it too. Cody pressed his lips together and breathed in sharply through his nose. "You're right. Just took us a while to figure it out."

"Happens." DeMetri shrugged and grinned at the same time.

Then the conversation switched to the Liberty football stadium and back to the droning English professor. They made small talk as they finished their lunch. Ten minutes later, Cody was collecting his taco wrappers when his cell phone rang.

"Hello?" He stood and walked toward the trashcan.

"Cody Coleman?" The voice was loud and distinct.

"Yes, sir?"

"Cody, this is Edwin Baylor, athletic director at Oaks Christian School, Thousand Oaks, California. Got your number from Jim Flanigan of the Indianapolis Colts." He spoke fast, his words choppy bursts. "I hope that's not a problem. Getting your number, calling you on your cell."

"No, sir. It's not a problem." Cody took a few steps away from the table where DeMetri sat watching him. Oaks Christian? The school was one of the most well known in the country. Its student body included the kids of several famous actors and athletes.

A group of loud students entered the outdoor area. Cody covered his free ear as Edwin Baylor continued. "Listen, our football coach stepped down last week. Taking an early retirement." A frustrated huff of air blew through Cody's phone. "The fact is we've really tanked these last few years. The kids are rich and lazy and complacent and we need . . . well, we need what you brought to that Lyle team. I figure you're committed out there, not looking to move." He came up for a quick breath. "But the fact is you're top of our list. We'd love you to at least consider the position."

Cody released a bewildered laugh as he glanced back at DeMetri. His player had gathered his lunch wrappers and was halfway back from the trashcan to the table. He shot Cody a curious glance, and Cody held up his hand, letting the kid know he wouldn't be long. "Wow . . . yes, sir. I can certainly consider it." He paused. "Do you have a time frame, a date when you need to know by?"

"Good question. Actually, I haven't thought about that. By the end of the semester, I guess. Our strength coach is running spring training with the boys. The decision with our former coach came rather quickly."

"I understand." Cody's mind raced. "I can tell you if I'm interested by the end of the week. Then we can go from there."

"Perfect." The man sounded optimistic. "You've got my number. Call me when you know something." Edwin thanked him again. "I think this school really needs you, Cody. Our team will be praying."

The call ended and Cody turned to find DeMetri, his brow raised, eyes curious. "Who was that?" The kid stood and met Cody halfway. "What are you certainly gonna consider, Coach?"

Cody slipped his hands into his back pockets and motioned for DeMetri to walk with him. "I'm not sure I'm supposed to stay at Lyle. Like maybe God is leading me somewhere else."

"What?" DeMetri rarely sounded angry. But this was one of those times. "You're not leaving us, Coach. Not after I prayed for you to come to Lyle." He stopped and stared at Cody, his eyes narrowed. "You're *our* coach. Those other schools, they can find their own guy."

They were out in front of DeMoss Hall on a shady tree-lined pathway. "Smitty, sometimes God calls us to a place and time

81

for a season." He stopped and looked around at the grand campus. "You're leaving Lyle because God is calling you here. But you won't be here forever." He put his hand on DeMetri's shoulder. "It's that way for all of us."

For a few seconds, anger framed Smitty's face and tension made the muscles in his arms tight. Then slowly the fight left him, and his shoulders relaxed. "The guys need you, Coach."

"They need each other." There was another detail Cody hadn't shared. "The team doesn't know this . . . but I talked with Coach Schroeder. His son starts high school this year, and Schroeder's crazy about the idea of being head coach. Something he's prayed and dreamed about since the boy was born."

DeMetri thought for a long moment. "Coach Schroeder has college experience." He gave the slightest shrug. "He'd be good, I guess."

"He'd be great. Plus he lives in Lyle and he loves it there."

"What?" Smitty looked shocked, but already the sparkle was back in his eyes. "You don't love Lyle?"

"Of course I do." Cody chuckled. "But I never planned to live there." He hesitated.

"Coach Schroeder . . . he'd coach the team for the next two decades if he could."

They started walking again, in less of a hurry than before. "Coach S'll do good," Smitty shot a slow, crooked grin in Cody's direction. "Must be nice, Coach. Getting big time offers from other schools." He puffed out his chest. "Just don't forget . . . we made you famous."

Laughter filled the air between them, and Smitty put his arm around Cody's shoulders. "Don't worry, Coach. I know what you're thinking. We didn't have anything to do with it, right?"

"That, and the fact that I'm not famous." Cody was grateful the kid wasn't still mad at him. "God did everything. Through Him and for His glory."

"His way."

"Exactly." Cody grinned and for a few seconds he relived the phone call. He had an offer on the table from Clear Creek High School in Bloomington and now this — a job possibility at Oaks Christian.

DeMetri removed his arm from Cody's shoulders and quickened his pace. "I wanna catch the lunch crowd at the café."

"We already ate." Cody kept up with the kid. "Don't tell me you're hungry again."

"Actually, I am." DeMetri winked at him.

"But I sorta want to see the kids, you know? Make sure I fit in."

For an instant Cody felt a flicker of heartache. He realized how much he'd miss the kid, miss the way he could brighten any room or lighten any mood. Miss having him around the apartment. "You'll fit in, Smitty. Like I said . . . fifty friends, easy."

"But what about a best friend, Coach . . . you think I'll find a best friend?"

"Of course." He elbowed the kid. "They'll be lining up for the spot."

"I don't know." DeMetri laughed. "I hope you're right."

They reached the café, and a couple of girls from the English class approached them. In no time they invited DeMetri and Cody to their packed table. Cody kept quiet while Smitty and the other students got to know each other. No, the kid wouldn't have a problem. Cody was sure.

As the day played out, Cody was even less concerned about Smitty's transition. Rather, he was concerned for himself, for the next step in his coaching career, and the decision he needed to make about where he would work. If he stayed in Lyle, he would forever see Cheyenne along the sidelines of their practice field, forever feel the memory of a beautiful girl whose life was cut short far too soon.

He could move to Bloomington, but there the memories would be worse.

It was a fact that made the phone call from Edwin Baylor very interesting. A move to Thousand Oaks outside Los Angeles might be the perfect solution. A few high school friends had wound up in Los Angeles, and last he'd heard Andi Ellison and her parents lived there too, though he hadn't talked to her since she left Bloomington. Of course, Bailey and Brandon would be there, but that didn't really impact his decision one way or the other. He doubted he'd run into them teaching and coaching. Yes, the move to Southern California was definitely a possibility. But, if he was supposed to take the Thousand Oaks position, he had the same question Smitty had. Not whether he'd fit in, but whether or not he would ever find a real friend.

FIVE

Bailey needed to talk to Brandon sooner than later.

He wasn't going to like what she had to say, and her heart hurt over what lay ahead. But she couldn't wait any longer. He had an open afternoon that day, and the two of them planned to meet at Will Rogers Beach — Bailey's new favorite spot. If they came in two different cars, they'd have a better chance of avoiding the paparazzi. They'd figured out that pictures of the two of them were much preferred by the media over either of them alone.

Bailey ran the towel once more over the clean kitchen countertop at Katy and Dayne's beach house. More than twenty-four hours had passed since Bailey had turned down the teacher part, but Brandon had worked late last night and this morning in the editing room with the production team from his New York movie. His busy schedule had given her more time to think, time to pray with Katy privately last night. And now — just a day after reading the script — she was sure she'd rushed her decision to move to LA. No matter how strong her feelings for Brandon.

Underlining the point were the two talks she'd had this week with Brandon's agent, Sid Chandler. Sid felt certain the right part would come along, but each time they spoke he treated her with a little more condescension. "You're very picky, Bailey," he'd told her yesterday over the phone. Like he was trying to hide his frustration. "You agreed to take the NTM role, and then you back out. Brandon told me you'd be selective, but I didn't expect anything like this."

The comment confused her. "I'm no pickier than Brandon." She didn't want to fight with the guy, but she wasn't sure what he expected.

"Well, now, I wouldn't say that." Sid seemed sure of himself. "I know Brandon. He's an actor first. Ultimately, he will be open to a lot of different roles, no matter what his contract eventually reads. That's why West Mark's willing to be patient with him." He paused. "Something to think about if you plan to work in this business. Don't confuse art with morality. Many times the two aren't exactly in sync. Walking away from a part will only hurt your reputation in the business."

His comments hurt, and now as she added soap to the dishwasher Bailey found herself analyzing them. She knew Brandon better than Sid knew him. He wanted creative control because he didn't want to make movies that compromised his faith. Sure, movies could deal with difficult topics and show the reality of hard issues facing the current culture. But Brandon wouldn't cross certain lines, no matter what Sid Chandler thought.

Bailey caught her long hair at the back of her neck and pulled a hair tie over it. The ponytail felt good, since her hair was still damp from the shower. She'd cleaned the kitchen and dining room earlier that morning and now she had half an hour before meeting up with Brandon. She poured a glass of water and was heading toward the back deck when Katy and little Sophie came through the front door. Their eyes met and instantly Bailey knew something was going on. The two had known each other long enough that Bailey could read her friend's eyes.

"What's up?" Bailey moved to Katy and took Sophie from her.

"Hold on." Katy set her bag down and began to make a quick tray of sandwich bites for Sophie. Along the way she stopped to stretch her back. She was five months pregnant now, and it looked like she was carrying a small soccer ball. They'd just found out they were having a boy, and Sophie often patted her mommy's tummy so she could talk to her brother.

While Katy worked to get Sophie situated, she looked back at Bailey. "It's so weird. I mean, we prayed about this yesterday and then today . . . today I get this crazy call from my CKT director back home."

Katy and Dayne owned Christian Kids Theater in Bloomington. They'd bought the business and the local theater with the intent of running it, but then they'd moved to Los Angeles to be involved in the development of Christian films. At this point they only attended CKT meetings a few times a year. Especially now that Katy was pregnant with their second child.

When Sophie was in her high chair eating, Bailey and Katy sat across from each other at the table. "So . . ." Bailey's heart beat harder than before.

"My director is quitting. She'll be around for another week, and then she's moving to Chicago." Katy sat back and crossed her arms. "We should probably sell it, what with this little one on the way." She rested her hand on her abdomen. "But I can't rush into a decision like that." She looked straight at Bailey. "Basically I need a director in a hurry. Someone to take over before we audition for the spring show in a week."

A week? Bailey swallowed. "So what were you thinking?"

"Well," Katy handed Sophie her cup of milk. "What are *you* thinking? You still see yourself moving back at some point?"

"Probably." Bailey felt a wave of sadness. "I haven't talked to Brandon yet. I go back and forth. We can handle long distance, but it's not ideal." She let out a shaky sigh. "At the same time . . . this isn't where I want to be." She stopped herself, dizzy and sick over the way the pieces seemed to swirl around. "All I'm sure about is Brandon."

"Good." Katy let that settle. "He loves you . . . very much."

"I love him too." Bailey's stomach still hurt at the thought of leaving him. She stared at the floor. What did her willingness to leave say about her? If she loved Brandon, shouldn't she be willing to stay? To sacrifice?

Katy leaned her forearms on the table so she was closer to Bailey, her eyes kind and understanding. "What are you thinking?"

"I should be willing to stay." She hesitated. "I mean, isn't that what love's supposed to look like? Two people sacrificing everything for each other?"

Katy's smile was gentle. She didn't need to answer, really. After all, Katy had made the sacrifice to move to LA for Dayne. Her answer took a few seconds, and during that time she gave Sophie some broken pieces of a graham cracker. The little girl was being so quiet she almost seemed caught up in the conversation. Katy faced Bailey. "Sometimes love looks like that."

Bailey hated this, feeling so scattered. One minute certain she should leave LA and return to Bloomington, take time to think through her life. The next desperate to stay here or wherever Brandon might be. She leaned her elbow on the table. "What's that mean? Sometimes?"

Again Katy took her time. "I remember when I was dead set against living here." A sad, quiet laugh came from her. "It wasn't really about LA or Bloomington for me. Back then . . . I loved Dayne, but I was scared too. I wasn't sure if I could spend the rest of my life in the limelight. I guess . . . love changed my mind."

The truth in Katy's words wrapped itself around Bailey and helped her see clearly for the first time in days. She loved Brandon, but did she love him enough to live in LA? To spend the rest of her life with him wherever that might be?

"See . . ." A new depth shone in Katy's eyes. "When you love someone for life, when your souls are at rest because they've spent a lifetime searching for each other, the places become irrelevant."

"Hmmm." Bailey blinked and stared out the back window at the distant sea.

"Because when you love like that, just being with that person means you're home." Her smile filled her face. "Home becomes a person, not a place."

Bailey and Brandon had discussed that very truth only a few months ago. She stood and hugged Katy. "Thank you." She pulled back and looked into her friend's eyes. "I needed to hear that."

"It's okay to not be sure." Katy's tone remained empathetic. "God will show you, Bailey."

"Whether it hurts or not." Bailey stepped back as Sophie clapped her hands and then slapped them on her high-chair tray. Bailey leaned down and kissed the little girl's cheek. "When you're older, listen to your mommy, Soph. She'll know what you need."

Katy looked touched. "Thank you." She

stood and ran her hand over her daughter's head, then paused. "If your decision really takes you back to Bloomington — even for a season — we'll miss you. But in the meantime, I need a director by Monday. Just so you know."

A smile warmed Bailey's heart. "It would be an honor." So many memories were tied up with the Bloomington theater and her time performing with CKT. Her and Connor auditioning for one play after another and Katy directing them, like that chapter in their lives would never end. But the one thing she couldn't do was rush into taking the position, thinking that just because the opportunity came along it was God's plan for her life. Instead she would take her time . . . talk to Brandon and pray. Maybe then the answers would be clearer.

Bailey grabbed her purse and gave Katy another quick hug. "I'll see you tonight."

"You're meeting him?"

"If I can use your car again, yes." She breathed in deep, steadying herself. "Pray for us."

Bailey called him on the way to Will Rogers State Beach, where she'd read the script and talked to her mom just the day before. "I'm on my way."

"Okay." Brandon hesitated. "You sound upset."

"I'm sorry." Bailey tightened her hand on the wheel. "I've been talking to Katy. About LA and Bloomington." She was quiet for a moment. "I have a lot on my mind."

"Hmmm." Concern weighed heavy in his tone. "Should I be worried?"

"I don't know. I'm not sure about anything." She sighed. "I just need to see you, that's all."

Twenty minutes of traffic later, Bailey pulled into the Will Rogers parking lot and saw Brandon's car parked close to the sand. His was the only one in the lot.

They were alone for now. Somehow the paparazzi must have missed him, or maybe they couldn't be bothered to hunt down celebrities at midday. *Thank you, God. We need this . . . please, give me wisdom, help us both hear Your voice.*

She parked next to his newly leased gray BMW, the latest in a series of vehicles he rotated through in an attempt to confuse the paparazzi. Her chest felt too tight to breathe deeply, so she didn't try. Instead she grabbed two water bottles from the backseat and stepped out of the car. The smell of saltwater was rich in the afternoon air, the sunshine on her shoulders warmer than it had been since last fall.

A strong wind blew off the Pacific, and Bailey shaded her eyes as she scanned the beach. She didn't see him at first, but then she spotted him on the lifeguard tower. He was standing at the railing, staring out at the water. His body language told her that he was deep in thought, as if maybe he had an idea about why she wanted to meet, how she was feeling unsure about staying in Los Angeles.

She set out across the sand, glad when the wind let up a little. He seemed to sense her presence, because he turned her direction when she was only part way to him. Without hesitating, he started down the stairs toward her. He stopped when they were a few feet apart, lost in her eyes. He looked broken, terrified of whatever she had come here to tell him. Their last conversation must've really made him think. But in a move that was classic Brandon, he smiled and seemed to force himself to let go of his fears. Then he pulled her into a hug that lasted a long time. Warm in his arms, Bailey doubted herself more than she had all week.

"This must be serious," he slid his face alongside hers, their cheeks brushing lightly together. He kissed her slowly, with a desperation she'd never seen in him. "Everything's okay, baby." He searched her face. "It is."

She allowed herself to live in his eyes for a long moment, but just when she was going to tell him about her thoughts of maybe returning to Bloomington, she heard the sound of cars screeching into the parking lot. "No!" She grabbed his arm and together they ran for their cars. "Why does this always happen?"

Brandon took the lead and kept to her pace. By the time they reached their cars, ten yards away the photographers squealed up in two sedans. They spilled out and grabbed cameras from the trunk and back-seat.

"Use my car," Brandon shouted, running with her toward the passenger door. The wind had picked up again and it was hard to hear above the sound. "Get in. I can lose them."

A scream rose in her throat but she swallowed it as she slid into the seat and he slammed the door. He ran around the front of the car, they had their cameras up. "Brandon, don't leave! Let us get some pictures," one of them yelled. "Why do you run? We always catch you."

Bailey slid lower in her seat, her heart pounding. She hated this, being chased whenever they were in public. She didn't have it in her to fake a smile, which meant the story would be about them breaking up. She couldn't handle that. Especially now, when she was trying to decide whether she could stay another week in Los Angeles.

Brandon jumped into the driver's seat, started the engine, and sped into a squealing U-turn away from them. Bailey looked over her shoulder and watched them run back to their cars. "They're gonna follow us."

"I'll lose them." He sounded angry. "I said I would, Bailey."

She sat back in her seat, shaken. He'd never talked to her like this, so what was happening between them? He sped across the parking lot and made a dramatic right turn on Pacific Coast Highway. She had no idea where he was going, but it didn't matter. Suddenly the photographers chasing them weren't nearly as important as one very obvious detail.

The question marks sucking the oxygen out of his BMW.

Six

Bailey glanced at Brandon's profile as he drove. He was clearly upset, focused on the road, speeding at the outer limits of safe. The intensity in his jaw told her this wasn't the time to talk. So she looked straight ahead. Her heart slammed around in her chest, faster and louder than when they'd been running up the sandy beach. Did he really expect her to be fine with this? With paparazzi chasing them along Pacific Coast Highway? Putting their lives in danger?

The moment had an uncanny, terrifying resemblance to the ones Dayne Matthews had once lived with. It was a time like this that had caused Dayne's nearly fatal accident on this very highway. She tried to breathe deeply, but she couldn't. Her heart raced faster than before. If the constant danger caused by the photographers wasn't trouble enough, there were the lies splashed across the tabloids.

Brandon shot her a quick, serious look. "I'm taking you out on my yacht."

She blinked and shifted so she could see him better. "You have a yacht?"

His face relaxed a little. "Yes." He smiled and it erased some of the anger in his eyes. "I thought I told you."

"Uh," Bailey uttered a bewildered sort of laugh. "No. You never told me."

"I don't use it much." He set his jaw again, glanced in the rearview mirror, and returned his eyes to the road once more. "Our first time out shouldn't be like this." He sighed. "I was going to surprise you with the trip today. The captain lives in Marina del Rey, and he's already on board, fueled up and ready to go."

Bailey felt the air around her grow thinner. He had planned this? A trip on his yacht? How could she tell him she might leave Monday for Bloomington when he cared so much, when he would do anything to connect with her and talk to her? She cracked the window and tried to take a full breath.

"What?" He didn't sound angry like before, but he wasn't happy. "Why the whole window thing? You're still worried about those guys." He clenched his teeth. "We've lost them. I told you . . . trust me."

"I'm not worried." She craned her neck around and searched the two-lane highway behind them. If they were still being chased, for the moment Brandon had lost them. No frantic drivers appeared to be gaining ground on Brandon's car. Bailey faced the front once more. She couldn't tell him how she really felt. Not yet, anyway. Her mind raced, searching for a safe topic. But none came to mind.

He kept the car at top speeds until they turned left into the gated marina parking lot. "They're gone. They'll never follow me onto the water. Takes a whole other level of paparazzi."

Bailey wanted to believe him. She stared out at the marina and the yachts lined up one after another. "It's beautiful here." Bailey turned to him. "I can't believe you never said anything."

"Well." He eased the car to a stop and settled back against his seat, his hand gripping the wheel. He looked more like himself now, but his tone still held a weary edge. "Compared with the ride I've been on since I met you, it didn't seem that important."

He had a point, and again Bailey's stomach ached at the thought of the conversation they needed to have. How could she tell him how she felt while they were out at sea together?

He parked in an underground lot, and as he killed the engine he leaned hard into his side door. "That whole race here . . . it wasn't how I planned this." He looked at her. "Please, Bailey . . . every time a photographer jumps out of a bush, it's not the end of the world." His frustration from earlier remained. "You make it exhausting."

"Because it is." She didn't want to fight, but she couldn't let the moment pass without at least trying to explain herself. Her voice grew louder. "It *is* exhausting. Always wondering who's following us or what kind of pictures they'll take and how they'll lie about them in grocery stores across the whole country."

"Who cares?" His tone matched hers, both of them more upset than they intended to be. "Nobody believes that trash."

"You can't be mad at me for wanting my privacy." She pressed her open hand to her chest. "I didn't grow up with this, Brandon."

"But you don't have to react to it." He lowered his voice, but clearly he wasn't giving up. Fear and determination mixed together in his expression. "Don't you see, baby? They want to break us up. If we let them . . . they win."

"We aren't breaking up." Bailey hated

even hearing him talk like that. Still, he had a point. Moments like this made the paparazzi the winners. They were creating the drama they liked telling people about. Even now the paparazzi had given her no time to explain herself, no time to ease into the conversation. It wasn't just the constant sense of being chased. The problem was with Hollywood itself, and the lack of projects she would even consider being a part of. And now CKT needed a director — at least while she thought about the big picture of her life. Like whether she should audition for Broadway shows again, among other possibilities.

Her head was spinning, so she closed her eyes and rested her forehead against her knuckles. "Please, Brandon . . . can we go? Can we get out onto the water?" She paused, dizzy from the sadness and confusion fast dancing in her mind. "I can't think in here."

Brandon released a burst of air, in a way that filled the car with defeat. He stepped out, and before she could open her door he was there, opening it for her. "Thank you." Her voice was weak, tired, because of how she dreaded the talk ahead. Maybe the struggle was all her fault, her fault she couldn't handle the photographers and her fault she didn't like LA.

He grabbed his bag from the backseat, shut the door, and locked the car. He started walking fast toward daylight, but then stopped and held his hand out to her. She hesitated, but only for a few seconds, then she caught up and let her fingers slip between his as they headed for the boat docks. Tears stung at her eyes, because everything about Brandon was still wonderful and amazing and full of the sort of love she'd never known before. And as they walked through the gated ramp and out to his yacht, she couldn't think of a single reason why she would mess things up between them now.

The sun was even warmer than it had been at Will Rogers, and though they walked in silence, the tension between them eased. Bailey could feel her heart start to relax. That didn't mean she should stay in LA, or that she could avoid the conversation ahead, but it made what she needed to say possible. After all, if she returned to Indiana, she wasn't breaking up with him, right? Just taking a step back. So she could be sure she was headed in the right direction.

Before they reached the boat, the sound of screeching tires sounded from behind them. Bailey whipped around, but Brandon tightened his grip on her hand. "Don't look. The gates are locked." He kept his gaze straight ahead. "They can't reach us. We'll be behind tinted glass before they can snap a picture."

Bailey's knees trembled, but she kept walking, following Brandon's lead.

He forced a smile, ignoring the commotion behind them in the parking lot. "This is it." Brandon led her onto the boat and toward a doorway to a living room on the main deck. He didn't exactly sound enthusiastic, but he was trying. Even behind the privacy glass, she could hear the paparazzi shouting at them. But Brandon was right. They couldn't get past the locked gate.

As if no one was shouting at them or snapping pictures of the yacht, Brandon motioned toward a small flight of stairs headed to the lowest deck. "The bedrooms are down there, and the top deck is sort of a covered observation area. The captain can pilot the boat from up there or here, on the main level."

"Wow." Bailey tried to put the paparazzi out of her mind. She sat on the built-in sofa. "It's beautiful, Brandon. Do you get out on it much?"

"Not really." He shrugged. "The studio uses it to entertain producers and other actors. I've only been out once in the last year." He stepped into the small kitchen. "I had them stock it with turkey and bread . . . fruit and avocados. Bottled water and iced green tea." He smiled at her. His expression was still weary from the past hour, but clearly he was trying to start fresh. "I thought maybe we'd sail along the coast and eat out by Paradise Cove. Spend a few hours on the ocean together."

Bailey felt her heart melt under his gaze and the sincerity of his words. He never would've taken her on his yacht to impress her. It had only come up now because she wanted to talk and he figured the ocean would give them time alone. Time away from the photographers. "I'm touched, Brandon . . . really." She ran her hand over the leather seat beside her. "That you would think of this. Today."

As they talked, the captain came down from the top deck and introduced himself. His name was Alex and he was a thirty-something guy from Ukraine. He turned to Brandon. "The paparazzi are aware of our trip."

"I'm not worried."

"Yes, sir." Alex smiled. "Ready, then?"

Brandon nodded. "Definitely."

The captain hurried up the stairs again

and in no time they were backing out of the slip, headed through the marina toward open sea, leaving the photographers behind them. Motion didn't usually bother Bailey, but between the craziness of the afternoon and the conversation she still needed to have with him, she quietly prayed she wouldn't get sick.

They sat inside, across from each other on separate sofas watching the marina pass by behind them, not saying much. Brandon pointed out the boats belonging to a few other celebrities — yachts much larger than his. "I like getting out here when I want to." His face looked relaxed, the way she was used to seeing him. "But I definitely couldn't live on the water."

"So you don't need a floating mansion." She understood him. The way she had always understood him since the day they met.

"Exactly."

When they cleared the breakwater, the sea grew choppy and Bailey grabbed a hand-hold anchored to the wall near the sofa. "Is this . . . normal?" She'd never been on a yacht. Her parents had taken the family on a cruise years ago and she remembered the gentle feel of the ocean beneath her. But the way the boat pitched and yawed now made it feel like they might capsize.

"Yes." He chuckled and moved carefully from his sofa to hers. "Come on . . . let's go up. It's a better view."

She felt the doubt in her expression. "When it's this rough?"

Brandon smiled. "You won't fall." He held out his hand. "Come on."

"You're crazy." She took tight hold of his hand, but when they reached the stairs she kept a death grip on both sides of the railing the whole way up. He followed her, and as she stepped onto the top deck, she turned back to him. "We're safe?"

"Yes. I promise." He laughed, but she barely heard him over the sound of rushing wind and water and the yacht's engine. Brandon yelled so he could be heard. "We're fine. I promise." When they reached the top deck, they fell together onto one of the cushioned bench seats.

The view from up top was stunning — they were alone, with sparkling deep blue water as far as she could see, the shoreline of Southern California far in the distance. Bailey held tight to the railing and relaxed a little. As she did, Brandon slipped his arm around her shoulders.

"I've got you, Bailey." He spoke close to her ear. "I won't let anything happen to you." He brushed a strand of hair from her face. "There." His voice mixed with the wind, soft against her skin. "Now I can see your eyes."

She waited, lingering in the moment. "What do you see?"

"Fear . . . walls." He hesitated. "You're ready to run." He soothed his hand over her hair, still close to her. "What's wrong, Bailey? What did I do?"

The boat was further out now, the water and wind less rough so she could hear him more easily. She didn't look away, didn't break the connection between them. "It isn't you." Still, Bailey held tighter to the handhold. How was she supposed to tell him she wanted to leave, that she wanted time? "I've been thinking about everything."

"About us?" Surprise and hurt shone in his eyes. "I thought this was because of the paparazzi, us being chased all the time."

"It's that. But it's all of it, everything about living here." Bailey put her hand alongside his face. "It feels so —"

Before she could finish her sentence, the rotating sound of helicopter blades broke the serenity of the early afternoon. "What in the —" Brandon stood, whirled around and caught himself on the frame of the canopy.

Bailey turned too, but she didn't stand. She didn't have to. The helicopter raced along the water straight for them and as it grew closer Bailey knew what was happening. There could be only one reason a helicopter would come after them. "Paparazzi." Bailey grabbed Brandon's hand and rushed to her feet. "Let's go back down."

"No!" Brandon stood straighter than before, glaring at the approaching chopper. "If they want pictures of us on my yacht, they can take them." He turned to her, the anger from earlier blazing in his eyes again. "Right? I mean, so what? Why should we move for them?"

"Brandon." Captain Alex hadn't said anything until now, but he adjusted his sunglasses and stared at the helicopter, "She's right. If you stay up here they'll come pretty close. Could be dangerous."

"It's fine." Brandon seethed, his body rigid, ready to fight.

She wanted to argue with him, but instead she sat down, her heart pounding so hard she could feel it through her whole body. He took the seat opposite her, so he could see the helicopter.

"Don't run, baby. We have a right to sit here." He clenched his teeth, his eyes locked on the chopper, which had almost caught up to them. Bailey shivered and crossed her arms, looking from the captain to Brandon. This was ridiculous, sitting out here like human targets.

The helicopter reached the yacht, and through the sound of the wind and waves, Bailey heard them. Loud familiar shouts and grunts, intended to get their attention. The staccato sound of the blades grew deafening, so close Bailey felt the wind from the propellers, the helicopter hovering what felt like inches above them.

Brandon stood again and cupped his hands around his mouth. "We're calling the police," he shouted. But even Bailey could barely make out his voice against the deafening noise.

Bailey looked over her shoulder again, and as she did she nearly fell to the deck. The chopper was much too close, dangerously close. The helicopter door was wide open and two photographers hung half out, their cameras aimed at them. Between shots they called out, as if Brandon and Bailey might pose or wave.

"Brandon!" Bailey's hair whipped at her face, making her dizzy. She yelled as loud as she could to be heard. "I can't do this! Let's get out of here."

He shot a final glare at the helicopter and then took her hand and hurried her back down the stairs to the main deck, safe behind the tinted windows. Even then the helicopter stayed, buzzing as close to the yacht as possible. So close that Bailey screamed over the roaring sound of the chopper, certain the chopper would clip its propellers and they'd all wind up sinking in the ocean.

Immediately Brandon wrapped her in his arms. He picked up the intercom from the captain's deck and called Alex, who was at the wheel downstairs. "Get us back. This isn't working." There was a pause. "Yeah, of course try to lose them and definitely call 9-1-1, but we're on our own for now. We need to get back. They've got the advantage."

Bailey felt safe with his arms around her, but her heart sank. Nothing about the day was how either of them pictured it. A quiet talk on the beach, the chance to sit side by side on the lifeguard tower savoring the ocean view and the warm salty air. That's what she'd wanted. Even if the conversation she needed to have was a tough one. Instead it felt like they'd slipped into an action movie where the director didn't know when to cut the scene.

Brandon slumped onto the sofa opposite her. "They'll find a way to get a picture. Even if it kills them."

For a long time they were quiet, allowing only the intense sound of the speeding engine as their background. Ten minutes passed while the helicopter stayed close, buzzing at the yacht again and again. Finally, when a coast guard boat with blaring sirens headed their direction, the chopper gave up and turned toward Malibu. By then Bailey was exhausted, drained physically and emotionally. Brandon looked like he felt the same way.

"I'm sorry." He raked his fingers through his hair and shook his head. "I don't blame you for hating this."

Bailey didn't need to say anything. The paparazzi, the chase down Pacific Coast Highway, and the harassment by the helicopter had said it for her. They were approaching the marina again and after a long while she stood and moved across the cabin to the spot next to Brandon. She took his hand and angled herself so she could see his eyes. "It's not your fault."

"But you hate it." His tone was gentle, wrapped in a sort of pain she hadn't seen in him before. "Right?"

She nodded. "I do." Her eyes met his and

held. With everything in her she hoped he could see inside her heart. "I love you, Brandon. This isn't about us . . . really."

He breathed in sharp through his nose and sat straighter. "But I live here. And you hate it here. That's what this is about." It wasn't a question. He could read her eyes as easily as she could read his.

Bailey wasn't ready to book a flight home, but she was close. She couldn't think about the idea now, so she put her hand alongside his face. "What's happening with your contract? Did they give you more control?"

"Not yet." He caught her hand in his and ran his thumb along her fingers. "They know I'm serious. They're postponing the announcement."

"Hmmm." Bailey wasn't sure why she asked. As if the contract could make a difference at this point. Whether Brandon had control or not, the deal would require Brandon to stay here for the next five years, maybe longer. She held her breath. *God, help me say the right thing . . . please.* "Brandon . . . I need to tell you something."

"This is it, then . . . the thing you wanted to tell me?" The anger from earlier was gone entirely. Instead Brandon looked sad.

So sad Bailey wanted to cry.

She swallowed her fear and hurt and

doubt and tried to explain herself. "The Christian Kids Theater back home needs a director for the spring show." She paused, but not for long. If she didn't say everything now, she might never say it. "I can't be here, Brandon." She took both his hands in hers and leaned close to him, desperate for his understanding. "I'm not doing the movie — you know that much. And there's nothing else on my schedule. Besides, you're leaving in a few weeks for Montana, right?" It was something she hadn't considered before now. The fact that maybe this would be a great time to spend a few months in Bloomington since he'd be gone, anyway.

"I am." Brandon looked paler than before. "So you're saying . . . you want to go back to Bloomington?"

"Maybe." Her answer was a painfully quiet whisper. "If I'm going to do this, I should leave Monday. Auditions for CKT are Tuesday."

Brandon pulled his hands free and stood, staring at her. He hadn't expected this, his shock proved that. "You would really do that? Leave on Monday?"

"Maybe. For now. Just while you're gone and until the play wraps up in a few months." She stood. "It's something I can do, directing CKT." She tried to take hold of his arm, but he avoided her. "Brandon . . . please. Try to understand." She waved her hand toward the ocean. "Running every day from the paparazzi and not having a life of my own. I can't live like this."

"You have a life here if you want one." He exhaled and his shoulders dropped a notch. He crossed his arms, still not willing to be close to her. "It's up to you. If you want to teach, you can teach here. If you're looking for a better movie, you can find it here." His tone filled with passion again. "Have you thought of that?"

He had a point. "You're right. If I want a life here, I can find it." She tried once more to put her hand on his shoulder, and this time he let her. "But I need to think about it, and I'll do that better back there. I don't want this craziness. Seeing my face in the tabloids every time I buy milk, running from paparazzi. It's not me." She couldn't stop now, not when the truth was knocking at the backside of her teeth trying to get out. "Honestly, Brandon . . ." her voice fell. "It might never be me."

Another level of understanding seemed to dawn on him. "Baby, we can figure it out. Don't decide everything right now." Tears filled his eyes, but he didn't blink, didn't look away. "I can't stand the thought of being away from you."

"Brandon . . ." This was killing her. She hated seeing him so upset.

He linked his hands at the back of his neck and looked down. When he lifted his face, a few tears slipped onto his cheeks. "We can't be long distance indefinitely. You move away and then what?" He lifted his eyes to hers, and the hurt there was more than she could take. "What happens to us if our homes are thousands of miles apart?"

Bailey hadn't thought about it that way. But if she was going home with no intention of coming back, he was right. Where did that leave them? She couldn't finish the thought. She only wanted to take him in her arms and reassure him. She felt breathless. "We'll figure something out."

"Maybe not." He came to her and pulled her into his arms. "If you're in Bloomington and I'm here . . . that could never work forever." His voice dropped to a whisper and he used his shoulder to catch another tear. "I have to be here. You know that."

"Maybe I'd only stay in Bloomington for a few months." She felt like she might be sick. They walked together back to the sofa, sat down, and faced each other, their hands joined once more. As Alex maneuvered the boat back into the harbor, the ride grew smooth again. Up ahead in the dock parking lot Bailey could already see two black cars waiting near the marina entrance.

Paparazzi.

"I don't know how to do this." Now the tears were hers, and she blinked twice so she could see him clearly. "I want to be with you." She studied him, holding on to him with her eyes. "I love you."

"Then stay." He swallowed hard, clearly trying to gain control of his emotions. "Stay, Bailey."

"I'm not sure I can." An avalanche of sorrow crashed in around her. She nodded to the waiting photographers. "Look at them."

There was nothing else to say. Brandon searched her eyes for a long time and kissed her, a kiss that hinted at defeat and goodbye. For now anyway. Their tears ran together, and Brandon put his arms around her, holding her close until they felt the boat come to a stop in the slip. Brandon paid the captain and they gathered their things. Brandon seemed determined not to let the paparazzi see them struggling. He forced a smile as they stepped out of the yacht, and he put his arm around her as they walked back to his car.

"Smile. Please, Bailey."

"I am."

The photographers stayed in their cars this time — their view of Bailey and Brandon exiting off the yacht unhindered. Bailey could feel the cameras trained on them, hear their shouts. The pressure to look happy made her feel like she was playing a role, and along with that came worse doubts. Crazy, irrational thoughts like maybe her whole relationship with Brandon had been nothing more than her own happy movie, and now . . . well, now the movie was over. Fade to black and roll credits.

The paparazzi didn't follow them to the private parking garage, apparently content to chase them wherever they were headed next. When they climbed into the car and the doors were shut, Brandon turned to her. "Can I ask one thing?"

"Of course." The sadness between them was almost more than she could take.

"If you leave Monday, can I drive you to the airport?"

"Yes." She leaned closer and hugged him for several seconds. "I'm sorry. I didn't see this coming, Brandon. Really. But if it's just for a few months maybe it makes the most sense."

He hesitated, but his eyes told her there were no guarantees. "I get it."

They were alone in the dark of the parking garage, the paparazzi waiting for them out on the street. So here, at least, this was real. For a couple minutes no one was taking pictures or tracking their every move. "I'm not breaking up with you."

He started the car and backed out of the space. A quick glance in her direction told her that she didn't need to verbally break up with him. Her actions would do that all on their own. The minute they were out in the open, the photographers were at it again — three cameras aimed out the windows of the car shooting in their direction.

Brandon acted like he didn't see them. He kept his expression the same, distant and desperate, as he drove by. Immediately the paparazzi flipped a U-turn and began following them. But Brandon didn't go faster. He only kept an even pace. "They can crash into us if they want to."

Bailey flipped down the mirror in her visor and studied them. "They're too close."

"We're fine. They won't really hit us."

But Brandon's refusal to react to the photographers didn't ease Bailey's fears. The paparazzi were willing to drive crazy, pulling into the wrong lane and cutting off other cars to stay immediately behind Brandon and Bailey. At any moment their actions could cause an accident. Finally

Bailey closed her eyes and leaned her head against the seat. *Father, help me ignore them, please. This fear . . . it isn't from You.*

I am with you, daughter . . . lean on Me.

The voice eased her fears and helped her breathe. She exhaled, feeling the peace that only God could bring. When she opened her eyes, she closed the mirror and kept her focus straight ahead, where the paparazzi couldn't be seen. But even as she did there was no denying the one very clear fact: as much as she loved Brandon, and as badly as she wanted to make things work, in this instant she could find peace just one way.

Picturing herself home in Bloomington, Indiana.

SEVEN

Brandon brought Bailey to his house for most of the weekend, taking her home after dark so that whatever pictures the paparazzi might take at least they wouldn't be clear. They talked and read the Bible together, and a few times they fought. Because Brandon couldn't believe this was really happening — that Bailey was leaving. And because of something else — if Bailey was committed to the CKT production, she wouldn't be able to visit him in Montana like they'd planned.

By Saturday she'd made up her mind. She could make no promises and there were no guarantees. By then they both knew that. This move back to Indiana felt different than anything they'd faced. If she wasn't willing to live in LA, then maybe they had nothing. At least as long as he was under contract with West Mark. The studio executives had made it clear that though some actors could take occasional movie deals and live outside California, this deal was different. West Mark executives wanted his movies to release several times a year and they planned on him attending weekly meetings.

Commuting from Indiana would never work.

The sun hadn't shown itself and wouldn't for an hour at least. At four in the morning — too late to photograph the bar crowd and too early for breakfast meetings — there was no traffic, no paparazzi following Brandon. Only a make-believe serenity that could never really exist in this city.

He pulled into the driveway at Dayne and Katy's house and Bailey stepped out from the shadows. Her flight out of LAX was at six. They'd get there ninety minutes early. Plenty of time for the goodbye Brandon couldn't imagine. The one he never saw coming.

He stepped out of the car and met her halfway. "Hi." He allowed himself to be instantly lost in her eyes. If this was their last time together for a while, he wanted to remember it.

"Hi." She let go of the handle of her bag and slipped her arms around his neck. "I don't want to leave you."

Brandon breathed in the smell of her, the hint of shampoo and the mint on her breath. He held on, not wanting to take a single step from here and from her in his arms. "Mmmm, baby. Why don't I go with you?" He pressed his face against hers and ran his hand over her hair. "We can fly off to some exotic island and never come back."

"Sounds amazing."

Brandon willed the moment to freeze, but someone laid on their horn as they passed by on the highway. He stepped back and smiled at her so he wouldn't break down and cry. There would be no exotic island, no freezing time. No way around the reality of the situation.

Bailey was leaving.

Brandon took hold of her suitcase and they walked slowly toward his car. As they did he couldn't help but steal glances at her — her long hair dancing in the breeze, her dancer legs, her beautiful profile. The way her eyes still took his breath when she caught him watching her.

They reached the car and he lifted her bag into the trunk. When they were in the car and headed for LAX, he took hold of her hand and kept his eyes on the road. If he looked at her now, as she left town, he wasn't sure he could hold it together.

"We can still Skype." Bailey squeezed his hand softly. "Okay? That'll help."

Brandon felt the sting of tears in his eyes. "Sure." He smiled at her. It was too late for anger or frustration or anything but love. "Maybe the right movie will come along and you'll come back in a couple months."

"Exactly." She looked at him, and her eyes couldn't hide her doubts.

Brandon sucked in a deep breath and tried to focus on the 405 Freeway. Bailey had never wanted to be in movies in the first place. Sure, she auditioned for *Unlocked.* But only because she hadn't found anything on Broadway. Even now she would pick New York over Los Angeles. At least in New York people left them alone.

He glanced at her again and his heart felt heavy. Hurt and sadness welled up within him. He felt like he was in a box with no windows and doors, no light, no way out. Nothing to give him hope that he might figure a way around what was ahead.

"Bailey?" He turned to her briefly and then looked at the road again. "Didn't you feel safe with me?"

She met his eyes and then looked down at her lap for several seconds. When she glanced up he saw that whatever pain he was feeling, she felt it too. "It wasn't about feeling safe. I don't like being chased." Her voice cracked and she put her hand to her throat, struggling for composure. "I don't like people running after us and taking our picture a hundred times a minute and never . . . never having privacy."

They'd been over this. Brandon nodded and gave her a quick, defeated smile. "I know. I understand." He held her gaze for a brief moment before looking ahead again. "Did I love you enough? I mean . . . did I show you how much I love you?" He wasn't ready for her answer. "Because you said a few times that in your darkest doubts you wondered if maybe it didn't all seem too perfect, too fast. Like what we had wasn't real somehow, right?"

"Sometimes." A long sigh came from her. "Brandon, don't do this." She placed her thumb and forefinger at her temples, covering her eyes. "You did everything right. Every time we were together. We aren't breaking up." She lowered her hand and touched his knee. "You love me. I know that." She paused. "But you have to admit everything happened fast. And it felt a little unreal. Like our own movie."

He wanted to remind her that her return to Bloomington had happened very quickly too. But he didn't want to fight. "We had fun together . . . and because of that it was unreal? Because we were happy?" For the first time that morning he felt angry. "What's wrong with being happy? Is it a problem, Bailey? Being too much in love? Are you really going to hold that against me?"

She withdrew her hand and crossed her arms. For a long time she said nothing, but as Brandon took the exit for LAX, she uttered another sigh, this time shakier than before. Goodbye was coming . . . they couldn't stop it. "What we have . . . it's real. Those were just crazy thoughts." She looked at him. "You and I aren't the problem." Her voice was as calm as it was heavy. "I need to be home, that's all. So I can think about what I'm doing . . . where God's calling me. Moving here, I didn't do that. I rushed things."

Again he resisted the urge to remind her that she was rushing things now. He pulled up in front of the United Airlines drop off area, killed the engine, and turned to her. "Bailey." He touched her cheek, his fingers light across her velvety skin. How could they be doing this? Walking away from all they shared? He squinted against the glare of his breaking heart. "I haven't known God as long as you. But why in the world would He call you away from me?"

She leaned in close to him and let her forehead rest against his. "I don't know." Her tone told him she was telling the truth. She didn't know why she needed to take the CKT position or why she was leaving now or how any of it made sense. But still she was going. "I'm sorry."

It was too late for many words. He took her face gently in his hands and kissed her. But the whole time his mind screamed the possibility: What if this was it? What if they never shared a moment like this again? "Don't leave." He breathed the words against her face, her hair. "Please, Bailey. Don't leave."

"Brandon." She kissed him again, and this time he could see that she was crying. Her body shook from the intensity of her sorrow. "I'm sorry."

"Baby, please . . ." He earned more money than he could spend in a lifetime and had the sort of life where if he wanted something he could have it. All except Bailey. He squeezed his eyes shut and let his head rest against hers again. Sure, he could fly out to see her, and maybe she could grab a few days to see him in Montana. But that wouldn't give them a long-term answer.

With everything inside him he felt the overwhelming reality that no matter what she told him, this was it. The breakup would only be a formality after this.

The goodbye he couldn't imagine saying.

She kissed him one more time and then, as if it took every bit of her strength, she pulled away and opened the car door. Even now darkness provided cover, and sunrise lay an hour or so ahead. Brandon was grateful, because for once they were alone. Their privacy was like a gift from God, because paparazzi always hung out at LAX. But in this moment they were truly alone in the crowd of people coming and going from the airport. Him and Bailey, like any other couple.

Brandon stepped out of the car, pulled her bag from the trunk, and met her on the curb. His eyes were blurry with tears, but he found a smile for her. "See? No paparazzi."

"God is good." She smiled too, but it didn't last long. Her expression fell, and again her pain shone through her sad eyes. "I have to go."

He nodded, and wiped at a few tears as they slid down his cheeks. "Did I ever tell you about the timing? How God brought you into my life at the right time?"

She tilted her head, and her look told him not to do this, not to make their goodbye harder than it already was.

"It won't take long." He moved in close to her, so their faces were only inches apart. All the world around them faded away as he spoke. "Four years ago I was in a dark place. Like, I shouldn't be here. That dark." He brushed a strand of her hair from her face and focused intently on her eyes. "I've never told anyone this. But when you came into my life I knew."

"Knew what?" Bailey was lost in his eyes, same as he was lost in hers. As if her flight were all but forgotten.

"I knew I'd made the right decision that dark day." He hesitated, careful not to say too much. This wasn't the time for details. "Because you taught me about Jesus . . . and you showed me what love looks like." He smiled despite the tears still filling his eyes. "Thanks for that, Bailey."

"You sound so final." She looked desperate. "I'm not breaking up with you." She searched his face, his soul. "We just need time."

"What if I move an hour out of Los Angeles? Two hours? I could commute, and we could find places in Camarillo or San Luis Obispo." The thought came to him in a rush. "What about that?"

"Brandon." She searched his face. "What would I do in Camarillo?"

He nodded, resigned. There would be no curbside debate here at LAX. She was leaving, nothing more needed to be said. "I love you."

Fresh tears flooded her eyes and ran down her face. "I love you too."

He couldn't imagine a greater pain if someone walked by and ripped his arm off. But he had to face it, so he stepped back and with a soundless whisper he said the only thing left to say. "Goodbye."

Her face twisted beneath her grief, and she waited until she could whisper the words too. "I'll call you."

For a split second he wanted to tell her not to make promises, not when she was leaving with no realistic hope of coming back. But he wanted to believe the possibilities, however slim, so he only waved, jogged around his car, and slid in behind the wheel once more. Their eyes held another long moment, and then she ran her fingertips beneath her eyes, took hold of her suitcase, and turned toward the airport. Brandon watched her go, but all he could think was how crazy this felt, how wrong it was.

Bailey shouldn't be leaving. He loved her,

and she loved him. They belonged together. He would prove that to her, prove that what they shared wasn't too perfect or too fast or too crazy. If Los Angeles was the problem, then he'd figure out a way around it. Hire more security or find a home further away, far from prying eyes and paparazzi. They couldn't walk away from what they shared, because God alone had brought them together. Whatever it took he would prove it to her.

If it took the rest of his life and every beat of his heart to do it.

Bailey couldn't see for her tears, and she had no idea how she checked in and got through security. Not until she was on the plane did it hit her exactly what she was doing: She was walking away from Brandon Paul, the one guy in her life who had fought for her and pursued her and gone to unthinkable lengths to show her how much he loved her.

The thought caused a rush of panic, and without thinking Bailey unbuckled her seat belt. She could still get off the plane, right? Still run back down the aisle and up the jetway and out into the concourse. She could call Brandon, and he'd be there to pick her up before she could reach curbside.

But even as she felt her legs tense up, felt herself move to stand and crawl over the two strangers in her row, her eyes fell on a magazine across the aisle. A teenage girl was reading a gossip rag and there . . . there on the front page was a picture of the two of them. Brandon and her. They were on the beach and Bailey had her face sheltered as much as possible. The headline screamed at her from across the aisle. "Rough Waters for B&B."

Bailey eased back and buckled her seat belt. Every day back in Bloomington was another day free from the paparazzi. Every week was one more where the tabloids would be forced to find other fodder. She turned toward the window and stared at the baggage guys. It looked difficult, tossing one suitcase after another onto a luggage cart or into the belly of a plane. But the guys laughed and joked with each other as they worked.

At least they get a normal life, she thought. They might not have a lot of money and maybe their circle of influence wasn't worldwide like it was for Brandon Paul. But they could work and live and date and marry without the world searching for trouble. They could have a life, even here in Los Angeles.

She closed her eyes and pictured Brandon, how she'd felt earlier in his arms, the way his cologne still lingered on her sweater.

Dear Lord, how can I leave him? Help me figure things out in Bloomington, please, Father. I can't live with him, but I can't live without him either. Being away from him, telling him goodbye . . . I'm not even sure I can breathe with him so far away.

Daughter, come to Me and I will give you rest . . . Do not worry about tomorrow.

Peace released a warmth through her body and Bailey felt herself relax. But even then fresh tears stung at her eyes. *I miss him already, God.*

There was no answer this time, and as Bailey gave herself over to sleep she remembered something Brandon said at their curbside goodbye. That she had confirmed to him how much God loved him. But he had helped her too. Because love never looked as beautiful as it had over the last year.

The year she'd spent with Brandon Paul.

EIGHT

Jenny was beginning to doubt everything she'd always believed about her daughter and the future God had for her. Some time ago she'd prayed about the certainty in her heart. The certainty that Bailey was and always would be with Cody Coleman. Back then she promised the Lord that this was not a story she would try to write. Rather, she would give God the pen and watch what He might do. After that, God seemed to show her that maybe Brandon was the one they'd been praying for, the right guy for Bailey.

Now Jenny wasn't sure about anything.

Bailey had been home from California for two weeks and not once had she seemed like herself. Sure, she was helpful and friendly, and she and Connor had found again the friendship that once mattered so much to both of them. But her heart remained broken. More wounded than Jenny had ever seen in her daughter. Even after Cody walked away from her the last time.

Jenny had been on deadline for a magazine article she'd written for *Reader's Digest,* and she was behind on the family's email. Now, on the first Friday afternoon in April, an hour before the boys would be home from school, Jenny headed for the computer. But even as she did, she pictured Bailey that morning. Her eyes were different, like they belonged to a person who couldn't find her way home. Even as she recounted the CKT auditions a couple weeks ago, she hadn't seemed like herself.

Like a part of her was absent or dead.

Clearly the impact missing Brandon Paul had made on her daughter's heart.

Jenny sat down at her desk, called up her Google account, and began looking at unopened emails. She was near the top of the list when a letter screamed for her attention. "Concerned about Bailey" the subject line read. Jenny opened it, confused. Who would've known something was wrong with Bailey? She was two lines into the letter when she realized who had written it. The area coordinator of CKT.

Dear Jenny, Just a quick note to let you know that several of us are worried about Bailey. She's doing her job — doing it bril-

liantly. But she's not the same girl. She isn't as open with the kids, and the light in her eyes isn't there.

The letter went on to ask if Bailey had been sick, or if maybe she was more upset about losing her role on Broadway than she'd let on at first. Jenny closed the email, sat back in her chair, and closed her eyes. Bailey didn't miss Broadway. She missed Brandon.

What can I do now, God? How can I help my daughter get past this heartache and loneliness?

The message came to her in a hurry, straight out of her Bible reading from earlier that day.

Trust me in all your ways . . . lean not on your own understanding.

Jenny let her hands fall to her lap. The words were exactly what she needed. She'd leaned on her own understanding long enough. She pictured Brandon, the way he hung on Bailey's laughter and conversation, the times she'd caught him gazing at Bailey when he didn't think anyone was watching. Brandon adored Bailey, no doubt. But the problem the two of them faced now was too great to fix. Jenny remembered a conversation she'd had with Bailey last night.

"I miss him more every day." She was

136

loading the dishwasher while Jenny rinsed the plates. "But I feel sane again. I couldn't take it, Mom . . . the frenzy and running and paparazzi everywhere we went."

"How does Katy handle it?"

"It's different now." Bailey leaned against the counter and tilted her head, thoughtful. "They're out of the limelight so the tabloids leave them alone. Most of the time, anyway."

Jenny had let that thought settle for a minute before she pointed out the obvious. "So that means at some point they won't be after you and Brandon either."

"But at what point?" The fear in Bailey's eyes was all-consuming. "After they run us off the road? Or when they turn the whole country against me for something I might say or do, for some dress I wear wrong or for taking a picture and looking heavier than I did a week ago?" She shook her head. "No. I don't want to live like that."

Jenny stood up from her computer, the conversation still playing in her mind. She didn't blame her daughter. But as real as the problem of living in Los Angeles was, it didn't erase the other problem. The bigger problem. The desperate way Bailey longed for Brandon Paul.

She wandered into the hallway and up the stairs to Bailey's room. There on her dresser was a photo of her and Brandon on the rooftop of the Keller's apartment — the place where Brandon had created a magical prom night for Bailey. The love and light in their eyes was enough to make anyone linger on the photograph, wishing and wanting for that kind of love.

Jenny understood. That was still the sort of love she and Jim shared — the kind that comes along once in a lifetime and makes everything and everyone else step aside for it. A love Cody Coleman never showed Bailey.

Jenny ran her finger over the top of the photo frame and sat down on the edge of Bailey's bed. Then she did the only thing she could do, the thing she'd done every day since Bailey returned home. She prayed for her daughter, and for the young man God had set apart for her to marry one day. That the Lord would protect him and guide him and direct his steps on a path that would in time come face-to-face with Bailey's. And as she prayed for her precious daughter, Jenny's mind filled with the face of a handsome actor, a young man who loved Bailey like no one else had ever loved her.

The face of Brandon Paul.

■ ■ ■ ■

Fifteen days had passed since Bailey pulled herself away from Brandon and somehow climbed aboard a jet plane bound for Indiana. Bailey knew because she was counting. She and Brandon had talked a few times and texted every day. But each time he asked her to Skype, she found a reason to say no. What was the point? She was completely involved with the CKT show *Peter Pan,* and already the area coordinator had talked to Katy about Bailey running a summer camp in Bloomington.

If it weren't for Brandon she could see spending her life here.

She could get through the days, keep herself busy, and find meaning and purpose working with the kids. Rehearsals reminded her of when she was an actor in the theater group herself. Back when she and Connor were kids. Some of the families who had been involved back then were still active in CKT now, and that, too, gave Bailey a sense of being home. Where she needed to be.

If only she could convince her heart.

Bailey pulled her family's car into the driveway and parked in the third bay. She was driving a used Acura, something her parents had bought for the kids to drive. Eventually, though, Bailey would have to get her own car. It only made sense. She stepped out, grabbed her things, and stretched. Rehearsal had gone later than usual, and as Bailey walked through the door and into the family room she felt beyond drained.

The house was dark, so her parents must've gone to bed. Her brothers too, except Connor. She could hear him softly playing the piano in the living room. She set her things down and allowed herself to be pulled toward the music. Their eyes met as she stepped into the room and took the chair next to the piano. Connor smiled with his eyes and kept playing, kept singing. He was working on a Michael Bublé piece for Clear Creek's talent show in a few weeks. A song called "Haven't Met You Yet," and Connor sang it beautifully.

When he finished, he relaxed his posture and turned toward her. "Rough night?"

"Yeah." She leaned on the piano. "Actually, no. The kids are great. We're already looking good for the opening number."

Connor smiled. "I remember *Peter Pan.* It was one of my favorite shows."

"You were the best Captain Hook ever." She grinned at her brother. "Everyone else can only try to come close."

"Aww, thanks." He chuckled. "I think my voice might've cracked a few times, but it was fun."

She let the silence settle between them for a few beats. Without warning she felt her eyes well up. "Nothing feels right."

"Finish the show and go back to LA." Connor understood her better than almost anyone except her mom. "You miss him bad, Bailey. It's all over your face. Every night . . . every day."

"I do miss him." Her whole body hurt from missing him. "When I lived in New York I let myself believe that someway . . . somehow it could work for us. But these past few months . . . I couldn't breathe, Connor. I mean, I thought taking the part in the NTM film would help, but really, I hated it. The whole celebrity thing, the paparazzi — then the way the studio changed the script on me. The whole thing . . . it's not me. It never will be."

"I guess you have just one question to answer then." Connor reached out and covered her hand with his. "What price will you pay for love?"

Bailey fell silent. It was the same question Katy had asked her. But why couldn't Brandon tell the studio he needed to live here? Where they could have a more sane life, and she could write her book or find a future with CKT? Were the meetings really that important? Couldn't he find a way to make it work if he loved her that much? She felt terrible thinking that way, but she couldn't help it.

"Whether you liked LA or not, you left a piece of yourself back in Southern California."

She nodded, trying to imagine ever going back. Her heart skittered around, slipping for a few seconds into an irregular rhythm at the thought. "I started doubting whether it was even real. But I can't do that. I love him too much."

Connor watched her, his face filled with empathy. "I'm sorry . . . I know it's not easy."

Two tears dropped onto the knees of her jeans. "No." Her phone buzzed in her back pocket and she pulled it out. The text message was from Brandon. *Baby, I can't stop thinking about you. Please . . . get on Skype with me. I need to see you.*

"Brandon?"

"Yes." Bailey stared at the text, and then slipped her phone back into her pocket again. "He wants to Skype."

"And . . ." Connor's tone was gentle.

"We will. We have to." She held out her hands and let them fall on her lap. "But sometimes — in my worst moments — I wonder what's the point? If we're living in different states, where is all this even going?"

Connor watched her for another few seconds, then he stood and came to her, pulling her up onto her feet and hugging her. When he stepped back, she could see he understood. "I read a verse in Matthew today. 'With God all things are possible.' " He shrugged. "Maybe that's something you can think about." He took his phone from the top of the piano and checked the time. "Class comes early. I better get to sleep."

Bailey hugged him again and the two of them headed upstairs together — the way they'd done as kids. At the top, Connor patted her back. "God will show you, Bailey. A way around the sadness."

She nodded. "I know. Thanks." She took a step back and managed to find a smile. "Goodnight, Connor."

"Goodnight."

After brushing her teeth and washing her face, Bailey slipped into sweats and a T-shirt and crawled into bed. Like every night since she'd been home she looked at the picture of Brandon and her. Before she turned off the light she took her phone from the nightstand and found Brandon's text message. She tapped her response out slowly, being careful with her words. *Sorry . . . not tonight. I miss you. I'm sorry about all this . . . it feels like it's all my fault.*

His response came almost immediately, as if he were somehow downstairs waiting for her and not across the country in California. *It's not your fault . . . it's not anyone's fault. But Bailey I need to see you, please. There has to be a way to make this work.*

She thought about the Scripture Connor reminded her of — with God all things were possible. How could that be true when, because of distance, it was only a matter of time before their relationship fell apart? Bailey read his last text again. *There has to be a way to make this work.*

She tapped her fingers across the screen again. *I'm praying. I can barely stand under the weight of missing you. Whatever else happens, you should know that. I definitely want to Skype.*

His response hit her at the deepest places of her heart. *Then let's Skype right now. Why wait? Remember, if you need me, say the word. I'll be right there, Bailey. Standing at your front door and ready to take you into my*

144

arms. *There has to be a way.*

Bailey didn't realize it until then, but she was crying again. The way she did almost every night since she'd been home. A few people had asked her if she was okay, and she always answered yes. She was okay. Glad to be home, certain that Bloomington was the sort of place she could live forever. But with Brandon she had been so much more than okay.

She dried her tears, climbed out of bed and grabbed her laptop. They skyped for a few minutes, and the feeling of his eyes on hers was like air to her lungs. But there were no answers, no absolutes, no solutions. After they finished the Skype session, she texted him. *Goodnight, Brandon. I love you.*

Maybe it wasn't smart to tell him so when the distance between them made everything feel so uncertain. But at this hour, she could only be honest.

Her phone buzzed with his text. *You have my heart, Bailey. I'll be in your dreams . . . the way you'll be in mine. I'll call you tomorrow.*

She typed quickly. *Brandon . . . you're amazing. I'm sorry again.*

Her phone felt cold in her hand, nothing like if she were sitting across from Brandon, his fingers intertwined with hers. His message came quickly. *Don't you get it, Bailey?*

145

I'm not letting you go. You can stay in Bloomington for a while, but every day while we're apart I'll pray for God to show you. That somehow you'll trust me enough to come back. I can protect you, Bailey. Give me a chance.

Her tears blurred the words as she tried to read them again. How could he know her heart so well? She typed one last text, because she couldn't go to sleep without telling him again. *I love you. That's all I know.*

One more time his response was almost instant. *I love you too, baby.*

The conversation needed to end. She couldn't let herself fall deeper in love with Brandon when she couldn't imagine a way for them to be together. Bailey turned her phone off, got back into bed, and flipped the light switch. Brandon was fighting for her even now. Like maybe he would always fight for her. She closed her eyes and imagined living in Camarillo or San Luis Obispo. That was possible, right? Maybe she needed to give the possibility more thought. She tried to fall asleep, tried to remember every promise from Scripture. But the one that repeated itself over and over and over in her mind was the one that gave her just the slightest permission to hold onto Bran-

don and his love for her.
With God all things were possible.

NINE

The girlish scream echoed across the prairie
and made Brandon's hair stand up on the
back of his neck. He grabbed the reins of
the muscled paint horse and swung himself
easily into the saddle. He pressed his heels
into the sides of the animal and moved with
him into a tense gallop. Forty acres ahead
of him on the open plain was a low-slung
house made of worn wood slats, a small
one-bedroom dwelling where the scream
came from.

"Molly!" He shouted the name of his
character's sister. "I'm coming. Hold on!"
He pressed his heels against the paint again.
"Giddyup!"

The horse responded and in a rush of dust
and pounding hooves, he brought the animal to a stop and hurdled himself off into a
dead run. "Molly!" As soon as he was
through the door he heard the director's
voice, but only barely above the sound of

his pounding heart.

"Cut! We got it. Check the gate." The director let loose an old-fashioned cowboy whoop. "Amazing work, Brandon. Everyone break for lunch."

Brandon dusted off his jeans and adjusted his white T-shirt. He'd been lifting weights for weeks leading up to this part and now he had heard from everyone on the team that he absolutely looked the part of Colt Granger. The movie was based on the true story of the high school senior whose parents were killed by robbers. Colt and his sisters were left to fend for themselves on a 500-acre ranch, even as the bad guys circled back around to kill them too. The movie was called *Eyewitness.* It was a fairly clean suspense picture, bound to be hugely popular with teens and college kids across America when it came out some time next year.

The movie wasn't the biggest budget film Brandon had ever been a part of, but his studio had pushed for him to take the role. Especially while they waited for the revised contract and the big announcement that Brandon would belong to West Mark Studio soon. *Eyewitness* would have very visible publicity, because of the true story angle, so his manager and agent figured it was one way to keep West Mark anxious to sign him.

Brandon walked back out to the horse and stroked his neck. Later on in the shoot, the real-life Colt would join them. Brandon was anxious to meet him. The way the kid had set a trap for the bad guys and saved the lives of his three sisters — even while his parents' dead bodies lay out back — was something the whole country was fascinated by. The real Colt had agreed to do interviews with Brandon when the movie released.

"Nice work." Molly Anderson came up alongside him and patted Brandon's horse. She was a pretty nineteen-year-old blonde who had made it clear from the first day on their Montana shoot two weeks ago that she was interested in him. She was playing Molly Granger, the oldest of Colt's sisters. Anyone who would listen had heard her explain how she was born for the part — what with her real name being Molly, same as the real-life girl.

Molly leaned close and breathed in. "Mmmm . . . I thought hard work and sweat was supposed to smell dirty." She laughed, teasing him. Trying to win him over. "You smell like every wonderful smell all wrapped in one."

"Wow." Brandon smiled and took a discreet step back. "Thanks, I guess." He paused. The girl was nice enough, and she was a talented actress. He just didn't want to mislead her in anyway. "And that scream . . . very nice."

"If that's what it takes to get you running my direction." She grinned at him and then seemed to notice his tanned arms again. She took hold of his bicep and squeezed it. "Are you kidding me? The girls are gonna go crazy over this new look, Brandon Paul."

He gently took her hand and removed it from his arm. "Only one girl matters."

"Come on." Molly put her hands on her hips and pretended to pout. "Bailey Flanigan's been gone for a month. At least according to the rags." She tossed her shoulder-length hair and took a few steps back. "She's not the only nice girl around, Brandon."

"She's the only one I want." He was finished with the conversation. A quick wave in her direction and he headed for the food truck.

Being on set in Montana had been the strangest experience. Most of the grips and techs were local, more easy going than crews in New York or Los Angeles. Almost like the cast and crew was more of a team, like they could work together and no one really stood out as the star.

All of which gave Brandon more time than ever to think about Bailey. Especially because they had only sketchy cell service on location. He'd only been able to text her a handful of times, and they hadn't talked once since he left for Montana. If that didn't make him miss her enough, there was the rest of the story line in the movie. Part of the plot was Colt's discovery that his parents' love had been extraordinary. A rare and passionate sort of love that most people only dream about, the kind where one heart doesn't feel complete without the other. In the movie, Colt learned this during periods of hiding with his sisters, when he stumbled onto a box of letters his parents had written to each other.

But every time they ran a scene dealing with Colt's parents' love, Brandon could only think of one thing: he and Bailey had that same kind of love. A love people would wait their whole lives for. A love they would die for. His heart was so full with missing her and the love story his character was discovering that Brandon had started writing to Bailey, but not in letters or emails or in mentions on Twitter. He'd brought a journal because he liked having a way to log his thoughts on set without using a laptop.

Already he'd filled a fourth of the book with his thoughts and feelings, with memories and funny anecdotes and dreams he would share with Bailey if she were here.

He decided to put off getting a barbecue beef sandwich from the food truck. First he wanted to meet the special guests who'd been invited on set today. He headed toward a small crowd gathered at the far end of the seating area. A few teenagers had been welcomed onto the set, kids who had been chosen because of their efforts helping others. Brandon walked up to one of the older teenage guys and held out his hand. "Hey, man, I'm Brandon."

"Hi." The kid was maybe seventeen, tall with a smile that lit up the plains. "I'm Brad Wright."

"Glad you could make it out. Tell me about your service project."

Brad proceeded to explain that a friend of his on the basketball team had suffered a severe brain injury in a car accident. "They needed a special van and their house needed to be handicap accessible."

Brandon was deeply touched as Brad shared how he spearheaded a fund-raising effort that brought in enough money to make life in his friend's house possible. His efforts had been noticed by the local news station and soon the production team for Brandon's movie took note and invited him to the movie set.

Brad was the kind of kid who could've easily ignored such a need. Athletic and intelligent, probably a star on his school's basketball team. But in this season of his life he was entirely focused on helping others.

After a great chat with Brad, Brandon shook the kid's hand and moved on to a teenage girl who looked to be fourteen or fifteen. Brandon introduced himself and she blushed, more nervous than Brad had been. "I'm Jade Gilbert. I love your movies."

"Okay, Jade . . . tell me about yourself."

Jade relaxed a little and told him how she loved singing and playing the flute and ballet dancing and karate. Her laughter rang sweet and pure through the spring air. "In my spare time I run marathons with my dad."

"You're a busy girl." Brandon liked her spunk, her love for life. She was probably a lot like Bailey must've been at her age.

She explained that she'd raised $1,000 for the pediatric oncology unit near her town. "I have so much." Jade's eyes shone brighter than the sun. "It's the least I can do to help others."

Brandon was touched deeply as another five teenagers shared how they had done something extraordinary for their community or peers. Several times Brandon blinked back tears, struck by one very clear thought: He hadn't looked for anything like this in Los Angeles. But he made a note to look into it. Certainly there were ways he could help others with his resources, more ways than acting that God could use him in his community.

He walked to the food truck, grabbed a sandwich, and headed for his trailer. The air was cool, so he slid his chair to a sunny spot near the door. From his bag, he pulled out his journal and a pen.

Brandon started at the top of the first blank page. He breathed in deeply before touching his pen to the paper, and he stared out at the wide-open spaces, the forever endless blue sky. Nothing in all his life had made him feel the way Montana made him feel. The few times he'd been to the store, people left him alone — if they noticed he was an actor at all. Like their lives were about only what was simple and strong — love and laughter, running a ranch, and raising a family. As if Hollywood didn't exist.

His eyes found the place at the top of the page and he began.

Dear Bailey, I sit here looking out over the Montana plains and a sky only God could've hung across it, and I dream. I'm always dreaming out here. I keep thinking, what if I gave it all up and we moved here? We could buy a ranch and raise paint horses or open a shop on Main Street — which is pretty much the only street, by the way.

Have I mentioned that I hate how we haven't talked? It's the last Friday in April, and I can't call you or text you. Too much time, Bailey. Far too much. There's no service out here, so I tell myself that you're trying to reach me. You just can't get through. But the truth is something different, right? You're still convinced we can't make it work. I know the paparazzi scares you, and I understand. Really, I do. But I think it was something more that made you run. Like maybe it hit you just how serious things were. For me, ever since the seaweed ring, all I can think about is one very important question — even though I rarely share that with you.

Wanna know a secret? I wanted to propose to you on Christmas Eve . . . you know that. But I planned to ask you again on Valentine's Day. I didn't do it, because Dayne Matthews told me to wait. He said you needed time to adjust to LA before considering something so forever. And now here we are all but broken up. Makes me wonder what if I'd ignored his advice and asked you anyway, the way I almost did on the beach that night.

Ahh, Bailey, I miss you. I feel like half my heart's in Bloomington, and I know — I absolutely know — that you feel the same way about me. Right? What I'd give to know if I was right. Like you can't imagine going your whole life with so much missing. Anyway, Bailey, you're all I think about. God didn't use you to save my life and bring me to Him only to take you away. I believe that. And I'll fight for you as long as I'm breathing.

One day . . . one day I'll give you this journal so you can see how much I care, how it wasn't only some romantic fling, what we shared. Wait, I have a better idea. I'll give you this journal on our wedding day. That's how strongly I feel that God will show us a way to be together. Until then, you have my heart. And I have yours. No matter what you say. Praying for you. Praying for us. Brandon.

He closed the journal and stared out at the horizon again. Lunch was almost over, and his toughest scenes so far were coming up, scenes where he had to fight off the bad guys to keep them from getting to the girls. Brandon slipped a pair of sunglasses on and wondered if Bailey's afternoon was this sunny. *Father, wherever she is, please let her think about me. If she's running, please don't let her get too far. I trust You, Lord. In Jesus' name, amen.*

Once the journal was safe in his bag again, he stood and walked up the steps to his trailer. Forty push-ups and thirty curls with the weight bar later, he was ready for the next round of scenes. There was only one way he would pull off the intensity and courage of the real-life Colt Granger when it came to protecting the girls this afternoon in front of the cameras.

He would pretend he was protecting Bailey.

Like most theater companies, CKT sometimes rehearsed scenes out of order. So it was on that Friday, still weeks before the run of the show, that Bailey and the rest of the artistic team were helping the kids catch the vision for the final scene of *Peter Pan*. The scene where Wendy is grown up and Peter returns for a brief moment.

The kids were about to go on break when

one of the kids playing a Lost Boy raised his hand. "How come Wendy can't stay in Neverland? That's where Peter is."

Bailey felt her heart react to the question. She looked at Ashley Baxter Blake, an old friend who was assisting her with this show, and then back at the little boy. "She had to return to the nursery so she could grow up, so she could find out what plans God had for her life."

"But she loved Peter." The child looked around as if hoping for some support from the rest of the cast. A few kids nodded, indignant at the way the story turned out. "She shoulda stayed with him. Even if it meant never growing up."

"Yeah, plus isn't that a good thing, Miss Bailey? Staying young?" The girl playing Tinker Bell stood and stuck her chin out. "Seems wrong that she would just leave Peter. Kind of selfish if you ask me."

Bailey gave a subtle nod to Ashley, and the young mom took over. "Actually . . . growing up is a good thing." She smiled at them. "You have time to find out what you're supposed to do and be, time to maybe fall in love and have a family one day. Wendy might've wanted that sort of life. A more normal life." She cast a quick look back at Bailey. Ashley knew about Bailey's choice to leave LA, and how badly she missed Brandon. Clearly she was using the moment to validate Bailey's decision.

But the kids would hear nothing of it.

"She was already in love with Peter!" It was the Lost Boy again. "I think when you love someone you should never, ever leave. Even if it means not growing up."

Brandon's face filled Bailey's mind, her heart. *When you love someone, you should never, ever leave.* His words spurred a debate between the kids, and after a few minutes Bailey stood and gave the classic CKT whistle, the sound they automatically knew to repeat and then quiet themselves down. "I think we would all spend a little more time in Neverland if we had the chance." She held up her clipboard and smiled at them. "Okay, let's have everyone take their places."

Throughout the rest of rehearsal, no matter how hard she tried, she couldn't rein her thoughts back in. The Lost Boy had a point, right? Wendy took the safe route by returning to the nursery, but she missed out on Peter Pan and a lifetime of adventures.

As she drove home that night, Bailey thought about Brandon, and their adventures in a different sort of Neverland — places like New York and Los Angeles. She could see again his face on the computer screen as they skyped when she was at the Kellers, and how one night, just like that, Brandon had walked into her room — surprising her with the fact that he wasn't really across the country but right there in the Kellers' apartment. Or the times when he'd taken her to the top of the Empire State Building or through Central Park. Together they'd gone on carriage rides and private jet excursions and even the more recent trip on his yacht. They'd played in the surf at Malibu and walked the streets of Manhattan.

The whole crazy ride felt like a trip through Neverland.

Bailey thought about that, and how in some ways coming home to Bloomington was like returning to the nursery. Safe and predictable. A way to find a career and maybe someday fall in love with someone ordinary, and raise a family in a place where she was comfortable. Which was the only option that made sense. The little Lost Boy was wrong about Wendy. She needed to leave Neverland to find her life and her career and to fall in love and raise a family. If she hadn't returned to the nursery, Wendy never would've known any sense of normal.

The kind of normal Bailey craved —

especially after dating Brandon.

Suddenly and certainly — like never before until this moment — Bailey knew without a doubt that she needed to let Brandon go. She loved him, she always would. But as she pulled into her family's driveway tears filled her eyes and she found a fresh sort of resolve. Found the determination to do the one thing she hadn't ever wanted to do. The time had come, no matter how great the hurt. She would call Brandon early next week, when he'd be back in Los Angeles. And she would tell him it was over, time for both of them to move on. Tears ran down her cheeks and her heart felt like it was being ripped in half. Breaking up with Brandon would be the hardest thing she'd ever done, but she loved him too much to keep him guessing. Too much to give him a sense of hope when there was none. She had no choice. Brandon's world was too crazy for her. It always would be. He lived in a sort of make-believe Neverland, and so she was right to move back to Bloomington. Because people didn't stay in Neverland with Peter Pan.

Not even in make-believe.

TEN

Since Cheyenne's death, Cody had spent every Sunday evening with Tara Collins. The woman was getting on, surviving this latest great loss the way they both were surviving: with God's help alone. Tonight the meal was chili, and Cody stood at the stove stirring the cooked ground beef and kidney beans while Tara mixed up a batch of homemade corn bread.

Music played in the background — the Anthem Lights album Cody couldn't get enough of. He'd made a fan of Tara too. She loved the same songs he loved: "Where the Light Is" and "Can't Get Over You," which was playing through the house now. Cody smiled as Tara crooned along with the chorus. Her voice grew louder and a little more off-key with every line she sang. She raised one hand to heaven and stirred the batter with the other as she belted out the words.

Suddenly Tara seemed to notice Cody grinning at her. She waved her spoon at him. "Now, there . . . don't go giving me that look. The Good Lord says to make a joyful noise and ain't nothin' more joyful than me singing in my very own kitchen."

"No argument here." Cody chuckled and held up one hand in mock surrender. "The Anthem Lights guys should take you on the road. Then everyone could be joyful."

"Cody Coleman!" She waved the spoon again, her eyes dancing. "Don't you make fun of me."

The song continued to play and Tara glanced at the kitchen speakers. "Then again . . . that's not a bad idea. Maybe I'll sing this song for the Ladies Tea next month."

"Only if I can watch."

They both laughed and the sound felt like life coursing through the old house. This was something new between them — the feeling that they had permission to laugh, that they'd mourned in quiet long enough. At first they'd met for Sunday dinner and talked in quiet tones, comfortable in the sad silence, each of them glad to have someone else who understood their pain. But now, so many months later, Cody enjoyed the change happening between them.

Like they were ready to live again.

The song faded and before the next one could start, Tara's smile dropped off a little. "I like to think Art and Cheyenne can see us, how we've figured out a way to laugh."

"Yes." Cody let the thought settle. "I like to think that too."

Tara breathed in sharp through her nose, clearly doing her best to keep the moment from becoming sad. "I miss them." Her smile filled her face again, even as her eyes glistened. "How good is God, letting them be in heaven together. Right?"

"Definitely." Cody pictured Cheyenne, the beautiful girl he had come to love, the way she spoke truth into his life. She had handled the wartime loss of her fiancé Art in a way that was nothing short of miraculous. Art was Tara's only son, Cody's best friend in Iraq. Cheyenne alone had been a light for Tara and Cody as they all lived with Art's death. And when the battle had become her own, Cheyenne again was the brave one, the voice of reason reminding them that heaven was the goal, the prize. And that death was not to be feared.

Now she and Art were together in heaven, and Cody was keeping his promise: making sure he looked after Tara in their absence.

A rush of nervousness shot through Cody's veins at the thought. What if he didn't always live in Indiana? Who would have Sunday dinner with Tara? For that matter, who would visit his own mother in prison? Cody had no answers yet.

He stirred the chili slowly and then set the spoon beside the pan. "Hey . . . I have to tell you something."

Tara was humming again, trying to find the words and the pitch of the next song. She raised her eyebrows at him. "Sounds serious."

"It could be." He leaned against the counter and crossed his arms. "I have an interview tomorrow afternoon in Southern California."

Surprise flashed in Tara's eyes, but she recovered quickly. "Well, good for you." Whatever she might be feeling, her voice remained positive, encouraging. "What sort of interview?"

"For head football coach. A school called Oaks Christian — one of the biggest Christian schools in the country. They want to talk to me about running their program." He almost winced, the sick feeling inside him spreading to his heart. After all, he had promised Cheyenne he would take care of

Tara. How could he do that thousands of miles from Indiana?

Tara stared him down and once more she pointed the corn bread spoon at him. "Hold on there, Cody Coleman. I see that look in your eyes." She shook her head, as serious as she'd ever been. "Don't you go thinking you have to stay here for me. I have my ladies' Bible study and my friends from the library program and —" She waved the spoon in circles. "Heavens, I can't think right now, but I could have Sunday dinner every week with someone new." Her brow lifted halfway up her forehead. "If God's calling you to California, then go. Go fast."

"Tara . . ." Cody loved the woman like she was his own family. He uttered a sad laugh. "I'm not leaving yet."

"I know." An intensity marked her tone. "But when you do get the call, you go. And don't give it another thought." She pierced the air with her spoon, as if adding an exclamation mark. Her posture relaxed. "Okay. Since we've got that out of the way, tell me about this school."

Another laugh made its way up from Cody's soul. "It's very wealthy." He picked up his own spoon and stirred the chili again. As the music played in the background, he told Tara about the challenges he might face at Oaks Christian. "It'll be work for sure. I'm excited to learn more about it."

Tara nodded, quiet for a moment. Then she cast Cody a wary look. "Southern California, you said?"

"Yes. Thousand Oaks, actually."

"How close is that to your Bailey Flanigan?"

Cody couldn't keep his heart from reacting to the sound of her name. The mix of missing her and regret that might always come over him when someone brought her up. He exhaled and then turned to Tara again. "When I first started talking to Oaks Christian, she was close by in LA. Dating Brandon Paul. Remember him? The actor from that movie, *Unlocked?*"

"Yes. Beautiful boy." Tara was merely making an observation. "I remember him."

The truth was undeniable. "Okay." Cody shrugged. "Yes. The beautiful boy. Him." He laughed softly. "Anyway, he and Bailey were very serious. Brandon lives in LA, of course." The next part was something Cody had only learned a few weeks ago when he called Jim Flanigan — the way he still sometimes did. "But she's back in Indiana now. Directing a kids theater program in Bloomington."

"Hmmm." Tara studied him. "You still

have feelings for her. I can see it in your eyes." She angled her head, trying to read his expression no doubt. "If she's here, then maybe you should go to California."

"Wow." Cody laughed out loud this time. "You never liked Bailey."

"I liked her." Tara made a knowing face. "I just liked Cheyenne better." Genuine concern filled Tara's eyes. "Besides . . . I guess I feel like Cheyenne felt. Remember what she said?" Tara poured the batter into a greased glass pan and looked over her shoulder at him. "You need a girl who makes you feel ten feet tall." She set the batter bowl down and pointed at him. "Don't settle, Cody. We can never settle."

"I know." He didn't want to talk about Bailey. If there was a chance he might move to Los Angeles, he wanted this night to be about his great concern for the older woman.

As the hours passed and they finished dinner, Cody and Tara found a way to talk about nearly every memory they had of Art and Cheyenne.

"You know what I love about being with you, Cody?" They were doing dishes, and Tara was at the sink. She smiled at him, and this time her expression was utterly serious. "When I'm with you it's like Art and Cheyenne are still here. Together we have their memories."

"We do." Cody dried his hands on his jeans and grabbed a towel from the closest drawer. "That's what I love about being with you too."

Cody hugged the woman and took hold of her shoulders. "No matter what happens tomorrow, you'll always be family to me, Tara. If I can't be here for Sunday dinners, we'll talk on Skype. Every Sunday night."

She put her warm hand against his cheek. "Don't you worry about me." She kissed his forehead the way she often did these days. "Go shine for Jesus, Cody. This is your time. I'll pray God makes the answers clear."

Sleep came in fits, and Cody barely had time to pack in the morning before setting out to the airport. Security lines were longer than usual, and Cody felt rushed until the moment he was buckled into his aisle seat. Only then did it hit him what he was doing. After a lifetime in Indiana, he was actually flying to Los Angeles International and interviewing for a coaching position in Southern California.

God . . . I know you have plans for me. But sometimes my life feels like a series of meaningless and costly moments. Like the real plans haven't even begun . . .

The response came from a poster that had hung in Cody's room when he lived with the Flanigans:

Be still, my son. Be still and wait on me.

Only God could've given him the reminder now. He thought about the seasons he'd been through. Living with the Flanigans. Loving Bailey. The hopes he'd had for his mother to stay clean and free of prison. His time in Iraq. And then his relationship with Cheyenne. All of it painful. None of it lasting.

He breathed in and let his lungs fill with the air of uncertainty. Was this step the one that would really count? The one where God would finally give him a glimpse of his long-term future plans? Cody felt unsure, but even as the doubts came at him, a peace began at the center of his soul. Whatever this step meant, and however God would use it in his life, this much was certain: God would be with him.

He remembered something then. He had connected with Andi Ellison last night on Facebook. Usually the two of them weren't online at the same time, but late yesterday they were. He had told her he was coming into town for an interview and they'd agreed to meet for coffee before his appointment at

Oaks Christian. It would be good to see her, good to catch up. Years had gone by since their time at Indiana University.

Cody closed his eyes and fell asleep before the plane left the gate. When he woke up, they were coming in for a landing and Cody checked his itinerary. He had been meticulous with the details and they played out just as he planned.

The shuttle van ride he'd arranged was at the curb waiting for him when he came out with his bag. An hour-long drive to Oaks Christian put him in Thousand Oaks two hours early for his three o'clock interview. Cody had the driver drop him at a Starbucks in Thousand Oaks. Sunshine beat on his shoulders and warmed his body as he walked up to the coffee shop's front entrance. Living in Southern California wasn't something he'd ever imagined, but this much was for sure: He could get used to the weather. He could hardly believe temperatures this warm when it wasn't quite May.

He looked around the busy shop and spotted Andi at one of the corner tables. She stood and he felt his breath catch in his throat. She was beautiful, more so than before. Only now there was something in her eyes that hadn't been there back at IU.

It was peace, a peace that proved she had come a long way in healing from the pain of her past. "Andi!" He made his way to her and they shared a long hug. Then he finally drew back and searched her eyes, her face. "I can't believe this."

"I know." She laughed. "It's been forever." She smiled at him, her cheeks slightly red. "I didn't think I'd ever see you again. How did you hear about a job in Thousand Oaks?"

"It's a long story." He laughed, his hand still on her shoulder. Without meaning to, Cody felt himself drawn to her. She had grown up, and something about her turned heads of the people around them. Not only her long blonde hair or her pale blue eyes, but something else. A maturity and faith emanated from her, and assured him again that she had grown much since college. "So you live around here?"

"Not far. I'm in one of my dad's movies. We're on location down the street from Oaks Christian." Her eyes narrowed. "So you're serious? You're looking at taking a job here?"

"They haven't offered it yet." Cody hadn't expected this, how happy he felt connecting with her again. "The interview's at three."

They ordered coffee and returned to the

corner table. "Listen . . . we both know they'll offer you the job. You're the best high school coach in America. My dad has the copy of *Sports Illustrated* with your picture on the cover framed on his office desk — where everyone can see it." Her voice became softer, and a new depth filled her tone. "We're all so proud of you, Cody."

He straightened and stuck his hands in his jeans pockets. "The hype's a little exaggerated." He shrugged. "God gets the glory. That, and I had a great team. No doubt."

"True." Andi didn't waver. "But you're gifted, Cody. Same as you always were, in so many areas."

Cody let her words wash over him, let them fill him with hope and encouragement. He searched her eyes, intrigued. "Hey, how long's your break?"

"An hour." Her eyes danced, but she held his gaze.

"Good. Then we have time to talk." He hadn't felt this lighthearted in forever.

"I'd like that." Her smile seemed to come from the depths of her heart. "I'll take you to the interview before I have to get back."

He laughed. "Yeah, I guess I didn't think about that."

She laughed, and again there was no question the years had brought her back, closer to God and to the girl she was supposed to be. "Sounds like a deal."

They ordered sandwiches and the hour slipped away. They talked about times gone by and how crazy she'd been back at Indiana University. "God taught me so much." Andi's eyes held a renewed innocence. "I had a baby. You know that, right?"

Cody knew about her pregnancy, but not many of the details surrounding the situation. He hurt for her, for the cost of her rebellion. "You gave it up, right?"

"Him." Andi leaned her forearms on the table and gazed out the window for a long moment. When she looked at him again, he could see that even in this she'd found healing. "I gave *him* up. He's living with the Baxters now. He belongs to Luke and Reagan."

"I think I might've heard that." Cody waited, letting her talk.

"Another long story." She smiled, tilting her head, studying him. "Maybe I'll tell you about it sometime."

"I'd like that."

Andi told him how she'd moved with her family to LA, and how her father's movie business was thriving. "I don't know why I ever walked away. But I wouldn't be the person I am today if God hadn't rescued me off that broken road."

Cody told her about his football season, and about his relationship with Cheyenne, how the cancer had taken her more quickly than any of them had expected.

"I'm sorry." Andi's tone was genuine. "I see you on Facebook every now and then. I figured you were going through something."

She was perceptive. He let that settle for a moment. "I never talked about it."

"I know." She smiled and there was a familiarity in her eyes that felt like home. "I guess I could see through your posts. And then Bailey told me about what happened. But I'd already guessed something was wrong by the look in your pictures. When you've been through pain, you can recognize it in someone else a little easier." A comfortable silence filled the space between them. "Did you know . . . Bailey's back in Bloomington?"

The mention of Bailey had to be intentional, and Cody understood. The last time they were together, Andi had been drunk and practically thrown herself at Cody. He hadn't been interested, of course, because she was a mess and because back then he'd only had eyes for Bailey alone. Things were different now all around, but it would be weird to have this conversation and not mention Bailey.

"I heard that. I haven't talked to her." Cody folded his hands and looked intently at Andi. "I learned something about Bailey Flanigan. Something Cheyenne taught me."

"What's that?" The vulnerability in Andi's eyes made the years fall away in so many heartbeats.

"We'll never be more than friends. Whether she stays with Brandon Paul or not."

Andi nodded slowly. "Another long story?"

Cody chuckled. "Definitely."

"I'd love to hear it. She and I don't talk about you, really. She's been . . . well, pretty down about leaving Brandon."

"I'm not surprised. She loves him. I saw that when I was in New York this past winter."

Everything about the moment — the warmth of the day and their easy conversation at the back of the coffee shop felt good to Cody. The years had clearly given Andi no choice but to be honest. He liked that about her. Too soon the hour was up and Andi checked the time on her phone. "I have to go."

"Do you have a big part? In the movie?"

"Small, but it's a start. I always knew I wanted to act. I just had to figure out how to do what I loved God's way."

"Hmmm. That's what I always tell the football boys. We have to do things His way."

They packed up their trash and walked out to her car in the parking lot. While she drove him to Oaks Christian, he pulled out his phone. "Maybe I could get your contact info." He grinned. "So we could hang out sometime. Especially if they offer me the job."

"Well, then," she laughed, "I guess you'll need my number. Because the job's yours. You don't need me to tell you that." She rattled off the digits as he punched them into his phone, then she parked her car at the back of the school.

"The head coach is giving me a ride to my hotel."

"Good." She smiled at him, studying his eyes. "I had fun."

"Me too." He leaned over and hugged her, then he opened the passenger door. "Okay, well . . . good seeing you."

"You too." She waved as she pulled away. "Call me when they make you an offer."

He nodded. And as he walked away he couldn't help think how long it had been since he'd felt this confident. The good feeling stayed with him for the next few hours, through the interview and into the meeting with Edwin Baylor, the Oaks Christian athletic director, and even later when they offered him the job.

"Take a week and let us know," Mr. Baylor shook his hand and smiled big. "We want you to take over the program here, Cody. You'll be the youngest head coach we've ever hired. But somehow I think you'll also be the best."

"Thank you, sir." Cody left the building feeling amazing. It was the job of course, and the fact that Tara had been praying for him. But it was something else too.

His time with Andi Ellison.

That was the only way he could explain how he felt as he headed to his hotel and the next morning as a driver took him back to the airport. He felt the way Cheyenne had wanted him to feel whenever he was ready to live again. The way Tara expected him to feel.

Like he was ten feet tall.

Andi could barely focus as she did her scenes that afternoon. Cody Coleman was interviewing for a job in town? Certainly Bailey hadn't said anything about this, which could only mean one thing: Her friend didn't know about Cody's job interview. But that wasn't the fact that stayed with her while she read her lines and acted out her part. Rather it was her time at a quiet corner table at Starbucks, and a lunch date with Cody Coleman that she never in a million years thought she'd have.

Back when she was at Indiana University her secret crush on Cody Coleman had been the greatest of her life. But there were problems. Cody had Bailey back then, and he wouldn't have been interested in her anyway. Not how she was back then. But all that had changed. Which was why she couldn't stop thinking about him.

Their coffee date, their conversation, the easy way they had together. All of it felt right. Natural. Just one thing troubled Andi as she finished out her day on set.

What would Bailey think?

ELEVEN

The shoot in Montana would last eight weeks, a couple weeks longer than most. But Brandon understood why. Many of the scenes required stunts — some Brandon could do, and some that required a stunt double. On top of that they were at the mercy of the weather.

Today was one of those times.

A thunderstorm brewed on the near horizon, threatening to cut short the scene they were currently filming. A scene between Brandon and Molly. The two of them rode on separate horses, moving slowly together around what was supposed to be the perimeter of their family's ranch. For now the plan was to go ahead with the scene.

"Okay," the director yelled from his place thirty yards away. "Let's roll it."

"Rolling." The assistant shouted above the sound of the increasing wind. "Action!"

Brandon walked his horse for a few seconds, easy and fluid in the saddle. After a few seconds he looked up at Molly. "I read the letters."

"What?" Her reaction was perfect. Surprise, and a little indignation. "Those were private."

"It doesn't matter. Mom and Dad are gone, Molly." He ran his fingers over his sweaty forehead and through his hair. "Besides . . . they'd want us to know."

She looked at her reins, her horse moving more slowly than before. When she looked up there were tears in her eyes, proof that her professionalism rather than her name was the reason she had won the part. "Know what?"

"About their love. Their love story."

Molly sat up taller in her saddle. "Like, the story of how they met?"

"Yes." Brandon set his eyes on the horizon. "It's like a movie or something."

More silence, and then Molly squinted at him. "So you'll show me?"

"I will. We should all read them." He flexed his jaw and allowed the hatred to come over him. A hatred befitting the part. "The killers — they stole that from us. Our parents and their love. They didn't get to finish." Thunder sounded in the distance, but the director didn't cut the scene. Brandon turned and stared at Molly, their horses still walking slowly. "I'm gonna get 'em, Molly. If it's the last thing I do."

"What if they get us first?"

Again he set his eyes straight ahead. "They won't." He clicked his heels against the horse's side and the paint took off running. Both of them had trained for the part, and both felt comfortable on horseback. Brandon knew that from conversations he'd had with Molly. But after the director yelled cut, as they rounded the corner into the stable yard, Molly's horse picked up speed and she lost her balance, falling hard onto the ground.

"Molly!" Brandon reigned in his horse, swung down quickly, and crossed in front of the animal to the place where his costar lay groaning in the dust. He motioned for help and then dropped to his knees. "Are you okay?"

"I think." She winced and rolled onto her side. "My ribs . . . they're killing me."

"Don't move." He kept his hand on her shoulder and while the team hurried over he leaned in close. "Can I pray for you?"

"What?"

Brandon wanted to hurry before the others reached them. "Just real quick. I wanna pray."

"Oh." Molly winced. "Of course."

"Just close your eyes." He did the same. "Dear God, be with Molly. Whatever's injured, heal her. She needs you, Father. In Jesus' name, amen."

The tension left Molly in as much time as it took Brandon to say amen. She lay back on the ground and looked up at him, amazed. "I can't believe that. No one's ever prayed for me."

Brandon shrugged one shoulder as he stepped back. "God knows what you need."

A paramedic and a nurse were the first to reach Molly. Even as they did, the storm moved in on top of them, spewing lightning bolts and blasting thunder louder than any Brandon had ever heard. The group carried Molly into the barn, but by then she was already feeling better. Within ten minutes she was back on her feet, laughing at herself for being so clumsy.

The director called off the shoot for the rest of the day. "Stay dry and safe. We'll meet again at seven in the morning. The storm should be gone by then."

As everyone cleared out, Brandon stayed to be sure Molly was okay. When he felt sure she was fine, he started off toward his trailer. But Molly came after him. "Brandon . . ."

He turned around. "Yeah?"

"I'm gonna watch a movie in my trailer." Her look wasn't suggestive like before. More open-eyed. As if by praying he had touched her in a different sort of way. But it was a way he had certainly not intended. He smiled at her, the way he would if she were his real sister. "Not this time. I'm heading into town, but thanks." He smiled. "See you tomorrow."

Her disappointment was as obvious as the storm raging around them, but she didn't put up a fight. Brandon gathered his things from his trailer and checked out one of the pickups with the crew. Town was a twenty-minute drive west and it consisted of little more than a single street, a few beaten-down bars, and a handful of storefronts: Bill's Grocer, Sandy Mae's Bistro, Jay's Java Shop, a few boutiques boasting used clothing, and at the far end of town a Super Wal-mart.

He had just one reason for going into town: Cell reception. Butte was the nearest big city, but at two hours away it was too far for an afternoon like this. The local town would do. Besides, Jay's coffee had grown on him and walking down Main Street gave him something to do. But most of all, he couldn't wait to use his cell phone, especially since it had been days since he'd gotten any service. No cell reception meant no Internet, no email, no way to update his Twitter or Facebook. But most of all it meant no communication with Bailey.

The road into town was bumpy, and combined with the driving storm, Brandon felt more like he was four-wheeling than headed to an actual destination. But even with the lightning and thunder and downpour, he realized as he drove that he hadn't felt this hopeful in weeks. Months, maybe.

Once he reached town, the storm let up and the rain stopped. Brandon parked a few blocks down from the coffee shop — a habit from years of living in LA. One way to keep the paparazzi guessing about which store he was actually in. Here, though, the walk gave Brandon time to take in the small-town feeling, time to imagine having the freedom to live somewhere like here.

Granted, he'd beefed up for this part, and he was more tan than usual. But in LA he would still be recognized everywhere he went. Brandon was sure about it. Here, people went about their business without giving him a second look. A couple women pushing baby strollers, a family with young children headed for the local restaurant, shopkeepers sitting out front of their stores swapping local news and gossip.

Brandon almost felt invisible. And that wasn't all. As he walked he was overwhelmed with a sense of freedom like he hadn't known in a very long time. Fame had hit him at such a young age, he barely remembered what it felt like to be normal. To walk along a street like this one without causing a commotion.

He slowed his pace, something else that didn't come naturally anymore. A glance over his shoulder told him what he already knew. No one was chasing him. There was no need to be in a hurry. He smiled and stopped at the nearest stretch of brick. For a long time he leaned against it and simply breathed. Just let the smell of rain and wet dirt fill his senses while the distant thunder added the gentlest backdrop. What would life be like in a town like this? Brandon gazed down the stretch of Main Street and chuckled. Okay, maybe he'd feel a little trapped in a town this small.

But what about Bloomington?

Sure the paparazzi had followed him to Bloomington when he filmed *Unlocked*. But they wouldn't bother him if he lived there. Not enough fodder to keep them in business. So if he didn't have so many movies to film for West Mark, he could move there and marry Bailey and find a life that would work for both of them. If it weren't for the pending contract.

The voice of his manager came back to him, the words from a phone call they'd had last time Brandon was in town. The studio was reworking his contract, making it stronger, better than before.

"They can sense your star is rising." His manager had sounded excited at the prospect. "I wouldn't be surprised if the deal's sweeter than the first time around." He laughed, like they'd accomplished something together. "Great move, making them think you'd walk if they didn't rework the details."

Brandon hated the insinuation, that he had hired Luke Baxter to give the contract a legal look-over just so they could get more money from the studio. "You know that isn't it."

"Whatever." The guy had laughed again. "It worked. That's all I'm saying."

Now a breeze stirred damp air between the storefronts, and again thunder sounded from wherever the storm had moved. Brandon lifted his eyes to the cloudy sky. So many movies in so many years. No matter what they paid him or how far they came to meeting Brandon's demands about creative control one truth remained.

He couldn't be West Mark's star actor from Bloomington, Indiana.

Suddenly a rush of buzzes hit his phone and he grabbed it from his back pocket. He had a signal! The texts would've been all that he hadn't received in the last few days. One after another they came and he could only wait until they stopped. Thirty-six messages in all. Brandon laughed quietly. Other than Bailey, maybe it was just as well he'd gone without service. How often did he get a break from the outside world like this one?

With a few taps he went to the message section of his phone and scrolled down until he saw her name. His heart pounded as he spotted her name. With another fast click her message appeared in the window. Actually it was a series of messages, and suddenly Brandon wasn't sure he wanted to read them. He checked the time and date at the top of the first one, but it was from only a few seconds ago. The price of poor cell coverage. No way to tell when she actually sent the message.

He walked to a bench a few feet away. *Please, God . . . let it be good. I need her, Father. Please . . .* But even as he sat down he felt his mouth go dry, his heart beat even harder. He found his place at the top of her message once more and began to read.

Brandon, I don't know where you are or if you're still in Montana. For some reason, I thought you'd be back in LA this week, so I thought I'd try you. If you're still on location, then you probably won't get this. Either way, I had to send it. The second text continued where that one left off. *First, I miss you. Not a day goes by where I don't think about you and us and how I can't imagine ever finding again what we've shared.*

But time has taught me something else. Brandon, we can no longer be together. I've thought about it a thousand hours and every time the answer is the same. I have to say goodbye. I tried to be like Katy, but I can't do it. I don't want to. The crazy life, running from the paparazzi, trying to figure out groceries and get-togethers between red-carpet events. All of it's just too insane for me.

I wish we could talk or Skype. I know this will hurt. It hurts me too. Maybe it always will. I'll be praying for you, believing in you. I love you. Bailey.

Brandon sat back hard on the bench and realized he wasn't breathing. A quick gasp filled his lungs and he checked the rest of the messages. In case there was another one from her telling him that she must've had a moment of insanity because she could never, ever break up with him.

He let his head fall back against the brick wall. What was she talking about? People didn't break up over text. Not at their age. She couldn't possibly rattle off a handful of text messages and expect him to understand.

He stood up and shoved the phone back in his pocket. First toward the coffee shop and then back toward his car he paced, fast angry steps while he replayed her words in his mind. She was breaking up with him because he lived in LA? How could that even be possible? Wasn't she the one who always talked about love being worth fighting for, how happy she'd been when he had stood up to the paparazzi for her. She wanted him to fight for her, and he'd done that.

But what about her?

"Come on, Bailey . . ." he groaned out loud, and then came to a sudden stop. For a long time he only stood there, staring straight ahead and trying to imagine that somewhere Bailey was going about her life content with her decision. Content because there were no other messages to the contrary. "You can't mean it, baby. No." He whispered the words, but they screamed through his heart. Across the street a couple walked by but they didn't look his direction.

His mind raced. What if they agreed to date for the next five years? So he could finish the contract and then leave movies altogether, move to Bloomington, and spend the rest of his life with her. Until then they could have a week here or there together, when he wasn't working and she wasn't in a show or directing. He thought back five years, to the time when he was still living with his aunt and uncle. Five years? It wasn't that long.

Brandon felt sick to his stomach, the way he felt too often these days. What was he thinking? He could never wait five years to enjoy life with Bailey, to marry her and love her the way he longed to love her. Five years would be an eternity.

His mind kept spinning, searching for answers, any way to refute her claim and find a way out of the mess they were in. Only there weren't any answers. No way to bridge his world and hers. He pulled his phone from his pocket again and dialed her number. If he could hear her voice, if he could make a case for their love, then maybe she would come to her senses. She wouldn't have broken up with him if he were on the other end of a phone call or if they'd been

loved splashing their pictures beneath sketchy headlines when they were together, they had also relished Bailey's departure from LA, pronouncing Brandon's depression and Bailey's sudden sickness. The lies would always be there.

But in the end only the truth mattered.

And now the days ahead stretched out like so many possibilities. No matter what Bailey said, he would believe. After all, God had brought them together. He would see them through this — even where it looked like there was no possible way. Brandon would believe that with every fiber of his being. Until he could look into her beautiful blue eyes and see for himself whether there was any truth in her text. Or if, like he suspected, she still loved him as much as he loved her.

The way he would always love her.

TWELVE

Bailey hadn't heard from Brandon, which surprised her. She googled him and found that she'd been wrong about his time in Los Angeles. He was still filming in Montana and would probably be there through the first few weeks of June. She had planned to spend a few weeks on the set, but her work with CKT left her no time, and she didn't see the point anyway. He hadn't responded to her texts, which could only mean he agreed with her reasoning.

There'd been nothing. Not even a voicemail. Only one missed call in the last four weeks. The reality caused her to feel right about her decision and heartbroken all at the same time. Maybe she shouldn't have broken up with him over text. But what other way was there when their cell connection was so poor? A few days after she sent her messages she saw his update on Twitter. She was pretty sure his words were directed at her. But there'd been no sign of what he was thinking then.

Bailey pushed away the sad thoughts and focused on the matter at hand as she parked her car in the CKT theater parking lot. Ten minutes before she needed to go inside. Enough time to update Facebook and Twitter. Even though it had been a while since *Unlocked,* Bailey still had tens of thousands of girls following her, asking for advice and trying to find what Bailey had in her relationship with God and her family. It was the reason she was thinking about writing a book. Most of them had figured out about the distance between her and Brandon, so Bailey was careful to keep her social media tone hopeful. After all, many of the girls following her were probably in the middle of a breakup too.

She went into her Instagram folder and found a photo of the morning sunlight splashing across the acreage in front of her parents' home. She edited the photo with a different filter, one that brought out the colors even more, then she added a caption. "When God says He has great plans for you, don't doubt Him. He's never been wrong yet . . . XOXO, Bailey."

She shut down her phone, gathered her things, and headed for the front doors of the theater. It was Monday of dress rehearsal week for *Peter Pan,* and Bailey's CKT kids were ready to shine. She could feel the energy as she stepped inside. Chaos abounded in every corner of the building. In the lobby a group of kids sat around a few moms working on makeup, and Bailey stopped to watch. Wasn't it just yesterday she'd been the one sitting in the group and her mom was the volunteer helping with makeup? She smiled and moved farther into the building. Again, everywhere she looked, the kids' excitement was bursting.

With the help of Ashley and the rest of the creative team, she managed to get them all seated, their attention on her. "This is dress rehearsal, and you all know what that means." Her tone was kind as she laid out the instructions, the dos and don'ts for this very important week. Again she was struck by how much fun this was, working with the CKT kids, taking a group of boys and girls and bringing a show to life. The work came easily for her, and the kids liked her. They listened and worked hard to please her, and along the way she and the kids had laughed a lot and made more memories than Bailey had expected. Especially when through it all her heart was breaking.

Still, the one certainty that would come

from directing this play was that she could do this work forever, if that was God's plan.

As she dismissed the kids to get ready for the first scene, she and Ashley took seats together in the front row. "What do you think?" Bailey felt a little overwhelmed. She hadn't done this before, and now they were opening the show on Friday.

"Are you serious?" Ashley gave her a bewildered look, one that showed she was amazed at how far they'd come. "You have an average cast, no real standouts, and somehow you've brought them together. Truthfully?" Ashley grinned. "I think we're further ahead than usual for first night of dress rehearsal."

"I'm not Katy Hart Matthews." Bailey knew her limitations. She had a lot to learn, even if she loved the work.

"But you're good. And in time you can be amazing at this, Bailey." Ashley turned in her seat so she could see Bailey better. "Is this what you want to do?"

Ashley's compliment warmed her heart. Bailey was grateful that despite the mess of her personal life, Ashley rarely touched on it. Almost as if she knew Bailey would rather focus on CKT while she was here. Bailey thought for a quiet moment. "Sometimes I think that. How rewarding it would be to direct one play after another. Getting to know the kids and the families involved. Bringing stories to life."

"But . . ." Ashley must've heard the hesitation in Bailey's voice.

"I don't know. Sometimes I think I'll write a book. A way to help all the girls out there who read my tweets and hang out on my Facebook page. Like a best friend's view on living life for God in today's culture."

"Hmmm. Sounds good." Ashley drew one foot up onto the wooden theater seat and hugged her knee. "I'd buy one. Us moms with daughters need all the help we can get. I wasn't close to my mom until the end. After I'd already rebelled against everyone who loved me."

Bailey listened, thoughtful. She knew about Ashley's past, but not the details. "It's hard. No one's perfect."

"No. But people watch you, Bailey. You and your mom . . . the way you carried yourself when you and Brandon were dating. Even the faith that has gotten you through your separation. They watch, and they want what you have."

"It's not that complicated." She smiled. "But yeah, sometimes I think it would make a good book. You should see the things girls are dealing with today. If I could help, I'd like to."

"Well, that settles it." Ashley checked her watch. "You'll write the book. How can you not?"

Bailey laughed. "First we better get this rehearsal under way."

"Let's do it."

The run-through that night didn't go as well as Bailey hoped. Peter Pan's cables broke before he could even climb into them, and Captain Hook's beard fell off every time he made any sudden movements on stage. The falling beard set off a sequence of giggles and halfway through rehearsal Bailey had to call a break so everyone could collect themselves.

She and Ashley stayed until almost midnight working on sets because a few parents had forgotten to paint the pirate ship. By the time she set off for home, she felt drained in every possible way. The house was dark again, her parents and brothers asleep — even Connor. Bailey dragged herself up the stairs and wondered like she did every night at this time what Brandon was doing, whether he ever thought about her.

The way she constantly thought about him.

She dropped to the edge of her bed, and her eyes fell on the old journal on the open bottom shelf of her nightstand. How long had it been since she'd opened it? She was in the process of starting a blog — the first step to writing her book. Even then, she wasn't sure if she had much to offer the hurting girls who looked up to her. She didn't have anything figured out, that was for sure.

A few seconds passed while she stared at the journal, but finally — even in her weary frame of mind — she decided she had to read it, had to walk through the pages one more time and remember who she had been back then. How far she had come — in good and bad ways. She flipped through the pages, running her fingers over the worn areas and knowing from memory the sections where her tears had blurred the ink.

Cody Coleman. Every entry was about him. This was the journal she'd kept when he joined the Army, when he was fighting in Iraq and she had no way to reach him. Back then she'd believed one day Cody would come home and they'd find their way together and someday . . . some wonderful day he would sit beside her and read this journal.

Instead Cody was out of her life completely. She still missed his friendship. Missed the way he was like a brother to her. She turned the pages slowly, looking for one specific entry. The one that haunted her and stayed with her and troubled her — even today.

She flipped through November and December and January, and finally . . . there on February 6, 2007, was the entry she was looking for. The one where she had felt compelled to pray for her future husband. The entry was intense, an emotional cry from her heart to the heart of God, begging Him to protect this guy, the guy she maybe didn't even know yet. Rereading the entry now reminded her of the sense of urgency she'd felt that day. She found the part that always got her.

I feel like he's in trouble, God . . . like You're telling me something's wrong and I have to pray for him as if my own life depended on it. So I'm praying, Father. Please . . . be with him, my future husband. Save him from whatever he's going through and breathe new life into him — however that looks. And as for Cody, Lord, You know I miss him and I'm worried about him. Rescue him from dangers all around him, and bring him home from the war soon. Thank You, God. I love You always. Bailey.

Not until last year had Bailey put the dates together and figured out the miracle of the entry. For it was February 6, 2007, that Cody had been caught in a firestorm as he escaped captivity in an Iraqi prison. That very day he had helped save the lives of a number of men and had suffered the injury that caused him to lose his lower left leg. But he had lived. Bailey had prayed for her future husband to be protected at a time when she sensed he was in danger. And at that very time, Cody Coleman had been spared death.

A tear slid down Bailey's face onto the page. Even now, with her heart still missing Brandon, she wasn't sure what to do with that truth. For so very long she had believed Cody was the guy God had brought into her life, the one who held her future. And if that wasn't true, then how could she explain the prayer? The proof was right there in front of her. The journal entry dated the exact same as the date of Cody's harrowing escape.

She closed the journal and heard her phone vibrate on the bed. Probably Ashley, reminding her about something for tomorrow. But when she picked up the phone she saw she was wrong.

The text was from Cody Coleman.

Bailey stared at his name for several seconds. He hadn't texted her since she'd returned from Los Angeles, even though it would've been just about impossible for him not to know. If he spent any time in a grocery store he'd seen the fact that she and Brandon had broken up. He also had to know she was back in Bloomington, because he kept in touch with her dad. Yet until now there'd been no word from him.

She tapped her phone a few times and his text came into view.

Hey, Bailey . . . thinking about you. God had you on my heart, so I prayed for you tonight. Hope you're well. Let's hang out sometime, okay?

A chill ran down Bailey's arms. She looked at her journal and back at the text. A coincidence? If not, what was God doing here? She and Cody had already agreed that they saw each other more as siblings. Bailey deleted the text and turned her phone off. Cody was the older brother she'd always wanted. She knew that was true, because as she fell asleep that night — like every night for the past two months — the face in her heart and mind wasn't Cody's.

It was Brandon Paul's.

Cody wasn't sure why he'd texted Bailey,

Cody assured her that when it was okay with her parole officer he would move her to California too. That way she could be near him and find a fresh start. Which was maybe what they both needed.

Tara knew too, and she had heard all Cody's thoughts and feelings. On every front the older woman was thrilled for him. "Thousand Oaks. Mmmm. Beautiful place."

"How do you know?" The conversation had happened yesterday over their last Sunday dinner.

"Google Earth, of course." She looked at him like he'd just asked her to spell her name. "I love Google Earth. Got to zoom in on the place and walk around with the little Google Man. Took myself a tour of the high school too." She waved her fork in the air. "I like flying. I ever tell you that, Cody?"

"You never did." Cody struggled to keep a straight face. "So you're saying you'll visit?"

"Visit? More like an extended stay!" She dug her fork back in the green beans. "You ain't getting rid of me that easy, Cody. No, sir."

Yes, all the loose ends in Indiana were tied up and ready for him to leave. He'd even talked to Jim Flanigan and explained the reasons he was taking the job over the one at Clear Creek. Jim understood. Oaks

Christian was the greater challenge. If he could build a winning program there, he could possibly coach at the college level.

"Maybe one day you'll be back." Jim had met him for coffee, and as they left he hugged Cody. "Coaching the Indianapolis Colts with me."

"That would be a dream." Tears burned at Cody's eyes as he said goodbye. The truth was he didn't know if he'd be back.

"Have you told Bailey?" It was the last thing Jim said. "I don't think she knows you interviewed in California."

Cody was glad Jim didn't share everything with his daughter. But at the same time the news presented the dilemma he was wrestling with now. The fact that Bailey didn't know he was leaving. And she didn't know about him and Andi.

His cell phone rang and he reached for it on the table next to his bed. "Hello?"

"Hey." It was Andi. "One week and you'll be here."

Her voice soothed his concerns and made his heart soar all at the same time. "I can't wait."

She laughed and then went into a story about her day and how one of the sets collapsed and nearly trapped two of the actors. The whole time she talked, Cody couldn't help but think how right this felt, this new connection with Andi. They had everything in common, after all. They understood what it meant to have a broken past, and to live with things about yesterday they would never be proud of. Andi wasn't a distant ideal, she was a girl he could relate to no matter what they talked about. And despite everything about their pasts, they shared a faith stronger than rock.

"Let me guess." Andi's story ended and she paused for a few beats. "You still haven't told Bailey."

"Hmm." He hated the thought. "I haven't. I'm sorry."

"It's awkward, that's all. I mean, Cody, we're just friends, you and me." Her voice was patient and understanding. But her concern was clear. "Please . . . it's getting weird not telling her. Like, I've talked to her twice since you and I started talking, and both times I couldn't bring you up."

"I know. I'm sorry. I really want to tell her." Cody massaged his temple with his thumb and forefinger. "I texted her tonight."

"Oh." Andi's tone held a level of caution that hadn't been there a moment ago. "What did you say?"

"Nothing, really. Just told her I was praying for her, thinking about her." Even as he said the words, he realized how they must've sounded to Andi. He was quick to clarify. "I mean, it was clearly a friend thing. Anyway, she didn't text back."

"But you're moving here in a week."

"Right." Cody sat up and leaned over his knees. "I'll take care of it. I'll talk to her."

"What do you think . . . I mean, how do you think she'll react?"

"I don't know. That's why I haven't made the call. I mean, she and I have both agreed we only want to be friends. But we're not friends."

Andi let that truth hang between them for a few seconds. "Maybe that's what we should pray for. Not just that she'll understand about our new friendship. But that we can all be friends."

Cody was amazed at Andi. In light of their past and how Cody had clearly been in love with Bailey back when they were in college, Andi had every reason to be jealous. But she wasn't. She was a new person in Christ, and she had full confidence in herself and the value her life held. The fact was hugely attractive to Cody. "You're very special. Have I said that lately?"

She giggled. "Every night, I think."

"That's crazy, right? We've talked every night."

As the call wound down, Cody pictured her, the way she had looked sitting across from him at Starbucks that day. "I can't wait till we can talk in person."

"Me too."

They talked a few more minutes and then said goodnight. Cody had to pack and clean his apartment and load everything in his truck, but if God was going to answer their prayers about a friendship being rekindled with Bailey, he had to do one more very important thing.'

He had to tell her about Andi.

THIRTEEN

The first weekend of *Peter Pan* was behind them, and Bailey was grateful for all the ways it had gone well. Captain Hook's beard had only fallen off once — during the Saturday night show — but the audience loved it and thought it was part of the act. They howled with laughter as the boy playing the part held it to his face through the remainder of the dance number and then gave them a funny look as he sprinted off stage.

Live theater would always be like that. The entire experience made Bailey realize that whether she was dancing on stage or directing, the thrill was the same. Being part of a musical made her feel alive, like she'd been created to be part of a theater troupe.

They still had one more weekend of shows, but they were on track with no injuries or major illnesses, and Bailey could hardly wait for tomorrow: Memorial Day.

She planned to hang out with her family and relax. Something she hadn't done much of since she returned home.

Bailey climbed into her sweats, cleaned up, and crawled into bed. For the sweetest moment she pictured Brandon, how much he would've liked the show and how happy he would've been that nothing had gone wrong. That there'd been no major disasters. He was still on set — finishing up his sixth week, if she'd counted right. So his tweets and Facebook status updates had been spotty at best. And once again they were cryptic, encouraging his fans to stay in the fight and hold tight to God and believe that He wasn't finished writing their story.

She was about to turn off her light when her phone rattled on the nightstand. Cody had started texting her nearly every night. Usually he'd give her a Bible verse or some sort of encouragement. She kept her answers short, thanking him and telling him it was good to hear from him. She had no idea why he'd renewed his interest in her. But there was one truth she couldn't hide from: seeing his name on her phone still made her smile. A quick look told her what she already knew. The text was from Cody again. She opened it and saw that it was longer than usual.

Hey, Bailey . . . you're probably wondering why I've been texting you this past week. I guess it's because I hate that we've lost touch. I still care about you, about your family. You'll always mean so much to me. And I'm sorry about you and Brandon. I know this can't be an easy time for you.

Anyway, here's what I was thinking. Can I pick you up tomorrow morning around nine and take you out to Lake Monroe? I think we need to talk, and . . . well, you know. That's where we go when we need to talk. What do you think?

Bailey had to read the message twice to figure out how her heart felt about the text. Cody was asking her to take a walk with him at Lake Monroe? What exactly did that mean? She tapped out her response. *Okay. I think you're right. We should talk. It feels wrong to be strangers. I'll see you at 9.*

A few seconds passed and another text came in. *See you then.*

Bailey stared at it and then turned her phone off. Sleep came in spurts, because usually she had a sense of where God was leading, how He was making His ways clear, His plans evident. But with Brandon gone and Cody finding his way back into her life, even in small doses, she didn't know His plans anymore. She only knew that she needed to take the walk with Cody.

Her mom spotted her when she came down the stairs that Monday morning dressed in a T-shirt and jeans. "Good morning." She smiled as she lowered her cup of coffee. "You're ready early."

"Cody's picking me up."

Surprise showed on her mom's face. "Is something wrong?"

"I don't think so." Bailey sighed and went to her mother. She looped one arm around her neck. "It's confusing. I mean, I still love Brandon. I do. But that can never work. And now I'm here and Cody's here and the other day I read the journal entry again, the one from that February. I don't feel about him the way I used to, but . . . I don't know. He wants to get together and talk, so I'm going."

"Aww, Bailey. I'm sorry." Her mom stood and hugged her, rocking her gently like she'd done when Bailey was a young teenager and every heartache possible seemed to crash in around her. "This can't be easy. You've hardly complained, but I know you." She pulled back and studied Bailey's face, her eyes. "God has a plan in this. You'll see it one day."

"Somehow I don't think today's that day." She blew at a wisp of hair that had fallen across her forehead.

"I'm not sure." The house was quiet, everyone else sleeping in on this holiday Monday. "But maybe it's part of the puzzle. One more answer."

Bailey shrugged. "I don't know." She leaned her head against her mother's. "I just wish Brandon would call. So I'd know what he's thinking."

Her mom was kind. She resisted what must've been the urge to remind Bailey that she had ended things with Brandon, not the other way around. Instead her mom stroked her hair. "I'll pray for you, Bailey. The answers will come."

They heard the sound of a car outside. "I better go." She kissed her mom's cheek and then hurried for the door. As she did she remembered what her mom said. The answers might not come today, but maybe part of the puzzle would become clear.

Please, God . . . let that be the case. Let me know where things stand with Cody. Where they will stand after today.

I am with you, daughter . . . whatever happens, do not be discouraged.

The answer seemed strange in light of the rustle of excitement stirring within her, but it was there nonetheless. Why would the Lord remind her not to be discouraged on a day when Cody only wanted to talk? She dismissed the thought and headed out front to Cody. Like every time he'd ever parked his truck on her circular driveway, Bailey felt the familiar thrill at seeing him. But this time as she reached his passenger door a thought occurred to her.

Why hadn't he gotten out and rung the doorbell? The way Brandon would have? Certainly a light knock wouldn't have woken anyone up, if that's what he was worried about.

Again, Bailey let the thought go. He wasn't taking her on a date, after all. She hurried to the passenger door and slid inside.

"Hi." He smiled at her, and the walls and weeks between them faded in a single breath.

"Hi." She leaned over and hugged him. "It's good to see you."

"You too." He let his eyes linger on hers, and then he put the truck into gear, grabbed the wheel, and headed toward the lake. Along the way he mainly asked her questions about CKT and the play.

"The kids are really talented." She settled into her seat. "You should come see it. We have one more weekend."

"Yeah." He kept his eyes straight ahead

and made no promises.

Funny, she told herself. He could at least agree that seeing the play was a good idea. She tried to keep her emotions even, steady. If they were finding their way back to friendship, she couldn't ask too much of him. They reached the lake and took their same parking spot, the one they'd used so many other times when they'd come here to talk or walk or figure out their feelings. Bailey felt butterflies in her stomach, more because she didn't know what was coming than because she was with Cody. The whole situation felt strangely unfamiliar. Bailey breathed in slowly.

Give me Your peace, Father . . . I need You.

The response wasn't audible. It simply was.

I am with you, daughter.

Like a constant assurance Bailey carried with her, God remained. All things might change. Love could come and go and friendships could fade. But God stayed. It was the truth that kept her company on the loneliest nights.

Not until they'd started down the path did Cody slow his pace and glance in her direction. That's when Bailey noticed something she hadn't before. He looked nervous. Whatever was going on, why ever he had wanted this time with her, the words weren't going to come easy. Not from Cody.

"Okay." He drew a deep breath. "You're probably wondering why the walk. Why now, right?"

"Of course." Bailey had no reason to be cold. The temperature was warm and getting warmer. But still she felt herself begin to shiver. "There has to be a reason."

"Yes." Cody let his eyes find some place on the ground ahead of his feet. For a long time he looked there and let a slightly uncomfortable silence hang between them as they walked. When he looked up, fear wasn't the only thing she saw. Sadness was there too. "There's a reason."

Bailey didn't feel like walking. Not if whatever Cody had to say was troubling him this much. There was a bench up ahead. "Let's sit."

He nodded and a few minutes later they sat down. Cody seemed careful to allow as much space between them as possible. Bailey did the same, leaning against the metal armrest. She had to work to keep her teeth from chattering. At least here the sun splashed through the tree branches and warmed their faces. "So talk to me, Cody. What's the reason?"

Again he seemed desperate to avoid whatever was coming. He shifted, restless and uneasy and after a few long seconds he lifted his eyes to hers. "I'm leaving. Tomorrow . . . for California."

Bailey felt the slow release of adrenaline. Once, a long time ago, Cody had helped Bailey's family spend an entire afternoon looking for the Flanigan's dog, Brownie. Slowly, with each passing hour, Bailey had the feeling something wasn't right. That the search wasn't going to end well. When she spotted her mom headed toward her and Cody, tears on her face, Bailey had known. Brownie was gone. It wasn't a sudden shock, but more of a slow fall. The way she felt now.

She worked to find her voice. "California? Like . . . for a visit?"

"No." Now that he'd started to explain himself, Cody seemed in a hurry for her to understand. "I'm taking a new job. Football coach for Oaks Christian High."

Her mind began to spin, and she pressed her spine into the armrest again. Anything to steady herself. "What about the kids at Lyle?"

"One of the dads is taking over. DeMetri and most of my team are graduating. I never planned to stay there more than a year." He sounded weary. "I was finished there. God made that very clear."

"So . . ." Bailey still felt dizzy. "You're moving where? To Los Angeles?" The irony was greater than any she had ever experienced. She couldn't stand LA, and now both the guys she'd ever loved would be there.

"Outside LA. The school's in Thousand Oaks." He angled his head, and for the first time that morning he looked at her. Really looked at her. "Near where Andi lives."

If Bailey had felt her world turning before, now she could barely catch her breath. "How . . . how did you know that?" She and Andi talked once a week or more. God had restored every bit of their friendship. But Cody? He hadn't mentioned Andi since their days in college.

"It's kind of a crazy story." Again Cody looked nervous, and once more he stared at the ground before finding the words. "We met up for coffee a month ago, the day I flew out for my interview."

"How'd that happen?" Bailey had no right to feel jealous or angry or sick to her stomach. But somehow every one of those feelings crowded the space in her heart.

"We talked on Facebook before I flew out." Cody explained that they had decided to meet for coffee. "We talked and remembered and . . . well, it was nice."

The confusion cleared a little. "Oaks Christian. Her dad was filming a movie not far from there."

"Exactly." Cody rubbed the back of his neck and again a strange silence squeezed in between them. "Anyway, we exchanged numbers and started talking."

Bailey closed her eyes for a long breath and when she opened them, she tried desperately not to feel hurt. "On the phone? Like the two of you have been talking?"

A long pause followed. "Every night." Cody looked guilty and if she knew anything about him, he felt as sick as she did. "I wanted to tell you all this, but I couldn't say it over text. Can you see that, Bailey? I had to tell you in person."

A hundred screaming thoughts battled for her attention, but Bailey could only deal with the one that got in her face the fastest. "So . . . are you two dating?"

Cody looked at her again, straight to her soul. As if whatever he was about to say was as honest as he could be. "Not yet. But . . . when I get there, to Thousand Oaks, I want to ask her out. See if what I'm feeling for her is real. Does that make sense?"

No, she wanted to scream. Of course it didn't make sense. Cody had been in love with her, not Andi. Back in college Andi had always liked Cody. The times when Bailey felt the furthest from her friend were the times when Andi would text Cody or call him or flirt with him. Like she had no shame.

"Bailey?"

She held up her hand. "Give me a minute." She stood and walked to the edge of the hillside, out where she had a better view of the lake. Cody was taking a job in Thousand Oaks. Where Andi Ellison lived. Anger and hurt and the pain of rejection — all of them assaulted her. But only for a minute.

God . . . help me. My feelings, they're wrong. I can't act like this. Please, help me.

His answer came again like earlier that morning, only this time it made sense.

I am with you, daughter . . . don't be afraid. Don't be discouraged.

The Lord didn't want her to be discouraged, although right now Bailey couldn't understand how she was supposed to feel any other way. Either way, she couldn't stand here much longer, letting Cody know how upset she was.

She straightened and turned to face him, holding her position a few yards away. "I'm sorry." She forced a laugh, but nothing was funny. "I didn't see this coming."

"I know." He stood, but he didn't make an attempt to come to her. "Andi wanted me to tell you a long time ago. Back when we met for coffee." He shrugged, but he didn't look away. And in his eyes she saw the familiar heart, the one she'd fallen so fully for back when she was a school girl. "But I couldn't, Bailey. I didn't want to hurt you. Not any more than I already have. Than I always have."

She didn't want to cry, but she was still breathing. And as long as there was breath in her lungs, the news he was sharing was bound to hurt. She couldn't stop that part. Tears clouded her view and she blinked so she could see him. "It's okay. I'm happy for you, Cody. Maybe . . ." Her voice cracked and she brought her hand to her throat, easing the tension of the muscles there. "Maybe she's the girl you've been waiting for."

"Back in college, things were . . . they were so different." His soul shone in his eyes, and he crossed his arms, struggling the same way she was. "Andi's . . . she's not the same girl she was."

But I am, Bailey wanted to shout. Instead she dabbed her fingertips beneath her eyes and nodded. "I know. She's wonderful. God's changed her." She fought the well of tears trying to find their way out. "Completely."

"Bailey, I don't know." He stood and took a few steps toward her.

"Don't, Cody." She held up her hand and shook her head. "I understand. We weren't right for each other. I agree with that. But please . . . don't say it."

The tears were his this time. He came to her, and though with everything in her she wanted to turn away from him, she could not. Instead she let him take her slowly in his arms and rock her the way her mother had earlier that morning. "I'm sorry, Bailey." He whispered the words in her hair. "If you only knew."

She sniffed and eased back enough to see him. Really see the hurt in his eyes. "If I only knew what?"

"How much . . . I still care about you." His tears fell onto his face, but he didn't blink, didn't look away. "I've missed you. But I haven't . . ." He dragged the back of his hand across his face, roughly, clearly angry at himself. "I haven't known what to say, or how to say it. You and Brandon apart from each other . . . you being back here in Bloomington just as I'm leaving."

Bailey bit her lip, willing herself to find

control. "Timing has never been our strong suit."

"No." The ocean of sadness remained in his eyes. "It never has."

"And now . . ." A rush of tears gathered in her throat, but she fought them. She searched his face and for a while she let the sad reality of missed chances and regret have their way. "Now you're friends with Andi and it's only a matter of time until —"

"Bailey —"

"Shhh." She put her finger to his lips and shook her head. "Don't say it. I know you. Remember, Cody? I always knew you."

He didn't try to argue. "Better than I knew myself, sometimes."

"Yes." She let herself get lost in his eyes, in the realness of him here with her on the path around Lake Monroe. His eyes were dry now, but he was still giving her a hundred apologies with the hurt in his eyes. "I'm sorry, Bailey. For all of it, for every time I ran and didn't get your feelings right." He sighed. "I'm sorry."

Gradually, like the sunrise after a particularly dark night, Bailey felt herself finding balance again. She took a step back from him. "It's okay. Really. It's the high school girl that still lives in here," she put her hand over her heart. "She's the one crying. When I have time, when I think it through, I'll be happy for you, Cody. Really."

"Which is one more thing I have to tell you." His eyes looked damp again. "Please, Bailey . . . call Brandon."

If her shock wasn't already great enough, this time Cody's words nearly pushed her over the edge. "What?"

"I mean it." Fresh pain darkened his expression. Obviously it was as hard for him to tell her to call Brandon as it was for her to hear about Andi. "You ran from him. That's what happened, isn't it?"

He still knew her, still could look into her eyes and see the truth no matter how badly she didn't want him to see it. Her sorrow was such that she couldn't speak, so she just nodded, her eyes locked on his. She had run, definitely. Cody was right.

"Bailey . . . learn from me." He sniffed, and a level of calm came over him. "When I was in New York . . . when I saw your show for the first time and you told me he'd been there every night, I knew. I never loved you like that. I wanted to, but I didn't." He took a slight step back, too, and rubbed his neck again, clearly distraught at the admission. When he looked up again anger mixed with the pain of his sadness. "I did it all wrong,

Bailey. But Brandon did it all right. When you walked away that night, I stayed." He took her hand and squeezed it lightly before releasing it. "I watched how he looked at you and took your hand and protected you from the crowd and the paparazzi." Cody stopped and let the sorrow wash over him for a painful moment. "He loves you, Bailey. Like I could never love you, he loves you. Don't run from that."

The idea that Cody Coleman was telling her this was more than Bailey could take. Not because she wanted Cody. But because he was right. She loved Brandon with everything inside her, and she'd done the same thing to him that Cody had done to her all those times.

She had run.

Her tears came in waves and she thought she might collapse here on the high hillside overlooking Lake Monroe. Instead she went to Cody one more time and clung to him, held him like her survival depended on it. They'd been through so much together. The missed moments and lost communication, the aching rejection he'd always managed to bring into her life. And now this — his determination to send her back into the arms of Brandon Paul.

"You're wrong, Cody . . ." She took gentle

hold of his shoulders and smiled straight to his soul. "You do love me. Otherwise you couldn't . . . have told me that."

He put his hand alongside her face and with his thumb he caught a few of her stray tears. "I have one more thing. Something I've been praying about all week."

Whatever it was, Bailey could see that this part mattered maybe most of all. Because the look on his face was the same one he'd had when he left her that summer before her senior year. When he headed off to Iraq. She waited, unable to find a voice in the sea of emotion.

"I want to be your friend again." The desperate fear and hope in his face told her his heart was breaking, that this was not a statement like he'd made the last time they were together. Back when it was a matter of being in love or being just friends. Cody didn't have to explain what he meant. He wanted her friendship. For real.

She squeezed her eyes shut and covered her face, trying desperately to quiet the teenager inside her, the one that saw this as the greatest ending of all. Finally, when her nose was so stuffy she could only breathe out of her mouth, she wiped her eyes and stared at him. "How would that look? How do we find that place and really mean it?"

"We talk. We text. You find your way back to Brandon and maybe one day when you're in LA we can all four get together and feel okay about it." The meaning in his voice grew. "Because no one can take away the history between us." He hesitated. "And just because all love is not the same, that doesn't make it less than love." He sniffed. "Right?"

His heart was breaking; she could feel it as clearly as it was happening inside herself. Because the reality played like a movie in her mind. No matter what they wished, time would have the final say. Once Cody was in love with Andi — if that's where God was leading him — there would rightfully be few times when it would make sense to talk or text. They would have their separate lives.

A friendship wouldn't be practical.

But they didn't have to say so right now. A greater calm filled her heart and spread through her body. She took his hands in hers and found a smile despite the tears still on her cheeks. "Right. It doesn't make it less than love."

They hugged again and without saying a word, Cody took her hand and led her back down the path to the car. They needed no conversation. Not then and not as he drove her home and dropped her off. It was like her mother had said. Maybe this wasn't the answer she had expected. But it was part of the puzzle. A door that wasn't only closed, but locked. And despite the rush of emotion, and the heartache his words had brought, deep down she knew Cody was right. Right to take the job in California and right to pursue Andi Ellison.

Right that she needed to find Brandon.

When they reached her house, she leaned in and gave him a hug. "I'll call Andi when I get inside."

Cody looked relieved. "Thank you." He searched her eyes. "You're always with me, Bailey." He pressed his fist to the place over his heart. "Right here. No matter how far."

Again she fought to keep herself from crying. "And you'll be with me. The same way." She leaned in and whispered close to his cheek. "Go find your future, Cody. The good plans God has for you." Then, without looking back, she stepped out, shut the door behind her, and ran lightly up the steps and through the front door.

If she didn't call Andi now, she might not do it. She'd find a way to be mad at her friend, as if Andi had sabotaged Bailey and Cody from the beginning and had always planned to wind up with Bailey's guy. But it wasn't that way, and Bailey begged God that the truth might stand tall in her heart. If this was the direction God was leading Andi, how could Bailey feel anything but happy for her.

She could've told me. The voice echoed back as she walked to the guest room to make the call. *We talked three times this month and she never said a word.* Again she fought for truth. Andi hadn't told her because Cody wanted to be the first to bring it up. And Cody hadn't been able to find the words or the will to do so until this morning.

Calm, Bailey . . . be calm. Show grace the way God shows it to you.

She breathed out and waited until she had a greater grip on her emotions. Then she called up Andi's number and hit the send button. On the third ring Andi answered.

"Hello?"

Did she sound nervous? Bailey tried not to think about it. She closed her eyes tight. "Hey . . . it's Bailey."

"Hi." A strange silence blared across the phone lines. Andi broke it first. "You talked to Cody."

"Yes." She didn't open her eyes. *Please, Lord . . . give me the right words, the right heart.* "I was . . . sort of shocked."

"I know. I told him to tell you a long time ago." She sounded troubled. "I'm sorry,

Bailey. It's not like I was trying to hide anything. We're just friends."

Not for long, Bailey wanted to say. She remembered something her mother had always told them growing up.

When Christ is in you, your life will bear the fruit of the Spirit. Love . . . joy . . . peace . . . patience . . . goodness . . . kindness —

The list played out in her mind and soul. "He likes you, Andi." She smiled, forcing her heart to go along with her decision to be happy for her friend. "He told me."

This time Andi was without words.

The news couldn't have come as a complete surprise to her. Bailey kept praying, kept seeking the right attitude. "I can't talk long right now, but . . . I want you to know you have my blessing, Andi. If the two of you get together, then I will be the first one cheering." She couldn't stop the new tears that slid down her cheeks. "From the sidelines. I'll be cheering. I promise."

"I never saw this coming." Andi's kind tone brought healing to the fresh hurt in Bailey's heart. "Please, don't let this come between us."

"It won't." She closed her eyes again. "You're one of my best friends, Andi. You always will be."

"You're the best friend I've ever had,

Bailey." There wasn't much more to say. "Thank you . . . for calling. For everything."

For giving her blessing. That's what Andi meant, and Bailey was okay with the fact that her friend struggled to say the words. No matter how they defined this conversation in years to come, it would always stand as just that: the time when Bailey gave her blessing for Andi to fall in love with Cody Coleman.

The call ended and Bailey opened her eyes. And there — like she'd always been, for all her life — stood her mom. The way she had always been there in hard times. There with that innate sense of knowing exactly when Bailey's world was falling apart. Bailey stood and without a word, her mother took her in her arms and soothed her hand along her hair and her back. "It'll be okay, Bailey. It will."

"I know." She felt tears in her eyes again, and she closed her eyes. But even then she felt a sense of hope. God had given her this bond with her mom, and now — despite all the pain and shock and heartache the day had already brought — Bailey knew she would survive this. With her faith and her mom, she would get through it. Which meant there was just one thing left to do.

She had to find a way to reach Brandon.

FOURTEEN

Even when he wasn't filming, Brandon liked getting around on his horse. The paint was a trained actor, but in the lonely hours when it was just the two of them, the animal had become his friend. Eight weeks out on the Montana plains had made Brandon wonder if he would ever fit in again once he returned to Los Angeles.

At first he hadn't been able to get past the lack of connection with the outside world. But after a while, he found a different sort of communication. The ability to talk to God at a deeper level and analyze where he had come from and where he was going in a way that he couldn't in the noise and pace of Hollywood. The open ranchland had turned out to be just what he needed.

Especially in light of the situation with Bailey.

They had one more week left on set, making the entire shoot almost nine weeks. May had been the stormiest one on record, and they'd lost far more days than they had anticipated. Brandon's agent had already assured him he'd be paid for the overtime — not that Brandon worried about that. He had more money than he could ever spend. The weather was only God's way of telling him he wasn't ready to go home yet.

He rode the horse to the arena and slowed him down, cooling him off and patting his neck as they walked. For once the sky overhead was clear and before he knew what was happening Molly rode up on her horse and fell in alongside him. "Hey . . . good day. The scenes, I mean."

Something about Molly had grown on him. Not that he had romantic feelings for her. But she had long since stopped playing the vixen and had instead become intrigued with his faith. Especially since the time when he prayed for her. Before they were finished with the shoot, he planned to ask her what she thought about Jesus.

She was quiet, so he glanced in her direction and saw tears on her cheeks. Maybe this was that time. He slowed his horse. "What's wrong?"

"I wasn't going to tell anyone." She brought her horse to a stop and held tight to the reins. Her eyes wouldn't meet his for several seconds. When she looked up there was a sense that in all the world he was the only person she could trust this with. Whatever it was. "I talked to my parents a few minutes ago." She wiped at her tears. "They filed for divorce." She bit her lip, beyond sad. "They've been fighting for a long time."

Brandon couldn't exactly hug her from atop the horse. But then, Molly needed his faith more than his arms. He waited, allowing the gravity of her pain. He took a slow breath and prayed for the right words. "My parents and I haven't talked in years. They . . . they didn't like that I was an actor. I'm not even sure if they're together."

She stared at him. "Brandon!" The surprise and hurt in her voice caught him off guard. "That's terrible."

He didn't want to tell her how his father thought he was gay because he liked acting. Only Bailey knew about that. Still, how shallow his faith must look to Molly now. If he couldn't even reach out to his own parents.

God, I think I just blew it . . .

But the answer that came breathed new hope into his heart.

My strength is made perfect in your weakness. Never forget that, my son.

"I know." He looked at her. "It is terrible." He waited, choosing his words carefully. "I have a long way to go in my faith. There's always something God's working on. My parents . . . the healing we need. Maybe that's next."

"It should be." Molly's expression eased. "You at least have to know how they're doing." She turned her gaze to the distant mountains. "The idea of my parents living in separate houses . . . it makes me feel like I don't have a home to go back to." Her eyes glistened again, but she was doing her best to keep control of her emotions. "You know?"

"I do." He thought about the scenes they'd run that day. "The Grangers . . . that's how love's supposed to look. For all of us."

"But it doesn't." She was quiet, and he could sense a question forming in her soul. "Can I ask you something?"

"Of course."

"Why would God let bad guys kill a couple like the Grangers? People who could've spent another forty years showing the world what love looked like?"

He might not have the exact answer, but this was something he had studied even in the last few weeks out here in the wide-open spaces. Here where so often Brandon felt it was just God and him, getting closer every day. "This is earth, Molly. Jesus promised we'd have trouble on earth." He sighed, hating the reality of that truth. "But He also promises that He has overcome the world."

His answer seemed to speak straight to her, because she let her guard down a little more, and a tear fell onto her horse's mane. "What about you and Bailey? You love her . . . you both have your faith. Why didn't that work?"

His answer was something God had laid on his heart recently. A reality he couldn't deny. "A few months ago I asked God to test me." He allowed a sad laugh. "I sat on the beach in front of my house and told Him I was ready. I didn't want to be a new Christian all my life. I wanted to put my faith to the test and let God grow me up. So that I could be the leader Bailey needed me to be. And even as I finished the prayer, I could feel Him telling me it would happen. The test would come."

Molly listened, thoughtful. "So . . . you think that's what this is? God's growing you stronger, so that one day . . . one day you'll get back together?"

"I can't speak for Bailey." He didn't show his frustration over the fact. "Cell service has been terrible, obviously. But I can say this. I'm out here surrounded by miles of open ranchland and every day, every hour, I feel myself getting closer to God. Even if He doesn't bring Bailey back to me, He's still enough. I never felt like that about my faith before."

"So it's working. He's growing you stronger."

"He is."

She managed a wary smile for the first time since she approached him. "Strong enough to call your parents?"

"Okay, yes." He liked her spunk. "Maybe even that strong."

The cast and crew had kept their distance throughout their conversation. Something Brandon appreciated. But now Molly's smile faded slowly, and a seriousness filled her expression. "Remember that time when I fell off my horse and you prayed for me?"

"Yeah."

"Well . . . what if I want that? The chance to talk to God and have this . . . this faith thing that you've got. It consumes you, Brandon. And it looks good on you — on your heart." A deeper sense of purpose rang in her tone. "I'm around actors all the time, but no one like you. No one with your peace and passion." She was baring her entire soul to him. "I want that, Brandon. Can you help me find it?"

"I'd love that." He patted his horse's neck. "Right here? Or you wanna go somewhere?"

Throughout the shoot Molly had tried to get Brandon into her trailer. But now that seemed to be the furthest thing from her mind. "Here is fine. I just want it, you know? The faith you have."

Brandon felt heaven as close as his next heartbeat. For the next half hour he explained to Molly the story of God's redemption, the way He longed for His creation to be restored, and how He'd sent Jesus as the atoning sacrifice, the one who would take the punishment of the world. "We have to admit our sin and our need for a Savior. From there we believe His word and try our best to live for Him"

"What about baptism? My friend back home got baptized."

"Jesus commands it, for sure. The Bible says believe and be baptized and you'll be saved."

"But baptism doesn't save us, right?"

Brandon laughed. He felt a little dizzy at the thought of tackling that question. "Jesus saves us, that much I know for sure. But the rest of it, I guess it's up to God to work out the details. Bottom line, He tells us to be baptized. You could do that here or when you get home. I could put you in touch with the pastor at our church."

Molly seemed to like that idea. "So can I do the other part now? Ask Jesus to be my Savior?"

"Of course." Brandon felt a rush of emotion like nothing he'd ever known, a sort of love for God and from Him that was more pure than anything he'd ever known. And in that moment, as he prayed with Molly to receive Christ as her Savior, Brandon understood why. Like all people, he had been created for moments like this. It was one thing to begin a relationship with Jesus, and another thing altogether to live it out. Part of God growing him up — so he could lead his own family one day — had to be moments like this. When he could share his precious faith with someone desperate for salvation.

Someone like Molly.

When they were finished praying, she had tears in her eyes again. She thanked him and then asked him one more question. "My friend . . . she gave me a Bible. It's in my trailer. If I wanted to read it, where should I start?"

"That's easy. The book of John. It's an eyewitness account of Christ's days on earth. It'll answer a lot of your questions."

"Okay." She smiled, but it was a smile of innocence. The smile of someone close to her Creator. "I think I'll go do that." She paused. "Thanks, Brandon. And I guess I have to thank my friend too. She's been praying."

"God is great." Brandon returned her smile. "I'll be around if you wanna talk about it some more."

"Okay." She checked her phone. "Hey! I have service." She raised her brow in his direction. "You probably do too. Maybe you should make a couple phone calls."

"A couple?"

"To your parents, of course." She hesitated long enough so that he would know how sincere she was. "And to Bailey. You love her too much to let her get away."

Brandon wanted to let loose a victory shout. Molly's friend had obviously been praying for her, and if she hadn't been on the set with Brandon all these weeks, she might never have taken time to think about God or the Bible or what it meant to give her life to Christ. But God had put all the pieces together, giving him yet another chance to grow and her a chance at new life.

Their Almighty God was amazing.

And after Molly was gone he checked his phone and found that she was right. His phone had full service — nothing short of a minor miracle. The first thing he did was check Bailey's Facebook page. She hadn't contacted him since breaking up with him over text, but maybe she'd said something about it in a status update. If so, he'd rather know before he tried to call her.

The app didn't respond quickly, but after a minute Bailey's profile came up. He scrolled down her wall and found Scripture references and words of encouragement. Not until he went back two weeks did he see a post by her that took his breath.

Had to let go of something I've held on to for far too long. Something that's been over for a very long time. God, help me move on. Help me accept new seasons in life. And please help me believe Your plans for my life are still good. XOXO, Bailey.

She couldn't be talking about Cody. The two of them never saw each other, never talked. Which meant she could only be referring to him. That had to be it. Somehow that Monday she had reached a point where she not only wanted to be broken up with him. She wanted to put him out of her life forever.

Molly's words came back to him, and he

realized how right she was about his parents. He needed to reach them. He missed them, no matter how they had treated him. And now that he understood forgiveness better, he needed to make the first move toward finding a relationship with them again. He would fight for restoration and hope and believe that one day in the not-so-distant future he might look in his mother's eyes and tell her he loved her. Not only that, but he would mean it. But where did that leave Bailey and him? She had made the decision to move on without ever talking to him.

Suddenly, Brandon knew he could walk across the plains and the mountains without sleep or food or water if it meant having the chance to tell her he still loved her. He tapped out a few clicks on his phone and called her. By the fourth ring, Brandon knew she wasn't going to pick up. Or maybe she wasn't with her phone. He was about to leave the most passionate, convincing message he'd ever dreamed of leaving when as quickly as it came, the service cut out.

Fine. He stared at his phone a long time. Waiting and waiting for the service to come back, hoping for it to come back. Finally he closed his eyes and felt once again the answer to his long ago prayer. God was growing him. He'd heard it said once that a teacher was always most silent during a test. That was definitely true for what God was teaching him now. How he had to have complete dependence on the Lord before he could truly pursue Bailey. This was one more way he was learning that. So if not now, if not with a message on her cell, Brandon would find another way to talk to her, to tell her how he thought about her every night and day and that he would always love her and fight for her. How he would go to the ends of the earth for her. He would die for her, if it took that. He had to tell her. Now he could only pray for the opportunity to hear her voice or see her face, and for one other thing.

That when he found her, she might stay with him long enough to listen.

FIFTEEN

Everything about Cody's new life made him feel like he'd slipped into some sort of dream. It was the fourth week of June and he was wrapping up another workout with the Oaks Christian players. They had a long way to go to be ready for fall, but he loved the chance to be part of the solution. Already he'd taught them the most important thing. As the guys ran off the field and huddled up, Cody's voice rang loud above the grunts of his breathless players. "Okay, men. Let's wrap this up. Whose way?"

"His way!"

"Whose way?" Cody's voice rang loud across the huddle, more passionate than before.

The guys responded with a renewed intensity. "His way!" They ran through the chant two more times before Cody dismissed them. Then he turned to the place where she was waiting, where she'd waited for him as often as she could since he moved to Thousand Oaks. He remembered how it touched him that Cheyenne would watch his Lyle practices, but this was different.

He wasn't only touched that Andi Ellison waited for him near the fence, her long blonde hair dancing in the summer breeze. He was grateful to spend time with her. With Andi he finally understood what Cheyenne had meant about Bailey. If he'd loved Bailey the way he once thought he had, he never would've run. He wouldn't have been afraid. Instead he would've wanted to fight for her and stay with her and never let her go.

The way he was beginning to feel about Andi.

They were dating now, a change that had happened his second week in town. But he still hadn't kissed her. He wanted her to know that his feelings for her were inspired by who she was as a person, the hardships she'd overcome, and how she'd found her way back with God's help. Same as him. They had both experienced things they shouldn't have. And for that reason too, Cody felt strongly that kissing could wait. The decision was one way he could honor Andi.

"Hi." He walked up to her and took her

in his arms, hugging her for several seconds before taking her hands in his. "We still on for the bike ride?"

"Look." She pointed to her convertible Volkswagen Beetle parked nearby. The top was down and two mountain bikes were piled into the backseat, rear wheels down, front wheels balanced against the back. "Hope you didn't wear yourself out coaching." Her tone was filled with teasing. "Seriously. The path goes on forever."

"And it's right on the beach?"

"Yep." Andi's eyes danced, and for a few seconds there was only the two of them in all the world. She took a deep breath and blinked. "When we moved here I was still finding my way back. Understanding what I'd done and why." Her smile made her look like an angel. "I'd drive down to Santa Monica, rent a bike, and ride for hours. Right along the water. Sometimes I'd stop and read my Bible before going back." Her eyes narrowed a little, the memory of that time clearly still very much alive for her. "It helped clear my head. Helped me forgive myself."

Cody wanted to hold her and erase every bit of pain and hurt she'd ever been through. But if things went the way he thought they would, there would be time for that. "I can't wait." He ran his thumbs along the sides of her hands. "I want to see this place."

He led her to the car. His truck wasn't the best vehicle for LA freeways and traffic, so most of the time they used her car, but she liked letting Cody drive. "I feel safe with you in charge," she'd told him a number of times. And always Cody took her words in like life to his bones. Andi needed him. That was this new thing he was feeling. She actually needed him. He smiled at her as they set out.

With her he had a purpose, no question.

They drove to Santa Monica and parked south of the pier. Along the path was the occasional bicyclist or in-line skater, but it was Tuesday and for the most part the beach was empty. Cody breathed in the salty sea air and grinned at her. "It's gorgeous."

"I told you." Andi put the car's top up while Cody took the bikes from the back-seat.

"You described it perfectly." Cody held onto both bike handlebars and took in the scene around them. "The path literally cuts right through the sand."

"For miles and miles and miles." She laughed. "I knew you'd love it."

The bikes Andi had brought were meant

for this sort of ride, and as soon as they set out Cody knew they'd be back often.

Andi explained that north of the pier was more scenic and remote, but south was busier and more interesting. "I usually ride south when I come by myself. It feels safer somehow."

"Let's go north." He grinned. "Remote sounds amazing."

"Yeah. With you it does."

"Hmmm." He put his arm around her and rested his head against hers. "Thanks for that." She made him feel whole and alive and sure about his faith and future. Just being with her.

He stepped back and they climbed on their bikes. As he did, he smiled at her and even with their sunglasses on he felt their eyes connect, felt the unshakable trust she had in him.

They rode under the pier and after only a few minutes Cody saw what Andi meant. The path ran along vast sections of open beach and breathtaking scenery. But they were the only ones on this section of the trail. "Andi, this is crazy." They rode side by side, their pace unhurried. "I didn't know something like this existed."

"Only in California." She lifted her face to the sun, her back straight, hair flying behind her in the wind. "I love living here." The path was far enough up from the water that the wind didn't make pedaling too difficult.

Neither of them said anything for a while. Cody pictured Andi taking this path in the opposite direction, trying to blend in with the other beachgoers, silently crying out to God for change and direction. "I wish I'd known you better back then, when you first moved here. Maybe I could've helped. You know, if we'd actually stayed friends after you left Indiana University."

Andi's expression grew thoughtful. "Such a dark time for me." She was quiet for a long moment. "I ran from Him as fast and hard as I could." She looked at him and then turned her attention back to the path ahead. "I knew better. I thought the world would be more fun than living for God." She paused. "When I moved here I was so lonely, so broken. I needed to be alone with the Lord. So I could remember how much He loved me. Even with all I'd done wrong, He loved me."

Cody stared out at the ocean for a stretch and then caught her eyes again. "That makes sense. I guess God's timing was perfect then. Bringing me here now."

"Yes. Always." She laughed, the sort of

childlike laugh that could only come from an untangled wholly healed heart. Her new feelings, the excitement of where this might go — all of it shone in her expression. "I'm glad you're here, Cody. Really glad."

"Me too." He held her eyes as long as he could without turning his attention back to the path. They rode for half an hour and then Cody saw a cove where the sand looked whiter and cleaner and the view even prettier than any they'd seen so far. "Wanna stop?"

"Sure." Andi didn't hesitate.

They rode down a driveway into an empty parking lot and set their bikes adjacent to the sand. "Will Rogers State Beach." He raised his brow at Andi. "We'll have to remember this."

"Look at all I missed, always heading south." Her tone held the familiar teasing. "See how good you are for me?"

And how good you are for me, Andi. He thought it, but he kept the words from crossing his lips. There was no need to rush what was happening between them. Not when they were enjoying these early magical moments so much. He took her hand and slipped his fingers between hers while they walked toward the water. A few feet from the surf, they sat down and for a while they only watched the ocean, the waves washing in one after another and the seagulls dipping low over the sea.

The silence between them felt easy and comfortable. Andi seemed deep in thought, and Cody didn't want to say anything to interrupt that. Instead he waited, and in time she turned to him. "God healed me of all of it, every bad choice, every rebellious thing I did." Sorrow hung in her hesitation. "But he's still working with me on one thing."

Whatever it was, Cody wanted to take it from her, take it into himself and handle it for her. So the kind girl beside him would never feel pain from her past again. He still had hold of her hand, and he squeezed it gently, waiting.

"It's my little boy." Tears gathered in her eyes and she turned toward the ocean again. "That's the hardest part."

In the silence that followed, Cody tried to imagine what that would be like. Giving away a firstborn child. His heart felt heavy, crushed in a different, stronger way by the reality of her courageous and difficult decision. A decision she would carry with her the rest of her life.

Andi's eyes narrowed, as if she were facing the pain all over again. "I didn't love the guy. I shouldn't have slept with him. But none of that was my little boy's fault."

"He's happy, you know that." Cody's voice was gentle, barely louder than the ocean breeze. "He's a Baxter now."

"Yes." Her smile was compassionate. She clearly didn't expect Cody to completely understand. "He's happy and loved. I did the right thing. I know that." She angled her head, and a sorrow so great it was tangible came across her. "I just miss him. And for a long time I believed that God wanted me to be alone. Just me and Him. Because I'd messed up so bad and maybe . . . maybe I didn't deserve love and a future. Maybe I didn't deserve a family someday." She sniffed and a tear slid down from beneath her sunglasses. "That's the part where He's still healing me."

A dozen quick responses came to Cody. How she couldn't possibly put that sort of sentence on herself, and how God would never punish her that way. He didn't only forgive, He *forgot* the things of her past. If she knew that giving up her baby boy had been the right thing, then she had to believe God was happy with her decision. That she had permission to move on and to love again and to believe in the life He had for her.

But somehow in the moment Cody knew better than to say anything at all. Instead he put his arm around her shoulders and hugged her to himself. They both watched the shoreline again and let the truth simply be. No matter how right her decision and no matter how real the promises of God, Andi still hurt. This was something that would take time. If anyone understood that, Cody did.

He had no idea how much time passed, but finally Andi stood and helped pull him to his feet. Her face told him she wouldn't hold on to the sad thoughts another moment longer. This day was to be lived. "Come on." The laughter was back on her lips. "I'll race you down the beach."

"You'll lose." He stood and walked toward her. What was it about this girl? He loved everything about her, about being with her.

She slipped her tennis shoes off and tossed her sunglasses on the sand. But before she could tell him to do the same she looked at his feet. As if she had just remembered his prosthetic left foot, the way his tennis shoe was part of an artificial lower limb that allowed him to run and walk and bike like anyone else. Her smile faded but only for half a second. Then she lifted teasing eyes to his. "You better leave your shoes on.

You'll need every advantage." Without waiting she took off running down the shore.

"Hey!" His foot didn't slow him down, but his laughter did. No one had ever felt comfortable talking to him about his leg the way she just had. Even with Bailey the topic never came up. He started running, yelling after her. "How about a fair start?"

Cody had run half marathons and triathlons since returning from Iraq, so catching up to her wasn't a problem. His shoes were such that water didn't hurt them, so if she challenged him to a swim, he could do that too. With God and technology Cody had no limits because of his injury. None whatsoever.

"You're done!" He passed her easily and when he was ten yards ahead of her he turned and ran backwards. "Maybe if I run like this . . . you know, so you have at least a chance." He laughed, enjoying the exertion, the way it felt to play with her. "I mean, come on, Andi. I thought you'd at least give me a challenge."

She slowed and bent over her knees, catching her breath and laughing. When he came close she suddenly sprang toward the sea and flicked foamy water at him. "Come on, Indiana boy. Come get me." She ran lightly through the surf, splashing back at him as she went. "I'll show you a challenge."

He didn't hesitate, running through the cold Pacific and easily reaching her again. With a single motion he swept her into his arms. But instead of kissing her the way he so badly wanted to, he picked her up and pretended to drop her into a small series of waves. "Really? That's all the speed you've got?" He yelled to be heard above the sound of the ocean.

"Cody!" She screamed, the happy sound ringing out across the water. "Put me down!"

"Okay." He started to drop her, but at the last second he kept her from falling. No matter how much he enjoyed the laughter and teasing, he had to make one point clear. "You are a challenge, Andi Ellison." He set her down gently in front of him and kept his arms around her waist. "And besides . . ." His face was close to hers, and he could feel her breath on his skin. "You've already won."

"Won what?" She was breathless, clearly as caught up in the closeness of him as he was with her.

Before he did something crazy like confess his feelings here in knee-deep ocean water, he stepped back and splashed her. "I'll tell you one day." He raised his eyebrows, flirt-

ing with her. "I guess you'll have to stick around to find out."

"You might be sorry you said that."

She was still laughing, but her answer hit him hard. Bailey would've teased and said something like, "Only if you're lucky." But Andi instantly went the other direction. Like she still wasn't quite sure of how great her worth, or her inner beauty, in light of the ugly marks life had left on her heart.

He brought her close again and hugged her. A larger wave slapped at their waists and their clothes were instantly wet. But Cody didn't care. What he had to say was more important than their wet clothes. "I would never be sorry." He moved a few strands of her wet blonde hair off her face. "Being with you . . . I've never felt like this, Andi. Never."

She sucked in a fast breath and held it. Finally she shook her head ever so slightly, her eyes locked on his. "I'm scared, Cody."

"Don't be." He spoke straight to her unforgiving doubts. Their faces were closer now, and as they hugged again their cheeks brushed against each other. He looked intently at her once more. "I'm not going anywhere."

She seemed to hold on to the promise and after a few heartbeats she nodded. Then, as if she was desperate to keep the moment light, to not venture where her heart wasn't quite ready to go, she took a few steps back and grinned. "Come on. I wanna show you something."

They ran back up the shore and held hands again while Andi led them up onto the dry sand and toward a closed-down lifeguard tower. They walked up the ramp and together leaned against the railing and looked out toward the horizon. "Bailey told me that when she lived here . . . she'd come to the beach," Andi looked around and shrugged. "Maybe even this beach. And she'd hide out here on the lifeguard stations. So the paparazzi wouldn't find her. It was one place she could breathe, she said."

Cody studied her, not sure why in the middle of this amazing day Andi would bring up Bailey. The fact didn't make him angry, but he didn't understand it. "That's why you brought me up here?"

"I guess. I miss her." Andi slipped her arm around Cody's waist. "We've been talking more. A couple times a week." She smiled up at him. "You don't come up all that much, to be honest. But when you do . . . I think she's okay with it. She's trying to figure out her feelings for Brandon. That's where her heart is."

"Hmmm." Cody felt himself relax again. "That's good. I told her she needed to talk to him."

"That's what she said." Andi turned toward the water. "We prayed about that, remember? That we'd all be friends again somehow."

"We did." Cody stood taller, remembering the sadness of that day at Lake Monroe. "It's different with me, I guess."

Andi's eyes held the hint of a question, but nothing more. "You and her, you don't talk much?"

"Not at all." His chuckle sounded sad. "It's different with guys and girls. Especially us."

"When you've been more than friends."

"Exactly." He turned and leaned his back against the railing, watching Andi, the way her heart was still afraid to love. "I'm over her . . . if that's what you're wondering."

"No, it's just . . ." Andi laughed, and her face told him she had been caught. "Okay, maybe. I mean . . . remember how you were back then, Cody? You were crazy about her."

"I was young." He tilted his head, praying she could see the depth of truth in this moment. "I'd never known anyone like her."

"She's very special." Andi seemed to slump a little. "I can never be her."

"I don't want her." The words came before Cody could think about them, before he could realize how there was a time when he wouldn't have dreamed he'd say such a thing. But now the statement was truer than the sunshine. "I care about her. I'll always care about her. But she wasn't the girl for me."

For a long time she looked at him, searching his eyes, like she was trying to believe him. "You mean it . . . don't you?"

"Yes." He pulled her close and hugged her once more. Then he eased back so she could see his eyes. "For all the things Bailey is . . . for all that she once was to me . . . with all the things she did right . . . she never . . . never made me feel like this." His voice was soft, each word a gentle touch against her face. "The way you make me feel."

Slowly, like the waves building toward shore, a smile lifted Andi's lips. She put her arms around his neck and held him — with her whole heart and soul she held him. When they stepped back their eyes stayed locked for several seconds. And as he took her hand and they walked back to their bikes, Cody felt they'd reached a new understanding: Bailey Flanigan was not now and never would be a problem for them. This was a new season and the questions they'd all had were being answered. Questions Cody hoped Andi would never have again. Because he'd told her the absolute truth.

The feelings he had for Andi were different.

They rode another half hour north and then turned around and headed back for the pier. When they stopped for a water break, Andi checked her phone and a concerned look filled her eyes. "My mom isn't feeling well." Her brow knit together. "She's had the flu for a week."

"Not good." Cody put his arm around her and looked at the text on her phone. He and Andi had planned to have dinner with her parents. But now she needed rest more than a night out. "Tell her we'll bring her soup. We can stop and pick some up. I found a place near my apartment."

"Really?" Her eyes lit up. "Cody, that's so nice."

"It's the least we can do."

They made their way back to the car, where Andi turned to him. "Next time I want to go south, at least for a while. So you can see where I used to ride." Her eyes were soft, thoughtful. "I'd like you to know. Maybe I can show you some of the letters I wrote to God."

"I'd like that." He realized the gift she was giving him, the gift of letting him see right into her heart where the walls between them were starting to crumble. The rush of open air around them only added to the moment, and Cody covered her hand with his, glancing at her as often as the road would allow.

On the drive to pick up soup, they talked about Andi's parents, the ministry they ran making Christian movies. After living with the Flanigans he hadn't thought he'd ever find a family he could feel so at home with. But from the first time he had dinner at the Ellisons' house, he knew he was wrong. He felt like he'd known Andi's parents all his life.

"I look up to your dad," he said now. "He's changing the world. How many of us would like to say that?"

Andi glowed beneath the praise for her father. "He's very special."

The older hillside home where Andi and her parents lived was in a modest Thousand Oaks neighborhood. They parked and carried the soup and a bag of homemade bread through the front door and into the kitchen. Her parents sat at the dining room table, and their faces showed their surprise at the food being brought in.

"Andi . . . you didn't have to do that."

Her mom stood slowly and pulled her robe tight around her waist. "Dad could've made something."

Andi grinned and waved her thumb at Cody. "It was his idea."

"Actually . . ." Cody shot her parents a quick smile. "I wanted to cook for you, but then I remembered you were trying to feel *better.*" He winced. "Figured we better pick up soup in that case."

They all laughed, and Cody was glad to see Andi's mother seemed to be feeling better than she had a few days ago. He set the food down and crossed the room, hugging first her dad, then her mom. "How are you feeling?"

"Better." She took a step back. "But I don't want you kids to get sick." She returned to the table and sat down. A sneeze caught her off guard, and she grabbed a tissue from the nearby box and held it to her nose. "A few more days of rest and I'll be my crazy self again."

"Good." Andi was in the kitchen unpacking the food. "That's what I like to hear."

The four of them ate together, despite Andi's mother protesting that they shouldn't be too close to her.

"Mom, you're not contagious. A person's only contagious the first few days of being sick." Andi took a spoonful of her soup. "Besides, we want to eat with you." She looked at Cody. "Right?"

"Definitely. Andi and I don't get sick. It's against the rules."

They all laughed. The conversation flowed after that, and Andi's dad told them about his latest project. An hour flew by and after they'd cleaned up, Cody noticed the time on his phone. "We better head out."

"Head out?" Andi looked surprised.

Cody loved this, the way he could create a plan and surprise her with one small act of kindness after another. "I'm taking you bowling. Didn't I tell you?"

"What?" She laughed and looked from her parents back to Cody. "How do you know I can bowl?"

Cody exchanged a knowing smile with Andi's mother. "A spy told me." He helped Andi to her feet and took her hand. Then he turned to her dad. "Andi's been looking for something she can beat me at." He gave her a quick smile. "We found out today it's not running or swimming."

Again Andi's face brightened and her eyes sparkled like the sun on the water earlier. "So maybe it's bowling!"

Her parents were already laughing and her dad held his hand up. "I can testify to this

— the girl can bowl. She beats me every time."

"That settles it." Cody winked at Andi. "Because I'm about as bad at bowling as anyone could be. Which will make this the perfect day, since you can actually be better at something."

"You crack me up." Andi grabbed her purse and waved at her parents. "I guess we're going bowling. Cheer me on!"

Cody hugged Andi's parents again and Andi did the same. As they walked down the hallway toward the front door Cody heard something that touched his heart. Talking in hushed tones, Andi's mother said, "I don't know what it is about that boy. I feel like I've known him for years."

Andi didn't seem to hear her parents, too caught up in the adventure ahead. But Cody let her mother's words find a permanent place in his heart. Andi had already told him that her parents had prayed for her future since she was born. For her choices and career path and for her future husband. So was it possible Andi's mom felt like she knew Cody because one day Cody and Andi would wind up together?

Any other season of his life the thought would've terrified him. He and Andi had only been dating a few weeks, after all. Still, they'd been good friends for more than a year at Indiana University, and those memories, along with their similar journeys of faith, made him feel like he'd known Andi forever. Maybe because of that, in this moment, her parents' words didn't scare him. They were like the greatest gift. Cody prayed all the time about Andi and his new relationship with her and always God pressed upon his heart the same thing. He had nothing to be afraid of, no worries this time around. And something else. Maybe all his life had led not only to his job at Oaks Christian.

But to her.

Sixteen

The first thing Bailey became aware of as she woke up was the smell of boiling potatoes drifting up the stairs. In a rush she realized what day it was and that she needed to get downstairs to help. This year July Fourth seemed to come more quickly than usual. Probably because Bailey had been taking Skype meetings with Dayne and Katy for the last few days, busy talking to them about her latest dream. The one she couldn't shake.

She wanted to buy CKT from them.

Bailey sat up in bed and ran her hand over her long hair. Already she'd talked to her parents extensively about the idea, and last Friday she'd put together a proposal and presented it to Dayne and Katy through overnight mail. By then, Katy was weeks away from delivering, and her doctor in LA didn't want her to travel. They had chosen a name — Egan Thomas — and Sophie was practically crazy with anticipation of meeting her little brother.

The birth of the Matthews' second baby made the timing perfect. Bailey smiled as she remembered that first virtual meeting. Katy and Dayne looked at each other, and almost at the same time they began to laugh. The kind of laugh that acknowledged some wild coincidence or unbelievable miracle. The way people laughed when they found out they'd won the lottery.

"You won't believe this." Dayne was the first to turn to her and explain. "For the last month we've been talking about selling CKT. With another baby, it just isn't practical. We'll only be back in Indiana a couple times a year to see family."

"We thought about you, Bailey, but we weren't sure." Katy's eyes allowed a seriousness that hadn't been there initially. "If you and Brandon figure things out, you might wind up back in LA."

"We're looking for someone who lives in town." Dayne sat back in his chair. He looked from Katy to Bailey. "But if you're interested, let's just say we're definitely ready to listen."

The meetings had gone very well after that. Bailey's dad had helped her put together the business plan, and she felt confident as she discussed it with Dayne and Katy during yet another Skype session. The one thing she refused to think about was what the decision meant to her and Brandon. How it would take Bailey one more step from what they had shared.

With all the time and energy she'd put into presenting her plans to Katy and Dayne, Bailey was glad that this was a holiday. She slid out of bed and hurried through getting ready. Brandon had left just one message on her cell since he'd returned to Los Angeles. She played it on speaker while she finished straightening her hair. "Bailey, this is crazy. I've been home for two weeks and we haven't talked. I want to see you, baby." He paused, his tone broken. "I'm not ready to give up on us. Please . . . call me back. I'll be waiting. I love you."

She closed her eyes and let his voice wash over her again. He loved her, he really did. And several times she started to call him back but then changed her mind. She wasn't sure what to say to him. It was wrong not to call him back, she just wasn't sure her heart could take the conversation. Maybe later today, when she and her family were at the lake.

She took the stairs slowly, aware again that making this decision to stay in Bloomington, to purchase CKT, might mean her being alone the rest of her days. Because she couldn't imagine another love like the one she'd shared with Brandon. But if that was what God was calling her to do, then she would live out that life in His strength.

The same as if she'd been called to Africa to spend her days on the mission field.

She reached the kitchen and saw her younger brothers Shawn and Justin chopping onions near the sink. A smile erased the sadness from a minute ago. She loved her brothers, how everyone in her family got along and appreciated this short season of life when they were all together under one roof again.

"Well, it's true." Justin dragged his wrist across his cheek. "Onions definitely make me cry, but I still don't get how a vegetable can make me sad."

Shawn chuckled and shook his head. "Yeah, it's not that kind of crying."

"Whatever it is, it's bad." He sniffed and wiped at his face again. "It's like the onion juice is going straight to my eyes."

Their mom was making coffee, and she laughed at the boys' exchange. "Onion juice is like that." She smiled at Bailey. "I've got coffee for both of us."

"Thanks." She walked to the pot of boiling potatoes. "Are these ready to cut up?"

"Pretty much." Her mom crossed the kitchen and slid a paring knife into one of the potatoes. "Yes. Definitely ready."

"I'll take care of them." This routine was as familiar as Fourth of July — the Flanigans making buckets of their mom's famous potato salad to take to the Baxter Family picnic at Lake Monroe.

Bailey drained the water from the pot as memories from the past July Fourths filled her heart and mind. The times when her old friend Tim Reed had joined them, and the Fourth of July when Cody first returned from the war. That year he knocked at the door and saw her for the first time since his injury in Iraq. That was the moment her mother always remembered — when she wondered whether anyone would ever love Bailey the way Cody did.

Of course there was the Fourth a few years back when she and Cody admitted their feelings for each other. The time he first kissed her when it seemed nothing would ever separate them. And then last year when Brandon joined her and everyone could see the attraction between them.

She sliced the potatoes without really seeing them. Hadn't she known back then it was a bad idea, falling for Brandon Paul?

Bailey had never wanted to live in Los Angeles. But he had been so amazing while she was in New York, so ready to come see her that their love had felt beyond magical. As if God Himself had given them the gift of each other.

Bailey looked out the window at her family's pool and beyond to the acreage that ran up against the forest. Why hadn't she thought about the reality? Which left just one question: Why had God allowed her to fall in love with Brandon in the first place?

Justin came up beside her and snagged a piece of potato. "Sometimes I like it without all the goopy stuff." He grinned at her. "And without those super strong onions."

Bailey laughed. She didn't blame him. But whatever their mom did to the recipe, it always turned out to be a hit. Onions and all.

They finished getting the meal ready and Bailey's dad brought the other boys home from their summer basketball workout. "It's going to be the best Fourth ever," her dad announced. "I have a feeling."

Another smile lifted Bailey's heart. Her dad said the same thing every year. "You're doing the fishing derby this year, right?"

"Of course." Her dad raised his fist in the air. "Enough of this Baxter domination. This

274

year a Flanigan man is going to win." He pointed at a few of the boys. "We have a plan, right?"

"Definitely." Justin raised his fist too. "It'll be the start of a dynasty."

Bailey could hardly wait to see what they had cooked up, but for now she helped her mom finish the potato salad, and then together with her brothers they loaded chairs and picnic supplies into the back of the Suburban. Like every other Fourth, they arrived at the lake around three that afternoon and began setting up. By then most of the Baxters were there. Katy and Dayne wouldn't be here this year, obviously, because Katy couldn't travel. But everyone planned to call them from the lake before the fireworks.

Luke and Reagan were the last to arrive, walking down the hillside with their three kids just after four. Bailey hadn't seen Luke and his family since last Fourth of July. As they came closer, Bailey watched them, especially Johnny, their youngest son. He was nearly two, still small enough that Reagan carried him in her arms while Luke brought their ice chest. Tommy and Malin, eleven and seven now, galloped along beside them.

But it was Johnny who held Bailey's attention. She and Andi talked all the time now, and often her friend opened up about the pain of giving the boy up. She stood by her decision, but she ached at the loss. Last time they talked, Andi had said she hoped for a chance to see the boy, see how happy and adjusted he was living with his family.

Bailey thought how it would feel to be Andi, to know that she'd given birth to a child who didn't know her. She watched as Reagan set Johnny down and took his hand as he slowly toddled along. He had Andi's blond hair and her fine features. No question he was her friend's son. But if Andi were here now, she would agree the same way everyone who saw Luke and Reagan and their kids would agree: Johnny was exactly where he was supposed to be. Bailey made a point to tell Andi later.

The smell of barbecue already filled the air around them as John Baxter and a few of the dads worked to get the burgers going. Connor ran up as Bailey was about to find Ashley Baxter Blake. "Come on!" He grabbed her hand, clearly excited about something. "It's a three-legged race. We're making teams and I pick you!"

Bailey laughed as they hurried down the hill to the shore. But no matter how much fun they had over the next hour doing crazy races and building stick forts along the water, Bailey couldn't shake the fact that something was missing. That no matter how badly she wanted to be content with being single in Bloomington, her heart was held hostage back in LA.

Or wherever Brandon was today.

She thought about calling him when the guys working the barbecue announced it was time to eat. She could slip off, head up the hill to the parking lot, and find a quiet place to call him. But even then the conflict remained. Why call him when the sound of his voice against her soul would only make her miss him more?

Connor walked beside her as everyone formed a circle. The largest circle they'd ever made, if Bailey's guess was right. A few of the Baxter kids had brought friends this year, and with all the families mixed together, the group was bigger than ever. They held hands and Bailey giggled when it took Ashley's son Devin a little longer to find his place in the circle.

"No . . . not here." He looked everyone over as he walked along the inside of the circle. As if he was sizing up each person trying to decide who to stand by for the prayer. When he reached Bailey he finally stopped and grinned. "There you are! I was looking for you!"

Bailey's heart melted. "You want to stand by me, buddy?"

"Yep." He looked over his shoulder and raised his eyebrows in Ashley's direction. "I can stand by Bailey, right, Mom? Because I'm gonna marry her one day, okay? So we should pray by each other, right?"

A trickle of laughter made its way around the circle. Ashley worked to keep a straight face. "Yes, Devin. Go ahead. I'm sure Bailey would love that."

The little boy beamed up at her. He was six this summer and his tanned dimples made him look beyond adorable. He slid in next to Bailey and took her hand. "Okay," he announced in a loud voice. "We can start."

Every year the dads prayed for their families. Some said only a few words, and others shared something deeper, more private. It was different each year. This time Luke Baxter started the prayer and he thanked God for the men and women who fought to keep America safe. Bailey kept her eyes closed, agreeing that they would not be a free nation if not for the military. Guys like Cody who had given everything they had for the cause of freedom.

Ashley's husband asked for God's protec-

and they had stolen a moment from yesterday.

"Don't say it." He smiled, but it didn't hide his sadness. "We'll talk later." He paused, allowing the full weight of his next words. "I leave in the morning. I have a meeting at the studio." For a moment he let that settle, the reality that this was nothing more than borrowed time. But then with another quick smile he glanced over his shoulder. "Anyway, right now it looks like dinner time."

Bailey leaned to the side and looked up the hill at the line of family and friends getting burgers from the place where the barbecues were set up. "I think you're right." She giggled and slipped her hand in his. She had missed him so much more than she realized. Brandon had come and he was here and they were going to share in the Fourth of July picnic.

What more could she ask?

They sat with Bailey's family for dinner and when they finished eating, Devin ran from table to table making a grand announcement: "Time for the fishing contest! Hurry, people. Gather 'round. Before it gets dark!"

Bailey didn't want to think about the fading sunlight or the way the clock refused to stand still. Not yet. Brandon had his arm around her, as if she'd never broken up with him. Once in a while she caught her mom giving her a look — nothing critical, but more of a sad, understanding glance. Because there was no happy ending to a moment like this.

Brandon spoke close to her cheek. "Who are we cheering for?"

"My dad." She gave her father a thumbs-up and yelled from where she sat. "This is your time, Dad. Go get 'em!"

"Right!" Bailey's dad, Jim, stood and yelled for his sons Justin and BJ. "Fishermen, report for duty! Let's do this!"

Bailey looked at Brandon and giggled, proof that at least for this moment her heart felt safe and whole and fully his. "We have to cheer loud. One of the Baxters always wins this thing."

"Got it." He took her hand as they walked down the hill and found a fallen log where they could watch the fishing battle. A chill ran down Bailey's arms and she pressed in close to Brandon's side. "I can't believe you're really here." She whispered the words like they were a secret. "I keep thinking I'm going to wake up."

For a long beat, Brandon only looked at her. But she knew him well enough to know what he was thinking. If this time together felt like a dream, then how could she consider breaking up? If being together was the only way either of them felt right, then why in a few hours would they have yet another goodbye?

A loud voice broke the moment. "Okay, everyone." It was Ryan Taylor, who was married to Kari Baxter Taylor — the second oldest of the Baxter sisters. "You all know how it works. This year we have three teams." He explained that he and Luke and John Baxter would form one team, three of the other Baxter guys would form another, and Jim and Justin and BJ would make up the third. Each of them would toss their lines in the water and after fifteen minutes, the team with the most fish would win. "Remember, it's not about the fish. It's about the bragging rights. Fourth of July champs means something around here."

From all around came applause and shouts of approval. Bailey snuggled closer to Brandon. "We take our fishing seriously."

"I remember that." He put his arm around her again. "Are you cold?"

"No." She lifted her eyes to his. "Not with you beside me."

The fishing battle grew heated long before the fifteen-minute mark. John Baxter's team reeled in three trout right away, and almost at the same time her dad and Justin caught two. "Way to go!" Bailey yelled her encouragement to her family. "You can do this, guys!"

"Maybe if they had you out there." Brandon nudged her, teasing.

In the end, it was the other Baxter team who won by catching five fish in the final five minutes, causing Justin to flop down on the bank like one more big trout. Bailey's dad helped him to his feet and brought both her brothers into a huddle. In no time a chant came from them. "Next year! Next year! Next year!"

"Yep." Brandon laughed. "I definitely want to see the rematch."

Bailey wanted to laugh, but his words hit her like so many rocks. Because next year at this time there was no telling whether or not they'd even be talking to each other. She wanted to ask him if he really thought he'd be here beside her next Fourth of July, but she couldn't make herself say the words.

Not when he couldn't possibly promise her anything of the sort.

SEVENTEEN

As darkness fell, Bailey felt time pressing in around them.

The picnic was fun, but she wanted to be alone with Brandon. They'd been apart for so long that if they didn't use the next few hours to talk, they might not have another chance. Before the fireworks show over the lake began, Brandon pulled her aside. "Bailey, can we get out of here? Please?"

She shrugged, and felt herself shiver a little. "Where should we go?"

"I know a spot."

Brandon waited while she told her parents where she was going. She'd done this once with Cody, before they were anything more than friends. But tonight was so different. She wasn't a high school girl now. She was grown up, desperate to find a way to make things work with the guy she loved.

When she returned to him, she slipped her sweatshirt on and with her hand in his they headed up the hill across the parking lot. "I've never been this way." She stayed close to him. Anything not to think of the heartache ahead.

"I found it the day after your dad baptized me. I needed somewhere to go, to pray and thank God for saving me." He smiled at her, but it didn't hide the tension in his expression. "I came here."

On the other side of the parking lot he helped her down a small but steep hill. At the bottom of it was a trail Bailey had never seen. "It's pretty here."

"One of the best spots on the lake." Night had fallen, but Brandon used his phone's flashlight app to light the path ahead of them.

"I bet it's gorgeous in the daytime."

"It is." They walked close together for another few minutes, and the path became a lookout, an area with an almost unobstructed view of the lake. "See over there?" He pointed toward the cliffy edge in front of them. "There's a fire pit."

"That's perfect."

"Yeah," he gave her a lopsided grin, "if I'd brought firewood and a match."

"That's okay." She shivered a little more, the cool air and the pending conversation leaving her colder than she liked. They talking on Skype. And certainly she couldn't have ended things if they'd been together in person.

He waited while the line rang. *Pick up, Bailey . . . please pick up.* But on the fourth ring the call went to her voicemail. "This is Bailey. I can't get to the phone right now. Leave me a message and —"

Brandon hit the end button. He wouldn't leave her a message. No way. He would wait until he could see her. Whether that was through Skype the next time he came into town or in person when he was finished up in Montana.

He looked down, half expecting to see a knife sticking out of his heart. The hurt was that bad. He wouldn't leave her a message, but he wouldn't give up either. He would pursue Bailey with every ounce of his strength, with all of his heart and soul. Once more he took his phone out and went to his Twitter app. It had been a week since he'd updated his feed, and now he opened a blank window and began to type. *I'm not letting go, not giving up, not taking no. The answers are out there . . . all we have to do is find them.* Then he hit the tweet icon. There. Let his million Twitter followers ponder that. By now they all knew that he and Bailey were apart. As much as the tabloids loved splashing their pictures beneath sketchy headlines when they were together, they had also relished Bailey's departure from LA, pronouncing Brandon's depression and Bailey's sudden sickness. The lies would always be there.

But in the end only the truth mattered.

And now the days ahead stretched out like so many possibilities. No matter what Bailey said, he would believe. After all, God had brought them together. He would see them through this — even where it looked like there was no possible way. Brandon would believe that with every fiber of his being. Until he could look into her beautiful blue eyes and see for himself whether there was any truth in her text. Or if, like he suspected, she still loved him as much as he loved her.

The way he would always love her.

and rested her forehead on his. "I can't do this."

"Baby, you have to. If you want me out of your life, then look at me and tell me so."

Over the lake, the first enormous firework exploded in the night sky. Bailey didn't need to look, she could hear it.

How could he ask this of her, ask her to break up with him this way? Brandon had never been anything but kind to her. He had showed her what love looked like, after all. She'd have to have ice in her veins to look in his loving eyes and end things.

"Bailey . . . please. Look at me." His tone was compassionate, as if he understood her struggle and, even more, he'd intended it. Because if she couldn't look him in the eye and break up with him, then what had really changed between them?

Finally she did what he asked. She opened her eyes and with all the strength remaining in her, she lifted her head from his and looked at him. Straight into the eyes that had talked to her on Skype and surprised her at the Empire State Building and danced with her at a rooftop prom. The eyes she had fallen asleep thinking about every night since their last time together.

Slowly and without looking away she shook her head. "I can't." With the sound of the fireworks, even she couldn't hear herself. His eyes told her he understood her, but she needed him to hear her all the way to his heart. "I can't look at you and break up with you, Brandon. Not when I've missed you with every breath."

He seemed to relax, as if her words had allowed little bits of his heart to return. "Okay, then." He worked his fingers into her hair and brought her close again, kissing her once more. "See?" His smile started in his eyes. "That's what I thought. Nothing's changed between us."

"Except I'm living here." She put her hands over his and lowered them. Then she linked her fingers with his. "I like this. Sitting with you. Hoping the morning never comes."

He faced her and held both her hands in his. She tried to think of an easy way to say what she still needed to tell him. But there was none. "We need to talk."

"I know." The light in his eyes refused to waver. "That's why I'm here. Because you suddenly have something against your phone."

She laughed and the release felt wonderful. It was impossible to stay completely serious around Brandon, even now. "Maybe I shouldn't tell you." She exhaled, the laughter still in her tone. "We could sit here and joke and kiss and pretend tomorrow isn't coming. That would be better."

A sigh came from him and he leaned closer. When the teasing was completely gone from his face, he spoke with a sincerity that surprised her. "I'm sorry. I want you to tell me. Really."

The breeze from the lake made the air cooler here, but with Brandon near her Bailey no longer felt cold. She took a long breath and for a moment they both turned and watched the fireworks. These were the best ones, triple shots of red and white and blue. But they didn't have time to take in the show. She looked at him again. "I've been praying, every day since I came home. I left because I was afraid."

"I know."

"But perfect love drives out fear. You and I already talked about that."

"Exactly." Relief seemed to come over him again. "That's why it didn't make sense when you left."

She hesitated, choosing her words with the care he deserved. "Fear wasn't the only reason, Brandon. I wanted to direct the show for CKT."

"And I wanted to see it. Every show." He shook his head. "There was no way I could leave the set. We had to get the movie shot."

"I know. That's okay." She held tighter to his hand. "Anyway, as I've prayed, God put a new passion on my heart." She paused. "I want to buy CKT, Brandon. Katy and Dayne are looking to sell it, and this weekend I showed them a business plan." She lifted her shoulders and let them fall again. "They loved it. We're talking about making the sale final before fall."

Her words couldn't have caught him more off guard if she'd told him she was taking a job in Devin's imaginary circus. "Baby . . . there's gotta be theater groups in LA where you could teach or direct. You could even start your own."

Pain radiated across her heart and into her veins. "That wouldn't be the same. I believe God wants me here. Running the same theater group I loved as a kid. It's everything I could possibly want for the future."

"Everything except me." Tears filled his eyes, but he didn't look away, wouldn't back down from the mountain that had just thrown itself between them. "Is that it?"

She wanted to stand up and scream her frustrations across the lake. "It's not how I want it." Her tone filled with the impossibility of the situation. "You have to know that, Brandon. I want you. But you're in LA, and no matter how many times I try to imagine it, I feel like God's calling me to stay here." The tears were hers now, and they came in a quiet wave. "What am I supposed to do with that?"

"There has to be a way." His tears came as if he refused to acknowledge them. "I need you. I don't care if I have to fly here every weekend, I need you."

For the first time since she stepped foot on the plane a month ago Bailey felt a glimmer of hope. Real hope. "You can't do that. Fly here every weekend."

"People do it. Lots of actors spend weeks in LA and weekends in New York. I've seen it."

She wanted to ask him if he'd seen it work, but she didn't want to dim the flicker of possibility when it had only just ignited. "What about your contract? You'll be busy making movies, right?"

"Planes go everywhere." He exhaled, and his eyes were already drier than before. "And the contract . . . they're supposed to make a big announcement the first of August."

"So . . . they worked out the problems?"

"I'm not sure." He looked suddenly uncomfortable. "August seems awfully soon.

But Luke Baxter is working with my agent and manager. My guys keep telling me everything's on track."

She let the reality sink in a little more. Seven movies over five years. Maybe more — at least according to the things West Mark had told Brandon initially. There would be location shoots and editing and reshoots and publicity and red-carpet events. Leaving LA or anywhere else to fly into Bloomington seemed unlikely. But then, he'd flown in today. Even just for a handful of hours. "We can't count on you having every weekend." Her voice was soft, and she realized the fireworks over the lake had stopped. The air was more still than before. "Even though it sounds amazing."

"We can count on God . . . and we can count on this." He moved in closer and once more he kissed her. When he drew back, when they both were breathless, he spoke words that calmed her soul. "I'm not leaving you. I'll fight for you, Bailey. Until you can look me in the eyes and tell me it's over."

She tried to breathe, tried to remember even a single bit of logic. But all she could do was breathe against his skin and hold onto the moment. "Okay . . . deal."

"All right then. Enough of that." He took

a full breath and laughed. "Now that my heart's beating again, tell me about *Peter Pan*. Don't miss a detail, baby. I mean it."

The flicker of hope became a flame. Bailey wasn't sure if it was the magic of the moment, the fireworks, the Fourth of July, or the fact that he'd surprised her with this visit. But suddenly everything that had felt final and finished seemed at least possible. Maybe they didn't have to have all the answers right now. If Brandon loved her this much, if he wasn't angry with her for wanting to purchase CKT and stay in Bloomington, then maybe they could somehow figure out the rest.

Or maybe they wouldn't figure it out, but they could at least have today. Here and now. In this moment with him, Bailey didn't care about tomorrow. They could live for the day, love for the day. The ending that might eventually come was somewhere off in the distance. For the first time she believed all of this and the feeling changed everything. She snuggled up to him as she told him about *Peter Pan* and her time with the CKT kids, holding on to every feeling Brandon's presence stirred within her.

Even if her feelings only lasted for tonight.

EIGHTEEN

Brandon headed north on the 405 Freeway to the West Mark offices. The past two weeks had been crazy busy — studio meetings and postproduction on his last two films — but even so he barely acknowledged that he was in Los Angeles. Not when his heart and soul were back in Bloomington with Bailey.

The idea of surprising her on the Fourth of July had come up suddenly. He arranged his flight that morning with a few phone calls and wondered the whole way there and back why he hadn't flown to see her sooner. Back when she was moving to New York he'd taken a plane to Indiana just to help her pack. But with his last two months in Montana and the constant meetings at West Mark Studios, somehow he'd forgotten that with even as little as a single day's time he could find a way to see her. Even if their time together lasted only a few hours.

Brandon gripped the steering wheel and checked his rearview mirror. Two cars full of paparazzi were on his tail. Another day in Los Angeles. Brandon stared straight ahead and tried to forget them. Matthew West's song "Strong Enough" played on the radio and he let the words and music speak straight to the center of his being.

He had to credit God alone for giving him the inspiration to fly to Indiana a couple weeks ago. By then it had been so long since he'd talked to Bailey that he could barely focus. He could feel their relationship slipping away and he had been desperate to connect with her again, to convince her they still had a chance. Only God had given him the strength to make the plan and carry it out so quickly. And now with God's help he would figure out a way to do the next thing pressing on his heart.

Take a trip to Bloomington and have a talk with Bailey's father.

But like the song playing on the radio there was no question about one thing: He could only take this next step with God's help, with the Lord speaking peace and assurance to Bailey that somehow they would figure out a way to be together. He would fly to see her as often as he could, but that wasn't the permanent answer. The schedule he'd kept for the last two weeks was a preview of how his life would be once he signed the contract with West Mark. He'd be lucky to find a couple days a month to fly to Indiana. *Work on her heart, God . . . change her mind about Los Angeles. I can't live without her for the next five years.*

Not when all he wanted with every waking moment was to marry her.

A screeching sound came from behind him and he looked over his shoulder in time to see the two cars full of photographers jockeying for position beside him. Was it really that important, getting a picture of him driving on the LA freeways? He exhaled, forcing himself to listen to the song. He needed God's strength for this too. Since returning from Montana he hadn't slipped into his LA life the way he thought he might. He was beyond annoyed at the intrusion of having paparazzi jockeying for position, cameras aimed at him wherever he was, whenever he stepped outside of his home. He glanced at the cars chasing him. No, he was more than annoyed. He was angry.

He needed a more private way of getting around — not just so Bailey would think about moving back here — but so that he himself could stand it. Back when he was journaling his thoughts and writing letters to Bailey in Montana, five years in Hollywood hadn't seemed like too long to ask of her, not too long to deal with the paparazzi. But here on the freeway this morning it felt like an eternity. Yes, he would definitely have to find a more private place to live, a better way of avoiding the constant chase.

The drive wore on, and Brandon hit traffic before he took the off-ramp for the West Mark offices. In the sanctuary of his car, another song filled his senses. "Walking Her Home" by Mark Schultz. The song told the story of a couple who had fallen in love young and lived out every day at each other's side. Small town guy and girl, love bigger than the skyline in New York City. The pleasure of simple nights together and raising a family and long walks through a local park. That was the sort of life the song made him think about.

Another loud screeching sound came and to his right one of the cars with paparazzi ran the other one off the freeway. Brandon sucked back a quick breath, careful to keep his car steady. In a cloud of dust, the second car veered off the road and down an embankment. From what he could see, the vehicle didn't flip, but it skidded broadside into a cement wall doing what must have been serious damage to the side of the vehicle.

"You've got to be kidding." Brandon uttered the words out loud, trying to focus on the halting freeway traffic. All around him people stared at the wreck, bringing the traffic to a nearly complete stop. Brandon peered through the passenger window and saw the photographers piling out of the damaged car, while the other carload lurched into the lane next to Brandon. The guy at the wheel was laughing, and two more in the back still had their cameras aimed at Brandon.

Rage ripped through Brandon and for a long moment he wanted to pull over and yell at the photographers, tell them what they were doing was insane. Instead he picked up his cell and dialed 9-1-1. He told the operator his name and how two cars had chased him, how they'd tried to run each other off the freeway and put everyone on the road in danger.

"And now one of them crashed into a wall."

"Is anyone injured?"

Brandon wanted to throw something. Only me, he wanted to say. But no one could know what it felt like to be hunted every day. He steadied himself. "They're out of the car walking around. But someone needs to be arrested over this. If you could send the police, I'd appreciate it."

"Yes, Mr. Paul." The woman promised to have authorities check out the incident and as the call ended, Brandon tossed his phone on the passenger seat. A conversation came to mind, one he'd had with Dayne when the two of them first became friends.

"I called the police all the time at first," Dayne's defeat sounded in his tone. "Most of the time the problem's too big for them. They could arrest a car of photographers, but there'd be two more taking that one's place fifteen minutes later."

The only time the law had helped Dayne was after his horrific accident — but even then the driver who caused the wreck only served a year in jail. Considering Dayne almost lost his life, the law wasn't enough of an answer to really help.

"Use a driver, get tinted windows, wear disguises," Dayne told him. "Even then there are no guarantees. But calling 9-1-1 only helps when something serious happens. And by then it's usually too late for us."

The memory of the conversation faded, but Brandon's frustration did not. Traffic inched along moving them further from the wreck, further from whatever police responded to his call. And all the while the second car stayed at his side, snapping pictures. Brandon wanted to flash an angry look their direction, but that would only give them something to sell. Instead he kept the practiced smile firmly in place. That way they couldn't say he was grieving the loss of Bailey or living in anger and reclusion. Of course, they could say what they'd said when they ran a picture of him talking to his costar Molly at LAX the day they returned from their shoot. *Brandon Paul, Happy and Loving the Single Life.*

Suddenly — in a way that had never hit him before — he was sick of this. Sick of being chased and photographed and described in any of a dozen untrue ways by the tabloids. As soon as the traffic let up, he cut in front of the paparazzi car and took the next off-ramp. Surface streets would be better than driving on the 405 with a camera aimed at his face. Mulholland was a two-lane option, so the photographers could stay behind him, but not beside him. That was at least a little better.

The ride to the studio took another ten minutes, and then he left his car with a valet attendant and ran up the steps and through the glass doors. He missed Bailey with every step, every heartbeat. But he put those thoughts aside for the next hour while he met with the studio executives. His manager Stephen Chase met him at the door and whispered a quick warning. "They're presenting you with the new contract. Luke Baxter's already given his approval." He paused, looking over his shoulder. "This is the moment when you act really grateful, Brandon. It's celebration time, okay?"

"Luke approved it? You're sure?" Brandon definitely had his doubts. Luke hadn't called, and usually he would hear from his attorney first.

"Look," Chase's patience seemed especially thin. "You hired me to manage your career. You either trust me or you've got the wrong guy." The conversation was still in whispered tones, just outside the boardroom.

"Fine." Brandon hadn't seen Chase act like this. "If Luke's okay with it, then we move ahead."

Chase stood a little straighter and smiled. "Perfect."

"Yeah." Brandon tried not to see dollar signs in the guy's eyes. "Let's get it over with." A heaviness weighed on him as he entered the room. If he didn't know better, he would've thought the walls were closing in on them.

He took his seat, but as the conversation began his mind went back to the night of the Fourth and how it felt to sit beside Bailey, the feel of her fingers soft between his, the sound of her voice filling his soul. The taste of her kiss on his lips.

"Brandon?" Across from him, his agent Sid Chandler cast him a strange look. "Did you have an opinion on that?"

Panic pushed through him. He didn't want to be here, didn't want to talk about the contract. Why hadn't Luke called him? And shouldn't his lawyer be here if he had approved of the contract? That way he'd have absolute certainty that the new contract gave Brandon the creative control he wanted. He cleared his throat and leaned closer to the table. "Sorry." He looked at Jack Randall, the top guy at West Mark. "Lots on my mind."

Randall hesitated, but then he gave Brandon a slightly condescending smile. "I guess I can understand that." He smiled at his assistants and at Brandon's management team. "This is without a doubt the best deal we've ever offered any actor." He chuckled, but the tone was more frustrated than humorous. "I guess I'd be a little distracted too."

"Yes." Brandon felt the heat in his face. If

the guy was trying to humiliate him, it was working. Everything about the meeting felt out of control, like he was merely a puppet watching other people make decisions about his life. Dayne had warned him about this. Something similar had happened to him years ago, right? Brandon blinked, trying to focus. "What . . . what were you saying?"

Another dry smile from Randall. "I was saying it's your call about the party. We'd like to see red carpet at Grauman's Chinese Theater." He nodded at Stephen Chase. "You wanna tell him the news?"

"Definitely." Chase made a show of taking a folder from his briefcase and laying it out on the table in front of him. "You've been given your own star, Brandon. On Hollywood's Walk of Fame."

A year ago the news might've made his day, but here in this setting it meant very little. It was the studio's doing, no doubt. A way to increase the publicity around the announcement of Brandon's deal. Even still, he knew the right response and the great honor the star held. He managed a surprised look and then glanced from Randall back to Chase and Sid Chandler. Whoever was behind the act, he needed to be grateful. "That's amazing. Seriously."

"Yes," Chandler raised his brow and

looked down at his notes. Clearly he was still irritated with Brandon, as if he thought Brandon should maybe have jumped from his chair in gratitude. "Anyway, now that your attorney has approved the contract, we'll have the announcement August first — that's less than two weeks from now."

"A Saturday," Chandler pointed out — in case anyone wasn't sure.

This part wasn't a surprise. Brandon listened but he felt like he was watching the meeting happen from some distant room. Like his role there was merely a token. All the work, all the decisions, everything about the announcement — all of it was already planned by his team and the brass at West Mark. He was about to make headlines everywhere. Greatest contract ever offered.

Brandon Paul — locked up with West Mark for the next five years.

Brandon tried to take a full breath, but the air in the room felt too thin.

"We'll start with the star ceremony. You'll put your hands in a fresh block of cement, and you'll be immortalized on the Walk of Fame forever." Randall looked proud of himself. He nodded at the others in the room. "The perfect way to start the night."

He went on to say that the party would then move into the theater, where by invitation and red-carpet arrival several hundred VIP guests and celebrities would help acknowledge the contract. "We'd like you to make a special announcement to your fans live on the Web that night. Your team will put it on your website, get it on Facebook and Twitter. We'll build it up with a count-down. Have millions of fans ready for your big news."

"Perfect." Chase nodded as he wrote something down on the pad of paper in front of him. He grinned. "This'll be big."

Brandon thought about that Saturday. First day of August. It was a day when, if he were any other guy in the world, he would be taking Bailey on a date, celebrating sum-mer, and enjoying private time with her. The voices of the people in the room blurred together until the sound was only a buzzing in his head, a clanging in his heart.

"That's perfect. Right, Brandon? The big party? Otherwise West Mark is okay to make it smaller, more intimate." Chase's look held a clear warning. This was that moment when Brandon was supposed to get excited.

"Yeah. Whatever."

Alarm flashed in the eyes of Chase and Chandler. They stared at him, waiting for him to say more, act more enthusiastic.

Brandon dug deep and found the smile he

was famous for. He flashed it at Randall, and then at the West Mark team. "I mean, it sounds amazing. I'm the most blessed guy in the business. No question." The words were true. Brandon really did appreciate the effort everyone was making. None of this was their fault — not what he was feeling about the paparazzi or the suffocating room or the way he missed Bailey. He felt sorry for not being more excited. "I'm beyond grateful guys. Seriously."

A feeling of peace came over the room, and everyone from Randall and his assistants to Chandler and Chase seemed to visibly relax. Small talk broke out and in a few minutes they wrapped up the meeting with promises to meet again a few days before the announcement. In the meantime Randall would work with Brandon's team to make sure every detail was addressed.

Brandon thanked everyone again and gave Chase and Chandler quick handshakes. Then he left in a hurry. On the walk down the hall to the elevator his next plan took shape. He didn't have another obligation in LA until Wednesday. Which meant he could fly out in the morning and make it to Bloomington by late tomorrow afternoon. He still had no idea how God was going to help him make this work, but he had to talk to Bailey's dad. It was more important than anything from the last hour. The conversation with Jim Flanigan would be one of the most crucial in his life, and the thought of it pounded at his heart and burst through his soul. Whatever it took, Brandon had to go there, had to talk with the man.

Before another day went by.

NINETEEN

The next day Brandon stepped off a private jet at the Indianapolis Airport just before two in the afternoon. By then he'd already called Bailey's dad and set up a meeting at his office with the Colts. Brandon had a private driver take him to the NFL team's headquarters and he walked into Jim Flanigan's office a full five minutes early.

For all the ways he felt disconnected and unable to breathe at the West Mark meeting yesterday, Brandon felt more alive than ever as he walked into this office. Like what was about to happen here was the most right thing he could do. He smiled big as he spotted Bailey's dad. "Hello, sir. Thanks for meeting with me."

"We didn't get to talk much on the Fourth. It's good to see you." Jim Flanigan's eyes were soft, his expression kind. He hugged Brandon and the two of them took seats on either side of Jim's desk. "This must be important." Jim leaned back in his chair. "I keep up with you. Things have been very busy."

"They have." The truth felt like weights on Brandon's ankles. "Very busy."

"And the big announcement. Bailey says that's coming August first, right?"

"It is." He sighed quietly. The last day had been so consumed with making plans for this talk, Brandon still hadn't called Luke to confirm his approval of the contract. "The studio's letting me have creative control." He nodded, anxious to get beyond this. "It's a great contract. God's worked out all the details for sure."

"I'm glad, Brandon. Really." Jim smiled, and the caring in his face was undeniable. "So what's on your mind?"

"Bailey, sir. She's on my mind all the time." Brandon swallowed, searching for the right words. He'd practiced this moment the whole flight here, but now every memorized line flew from view. Instead there was only his heart and the heart of Jim Flanigan. Brandon looked straight at the man, grateful for the friendship they already shared. Now that he'd started, his words came quickly and in a rush. "Whether I'm filming or at a meeting or discussing my upcoming contract, she's always on my

311

mind. Not just since the Fourth of July, but since I met her. She's, well, she's the most amazing girl I've ever met, sir, and I can't stand being away from her even though right now my work keeps me in Los Angeles and —"

"Brandon." Jim leaned forward and a gentle bit of laughter came from him. "Breathe, son. Don't forget to breathe."

Yes. Breathing. That was a good idea. Brandon sank back just a little in his seat and exhaled. "Sorry." He raked his fingers through his hair and chuckled, dizzy with the enormity of the moment. "I've been thinking about what to say for a few weeks now. Definitely the whole way here this morning."

"I know. It's okay." Jim rested his forearms on the desk. "Go ahead. But remember to breathe."

"All right." He took in some air and felt a warm peace come over him. "Anyway, I guess what I'm trying to say is I'd like to ask for Bailey's hand in marriage." He felt his smile start at his eyes and work its way through his face. Just saying it made him happier than he'd ever been. "I love her. I want to marry her and make a life with her." He had never meant any words more. "I'd like your permission, sir."

The man didn't seem shocked. He nodded slowly and drew a long breath. "I sort of thought that might be why you wanted to talk." His kind eyes were still intent on Brandon's. "Bailey means everything to me, Brandon. She's our only daughter, and very different from so many girls her age."

"I know." Brandon listened, hanging on every word Jim Flanigan spoke. "She's unbelievable."

"She's not perfect, of course. You can never expect that of her any more than she could expect it of you."

"Definitely not." Brandon's mouth was dry. "I would never expect more of her than she could ask of me."

"And something else. We raised Bailey to believe that one day when she got married, she'd need to see her husband as a godly leader, someone she could trust not only with her heart, but with her soul." He paused, his voice soft, compassion shining in his eyes. "Have you thought about that?"

"I have." Brandon had come this far to talk, so he wouldn't leave out the explanation. In a conversation this important they had time for specifics. "A few months ago I prayed that God would test me." He shared about that night on the beach, and how he believed God spoke to him, telling him that testing would surely come. "And it did. Every day I was in Montana was a test." His heart fell a few notches. "Bailey tried to break up with me while I was there."

"That's what she said." Jim's response proved that Bailey wasn't only close to her mother. She shared her life with both her parents.

The way Brandon wished he had been able to do through the years with his.

He kept his eyes steady, his intentions absolute. "I feel ready to lead her, sir. I never thought I could love anyone like I love her. But my love for God is even greater. It's the most important thing I can bring her."

Jim smiled. "I believe you."

"Thanks." Again Brandon felt himself relax. He went on about how he'd kept a journal of letters to Bailey and how every time he prayed he felt God telling him to fight for her, not to give up but to find a way to make things work.

"Have you figured that out?"

Brandon hesitated, wishing he had a perfect response, some formula that would prove to Jim Flanigan how carefully Brandon had made his plans and how easily marrying Bailey fit into that. He sighed, defeated. "No, sir. I haven't." He raised his brow. "But I will. I think if I talk to Bailey I can convince her to live in LA for the next five years. She can still buy CKT, but maybe have someone else run it until I'm finished with the contract."

Jim nodded slowly. "That could work." His smile looked more sympathetic than hopeful. "It'll be up to Bailey."

"Yes, sir."

"Brandon." Jim chuckled lightly. "Call me Jim. If you're going to be my son-in-law, we need to drop the formalities." He grinned. "I baptized you, remember? We were practically family, even before today."

Blue skies and sunshine seemed to fill the sterile office space. "Really?"

"Yes."

A quick laugh came from Brandon, one that expressed his sudden great relief. A thought dawned on him at almost the same time. "So . . . you're saying I have your blessing?"

Jim pushed back from his desk, stood, and walked around as Brandon stood. Without hesitating Jim Flanigan hugged him again — the sort of hug Brandon would remember forever. When Jim stepped back he put one hand on Brandon's shoulder and with the other he shook Brandon's hand. "You have my blessing, son. Bailey's mother and I have talked about this, and we believe you two love each other and that God brought you together." His smile fell a little. "We aren't sure how it'll work. That part seems a little difficult."

"It does." Brandon didn't want to think about it. If he had Jim Flanigan's blessing then God would change Bailey's mind about LA. At least for five years. Brandon had to believe that. "Maybe you could pray for us. That she'll be okay with LA, at least while I work through my new contract."

Jim took a step back and leaned against his office wall. "We'll pray." He raised an eyebrow. "But Bailey's pretty sure about not wanting to live in LA. Just to warn you."

"I know." Brandon tried not to feel afraid. "I guess I'm praying for a miracle."

They talked for a few more minutes about how deeply Brandon loved Bailey and how he planned to care for her and protect her all his life. As he spoke, he watched Jim's eyes grow damp. "I always wondered what this day would feel like. A young man asking for my daughter's hand in marriage." He blinked back tears and uttered a sad laugh. "I can still picture Bailey on her first day of kindergarten. It was easy to forget this day would ever come."

Brandon tried to imagine having a baby

girl with Bailey someday and having this conversation with a young man. Having to embrace the idea of giving her away. The picture made his throat tighten and brought a wave of emotion. "It's a big day."

"It is." Jim put his hand on Brandon's shoulder again. "After I baptized you, I prayed for you every day, Brandon. Knowing what you faced working in Hollywood and the challenges of being around so many pressures." Jim paused, and the set of his jaw made it clear he was still struggling with his emotions. "But if you and Bailey can work through the obstacles, that means I haven't only been praying for you since then."

A slight confusion came over Brandon, but he waited.

Jim smiled. "I've been praying for you all her life." He gave Brandon one more hug. "Go figure out your plan and pray for a miracle. Let me know if there's anything I can do."

"There is one thing." Brandon wanted to stop by the Flanigan house and leave something for Bailey in her room. "I need to leave something in her room. She's working at the theater today. So she won't see me. And then I have to fly back to LA in a few hours. But this part's important if that's okay."

Jim agreed and explained where to find a spare key hidden not far from their front door. "Use that in case no one's home."

He thanked Bailey's father, and as he headed back to his waiting car, Brandon rejoiced at how the day had gone so far. Nothing could dim his joy and gratitude. He wanted to stand on the corner and shout to all the world that he'd done it! He'd asked Jim Flanigan for permission to marry Bailey, and the man had said yes! Brandon hadn't dreamed the conversation would go so well, and now he knew something else. He not only had Jim Flanigan's blessing, he had the man's love and respect. Jim and Jenny Flanigan were ready to accept him as a son-in-law, ready to see him as the guy God had set apart for their daughter. They were ready to see him marry Bailey!

Brandon felt giddy with hope and possibility and God's undeserved blessing. He stayed on that high while his driver took him to the Flanigan house and as he left the surprise in her room. This wasn't a trip where he planned to see her. He'd be back soon enough, if he had his way. The trip to see her father was one rooted in hours of prayer. Brandon had never prayed so much in all his life — that her father would approve, and for his timing and courage about what might come next, and for Bailey. Prayers for her most of all.

Brandon smiled to himself. That's what this trip was about — laying every part of his love for Bailey at the feet of God.

It took half the drive back to the airport before Brandon felt his excitement dim a little. Because for all the ways the talk with Jim Flanigan had gone brilliantly well, for as excited as he was for her to come home and see what he'd done for her, and as thrilled as he was about the prospects of marrying the girl he loved, the toughest part was still ahead.

Convincing Bailey.

The bank meetings had dragged on all day, but as Bailey walked through the front door of her parents' house she felt more excited than weary. Everything was coming together for the purchase, and Bailey had even looked into buying a small condo in the downtown area, not too far from the theater. The condo wouldn't lock her into staying in Bloomington. It was in foreclosure so the price was lower than it would probably ever be again. She still planned to spend a lot of time at her parents' house, but having her own home near the theater would be a good idea. At least she was starting to think so.

Even while she was going through false contractions in Los Angeles, Katy had managed to hire an intern to help with direction for the coming year — a college girl from Indiana University. Bailey hadn't met the girl, but she figured maybe the two of them could room together.

Bailey wasn't sure, except that she could see her life in Bloomington becoming more certain, more a reality with God opening doors and working out details. The only problem, of course, was Brandon.

Bailey set her things down just inside the door and felt her phone vibrate in her pocket. She pulled it out.

I love you, Bailey. I'm praying for you, for us. Maybe by now you know how much.

She looked at the message again and felt the familiar thrill of the unknown, how with Brandon anything was possible. A quick look into the living room told her he wasn't waiting there. "Brandon?" She called out his name and waited, but there was no response. Her mom had texted that the family would be out that night at a summer league basketball game. So the house was empty.

Silence followed, so she tried again.

Louder this time. "Brandon? Are you here?"

There was only the sound of her increasingly louder heartbeat. With Brandon she never knew what to expect. Since the Fourth of July they'd talked on Skype nearly every night and several times he'd mentioned that he wished he could just walk around the corner and be with her. But he'd told her he was too busy.

Bailey walked down the hallway, into the kitchen, and up the middle staircase to her bedroom. "Brandon?" She felt a slight disappointment as she rounded the stairs at the landing. He wasn't here. By now he would've come out and taken her into his arms. He wouldn't have made her wait like this.

A sad sigh drifted from her heart. She missed him more than she ever imagined. And with every day of missing came a realization she hadn't quite acknowledged fully: She hadn't rushed things. What she and Brandon shared wasn't too magical or too fast or too anything. Their love was amazing. Which was why Bailey kept getting on Skype every night, allowing the hour of virtual together time to get her through another day. Because she believed, like Brandon, that there had to be a way.

Even if nothing seemed possible just yet.

She turned the corner into her room and came to a sudden stop. Throughout her room were bouquets of the most beautiful red roses she'd ever seen. Two on either end of her built-in bookcase, one on her desk, and another on the table by her bed. Bailey gasped softly and put her hand to her mouth. He'd been here. He had to have been.

She moved slowly to the first bouquet, the one on the table not far from her pillow. Only then did she notice something else, something that made her suck in another quick breath.

Around her room, taped to the walls and windowsill and door frames were a dozen index cards, each of which held a handwritten note. Bailey looked closely at the one that lay on her pillow. This time she didn't gasp. As she reached for the card and realized what he'd done, her eyes welled up even as her heart rejoiced.

On the card was a prayer. Brandon's prayer to God on her behalf.

Her movements came slowly, like she'd slipped into a trance. She sat on the edge of her bed and read the card that had been on her pillow.

Dear God, please be with Bailey as she sleeps. Help her to trust You and not worry about the days ahead. Help her believe that You are working even while we sleep, and that You have a plan. Let her nighttime thoughts be filled with beautiful, wonderful possibilities, and let me be the guy she dreams about. In Jesus' name, amen.

Bailey felt her mouth open and she shook her head, unable to believe the gift he'd given her. She read the prayer one more time and then she walked around the room to read each of them. On the card near the bookcase Brandon wrote a prayer asking God to help Bailey always learn, always grow, and to fill her mind with truth. The card near her closet held Brandon's prayer that Bailey would never find her identity in her wardrobe, but rather that she would always stay as she was today — clothed in kindness and humility. The most beautiful clothes of all.

In all, there were twelve prayers posted around her room, all of them Brandon's way of holding her up to the Lord, and asking for His divine intervention regarding the impossible aspects of their relationship. Tears slipped down Bailey's cheeks, and her smile grew until she wasn't sure she could feel any stronger mix of pure joy and aching loss. Because Brandon had obviously been here, but he hadn't stayed. He could never stay.

The whole room smelled like the freshest roses, and Bailey tried to picture Brandon flying in, buying the flowers, and setting them up in her room. Sitting here — probably at her desk — writing out the prayer cards and carefully posting them around her room. Could anyone ever love her that much?

Another text buzzed through her phone and she read it quickly.

I'm sorry I couldn't stay, baby. I have meetings in the morning. Just wanted to stop in and tell you I'm praying for you.

Bailey was still reading the words when a third text flashed on the screen.

If you're in your room . . . then you see that now, right? ☺

"Brandon . . . I can't believe you," she whispered as if somehow he could hear her. Then she set her purse down on the bed and took the bank folder from inside. What was she doing buying CKT here in Bloomington? Thinking she could be happy running the children's theater when Brandon was across the country in Los Angeles? She could always run a theater company, right? If he loved her this much, if he was willing to come here just to let her know he was praying for her, then she needed to do whatever it took to be with him. Which meant maybe when God led her back to Bloomington for the CKT position, He wasn't asking her to buy the organization. Maybe God only wanted her to take a few months to reflect and pray and truly appreciate what she had in Brandon Paul. If that was the case, then she needed to pray now more than ever.

In case God might be leading her back to Los Angeles.

TWENTY

Jenny saw the announcement on Foxnews
.com where she was checking for stories on
her husband's Indianapolis Colts. She
didn't find anything on the football team
but at the top of the website a different story
caught her attention. The headline read,
*"Brandon Paul Cancels Huge Celebration; Will
Announce Contract to Fans Live Online."*

The house was quiet that Friday morning, the last day of July. Bailey was doing
her online studies in the other room and
the boys were at school. Jim had summer
workouts at the facility in Indianapolis. So
Jenny had no trouble hearing the way her
heart beat harder in her chest at the sight of
the headline. Why would Brandon cancel
the party? From what Bailey had said the
studio had spent a fortune putting it together. Red carpet, live television feeds, and
performances by some of the top acts in
music. He was even getting his own Holly-

wood star.

She found the first line in the story and flew through the article. Apparently there was some air of mystery surrounding Brandon's announcement and no one interviewed could understand why he wouldn't want the party. One studio executive suggested maybe Brandon wanted to save the money that would otherwise be wasted on the party. "Brandon's a very conscientious young man," the West Mark Studio representative was quoted saying in the article. "In the last year or so he's been much less into the flashy Hollywood lifestyle."

Brandon's manager Stephen Chase had another take. "The focus here is on Brandon's fans," he was quoted saying. "He wants to celebrate with the people who put him in this position. Believe me, the news will be very dramatic."

The article went on to say that some experts believed the contract might be worth a hefty eight-figures. Speculation also ran high that the deal involved a lengthy period of time, possibly locking Brandon with West Mark Studios for many years. An uncommon move for big actors in today's world. At the end of the story, readers were given a link to Brandon's website where the announcement would be seen live at five o'clock Pacific Time on the first of August.

Jenny wanted to call Bailey into the room, but she could show her later. Her Historic Literature essay was due in a few hours. Still, as Jenny stared at the screen she could barely keep from running and finding her daughter. Because whatever deal Brandon planned to announce to his fans tomorrow, his future would hinge on it. And not only his.

But quite possibly Bailey's future too.

An hour before her essay was due, Bailey filed the document online and signed out of the virtual classroom. Only then did she find her mom and learn about the change in Brandon's plans. She'd texted him twice since then but he hadn't responded. They hadn't talked on Skype as often over the last week because his meetings at West Mark had been so demanding. And though they didn't talk about the gala the studio was throwing to celebrate the contract, Bailey was well aware of it.

It was the one subject she and Brandon had struggled with lately. When he'd asked her to be his date at the party, she couldn't bring herself to say yes, and Brandon didn't ask again. He understood. The paparazzi would have a field day if she returned for the announcement. The tabloids would splash her return across the headlines and there would be three times as many photographers chasing her as before.

Not only that, but the contract didn't make her feel like celebrating. It was more of a prison term for the two of them. Five years where Brandon wouldn't be able to spend more than a few days at a time with her in Bloomington. Or five years where she'd have to find a way to be with him in California. Either way it wasn't the life she wanted, the normalcy she dreamed of sharing with him. No, Bailey couldn't stand beside him and smile as everyone in Hollywood took their picture and cheered for Brandon's new contract.

But now, as her mom pointed out the story on the Internet, Bailey was shocked. Other than the fact that she didn't want to attend, the two of them hadn't talked much about the party. She'd seen rumors online or on the cover of tabloids that the celebration would be the event of the year. And now it was canceled?

"He didn't tell me," she looked at her mom, her mind racing. "I can't believe the studio decided it was overkill. Something weird must've happened behind the scenes."

"You're right." Her mom lowered her

brow, as confused as Bailey. "They've been working on this deal for almost a year."

Bailey felt a strange buzz work its way through her. "I wish he would text me."

"He probably has a dozen people around him, coaching him what to say tomorrow when he goes live on the Internet, or walking him through the signing process."

That hadn't occurred to Bailey, that maybe he was signing the contract today. The idea made sense. Tomorrow was the announcement, so by then both Brandon and the studio would probably need a completed deal.

They both stood there, lost in the implications of the news when the house phone rang. Jenny grabbed it while Bailey stared at the computer. "Hello?"

"Really? Okay, for sure." She paused. "That's so exciting, Ashley. I'll tell everyone." Her mom hung up the phone and her eyes lit up. "Katy's in labor!" She grinned. "Everything's great, but Ashley wants us to pray." She checked the time on the computer and grabbed her car keys from the desktop. "I have to get the boys. Football practice lets out early this week."

"Okay," Bailey kissed her cheek and bid her goodbye. But she remained distracted. By the fact that her friend was in labor and needed prayer, and by the story. What was Brandon going through right now and how was he feeling? She reached for her phone to text him again when her ringtone went off. The Caller ID told her it was Andi, and Bailey smiled. She no longer felt the sad sinking in her heart when she saw her friend's number, the way she'd felt it the first few times they'd talked after that one painful day.

Now it was more of a knowing, the sort that came from growing up and realizing life would never again be what it once was. "Hello?"

"Hi." Andi's tone was warm. Proof of the strong friendship that remained between them. "Did you see the news about Brandon?"

"No party? Yeah, I saw it. Crazy." Bailey sat in the chair in front of the computer and absently typed Brandon's name into the search line. Then she hit the enter key and watched a list of recent news stories about Brandon fill the screen.

"Why'd he do it? I mean, like, is he coming to see you this weekend?"

"I don't think so. He has lots of studio people to meet. If he doesn't have the big party, he'll have a smaller one at West Mark, for sure."

Andi thought about that for a moment. "Hmmm." Her tone sounded disappointed. "I thought for sure it meant he was coming to Indiana."

"Maybe next week." Bailey felt more discouraged than she'd felt since the Fourth of July. "I don't know, actually. We haven't talked about it." Bailey turned her chair so her back was to the computer. "How are things with Cody?"

"Good." There was a depth in Andi's voice, something softer and dreamy. "Really good, actually." They chatted for a few minutes about Cody, how the two of them had been taking bike rides on the beach and spending more time together.

Bailey checked her heart as she and Andi spoke, and she found herself truly happy for her friend. No question Andi was in love with Cody. She hadn't said so, and Bailey hadn't talked to Cody, but Bailey absolutely knew. Never mind that they'd only been dating a short while. The strength of Andi's feelings for Cody was obvious and further proof that the two of them were meant for each other. Even if picturing Cody still took Bailey back in time.

Toward the end of the conversation Andi paused for a long beat. "Bailey . . . you haven't talked to Cody."

The comment puzzled her, and she leaned forward, pressing her forearms onto her knees. "Was I supposed to?"

"Well," Andi sounded conflicted. "I mean, the two of you need to be friends. It's weird not to have you talking to each other."

"Not really." Maybe her friend didn't understand the way things had been. "Cody and I haven't talked much in more than a year. Almost two years."

"Hmm." Andi hesitated. "Through the whole Cheyenne thing, you mean?"

"Yes. That and just, well . . . he moved on a long time ago."

"I guess." Andi seemed to search her heart for a way to make herself clear. "I think it'd be better if you talked once in a while. Sort of practicing being friends again."

Practicing being friends. Bailey let the thought play in her mind and after a few seconds she stood and walked to the kitchen window. A thunderstorm was passing overhead, and rain poured down on the pool out back. "Maybe." She didn't want to commit to the idea, but it was growing on her. "We said we'd be friends. We just never really do anything about it."

"I just want us all to get along. You know . . . when you're out here next time." Andi couldn't have sounded kinder, but at the same time a peaceful confidence rang in her tone. As if she had no doubts that by talking, Bailey and Cody would rekindle what they once had.

"We'll see."

Before they hung up, Andi talked about making a visit to Bloomington. "I want to see you. It's been too long."

"It has." Bailey thought of another reason Andi might want to take a trip to Indiana. "Maybe you could meet up with Luke and Reagan."

Andi didn't hesitate. "That's what I was thinking. Reagan said I could visit Johnny whenever." She paused. "He'd be two now."

Bailey felt the sadness of her friend's loss as strongly as she felt the joy of her decision. Johnny Baxter was thriving from everything Bailey had seen and heard. She had shared with her friend the details after the picnic on the Fourth, how Johnny's hair was pale blond like Andi's and how happy he looked. But it would be good for Andi to see that for herself.

When they hung up, Bailey wandered to the sink and did the dishes. Her mom had a lasagna casserole in the oven and the whole house smelled wonderful. The perfect dinner. Especially on a day with thunderstorms and driving rain.

A restlessness filled Bailey's soul and she walked out back. There, on the covered patio, she leaned against the outdoor wall of their house and stared at the stormy sky. The idea of contacting Cody every now and then sounded a little crazy, but maybe Andi was right. They wouldn't talk often and even if Bailey spent time in Los Angeles, they would rarely have a reason to see each other. But when they did? Cody had been a part of Bailey's life, a part of her childhood and teenage years when no other guy ever could've made the impact he did. So Andi had a point, allowing time to turn them into strangers seemed wrong.

Lightning pierced the sky in the distance and after a few seconds thunder rumbled across the sky over Bloomington. Bailey pulled her phone from her pocket and called up the most recent text conversation with Cody. The last time they'd texted was when he had wanted to walk with her around Lake Monroe. When he needed to tell her about his feelings for Andi. She read over the last part of the conversation and then lowered her phone. She drew a slow breath and steadied herself. If she texted him now it would be the beginning of a new season for them. One that was bound to be spotty and infrequent. But at least it would do what they still hadn't done yet.

Bring them into a period of friendship. Real friendship. The kind they had started out with. She lifted her phone again and with another shaky breath she began to tap.

Andi said the two of you are . . .

She paused. No, that wasn't how she wanted to start. If they were going to be friends, they needed to make a start without pressure from Andi or anyone else, but with only the memories of where they'd come from. Where they began. She started again.

Hi there. It's been a few months since our talk that day, and from what I hear life is going amazingly well. I'm so glad, Cody. Really. The idea of you being truly happy for maybe the first time in your life makes me smile. Just wanted to say hey.

Bailey reread the text and sent it. Then, as another flash of lightning sliced the sky, she thought about what she'd said. A strange truth began to warm her and work its way from her mind to her heart: Everything she'd texted was true. A smile tugged at her lips and she stared at the sky, convinced. She really was happy for Cody. And in this moment she felt more ready than she had in years to find her way back to friendship.

His response flashed on the window of her phone.

Hey there, Bailey. It's good to hear your voice. ☺ Andi tells me you and Brandon are talking. I'm proud of you. I knew you wouldn't run forever. That never was your style. Anyway, yes, I'm doing well. Spending a lot of time with Andi. God is good. Have a good night, friend.

Bailey's eyes fell on the last word and she thought long about how it felt to have Cody Coleman call her friend. Again a warmth came over her and she realized for the first time in years that it felt great. Being called a friend by Cody was exactly where she wanted to be. Far better than being strangers or having some awkward broken relationship as the only recent memory between them.

She slipped her phone back in her pocket and watched another couple rounds of lightning. The storm was moving closer and in a few minutes Bailey would have to go inside. But for now standing out here made her feel closer to God, closer to Brandon. Whatever Brandon was doing, she wished more than anything she could be with him. She should've told him she'd go to the party. He deserved her support, and maybe then he wouldn't have canceled it. A couple days under scrutiny wouldn't hurt. They could've hired a driver and stayed in at Katy and Dayne's house, right?

Bailey jumped a little when the clap of thunder followed right on the heels of a lightning bolt. Both their dogs came jogging from the other side of the house and lay on their mats close to the patio door, under the covered porch. Bailey took a few steps back. This was how she felt about Brandon. Like the storm was raging right in front of her, all around her. The more time she spent with him, the more she loved him. There was no denying the fact. Which meant that the impossibility of their situation was only getting worse.

Call me, Brandon . . . where are you?

The thought hung around in her mind for a while. She wasn't going to text him again. In Brandon's world he could be in any of a hundred situations where he couldn't be on his phone. In light of the canceled party, he might be having a more intimate celebration with the people at West Mark or maybe meeting with his agent and manager. He'd get back to her when he had time. She only wished she knew what was behind the canceled event. It was hard to see such big news about Brandon on the Internet before hearing it from him.

For a moment she had a worse thought: What if he was sick or he'd been in an accident? His people might've canceled the event and kept the truth hidden from the fans. She thought hard about the last time they'd talked and finally she checked her phone. The last call from him had been Wednesday night. He'd texted her Thursday morning but only once. Anxiety kicked a wave of adrenaline through her body.

But then she remembered his announcement. If he was going to broadcast his news live on his website tomorrow night, then he must be fine.

Still . . .

A flash of light and thunder boomed all around her, shaking the patio and the walls of the house. Bailey jumped and this time she hurried inside and shut the heavy glass door behind her. Inside, out of the storm, she felt even more aware of the heaviness in her heart. Only this time the hurt had nothing to do with her friend, Cody. It had to do with Brandon.

And what tomorrow night's announcement would mean for both of them.

TWENTY-ONE

From the vantage point of that Friday evening, the crash in what had previously been Brandon's rock-solid career started with a simple phone call earlier in the week.

A call from Luke Baxter.

Brandon had played the conversation over in his mind twenty times since then. Luke had sounded pleasant and upbeat, if a little concerned. "I know you're busy, but I'm still waiting on that edited version." He allowed a nervous chuckle. "Wasn't the studio hoping to make an announcement this week?"

Brandon stood on the deck of his Malibu home where he had been praying about the importance of the coming days, and at Luke's question he literally couldn't respond for several seconds. His mind raced, trying to make sense of Luke's words. Finally he leaned hard into the railing, his phone tight to his ear. "The edited version of what?"

The question was all he could come up with.

Luke paused. "The West Mark contract." This time the guy's laugh made it clear he was at least a little worried about Brandon. "I gave you the red-lined copy months ago. You said they were going to make changes and let us see the edited version. The correct version."

By then the blood was leaving Brandon's face so quickly, the back deck seemed to sway beneath his feet. "Luke." His strength rallied, and anger swirled up from deep inside him. "The studio execs presented me with that contract weeks ago. They said you approved it."

Brandon would always remember how furious he was with himself for not following up and calling Luke, seeing if his attorney had really given his approval.

On the other end Luke was just as angry. "What? They told you I gave my approval? That's completely wrong." He released a burst of air. "Are they crazy? Lying about a lawyer's okay on something this big?"

Brandon had searched his mind trying desperately to remember the wording from that meeting but he couldn't be sure. "Maybe they didn't say it that way." He had never felt younger and more inexperienced. "It was something like, 'Luke knows about the changes.' I mean, I definitely had the impression you'd seen the revised contract and approved it."

"Wow. Unbelievable." His lawyer muttered the words under his breath, but he might as well have been standing in front of him. Brandon could see his disappointment that keenly. "If they said it like that — and they probably did — then they only mean I ordered the changes in the first place. So of course I know about them."

Over the next hour Brandon faxed the new contract to Luke, who read it and immediately called back. "It's better. You have more control than before. But they left clauses in that basically counteract anything they gave up. As is, I wouldn't sign it." Luke paused. "I can call the head of legal at West Mark and get it ironed out this afternoon."

Like in several West Mark meetings, once more Brandon felt himself suffocating, like the walls of his world were truly closing in on him. The idea that Luke would have to call West Mark yet again to get the contract where it needed to be. And to think this was happening days before the announcement. Worse, he was about to trust these same people with his next five years. "Don't call. I need to pray about all this." Brandon didn't mean to be short, but his thoughts were coming together as quickly as the waves crashing on the beach below.

Not until the call was over did another blow hit Brandon square in his gut. His team — his agent Sid Chandler and certainly Stephen Chase, his manager — must've known about the contract, the fact that Luke hadn't actually signed off on the revised version. So they were a part of the duplicity as well.

Suddenly Brandon couldn't think of a person in Los Angeles that he could trust. Not the studio or its legal staff or his own team. All of them stood to receive such great financial gain when he signed the contract that they'd stopped being loyal.

Or maybe they never were.

That reality stayed with Brandon, stirring up new thoughts and plans and possibilities and on Thursday he placed an emergency conference call to his team and the brass at West Mark. In a one-sided conversation that lasted only a few minutes, he canceled the celebration.

"Call it off . . . the whole thing's too extreme." Brandon still didn't have his ultimate plan fully formed, so he kept his voice neutral. That way he had options about the rest of the week and the announcement he needed to make. "The contract is something private." He paused. "So there's no need for a red carpet or all the artists you've hired. Right?"

"Brandon . . ." Jack Randall made a sound that was more shock than quiet laughter. "We have the entertainers booked. It's two days before the event. And what about the star you're getting?"

"Ask everyone to take a rain check." Brandon worked to sound respectful. "There's bound to be another gala next month or next year, right?" He knew the business well enough to know that canceling an artist wasn't always that simple. But West Mark ruled the movie world. Managers for the various pop acts would understand. Same with the people in charge of getting a star outside Grauman's Chinese Theater.

"What does this say about the contract?" The fear in Randall's voice was undeniable. "We've worked hard on this, Brandon. Don't go crazy on us, now."

"Right. And Luke Baxter's on board?" Brandon resisted the urge to sound sarcastic. But this was one more chance for the studio or his team to come clean with the truth. "He's seen the changes?"

Brandon's team of Chase and Chandler remained silent. Tellingly so. And this time when Randall's laugh rang through the conference call, he was clearly more nervous than shocked. "Brandon, you should know the answer there. Luke ordered the changes. Of course he's familiar with them."

A sick feeling twisted itself around Brandon's stomach. They were working around the truth, just like Luke had warned him. "That's what I thought." This time the laugh was Brandon's. "Anyway, the party's off. Just wanted to let you know in case you had calls to make."

The studio execs must've been on the phone making calls the moment Brandon hung up because by Friday morning the news was everywhere. Brandon Paul had canceled his own party. No gala, no red-carpet event, no epic celebration. It had occurred to him sometime after the conference call that if the entire nation knew basically what to expect of his announcement, then certainly the studio hadn't kept silent about the details, the way they were supposed to from the beginning.

By Friday afternoon Brandon felt like little more than a puppet. He made his team and the studio a ton of money as long as he did everything their way, as long as they could set the rules and break them at will. The West Mark deal would be lucrative and it could possibly build his career to a level no other actor had reached.

But at what cost?

Brandon wanted to walk along the beach and think, pray about the decision at hand and the announcement tomorrow. But on a Friday in late July the beaches would be packed. Paparazzi would follow him or show up within minutes and his quiet time of seeking God would become a circus.

Brandon walked out onto his back deck into the bright sunshine and crossed to the railing. For the first time he could understand how Bailey felt. Exactly how she felt. For all his money and for all the beachfront beauty around him, he was a prisoner in his own house.

He breathed in and tried to find peace in the situation, patience in it. But there was none. He thought again about Montana and how he wished Bailey could've come to the set at least once. They could've walked Main Street and shared coffee dates and grabbed pizza at Pete's on the corner. And no one would've bothered them. Molly had private messaged him on Facebook the other day and told him she felt the same way. Like the serenity of that small Montana town was something that couldn't be bought or found in LA, no matter how much power, money, and influence a person might have.

He smiled because Molly was dating a Christian guy now. Someone behind the scenes in the movie business. God was still drawing her close, and Brandon was grateful he'd been in the right place at the right time to make a difference. Those days remained part of how God continued to grow him, stretch him. He sighed and squinted out at the brilliance of the sunlight on the water. Like a million diamonds all promising fame and fortune and heaven on earth. But if he walked down the path behind his house and over the sand dune down the beach to the water, if he swam out to where the diamonds seemed to lay on the ocean's surface, he knew what he would find.

Water. Nothing more.

The brilliant splash of diamonds across the sea was a mirage. Just like living a celebrity life in California. However it looked to the public, however glamorous it seemed and however envious millions of people might've been for the life Brandon lived, the truth was this: He couldn't even leave his house.

Brandon held tight to the railing and thought about his last conversation with

Bailey. She'd reminded him that whatever happened between the two of them, God had great plans for both of them. "If we don't work out, if we don't find a way . . . we have to leave this season still caring about each other. We can never be angry."

Her words had sliced at him like so many knives. If they didn't work out? Sure, she didn't know about his asking her father for her hand. But was that really how she felt? That there was a possibility they might not find a way? Brandon reminded himself about the past week, the deceit and trickery, the manipulation for the sake of money and fame. The way he couldn't go to the beach today no matter what. Like a light flipping on in the dark places of his heart, Brandon understood Bailey like never before.

Of course she wanted to live in Bloomington.

Something about the wind off the ocean and the sun on his face took Brandon back, back to the time when he first started acting. He had graduated high school early and moved to LA where one of his first auditions was for NTM Studios and a series they were putting together for teens. His place among Hollywood's elite happened quickly, but that first year was tough. He was alone in LA and his relationship with his parents was utterly severed. Most nights he felt alone and unsure, not convinced of the sincerity of the people gushing over him. Often times he wished he could pick up the phone and call home. The way other young people did when they set out on their own.

Loneliness from those days drew him further into the past and as he looked out over the ocean he could see himself in his first apartment, see the very dark night when he had gone out with some of the cast from a movie that had been filming in LA at the time. One of the girls — an actress Brandon didn't know — invited him through their managers. Brandon was thrilled. It was his first time partying with Tinseltown's A-list. He'd never really drank, but that night he and a few girls finished off a couple bottles of champagne. The girl who invited him took him back to her house and when Brandon woke up he was in her bed.

He was seventeen.

The memory made him both disgusted and deeply sad for the childhood he'd lost out on. What happened next that day had haunted Brandon ever since. After the wild night he'd walked back in his apartment and found a bottle of pain pills in the cupboard. *In case you have trouble sleeping*, his pro-ducer at the time had written on them. *Just keep them around.*

Everything about that terrible time seemed more vivid now. Brandon hadn't been able to shake the filthiness that consumed him. What if the girl had given him a disease? Or what if she got pregnant? Was this how things were in Hollywood? Partying and sleeping around like it was nothing more than a typical weekend?

He could feel the bottle of pills in his hand all over again, sense deeply the way the idea had come in a rush and consumed him. In that moment, nothing had felt real and he had no idea how to handle the fact that suddenly everyone wanted a piece of him. So why stick around? He could take half the pills and in minutes be done with missing his parents and finding his way in LA and trying to feel clean again.

He could see himself now, opening the bottle and pouring most of the contents into the palm of his hand. He had set the nearly empty bottle on the counter in his apartment and grabbed a glass of water. In that instant, voices had begun to scream at him and he couldn't tell if they were real or not. *Hurry up, you coward. Your father was right to get rid of you. Hurry! Get it over with! You're filthy and you don't matter to anyone, anyway.*

Brandon had nodded then, believing every word.

Just do it! What's the point in living? Take the easy way out.

The questions shouted at him and surrounded him, and slowly . . . slowly he had raised the handful of pills to his mouth.

And at that instant, less than a heartbeat from when Brandon would have ended it all, there came a knock at the door. Brandon froze and he remembered feeling the blood rush to his face. He set the water down and slipped the pills back into the bottle. Then he answered the door. It was a delivery guy with a basket of fruit and a card from his uncle. The one he'd lived with after he ran away from home, after his parents no longer wanted him.

He could see the words on the card as easily as if he were holding it in his hand again: *Congratulations on your success, Brandon! Your life is just beginning!*

That afternoon so long ago, Brandon had read the words over and over and over again, and in a flood of horror, the idea of killing himself suddenly felt like pure insanity. Like for a few minutes he'd fallen into some dark trance where he had briefly and fully lost control of his own mind. He had hurried to the sink, grabbed the bottle of pills, and washed them down the drain.

But then and a thousand times since when he thought about that moment, he felt certain about one thing: Someone, somewhere in that crucial moment in time had been praying for him. Probably not his parents — since they had basically disowned him. Most likely not his uncle, since the man and his family hadn't come to know faith in Christ until this year.

Still, only a miracle could account for the way the knock on the door came only a second or two before he took the pills. And the message on the card seemed like divine intervention. His life was just beginning? When he was ready to down half a bottle of pain pills? Then and now Brandon was convinced.

Someone was praying.

And whoever in all the world had thought to pray for Brandon Paul that day, he could also credit them for praying for him through the next few years, through his dark days of partying and girls and one regretful decision after another. That person must've been storming heaven's gates on his behalf, because God in all his mercy had done the one thing that had changed Brandon's life forever.

He had led him to Bailey Flanigan.

Brandon straightened and stretched, allowing the breeze to take with it memories of his past. Back on the day Brandon had talked about his darker days to Bailey at Lake Monroe he had stopped short from telling her this part. The fact that he had nearly killed himself. But that day she had said something to him that haunted him, especially now in light of his West Mark contract. She'd told him God had brought him to Bloomington to film *Unlocked* with her because of his soul, not his senses. She was trying to make the point that Brandon didn't really want her, but her faith. The peace and love and joy that marked her life.

Back then he had to agree to some extent. When he first met Bailey, that's what he needed. But now that he shared her faith, he couldn't help but think of the rest of what she'd said that day. He closed his eyes, and the memory of her voice in that moment brushed soft against his heart.

"You're a tremendously talented actor, Brandon. Can you imagine how this world could be changed if someone like you really lived for God?" She had been kind, as always. But her tone held the enormity of the possibilities. "There'd be no way to measure the number of people you could touch."

Brandon had said that maybe that was a lot to ask of an actor in his early twenties. But at the same time he had asked Bailey to pray for him. That if God was calling him to do something big and extraordinary for him, then somehow that would be obvious. That God would show him.

For a long time Brandon thought about that, how he'd asked Bailey to pray and about the events of the past week. And suddenly — like a blind person receiving sight — Brandon could see what he hadn't been able to see until now. The big and extraordinary thing was right in front of him, so close he could touch it. God was making it abundantly clear, just like he'd asked Bailey to pray about.

After more than an hour of knowing no way out, of feeling trapped in his own house, Brandon felt himself smile, felt the invisible walls around him fall away. Then he did what he should've done a long time ago, or at least the moment he'd learned about how they'd lied to him. He called Sid Chandler and then patched in Stephen Chase.

Then in no uncertain terms he fired them both.

"I care about you as people. I pray you'll find integrity in the places you go from here.

But I cannot have my own team lie to me. You should've told me Luke Baxter hadn't signed off on that revised contract."

Sid started to speak, but Brandon stopped him. "I have things to do. Busy day tomorrow, you know." This time Stephen tried to speak, but Brandon was already a step ahead of him. "Don't worry. You'll get your cut of the contract. Both of you." He paused. "That's all you cared about, anyway."

As he hung up, he felt something he hadn't felt all afternoon. Something Bailey once said mattered very much to her. The ability to breathe in and out. Like normal.

It was late by the time Brandon called the studio to talk about his decision to fire his team. After the wildest day in his professional career, he didn't walk into his bedroom until midnight. No way he could call Bailey now. She would've been asleep for hours. But maybe that was just as well. He had to get through tomorrow night's big news first, before he could think about seeing her, the way he was dying to see her.

The meetings that day had been exhausting, draining him of everything creative. When he set out to be an actor he never dreamed about having strong business and marketing skills. Never thought about having a team of his own people lie to him or having to fire that same team. But these days his life was mostly meetings. It was why he'd need to be in LA full-time for every bit of the five-year contract.

Brandon stared at himself in the mirror and again he couldn't keep from smiling. What was that look in his eyes? He studied his reflection until he realized the answer. It was peace. Peace and victory and excitement about the announcement he would make on his website. No question he was doing the right thing.

Now he could hardly wait for tomorrow.

TWENTY-TWO

Bailey couldn't shake the sick feeling. She was home alone, sitting at the family's kitchen computer watching updates and tabloid speculation about Brandon's big announcement. Her parents and brothers were at Ashley and Landon's house for a summer barbecue, which was perfect. Bailey would go over later, but for now she didn't want any distractions. Not when she couldn't pull herself from the computer screen.

Brandon would go live on his website in just one hour.

Over the next few minutes, her mom called her twice, first with a task for Bailey — a load of laundry that needed moving from the washer to the dryer. The second call was more exciting. Katy's baby had been born.

"Everyone's healthy. Egan Thomas is beautiful. Dayne sent us a picture. I'll text it to you."

"That's wonderful." Bailey silently thanked God. Some of the pregnancies in the Baxter family had been so difficult. They were probably all very thankful that this little boy had come without a struggle. "I'll call the hospital gift shop and order flowers from our family."

"Perfect." Her mom paused, her tone hesitant. "You okay?"

"Yes, Mom." Bailey sighed. Her happiness over the birth of Katy and Dayne's baby dimmed as she remembered Brandon. "I just wish he'd call. Something doesn't feel right."

"He will. He'll be in touch as soon as he can. Things must be crazy for him right now."

"I know." They talked a few more minutes about the barbecue at the old Baxter farmhouse and after the call Bailey looked at the time on the computer. The time switched from 7:27 to 7:28. In a little more than thirty minutes the whole world would know about Brandon's next five years. Bailey looked up the address for the hospital where Katy was a patient and paid for flowers from the gift shop. At about the same time a picture text lit up her phone screen. Bailey opened the photo and smiled at the image for a long time. Egan Thomas looked like a miniature Dayne. Tears blurred her eyes as she thought about the joy they must be feeling right now. *Thank you, Lord. I can't imagine a day when that will be me.*

She looked at the time on the computer again. It was 7:36 p.m. Instantly Bailey's thoughts were consumed once more with Brandon's message. She surfed through a few Facebook pages and checked Twitter to see if Brandon had left any messages. The last one was from yesterday and it only said, *When you ask God to show you something, keep your eyes open. Sooner or later He'll make the truth known.* Bailey stared at the tweet for a few seconds and then switched to the comments people could leave for him, the things people had tweeted in response.

There, just a few from the top, was a message from Molly, his costar from the Montana shoot. Her tweet read: *@BrandonPaul so true!! And then once you can see it, you wonder why you couldn't see it sooner! Speaking of . . . can't wait to see YOU!*

Bailey felt herself grow dizzy, felt the sound of her heartbeat pulsing in her ears and temple. Was this really happening? Was Molly making plans to see Brandon later today? Maybe to celebrate his news? Again she wished she had gone to LA for this weekend, just to be with him. Her throat felt parched, and she couldn't swallow, couldn't feel the chair beneath her. In a flurry of keystrokes, she found her way to Molly's blog. The latest entry read, "Love at Last."

The entry was shorter than Molly's usual ones. She went on about how all of life she had wondered and planned and dreamed about love. But nothing could have prepared her for the way she felt now. "I found it! I found love at last and I couldn't be happier. Even more, he's a man of God, this guy of mine. Can't wait to introduce you to him!"

She couldn't be talking about Brandon, absolutely not. Bailey ordered her mind to stop playing tricks on her. Whatever new love God had brought into Molly's life, Bailey forced herself to feel happy for the actress. Brandon would never go behind her back. Humidity and heat and the still of the air in the house wrapped her in a suffocating cocoon. Bailey's heart raced in her chest and she couldn't draw a breath, couldn't find even the slightest relief for her aching lungs.

Why wouldn't he call?

The air grew thicker, and she needed to be outside before she dropped to the floor.

She pushed away from the computer and jogged to the back door. She burst out onto the patio and ran until she was on the other side of the pool, where she fell into the nearest chair. Only then did her next breath come, and with it a rush of tears.

Why wasn't she in LA for Brandon's announcement? She thought about how many times she'd told Brandon that the two of them might not work. If she held her ground, determined to stay in Bloomington, then eventually he was bound to fall in love with someone in LA. Bailey clenched her fists. What was she doing here when he was about to make the biggest announcement of his career? She asked the question a dozen times in her mind until eventually she had a sense about the situation.

A sense that Brandon's silence meant something big. Something Bailey figured would be answered at least in part in the next few minutes. She breathed in deeply, the humid summer night air filling her with the strength she needed. Before she went inside she gazed at the moon in the distant sky. It was still light out, but a sliver of the moon was visible. What was Brandon thinking right now, sitting in an LA studio ready to go live before millions of fans? Couldn't he have at least called her or texted? Maybe not this close to the announcement, but earlier today or yesterday?

God, I don't understand what's happening. I've prayed about Brandon since we met on the set of Unlocked, *and now I lift him to You again. I never meant to fall in love with him, You know that.* Bailey crossed her arms and pressed her fists into her stomach so the knots wouldn't hurt so bad. *If You're taking him from me, I understand. I'll hate it, but I understand. You haven't given me a peace about going back to LA and with his contract I don't see a way for us.* Tears filled her eyes. And maybe he's having doubts about me, anyway. She stood taller, steeling herself against the pain she felt certain was coming — both in a few minutes and later tonight if they talked. *Anyway, be with him as he makes his announcement and remind him about me. So that together we can end this and get on with our lives — if that's where You're leading. And if not . . . well, if not then I guess I'm praying for a miracle. Be with me, Father . . . please. I need You tonight. More than ever.*

My daughter . . . your ways are not My ways. Do not be anxious . . . I am with you.

The words came in waves across the broken places in her soul. Words from the Bible promises app Bailey had spent time on earlier today. How great that God would

362

remind her now, when she needed His promises most of all.

She dragged herself back inside, dreading the announcement and drawn to it all the same. The computer time showed 7:56. Brandon would go live in four minutes. Her hands trembled as she poised them over the keys and typed in his web address. There on his home page was a dark box with a bright red countdown clock just above it. Bailey remembered the whispers of holy assurance from a few minutes ago.

Whatever he would tell the world, it was part of God's plan.

The funny thing about the announcement was that someone from West Mark had to have leaked information. Most of the details seemed to need confirming rather than announcing. Of course, at the last minute anything could've happened. They might've agreed to a shorter deal or . . . worse . . . more years.

Bailey watched the countdown clock, watched the numbers fall away. *Breathe, Bailey,* she reminded herself. *You have to breathe.* Finally the time expired, and the box on Brandon's page came to life. Just like that he was there, sitting on a barstool, the camera close-up enough that she could see into his eyes, read his face.

She expected him to look nervous or at least conflicted. Instead his expression was a familiar one, the look he wore when they were together and away from the paparazzi and all was right with the world. Whatever West Mark had done to the contract in the final days, Brandon was happy about it. That much was clear.

He began to talk and she turned up the volume. "Hi everyone," he gave a slight wave and his smile made her hands shake a little more. She hated that he was so far away. How could she not be there? Nothing but selfishness on her part. No wonder he hadn't called, when she couldn't even make the slightest sacrifice on his behalf. Her tears came again and she felt angry with herself. She would apologize later. If there was a later.

Brandon sat up a little and looked straight into the camera, straight into her heart. "Okay, so there's been all this build up about my next contract." Again he looked relaxed, at peace with whatever was coming. "You knew about the party, but, yeah . . . that wasn't me. Maybe we can celebrate like that if I win an Academy Award someday."

Please, Brandon . . . get to the point. She wiped her palms on her jeans and gripped her knees, forcing her hands to be still. Her eyes never left the computer screen, the place where he sat so handsome and sure of himself, relating so easily to the millions of people probably tuned in right now.

"Here's the reason I canceled the party." He shrugged, his eyes bright. "It's because of you. I thought you deserved to hear the news from me first. Because you're the ones I care about, my fans who have been loyal to me all these years."

Bailey hung her head for a few seconds and then looked up again. She couldn't take this. Not when so much depended on his next words.

"Before I go any further, I need to say that West Mark Studios has been wonderful through this whole process. In the right scenario, I'd definitely work with them again."

The first flicker of confusion rattled Bailey's already jagged nerves. Again? Why didn't he talk about the next five years before he talked about what happened after that?

"Because my announcement is this: I didn't sign the contract." His look softened. "I prayed about it and read my Bible and asked God if it was the right thing." He hesitated. "But I never felt peace."

The stress Bailey had felt before the announcement was nothing to the shock racing through her system now. Had she stumbled onto some sort of phony website? Because the words Brandon was saying didn't make sense, not when all the world was waiting for something else. She glanced up and checked the website address. It was the right one. Her eyes found his again.

He was finishing up. "I won't make this long. But I want you to know I plan to do movies in the future. The thing is, it'll be one film at a time, and I'll have to consider what we film . . . and where. Because I'll be leaving Los Angeles soon." His smile this time was the one America loved. "I've kept the tabloids in business long enough. Now I need to be somewhere else, and here's the reason."

Breathe, Bailey told herself. She touched her fingers to the screen and didn't dare look away.

"I'm in love with a girl from Indiana." He leaned forward, his hands on his knees. "For all you praying fans out there, if you could pray for me and her, I'd appreciate it." His expression grew slightly more serious. "Pray that I'll have the chance to love her for the rest of my life."

What? Bailey grabbed the arms of the

chair and held on tight. He was talking about her! She couldn't look away, couldn't move. She barely noticed the tears splashing onto her jeans. Was this happening? This was his announcement . . . that he wasn't going to sign the contract? Her heart danced and twirled and spun around inside her but still she sat motionless, waiting. She didn't want to miss a word.

The screen held her attention so completely she barely heard the sound of the front door open and shut, didn't care to turn around at the soft thud of shoes on the tiled floor. Connor had probably come home earlier than the others. He was working on a song, and he hadn't expected to stay out late.

She kept her eyes glued to the computer. Brandon was going on about how he cared for the fans and wanted them to know that any project he took would be with them in mind and —

"Bailey." The voice was close and it didn't sound like Connor. Suddenly she felt two hands on her shoulders.

Her gasp came faster than she could spin around and jump to her feet. "Brandon!" He was here! He had come and now he was right in front of her, taking her into his arms. Fresh tears filled her eyes in a rush.

"How did you . . . ?"

"Baby, shhhh . . . it's okay." He rocked her, brushing his face against hers. "I love you, Bailey. I love you."

She gripped his shoulders and stared at him, trying to believe this was really happening. "I love you too." She wiped her tears and laughed so she wouldn't break down and cry. Then she looked at the computer screen, where he was still talking about staying in touch with fans through Twitter and Facebook. "You taped it?"

"I did." He pointed to the screen. "See . . . the word 'live' isn't anywhere." He angled his face, studying her like he, too, couldn't believe they were standing here. Finally face-to-face. "I never said it was live." He looked at her again. "That was my manager's idea." His smile faded. "My *former* manager."

"Brandon . . . what happened? To the contract . . . to your plans?" She could only figure the studio had played hardball, unwilling to let him have creative control. "I mean . . . how is any of this real?"

"It's a long story." He gently took hold of her face and eased his fingers into her hair. "Come with me, Bailey." There was a depth in his eyes that had never been there before. As if the last few months had grown him in ways that were only now coming to light. "Please . . . I need to show you something."

"I'll go." She didn't blink, didn't look away. "Wherever you take me I'll go."

He took her hand and led her toward the front door. As they left the room she realized something that sent a smile through her heart and soul. The words she'd said to Brandon didn't only apply to this moment. If he loved her this much, if he could walk away from the West Mark contract and ask the whole world to pray that he'd have a chance to love her all her life, then this much was certain.

She would follow Brandon Paul anywhere.

TWENTY-THREE

As they walked down the porch steps to Brandon's rented Chevy Tahoe, Bailey still couldn't believe any of it. Brandon refusing his contract and flying here to be with her. He had even said on the announcement that he was leaving Los Angeles. Bailey's head was spinning with questions, but for now it was enough to have him beside her. He opened the door for her before climbing behind the wheel, and she had the most wonderful thought: This was what life would feel like if she and Brandon could ever have normalcy. He would pick her up and open the door for her and they would drive somewhere in a normal car and have a normal night out on the town.

"So you really fired your manager?" Bailey winced in Brandon's direction.

"And my agent." Brandon's jaw flexed and he kept his eyes straight ahead. "They weren't honest with me. I had to let them go."

Brandon explained how they had kept the truth from him regarding Luke's involvement in the final stage of the contract.

"They got crazy over the money." He glanced at her, his eyes full of peace and only the slightest sorrow over the way things had played out with his team.

"You trusted them." She reached out and put her hand over his. "No wonder I didn't hear from you."

"I know." His expression filled with remorse. "I couldn't call you, baby. I spent my time praying and in meetings right up until I boarded the plane."

"Are they mad at you? The team at West Mark?" Her words ran together, the questions coming faster than she could get them out. "Like how long before they give you whatever contract comes next?"

"Next?" He looked at her. "What do you mean?"

"Well . . ." Bailey absently twisted a long strand of her hair. He'd mentioned something in the announcement about doing movies one at a time. But she figured that was just what he had to say for now. Something his team had insisted on until the legalities with West Mark could be worked out. She turned slightly so she could see his profile better. "Isn't the studio working on another revision, a scenario you can live with?"

They were still on the road that led out of her neighborhood. Brandon eased the car to a stop on the side of the road. He slipped the gear into park. "Bailey." He put his hand on the side of her face, his tone so sincere it was like she had a front row seat in the arena of his heart.

"Yes." Her voice was a whisper. She was afraid, afraid to know the details of what lay ahead.

Brandon's tone was gentle, a caress that soothed every jagged nerve inside her. "There's only one scenario I can truly live with." The look in his eyes told her the depth of his sincerity. "I can only live if I have you. If I'm here with you." His smile shone deep in his eyes. "I'm not signing a long-term contract. Not ever."

"What?" The word was little more than a breath.

"No, baby." He ran his thumb along her cheekbone. "Never. One movie at a time, and even then, maybe not for a while." He looked at her, grabbed hold of the gear again, and his eyes sparkled with the kindness that had won her over from the beginning. "You'll understand more in a little while."

Her heart struggled to grasp what he was saying. But right now she could only believe him. She could understand later. The way she trusted him must've showed in her eyes, because he seemed to visibly relax. From her neighborhood he drove into town toward the university and the Starbucks not far from campus. He parked across the street and stared at the entrance. "This is it." He turned to her. "Remember this?"

A memory came to life, starting deep within her and working its way to the surface. "The first time we hung out." The moment seemed like a lifetime ago. He had flown into town to read with her for her role of Ella in *Unlocked.* "You private messaged me that you were looking forward to it." She laughed and the release felt so good. After the day of waiting and wondering, this felt like a dream. "My brothers couldn't believe it."

He reached for her hand. "And then I strutted into the audition room all full of myself."

"You were pretty arrogant." She glanced at the Starbucks awning. "When we walked in here that day I was like, 'I could never be interested in a celebrity like him.'"

"And I was thinking, 'Whoever this Cody is, he's the luckiest guy in the world.' " His smile fell off. "I figured he'd be crazy to ever let you go."

"Hmmm." The truth would always be telling. The fact that Cody had walked away. But then if he hadn't run from her, her heart never would've been open to love Brandon. "So weird how much has happened since then."

"Come on," he nodded at the Starbucks. "Let's get coffee."

Bailey felt herself tense up the minute they stepped out of the Tahoe. This would normally be the moment when, from several surrounding cars, photographers would spill out and run after them, shouting and firing off rapid camera shots. Instead, a couple of strangers walked slowly by, arm in arm, unaware of Bailey and Brandon. As they crossed the street there was only the sound of happy voices from college kids as they sat at the outdoor tables in front of the coffee shop and an adjacent café.

"This sort of proves my theory." He grinned at her as they walked inside. "No one notices us here. That, or they don't care."

It was true. Bailey felt the instant tension in her shoulders ease and as they got to the end of a line of ten people, no one even did a double take. She looked at him, confused. "But . . . when you were here filming people lined up six deep to see you."

"The papers told everyone I was here filming, that something big was going on downtown." He chuckled. "Of course they came."

They were in line three minutes before two teenage girls walked by, paused, and hurried out giggling with their drinks. The first of the two gave Brandon a slight wave, her cheeks red. "Hi!" The word was more of a squeal. She definitely recognized him, but she didn't stop for an autograph or a picture. Her friend simply pushed her along and gave Bailey and Brandon an apologetic look. "She's crazy. Don't mind her." And like that the two girls left the coffee shop.

Bailey glanced at the other patrons. They were all busy in their own conversations, caught up in their homework or phone calls or personal lives. "Are you kidding me?" Her laugh held proof of her disbelief.

"I know." He slipped his arm around her. "We could live with this, right? That's how life would be here."

It was their turn to order, so she didn't have time to think deeply about what he'd said. It wasn't the first time that night he'd referred to living in Bloomington. Or was he only saying that rhetorically? Like he would be here with her more often? The answers were coming, that's what he'd told her. So they ordered and took their drinks back to the SUV and this time they headed back toward Clear Creek.

"I'll never forget those weeks working with you on the set of *Unlocked*." He angled his head, a tenderness in his eyes that hadn't been there before. "I was one way when we started that movie, and completely changed by the time we finished it. A new person." He set his drink in the cup holder. "Literally. And you know where it all began?"

Bailey realized they had reached Clear Creek High School. She looked at the series of buildings and the football stadium in the distance and she remembered everything this place meant to her. The buildings held memories of four years of high school, four years of homecomings and winter dances and too many football games to count. It was where she had first fallen for Cody Coleman. But with all that her eyes found his. They had filmed *Unlocked* here, after all. "That time . . . here, with you. Best memories I have at Clear Creek." She meant every word. "You always made me laugh."

"Which was a little awkward." He gave her a silly look. "I mean, it wasn't a comedy."

"It's amazing I could say my lines at all."

He slipped the car into park and took both her hands in his. "Wanna know my favorite memory here?"

"Let me guess." She let herself get lost in his eyes, and the picture he made with the moonlight shining on his face. "When you were teasing me. Like you always were." He would even joke about her pretend boyfriend, because Cody never showed up on set, never called when she was around Brandon. Another telling sign she'd struggled to see back then. She smiled at him. "Or the time it took eleven takes to get our hallway scene right? I thought they were going to fire us both."

The memory started a bout of laughter for the two of them, and Brandon let his head lean back against the seat until he could catch his breath. "I can imagine how I must've looked. Thinking I could flirt with you and win you over in a minute. Like you were any other girl." His laughter died down and he stared at her. In a moment that stopped time, he leaned closer and kissed her. As he drew back, his eyes were the same as when they'd danced on the Kellers' roof.

Completely and totally lost in hers. "But you, Bailey . . . you were never like any other girl."

She felt the thrill of his words, his eyes on hers, the nearness of him. "So tell me . . . your favorite memory."

"Mmmm." He didn't look away. "That's easy. The time you and I went to Lake Monroe Beach. The things I told you that day, I'd never told anyone before."

"It was the first time I saw you as more than a costar." She gave his hands a gentle squeeze. "After that, you were my friend."

"And after that I wasn't crushing on you." His smile was gone, and he looked utterly taken by her. "I was in love with you." He didn't pause long. "You had Cody, so I couldn't tell you."

"Really?" Bailey never would've guessed. After that day at the lake and in Cody's constant absence, of course she and Brandon had grown closer. "I didn't think you had real feelings for me until you flew here to help me pack for New York." She leaned her forehead against his so that his eyes were all she could see. "I mean . . . who does that?"

He took tender hold of her face, his movements slow and deliberate, and again he kissed her. "I would've flown to the moon and back for you, Bailey. Then . . . and now." He kissed her once more. "Always."

How good it felt to be wanted like this, to be cared for and loved and pursued and fought for. She put her arms around his neck and for a long time they stayed that way, holding on to each other so that nothing and no one could ever pull them apart again. Finally Brandon drew a deep breath and sat back in his seat. "One more place to go."

As they drove, Bailey's heart felt like it might burst from joy, from the unbelievable reality this night had turned into. Before they pulled out of the parking lot, Brandon slipped a CD into the car stereo. "I made a playlist for tonight. The first song . . . 'Forever Love' is from Francesca Battistelli," he explained. "It's how I've felt since I met you."

Her eyes welled up. She stared at him, and couldn't look away as he started the song. She hadn't heard it before, but it was beautiful from the first line, talking about a forever kind of love, the love of God and ultimately — from Brandon's perspective — the sort of love he had for her. The windows were partially down and Bailey felt the summer wind play in her hair. She smiled at Brandon and she could see in his eyes exactly when he forget everything but her. By the time the song reached the chorus, Bailey could feel tears on her cheeks. She absorbed the beauty of the lyrics, telling about a love that fully and wholly consumed the heart. Between the lines she could see in Brandon's expression his prayers, his hopes and dreams, and how very much he loved her.

You are my forever love . . . from the bottom of my heart I'll sing to you, from the depths of who I am I'll love you . . .

Brandon glanced at her as he drove, and it was as if he were singing straight to her soul. The chorus played out and as it finished, every word seemed written for them. And as the song wrapped up, Bailey lived in every line.

Bailey could barely breathe. The song wasn't talking about any sort of love, it was talking about the rare sort of love God had for them, and their love for Him. And because of that very great love, the song celebrated the way the two of them felt for each other. No question the song was talking about a forever that could only come through faith and commitment. Maybe even a lifelong commitment.

Tears shone in Brandon's eyes too, and as the song ended he reached for her hand once more. He turned the stereo off and for a long time neither of them said anything. He was taking her to Lake Monroe, she could see that. And as he pulled into the upper lot, she remembered the last time they were here, the walk they'd taken and the fire pit they'd found. He parked the Tahoe and turned to her. "This is the last stop."

They left their coffees and again he opened the door for her. The night air was still warm, still humid the way summers in Indiana always were. But a breeze stirred in the trees and Bailey felt wonderful. Every second, every breath absolutely in sync with Brandon's.

Night was falling over Bloomington, so he took a backpack from the seat behind her and pulled a flashlight out before he slipped the pack over his shoulders. He smiled and took her hand. Everything about the moment felt sacred, like words would only interrupt the connection they shared here now. He used the flashlight so they could see clearly, and he led her to the same path they'd walked on the Fourth of July, toward the fire pit.

As they neared it Bailey spotted the lights. Two soft spotlights aimed at the pit and the lake. The area around it looked lit up like something from a movie set. Bailey looked around, but they were the only ones here. She looked at him. "Brandon?"

"I'm tired of being in the dark." He grinned, but the depth, the intensity of the moment remained. He turned off the flashlight. "Come sit with me."

Her heart beat harder than before. She followed him and sat down. As she did, he opened the backpack and pulled out a manila envelope. Again she didn't feel the need for questions or words. Whatever was happening, Brandon had planned this out. Right down to the lights.

He took the envelope to the fire pit and only then did she notice the small pile of fresh-cut logs and brittle branches. And something else — something that made her breath stop for a few seconds. Beside the fire pit was a table and on it was a pack of matches, a bucket of ice, and two long-stemmed glasses. And in the ice bucket was a bottle of orange soda — just like Brandon had brought to their rooftop prom.

Bailey's senses were heightened, her heart and soul aware of Brandon's every move. He looked at her, his eyes sparkling in the pretty light from the lamps behind them. For a few seconds he seemed to struggle for words, but then he held up the envelope.

"Inside is the contract. The one thing —" He paused and looked down. When he looked up his eyes were damp again. "The one thing that could've stopped me from being with you." With shaking hands he ripped the envelope open and sifted handfuls of little white pieces over the logs in the fire pit.

Without saying a word he took the matches and almost ceremoniously lit one. Then he held it near the paper. Bailey felt her knees tremble. She'd never felt like this in all her life. She was on her feet, drawn to the scene; mesmerized as she moved to the edge of the fire pit. She watched as the ripped-apart contract acted as kindling for the fire. A fire that Bailey understood now would never go out.

"Baby . . ." He stood slowly and came to her. With the fire crackling beside them, he took her hands. "Nothing is going to come between us again." The tears in his eyes fell onto his cheeks. "I don't need another movie or another dollar . . . or another day being chased by paparazzi." He put his hand alongside her face, lost in her eyes. "I must've been crazy not to see it before."

"It was me too." She wiped at the tears on her own cheeks. "I never should've left you. If you wanted to live on the moon I should've been willing." She put her hands on his shoulders. "I love you that much, Brandon. I do."

They came together in a hug and Bailey could no longer tell where her soul ended and his began. No one had ever understood her like Brandon did.

As he stepped back, he searched her eyes. "You deserve better than me, Bailey. My past . . . it's so different from yours."

"That's not —"

He shook his head slightly and touched his finger softly to her lips. "Wait." He looked more intent, more serious than before. "Here's the thing." He looked at her in a way that saw all of her heart. "I know I'm undeserving, but I'm a new man in Christ. That's why I haven't stopped fighting for you, going after you, and believing . . . that with God's forever kind of love I can be the one-in-a-million guy you deserve. Because that's what redemption looks like."

Her tears came harder now. Wasn't this what she had wanted for so many years? A love that would go after her, fight for her, lay itself bare for her? "I'm not perfect either. No one is."

"You're close." He smiled and ran his thumb lightly over her cheek. "Remember when we came to the lake that first time? You told me I didn't really want you . . . I wanted your faith. Remember that?"

Bailey nodded. "Yes." With all her being she never wanted this moment or the closeness between them to end. "I remember."

"You were right. What I was drawn to in you . . . what I'm still drawn to is your faith, the way you love God and people. That's why you deserve so much." He smiled again. "Not really because you're perfect. But because He is."

Every word, everything he said was exactly how she had always felt. It was how she had hoped Cody would feel, only Cody never got this very simple truth and so he had run from her. Brandon ran too. But because he understood about redemption, he had run toward her.

Always toward her.

They hugged again and this time he framed her face with his hands. As he did, from somewhere in the nearby bushes came the beautiful sound of the same song Brandon had played for her in the car. Francesca Battistelli's "Forever Love." The music wasn't too loud or overwhelming. But it made the entire moment feel like a scene from the most beautiful love story ever written.

Brandon searched her eyes and quietly sang along. "You are my forever love . . . you're my forever love."

"I love you." She clung to him, her face close to his. "I always will."

And with that, as if all her life had led to this moment, his eyes welled up again and he dropped slowly to one knee.

Bailey's hand flew to her mouth and she took a half step backwards. Because how could God love her enough to clear away every obstacle, every hesitation, and bring her to this moment? All her life she'd prayed about the man she would marry, prayed for him and dreamed of him and asked God to lead him to her.

And now . . .

She held her breath and watched as he pulled a small box from his pocket. No matter what else happened in all her life she would remember this moment, every rustle of wind in the trees and the smell and sound of the fire. Honeysuckle sweet in the summer air, the soft lighting all around and the song filling the spaces between them. And the absolute pure and all-consuming look of love on Brandon Paul's face.

She would remember all of it.

"Bailey . . ." He held out the ring to her. The glow from the moon on the lake and the fire beside them shone on his face, while the soft lights on the other side erased any shadows that might have otherwise fallen over the moment. "Let me love you, let me lead you and protect you. Marry me, Bailey . . . Please marry me?"

There was no hesitating. "Yes, Brandon. Yes, a million times, yes." She put her hands on his shoulders so she wouldn't fall from the weight of emotion and love and caring she felt overflowing from her heart. Here on this sacred lakeside path God was giving them both a miracle and her yes was as easy as her next breath.

He was still lost in her eyes, but he stood now and slipped the ring on her finger. Only then did Bailey notice details of the diamond. It was beautiful, a circle so multifaceted that it caught every sort of light and shone it to the heavens, the way their love would always shine as long as her heart beat. And the spray of light from the stone would always celebrate the love they had found in each other.

With that he raised his fist in the air and stared up at the starry night sky. "She said yes!" After shouting his excitement, he pulled her close and kissed her, the sort of kiss that took her breath and made her forget where they were. He hugged her and then picked her up and twirled her in a circle. "Yes!" His voice rang with a deep and very great joy. "I'm marrying Bailey Flanigan!"

Bailey laughed with him and when he settled down again she held his face in her hands and let herself get lost in his eyes. "And I'm marrying Brandon Paul." She wasn't loud like him, but victory rang in her tone as well. She was finally past all the wondering and doubting and trying to move on without him. She put her hands on his shoulders and wondered if she'd ever mean any words more in all her life. "I will love you till the day I die." For a few seconds she laughed in disbelief. "I can't believe this. I thought you were mad at me. I thought I'd spend the rest of my days regretting not flying to LA this weekend. I was so afraid, Brandon."

"No, baby. You had nothing to worry about." He kissed her and his tone grew softer, more serious again. "Because perfect love drives out fear. Remember?"

This was a new and more mature Brandon Paul, and Bailey could feel herself falling hard for him, finding new ways to love him and want him and believe in him. "Forever love." She smiled. "Nothing could be more perfect than that."

"You know what else forever love does?" His eyes danced and he became again the familiar fun-loving Brandon, the one who made her laugh and love life and see colors where before there were only grays.

"What?" She caught the teasing vibe and took a step back. The ring on her finger felt absolutely wonderful and she glanced at it for a few seconds.

"Well . . ." He shaded his eyes and squinted in the direction of the bushes between the two light posts. "Perfect love looks great on video."

"What?" She grabbed a quick breath and looked to her right. "Video?"

At that moment Bailey's brother Connor and a friend of his from the football team stepped out of the bushes, laughing and clapping and beaming with joy. Connor raised a small video camera high in the air. "I always wanted to be a director."

Bailey couldn't believe the extent of Brandon's surprise. "You videotaped this?"

Connor answered for him, "Yep. Got the whole thing." He set the camera down on the log bench. At the same time, Connor's expression softened, and his eyes met Bailey's. "Congratulations!" He hugged her. "I'm so happy for you guys." Connor looked at Brandon and back to Bailey. "You've been through a lot. But no one's ever appreciated you and loved you the way Brandon does."

The night would've been perfect without her brother's words, but this only made the moment that much better. The fact that her brother — who knew everything about her past — could see Brandon was the right guy. The one who understood her and loved her the most.

Connor's friend held both fists in the air. "I can't believe we got to watch!" The kid had been over to the house before, and he'd met Brandon a few weeks ago. He shook his head, his grin filling his face. "Seriously. This is the coolest thing!"

Bailey laughed and slipped her arms around Brandon's waist. He held her in a way that made her feel safe and special and cherished and loved. She leaned on his shoulder while Connor launched into an explanation of how they'd set up the scene and how his friend's amateur moviemaking helped him get the perfect lighting and how amazing it was to watch the scene from the bushes. The whole time a million thoughts fought for position in Bailey's heart. But at the top of the list was the most obvious: They needed to stop and thank God, now before the moment got away.

At a brief break in Connor's story, Bailey opened her mouth to suggest they all pray, but at the same time she felt a stirring of the Holy Spirit in her soul.

Wait, daughter . . . let him lead.

She closed her mouth and stayed where she was, listening to Connor's story.

Yes, Lord . . .

As soon as Connor finished, Brandon looked at the boys and finally to her, where his eyes remained. "Would it be okay if we prayed? All of us?"

Bailey loved the way Brandon included her brother in this moment. The two of them would be family soon, and this would be a time they would all remember forever. They held hands as Brandon led the prayer. His voice confident and clear and brimming with an otherworldly joy, he thanked God and asked for His blessing over their engagement and their marriage. He promised to love and lead Bailey through every season of life, and he asked God to keep men like Dayne Matthews close by so he could continue to grow as a man and as the husband Bailey needed.

Through it all Bailey could only stay close to Brandon, amazed at it all. Through the prayer and as they drove back into town and stopped at Ashley and Landon's old Baxter farmhouse, and through the surprise engagement party with her family and the Baxters that Brandon had secretly staged for her. Through telling her parents and watching the video Connor and his friend had shot and while showing off her ring and retelling the story of his proposal again and again and again.

As the party wound down, Brandon wrapped his arms around her. "I'll never forget tonight, the way love felt looking in your eyes."

She grinned. This was why she never wanted to spend another day away from Brandon Paul. The way he talked to her, the way love felt fresh with him and like they were the only two people in the world. "I'm still trying to believe it." She smiled. "That you love me this much."

"Or that a girl like you would really love me back."

They hugged once more, not wanting to let go. Again awe and wonder spread like adrenaline through her heart and chill bumps ran down her arms. God was right — she needed to give Brandon the chance to lead. The guy she loved had grown so much deeper in his beliefs, gone through so much these past months while they were apart. Bailey could rest in the safety of his faith for a lifetime and here in this moment. She had nothing to fear about that or anything else when she was with Brandon. Because God had brought him to her, and He had given them this:

Forever love.

TWENTY-FOUR

Jenny had always known that when the time came for Bailey's wedding, the two of them would find a way to be even closer than they'd been all her life. By mid-October, life was playing out exactly that way. She and Bailey and Brandon had already shared so many beautiful moments thinking about and planning the wedding day that Jenny woke each morning thanking God for this season.

She sat with Bailey that Saturday morning at Starbucks across from the Indiana University campus going over the details already in place. The smell of coffee and the comfortable sound of half a dozen quiet conversations filled the air. Outside the sun shone against the bluest sky, while leaves in every shade of red and yellow and orange fluttered from the trees outside. October shouting to all the world that God would make all things beautiful in His time.

Bailey had the notebook in front of her, the one Jenny had made for her and Brandon to hold contracts and documents associated with the wedding. They had opted to do the planning themselves and not seek help with details until the last month. So far they were all glad for the chance to work together.

For a minute, Bailey thumbed through the book and Jenny simply watched her, the way her long hair hung in pretty layers around her face and how the glow since her proposal had stayed with her. *No bride-to-be ever looked more beautiful,* Jenny thought.

Bailey flipped to the page with the church contract. "I know we have the documents here, but the secretary at church called last week and thought they had a conflict for March sixteenth." She uttered a nervous laugh. "That would've changed everything."

Jenny wasn't worried. "We would've worked something out. Especially since we already have the contract." It was the first detail they'd nailed down, especially after Bailey and Brandon decided they didn't want to wait a long time before the wedding. "This is half the fun, dealing with the little conflicts."

Bailey took a sip of her coffee and smiled. "That's what I love about you, Mom. You see the good in every situation."

"Most of the time." She made a silly face. "That lady at IU in charge of the ballroom? Definitely more of a struggle."

"Dear old Tammy." Bailey smiled, and her eyes sparkled with a hint of teasing. "She's just had a lot of bad days."

"But we've got the ballroom." Jenny gave her daughter two thumbs up. "That one's locked in too."

In all, the wedding was coming together better and faster than Jenny expected. It really wasn't that hard, planning such a beautiful event. They expected around three hundred guests — extended family, of course, and special people like the Baxters and the Kellers, along with close connections from the Indianapolis Colts organization and Clear Creek High and Christian Kids Theater. Of course, some of Brandon's long-term Los Angeles friends would be invited, too. The media had covered the story like it was the hottest news of the year. Brandon Paul was officially off the market. Talk in the tabloids had every rag guessing about their wedding day. Everyone figured it would be unforgettable.

Jenny sipped her latte and thanked God that she could be here, sharing this time with her only daughter. Especially after the sad goodbye they'd shared a few years ago. Again, God had made all things work together in His timing.

"Okay." Jenny folded her hands on the table. "Why don't you go over what we're sure about?"

Bailey turned to the beginning of the book. "Besides the church and reception sites, we have the mobile coffee people." She looked up. "Which I love, by the way. That's going to be so great."

"I agree." Neither Bailey nor Brandon wanted alcohol at their wedding — not because they had a problem with other people having a drink. But because in light of Brandon's past they wanted to mark their wedding date without it. The coffee bar had been Brandon's idea, and everyone loved it.

Bailey stopped and her expression changed. "Speaking of coffee. Did I tell you I talked to Brandon's parents?"

"What?" Jenny brought her voice down a notch. Brandon's parents hadn't been part of any discussions. He hadn't talked to them yet, despite Bailey's occasional suggestion that he do so. "Does he know?"

"I told him I might do it!" She smiled, clearly at peace with the decision. "He wasn't sure, but he told me if God led me to make the call I could find their number

397

in his phone. So when he was working at the computer one day, I found their number and called."

"Were they surprised."

"Shocked." Her eyes softened. "I told them we were engaged and that I wanted them at the wedding." She hesitated. "His mom started crying when I said that part. Then she said she didn't think Brandon would want them there."

"What'd you say?"

"I told her Brandon wanted reconciliation. And maybe the wedding was the perfect chance to find it."

"Wow!" Jenny set her coffee down. "I don't know. Maybe sooner. That's a lot of emotion for one day."

"That's what Brandon said. He's going to call them soon, maybe work out something where they can fly out sooner." She took another sip of her drink. "He asked me to ask you and Dad to pray. For reconciliation and a new start. It's hard on Brandon, the distance between him and his parents." She still looked sad. "He doesn't talk about it, but the silence between them breaks his heart. Mine, too. He's wanted to call them . . . but it's never felt like the right time." A smile lifted her lips. "He was glad I made the first move."

"We'll pray." Jenny thought about her daughter's bold determination to see healing in this part of Brandon's life. "For all of it."

"Thanks." Bailey smiled and gradually the hurt lifted. "Let's see." She flipped through a few pages of the book. "We have the videographer and photographer contracts here. I'm so, so excited about that, Mom." She angled her head, giving Jenny the sweetest look. "That was amazing, doing that for us."

"It was fun." Jenny remembered her and Bailey looking through one website after another trying to find a photographer who seemed to have the ability to capture the kind of love Bailey and Brandon shared. "I think we have the perfect team lined up."

"Definitely." Bailey studied the paperwork in front of her. "The florist is working up a bid . . . the twinkling-lights people are doing the same."

"I love that you're getting twinkling lights."

"The whole reception will be magical." She grinned at Jenny. "Twinkling lights will be perfect."

Even so, Jenny thought, *they could never match the light in Bailey's eyes.* The way her grown-up daughter would look that night.

As they finished their coffee they talked about having a runner down the center aisle of the church, and how Bailey was hoping for bows draped from one pew to the next along either side.

"Of course, there's still the dress." Jenny raised her brow and laughed. "We never seem to talk about that."

"I know." Bailey's grin turned sheepish. "We've looked through every wedding magazine." She shrugged lightly. "I still haven't found one I like."

"Maybe if we went in person." Jenny wasn't worried yet, but if Bailey didn't find something by the end of November they could run into some time constraints.

"We will. Very soon." Bailey sat back as if the idea almost exhausted her. "I think I'm avoiding it. Like, what if I don't find one? Maybe I'll just get married in something comfortable."

Jenny smiled. "Okay. Jeans and a T-shirt." She stifled a laugh. "Is that what you want?"

Bailey giggled. "You know me too well." She sighed. "I want the pretty dress, the train, something timeless and elegant and vintage and sexy and fashionable." She flashed a weak smile. "All in one dress. Which is why I'm avoiding shopping."

"We could look this afternoon." Jenny

liked the idea. "There's that boutique just off town square a few blocks away. Ashley told me they have hundreds of dresses. From designer to originals made right here in Bloomington."

"No." Bailey let the last part of the word trail off for a moment, like the note of a song. She closed the book and her face lit up. "I have an idea." The joy in her voice was contagious. "Let's get pedicures. We haven't done that in so long."

"Hmmm." Jenny checked the time on her phone. Just after four. The guys would want dinner at home in an hour or so. "Maybe if we just ran into the boutique for a few minutes. They close at five, so we wouldn't have long."

Bailey wrinkled her nose and gave a polite shake of her head. "Pedicures sounds more fun."

"We might not have time." Jenny did her best to sound enthusiastic. "Come on . . . you don't have to try anything on. Just take a look. If you don't like anything, we at least know we need to go into the city, or maybe do something crazy like take a mother-daughter shopping trip to New York. A quick look would at least give us a little direction."

"That's very nice, Mom. But I don't

know." Bailey looked about as excited as when she spent the day cleaning her room. "Can I admit something?"

"Sure." Jenny sat back, trying to hear her daughter's heart. Bailey had always been different from other girls her age, and this was one of those moments. She hadn't kept a scrapbook of wedding-dress styles and floral arrangements dreaming of her perfect wedding. Instead she'd kept a journal, dreaming about her perfect guy.

Bailey took a deep breath. "Okay, the thing is, even though I love the thought of shopping with you for my wedding dress, I think I'd rather walk in and find it right away. Then we can have fun with other things and I won't be stressed about the dress."

"Hmmm. Could be a new reality show. 'Stressed About the Dress.' " Jenny laughed, and Bailey did the same.

Finally Bailey dragged herself to her feet. "I won't find one." She gave Jenny a wary smile. "But okay, fine. Let's go look."

"Just a look!" Jenny felt a thrill at the idea. She hadn't dreamed about this for Bailey, either. But now that they were in this special time, she cherished the idea of sorting through bridal gowns looking for the right

402

dress for her only girl.

At least this would be a start.

TWENTY-FIVE

By the time they parked outside the boutique and headed inside, the store was closing in just thirty minutes. At the front door, blocking their ability to go further inside, was a long table and a thin man with a trim suit and black rimmed glasses. "Yes?" He studied them with a sort of disdain, as if they maybe smelled bad.

Not the sort of greeting Jenny expected. "Uh . . ." She felt the giggles rising inside her. A quick look at Bailey confirmed her daughter felt the same way. Jenny turned to the man again. "We'd like to . . . look at a few dresses. If that's okay?"

With great flair, the man checked his watch. "It's very late."

"I'm sorry." Jenny bit her lip.

He checked a clipboard and then peered at her over his glasses. "Do you have an appointment?"

"Nope." Jenny felt like she'd committed

some sort of misdemeanor. Like the guy was about to order both of them to leave and never come back. She shook her head, and again she worked to keep from laughing. Was the man for real? "No appointment, sir."

"Novices." He released an exaggerated sigh. "Fine. I'll see if Gwen can help you." He huffed and allowed his tone to do most of the talking as he placed a call to what must've been a back room. When he hung up he found his most professional, practiced smile. It never came close to reaching his eyes. "Gwen will be up in a moment." He looked at Bailey, studying her like she was a lopsided Christmas tree. "Until then maybe sort through that rack there."

Jenny thanked him and linked arms with Bailey. When they were around the corner down the aisle where he'd suggested they go, they both stopped and burst into quiet laughter. "He hates us!" Jenny whispered. "What did we do?"

"I don't think it's us." Bailey covered her mouth, her eyes dancing. "He doesn't like customers." She, too, kept her voice to a whisper. "Like they have a customer avoidance program or something."

After a minute they caught their breath and began sorting through the dresses on the rack. The first had an empire waist and a high neck. Bailey studied it for a moment, thoughtful. "No . . . not that one."

It went that way through a simple country dress of antique silk and lace and another one with a dramatic ten-foot train. The moment felt familiar in a long-ago sort of way. And suddenly Jenny remembered. "I was just like this." She gave Bailey a side hug. "I hated looking for my wedding dress. I didn't think I would look good in any of them."

Before Jenny could explain further, a round woman with a warm smile and red cheeks came around the corner. "Sorry to keep you waiting. I'm Gwen." She winced. "You met Albert?"

"Yes." Jenny and Bailey swapped nervous looks. "He didn't like us."

"He doesn't like brides." She waved at something in the air in front of her. "Shucks, he doesn't like weddings."

Their confused faces must've propelled her to finish the thought. "He owns the place. Inherited it from his parents, who loved weddings. His frown's nothing personal. It's part of him."

"Whew." Bailey looked glad. "I thought maybe it was us."

"Not at all." Gwen adjusted a few dresses on the rack. "Anyway, what have we found so far? We can only take three dresses into a fitting room at a time. Otherwise it gets overwhelming. This is a big moment, big day. Most important dress you'll ever wear." Gwen squealed a little. She was a fast talker, whose enthusiasm for wedding dresses and brides more than made up for her boss's shortcomings. She raised her brow, hopeful. "Did we find any?"

"We aren't really —"

"It's late to try on any —"

Jenny and Bailey spoke at the same time, and the combination of their excuses only made Gwen happier.

She clapped her hands a few times. "I love when brides aren't sure." In an efficient matter of seconds she selected three gowns from various spots on the rack and took off for the dressing room. "These look about your size. Follow me," she called over her shoulder. "This will be fun!"

Jenny looked at Bailey. "It can't hurt."

"Albert will be furious. He'll have us arrested." Bailey didn't look sure about any of this. "We'll make him late for dinner."

"Girls!" Gwen's shrill voice called out to them.

"I guess we don't have a choice." Jenny giggled and then cleared her voice, smoothing out the wrinkles in her sweater. "Coming!"

From the moment they reached the fitting room, Gwen was completely in charge. "I'm working with two brides at once so I'll have to be on my A-game." She looked at a late thirty-something bride-to-be standing on the pedestal next to the one Bailey would use who was admiring the wedding dress she was wearing. Gwen supervised an exchange of names and wedding dates. The other bride — Betsie — was getting married in June.

And with that, Gwen flashed a practiced smile at Jenny. "You'll wait over there. I'll help Bailey with each dress."

Jenny felt the slightest sense of disappointment. Since Bailey's engagement, when she thought about this day, she pictured being the one to help Bailey slip in and out of each dress. *That's okay,* she told herself. *I can be patient.* But as Bailey and Gwen came out of the dressing room with the first dress Jenny could tell immediately from Bailey's pained smile that she didn't want a stranger helping her.

The dress was very pretty, strapless with a flair into an A-frame skirt that was embellished with swirled sequins. Bailey waited until Gwen's attention was on the other bride. "Mom!" Her whisper was beyond urgent. "Help! I look like I'm playing dress up."

Jenny felt along her daughter's middle. "What're you wearing underneath?"

"I have no idea." Her whisper remained intense. "Some kind of corset thing. It's cutting into my ribs."

Jenny was trying to think of a way to sneak Bailey back into the dressing room to remove the cumbersome undergarments Gwen had chosen, when the other bride let out a scream. "Is that blood?"

"What?" Gwen jumped back, and sure enough there was a red smear around the waist of Betsie's dress. "My goodness this is awful." She looked down and grabbed her finger. "Oh, dear, I seem to have cut myself. Paper cut from the tags maybe. I'm so sorry. Heavens, this is terrible." She hurried off holding her finger and talking to herself.

Betsie looked horrified and at the same time the grumpy guy up front caught wind of the disaster and hurried to the scene. As Gwen disappeared into the back room, Jenny hurried to Bailey's side.

"This is our moment," she whispered. She took her hand and ushered her into the dressing room. "Let's get you out of all those under things."

Bailey's eyes were wide. "Glad it's only a paper cut." She shut the door behind them. "Can you imagine? Poor Betsie!"

Jenny helped Bailey out of the dress and the various corsets and hip-trimmers Gwen had instructed her to use. "There." Bailey exhaled. "I can breathe. Okay . . ." She thumbed through the other two choices. "How about that one?"

It was a simpler dress without a train, antique white with layered lace and cap sleeves. Jenny helped her daughter hang up the other dress, and then she unzipped the second one and slipped it over her head. As she eased it past Bailey's long hair, the zipper snagged and Bailey dropped with the dress to the floor of the fitting room.

"Help!" Bailey laughed as she quietly cried out. "I'm caught!"

This whole experience was becoming a comedy of errors. Jenny worked quickly trying to untangle Bailey's hair from the zipper. "Now I see why Gwen has this job."

"No, it's okay. I want you." Bailey was crouched on the floor, the dress gathered around her like an off-white tent. "Am I free?"

Jenny worked another few seconds. "There. I think so."

Tentatively Bailey stood. Jenny eased the

dress up and zipped it, and together they walked out of the fitting room looking a little guilty, like the class troublemakers. Neither Gwen nor Albert were in sight, and Betsie was talking to an older woman — probably her own mother.

"Here." Jenny pointed to the pedestal. "Step up."

Jenny straightened the back of the dress as Bailey positioned herself. But almost immediately she shook her head. "No. It's wrong."

"It *is* beautiful." Jenny offered, one brow raised, doubt ringing in her voice. "Maybe for someone else?"

"Yes. Definitely." Bailey's shoulders sank. "I don't like the other one in there either, Mom. Let's go. This isn't the place."

Jenny was about to agree when from behind Bailey she spotted a row of gowns they hadn't seen before. "Hmm. What are those?"

"What?" Bailey turned and looked. A mild interest showed in her eyes. "Probably nothing."

"There's a few white ones mixed in."

"See if you can find one. Just one." Bailey didn't sound hopeful. "Then we need to go, please?"

"Okay." Jenny thought about the last half

hour as she hurried to the new section of dresses. This wasn't the dreamy memorable trip she had pictured, but they would remember it all the same. Gwen was still missing, still tending to her paper cut, no doubt. But Jenny didn't have long until she'd be back. And then she'd lose this chance to work with Bailey. She sorted quickly through five dresses, and a sixth, and as she came to the seventh she stopped. The dress was white, strapless with a sweetheart neckline, the kind Bailey had admired a few times in magazine ads. The skirt was hard to make out in the thick plastic bag, but it looked lovely, a mass of silk lace and layers that came out from a banded waist, just above the hip. Jenny stared at the gown. She had a feeling about this one. "Bailey," she took it from the garment bar and held it up. It was heavier than the others, for sure. "What do you think?"

"That?" Bailey hesitated but she shook her head. "It's pretty, but I don't know. Maybe we should come back another day. Gwen'll be back and then she'll take over."

Jenny studied the dress again. "You're already here. It'll just take a minute."

"Mom . . ." Bailey allowed a little whine in her tone. "That's not it. I can tell."

"Think of it this way." Jenny carried the

412

dress to Bailey. "Try it on and you can rule out this style. That'll take us one step closer to figuring out what you *do* like."

They watched Gwen hurry from one back room to another. She still seemed to be talking to herself. Bailey giggled and it was proof that she'd given in. "Okay. Let's go fast."

Together they took the new dress into the room and when Bailey was out of the simple off-white one, Jenny helped her into the new one. "The skirt weighs a ton." She was careful not to catch Bailey's hair this time. "It's so pretty, Bailey."

"I don't know." There were no mirrors in the small dressing room, so it was tough to tell.

Jenny zipped it up and admired the round silk buttons that ran down the center of the back. "Okay . . . let's see."

The dress had a pretty train that trailed maybe four feet behind her. Jenny picked it up and walked behind Bailey as they left the fitting room and headed for the pedestal. Bailey stood on it and faced the myriad of mirrors. Jenny fanned out the train and together they took in the sight of her.

Bailey breathed in sharp and held it. Her eyes softened and lit up all at the same time. "Mom!" She sounded dreamy and shocked at the sight of herself. "It's absolutely perfect."

"Wow . . ." A smile started in Jenny's heart and quickly became tears in her eyes. "It's like it was made for you, honey." The waist cut at an angle, and the satin that made up the middle of the dress shirred and gathered at the same angle. The effect was everything Bailey had hoped for in a dress.

"I can't believe it." Bailey turned one way and then the other, clearly disbelieving what she was seeing. "It's timeless and elegant and vintage and sexy and fashionable."

Jenny laughed through her tears. "Probably the only one in all the world."

Just then Gwen bustled over, her face a mask of embarrassment. "I'm so sorry about that terrible cut. So nasty. I've never had anything like that happen in all my days as a consultant and this would be just the time when —"

She stopped cold, stopped moving and talking and by the looks of it she might've even stopped breathing. "Bailey!" She stared at the image in the mirror. "You . . . you look like a vision." She called to the back. "Coco . . . hurry. You have to see this." She looked at Jenny. "Coco is our seamstress."

An older woman appeared from the back. She had a pincushion in her hand. "Yes?"

She walked toward them and as she reached Bailey, like Gwen she made a sudden stop. "My goodness . . . are you a model, dear?"

Bailey laughed, but even she couldn't take her eyes off the dress. "No."

"Well, no one's ever worn that dress the way you're wearing it." Gwen's words came more slowly now. "This is why I do this job." She seemed choked up as she looked at Jenny. "I could just cry. Your daughter is stunning."

Jenny couldn't think what to say or how to hold on to this most precious moment. She took a veil from a rack a few feet away and carefully placed it at the crown of Bailey's head. Her tears were immediate and she blinked to keep them from falling. In the mirror, her eyes locked onto Bailey's and like so many times over the years since Bailey was a very little girl, there were no words necessary.

Jenny knew only that here and now her daughter had found the dress. The perfect dress. The one she would wear to change her name and become Brandon Paul's wife. It had happened in a single instant, at the most unexpected place and the most unexpected time. On a day when they had laughed till they cried and when there had been no warning or signs that something deeply significant was about to happen.

Jenny came alongside Bailey and hugged her. "This is it."

"Yes." Bailey dabbed her fingers beneath her eyes again. "Brandon will love it."

And like that Gwen began talking about payment plans and how the dress was made by a designer, so they would order Bailey her very own and that the process might take three months and . . .

Jenny could only see Bailey . . . her sweet blue eyes and the love that was so clearly inside her. For God and her family, and at this moment for Brandon. Here in her wedding dress, for him most of all.

Never mind if this wasn't the dreamy way either of them pictured Bailey finding her dress. They were together, and because of that this day would always be special. The way every day with Bailey had been special in its own way since she was a little girl.

In no sort of hurry, Jenny helped her out of the dress, listening while Bailey gushed about the gown and about how she would feel on her wedding day when Brandon would see it.

Jenny listened, but deep inside she was seeing Bailey at two years old walking around in Jim's cowboy boots singing "Onward Christian Soldiers." And at six when she was being dropped off at her first day of kindergarten, looking nervously back at the classroom door because she didn't want Jenny to leave, and when she was eight years old coming home from school saying that she wanted Jesus as her Savior. Only Jesus. Always Jesus. And at thirteen with braces, crying because the boy she liked had liked someone else and a few blinks later when she was smiling for her high school senior portraits.

Where the time went, Jenny had no idea. Because here they were buying a wedding gown. Her sweet Bailey, her precious one-in-a-million girl, was getting married. The wonderful truth seemed much more real now that she'd found the dress. In no time Bailey would be married and she would start her life with Brandon. But despite all the times gone by, Bailey's wedding could never be an ending to what she shared with her only daughter. Rather it would be a beginning.

The most beautiful beginning of all.

TWENTY-SIX

Brandon was about to put his plan into motion, and he could hardly wait. He pulled up in front of Bailey's house and climbed out of his new Acura. He had moved to Indiana fulltime now, especially in light of the deal he had worked out last week. The same week Bailey found her wedding dress.

He smiled to himself as he jogged up the steps to her front door. She wouldn't tell him any details — which was fine with him — only that he would love it. The idea of Bailey walking down the aisle toward him in her dream wedding dress was almost more than he could take. He was filled with passion and desire and at the same time an ocean of love he couldn't begin to fully grasp.

For now he lived with Ashley and Landon in their spare bedroom. But in a few weeks he would move into a house. Their new home. Which was the surprise he had for her today. He'd been back and forth to Los Angeles wrapping up loose ends until just this week. Still, the amazing thought of not having to say goodbye for a very long time didn't seem real.

She appeared at the front door and for a long time they only looked at each other, their eyes lost to everything except each other. "Every time you pick me up it's something crazy, some wild surprise or dramatic moment." Her voice was soft. "But not today."

"Not today?" He stifled a laugh. If she only knew.

"No." Without looking away, she came closer and eased her hands around his waist. "Starting today we get to do life together." She leaned up and kissed him. "Because you live here. You really live here."

He looked into her eyes, at the trust she had for him. "I don't care if I ever see Los Angeles again." Laughter came from him but he was more amazed than humored. "Paparazzi even chased me to the airport." He hesitated, because their closeness didn't need constant conversation. "And guess what?"

"What?" They swayed slightly, neither of them wanting to let go.

"My realtor says he has someone interested."

Bailey stepped back, her brow raised.
"Really? Brandon, that's wonderful!"

"They might want it quickly. A month-
long escrow."

"That's great!"

Brandon had expected the sale to take a
year or longer. Either way he didn't care.
He would have a few of his things moved
here, the ones he'd designated for his new
life in Bloomington. Otherwise he would
enjoy shopping with Bailey, walking through
antique stores and furniture showrooms
looking for the pieces that would bring their
touch to the place he'd just bought. Whether
the offer came through now or not, Brandon
was willing to wait. He saw no reason to
hold onto the Malibu house. He wasn't
Dayne Matthews. No matter what offer
came up, he and Bailey would not move to
LA. Not unless God sent them a direct message telling them to go.

Otherwise they were here, and they were
home.

"Let's go." He ran a little ahead of her,
loving the way he could tease her and play
with her. They had more fun together than
any couple he knew. At least it seemed that
way. "The surprise might not be there if we

don't hurry."

She laughed and easily caught up to him. Once they were in his vehicle she turned smiling eyes to him, eyes that became more serious. "I don't need another surprise. Having you here, that's all I need. Not having to Skype and steal moments on top of the Empire State Building." She took his hand. "I couldn't want more than this."

"Still . . ." He couldn't stop smiling around her. "The surprise is waiting." He lifted his shoulders and let them fall again. "Whether you want it or not."

"Then let's hurry." She buckled her seat belt.

He played the list of songs he'd put together for their engagement. The one with "Angel" by Casting Crowns, and several other songs they'd come to love. Songs like "I Will Be Here" by Steven Curtis Chapman, and Newsong's "When God Made You." As that song came on Brandon thought how true the words were. When God made Bailey Flanigan, He must've been thinking about him — Brandon Paul.

Another song came on — Lady Antebellum's "Just a Kiss." A song that spoke of purity and passion and the importance of waiting for more of a physical relationship until marriage.

They sang along and Brandon caught glimpses of Bailey, the way she moved with the music, and her eyes when she looked at him. "We sound good together," he smiled. "Singing this song."

Bailey laughed, but he had a point. Their voices sounded beautiful together — Bailey singing along with the lead female singer and Brandon singing the guy's part. "Maybe you should quit acting and we'll hit the road. Brandon and Bailey."

"People would line up." Brandon was laughing, too, but more because it felt so wonderful to be together than because there was a thread of anything serious in the discussion.

He watched her again, drawn to her. Yes, the songs and scriptures were right. If they could survive from here to the wedding, sharing this beautiful passion without the physical love that would come after they were married, then they would be blessed for waiting. If they could hold to just a kiss goodnight, like the lyrics said, then God would bless them. With everything inside them they believed that and were determined to keep their commitment to stay pure with each other. Brandon talked to Dayne about it often, asking his older friend to pray for them and to hold him accountable. Bailey talked to her mom about ways they could avoid falling in any way, and Brandon was grateful. Because the chemistry between them was so intense Brandon knew they could only wait until the wedding with the help of God and the people who loved them.

"I get it. We're going to the lake." Bailey smiled and settled back in her seat. "That's a great surprise. Let's go back to where we got engaged. I love that place."

He smiled and let her talk. She had absolutely no idea. When they drove past the entrance to Lake Monroe, Bailey turned to him, clearly puzzled. "Where are we going?"

"You'll see." He could hardly wait to watch her reaction. The sun was setting quickly, so he kept his eyes on the road, his speed a few miles over the limit. "Any guesses?"

Bailey peered at the winding road ahead. "A hike?" She twisted her face, confused. "No. That wouldn't make sense. It's getting too dark."

"And it's cold." He shivered. "This LA boy has a long way to go to get used to Indiana falls. Hopefully the winter won't kill me." He grinned. "I picture wearing four or five layers at least."

They both laughed at the picture, and

then almost without warning the house was upon them. Brandon slowed down and pulled into a long driveway. At the end of it was a beautiful lakefront house, one with a wraparound porch and more windows than Brandon had counted yet — even though he had lived here with Katy and Dayne during the shooting of *Unlocked.*

"Brandon." She looked at him, unsure, like maybe he'd taken a wrong turn. "This is Katy and Dayne's house." Leaning over her knees she peered out the window at it, staring at the pretty roof as they pulled up near the porch and parked. "I love this place. I always see you when I drive by it. How long did you live here?"

"Most of the shoot. A couple months."

Bailey smiled at the house. "And I helped build it. It's the perfect place to talk."

He smiled. She had no idea. "Definitely perfect."

"So they're home? That's the surprise?" The idea clearly warmed her heart. "I haven't seen them since before we got engaged. I'd love to see their baby!" She started to step out, but before she could he put his hand on her knee.

"Hey." His tone was soft, and it was one more moment he knew he'd remember. "Katy and Dayne aren't here. That's not the surprise."

She sat back in the seat and studied him. "What do you mean? Like, we're walking down to the lake?"

"Well, yes. We'll definitely do that."

"Tonight?" She glanced at the sky.

"Maybe not tonight." He chuckled. "That's what I meant when I said it would go away. Because if we got here much later you wouldn't have been able to see it."

She looked dizzy, like he was talking in circles for all the sense she could make of the conversation. "See what?"

He couldn't string her along another second. "Reach in there." He pointed to the console between their seats. "See what you find."

"Brandon," she laughed, but it sounded more nervous than funny. "What are you doing?"

"You'll see." He watched her, realizing that this was the first of countless times they would park in this spot and hold a conversation. "Look."

Tentatively, like something living might jump out at her, she opened the console and looked inside. Again a puzzled look filled her face as she pulled out a set of keys. "We're going inside?" A light dawned on her face. "Oh . . . you made me dinner?

Here at Katy and Dayne's house? Where you used to live? I love that!" She started to come to him, as if she might hug him and thank him, but he tenderly caught the side of her face. As their eyes met he shook his head. "No."

"No?"

"Not Katy and Dayne's house." He hesitated. "It's ours, baby. Our house." He looked from her to the house and back to her again. "This is where we'll begin our life together."

"What?" She blinked a few times, the reality not even close to sinking in. "How . . . how is that possible?"

"They wanted to sell it. People do that." He chuckled, and quickly climbed out and went around to her door. "Come on. Come see your new house."

"Brandon . . ." She started laughing, but it was more the sound of disbelief. Slowly she stepped out of the Acura and for a long time she stared at the house and then back at him. "Are you serious?"

"Yes." He allowed a slightly nervous laugh. "You like it . . . I like it." He gave her a lopsided grin. "I figured it was an easy yes, right?"

"You're really serious?"

"Yes."

Suddenly she flung her arms around his neck and held on so tight he had to lightly take hold of her hands to see her. She caught her breath, her mouth still open from the shock of it. "Baby, thank you. I love it." She took hold of his face with both hands and he couldn't tell what was more beautiful: the gratitude shining in her eyes or the look of forever in her expression.

"I'm glad you're happy." He led the way up the porch steps and after a few seconds she put her hand on one of the sections of porch rail. "I painted this. All of us . . . we worked together to make this house ready for Katy and Dayne, after his car accident."

"I remember you saying that during the movie." He stopped, pensive. "Wish I could've seen it. Sounds like a home make-over episode."

"It was!" She blinked away the tears that were gathering in her eyes. "And now it's ours?"

"Yes."

She wrapped her arms around his neck again. After a long time she kissed him, searching his heart, seeing straight through him. "I can't believe it. I can't believe any of it's real."

"Well . . ." He rocked her in his arms, his tone leading her back to laughter. "The dirt inside's bound to make it feel real. Dreams don't usually come with dirty sinks."

"Oooh." Bailey winced, her eyes sparkling. "They haven't lived here for a year."

"A lot longer than that."

"Yikes."

"Yep." Brandon walked her up the porch steps. "We better get a broom and some bleach."

Laughter rang through the air as they walked into the house and he flipped on the lights. Brandon could see by Bailey's expression that she didn't mind the dirt. He had already hired a cleaning crew, but getting the garden out back planted come spring, or painting a couple walls, might be more fun to do on their own, together.

They walked through the house, and Bailey grew more excited with each room. Especially when they stopped in the master bedroom.

Katy and Dayne still had furniture in the house, things they planned to donate to an auction to raise money for World Vision. Dayne and Katy had become spokespersons for the group, and Brandon hoped he and Bailey could join them after the wedding. But for now, the bed was still here.

They sat together on the edge, and looked at each other. Without warning the air around them seemed to change. The windows had been closed, but other than a stale smell, the room was pretty clean. Brandon put his arm around her and kissed her, more slowly than before. "Baby . . . I wish it were March sixteenth."

"Mmm." She returned his kiss. "Me too."

He wanted to stay here, wanted to lay her gently down on the bed and kiss her. Just that. Because they'd never been in a bed together and right now the idea felt irresistible. Laying there on top of the covers, just being together. Nothing that would cross any lines, right? He closed his eyes briefly, struggling with the feelings warring within him. When he opened them he knew the answer. "We have to go." The words weren't his own, neither was the strength to say them. He stood and helped her to her feet. Her eyes told him she wanted to stay as badly as he did. But no matter what lie they told themselves about not letting things get crazy or out of hand, it was just that.

A lie.

Flee this, My son . . . seek My best.

"Brandon . . ." She put her arms around his neck and whispered in his ear. "I love you."

"I love you too." They were so alone, together here in the room where one day soon they would share the very great depths of their love. He drew her close and once more he felt the pull, felt it stronger than he had since he'd known her. He wanted her so badly. Laying down wouldn't hurt anything, would it? The temptation was persistent. But it was nothing next to the voice of God resonating in his soul. This was new for him, hearing God's voice or remembering a Bible verse in key moments like this. Right when he needed it. Scripture was right about this too. The only way to keep their promise to God and each other was to leave. Take the escape route God always provided for those who faced sin struggles.

I get it, Lord . . . I do. Thank You for Your truth. Help me find the way out.

From where they stood Brandon could see out the patio door onto the deck overlooking the lake. That's where they needed to be. Now, before he gave himself permission to compromise even a little. He kissed her again, their bodies close. The temptation had a way of gaining ground in seconds. He inched back, shaking a little, and he set his hands on her shoulders. "I have an idea." His desire was so great he almost didn't recognize his own voice. "Let's check out the view."

"I know the view." She didn't flinch,

didn't even look toward the window. "I worked on the deck. Remember."

He was losing ground. "Bailey . . ." He felt himself breathing just a little harder. He could fight this, but he'd need a miracle without her help.

Then almost as quickly as desire had seized the moment, Brandon watched Bailey's intentions shift, watched the rock-solid faith inside her rise to the surface. "Sorry." Her voice was barely audible, her smile more empathetic. She stood and stepped back, drawing a deep breath. "The important thing is, *we* haven't seen the view. Together." Her switch to innocent was beyond adorable. On her way out she looked back at him. "It's amazing out here. Come watch the sunset on the water."

Brandon exhaled and took hold of the bedpost as his resolve returned in full. Moments like this had to be avoided. He hadn't seen how quickly temptation could hit, but he would be smarter next time. No more bedrooms for them until after the wedding.

Bailey had left the door open, and once he was out on the deck he shut it behind them. Out back the view was familiar for both of them, but even fifty years from now he knew it wouldn't get old. They stood side by side, facing the water through the trees and staring at the setting sunlight against the lake. "So pretty." Bailey turned to him and smiled. "This is really ours?"

He only watched her, grateful again to be outside, to have avoided a scene they both would have regretted. "You're beautiful. Do I tell you enough?"

"You do." She leaned her head on his shoulder and looked at the view again. "It's so easy to think out here. Like I could sit on this deck and write a novel if I wanted to."

"Which you might want to someday." He nudged her, playing with her the way he loved to do. "I've probably given you enough material for a series."

Her laughter sounded wonderful. "Definitely."

For a while he didn't say anything, but then something hit him. He still hadn't finished telling her his own story, the one he'd started that day at the airport when she left for Indiana. The part of his story he'd remembered in detail on his Malibu back deck before turning down the contract. "Remember at the airport, how I told you God brought you into my life at the right time. How I'd been through a dark period four years ago?"

"Yes." She turned and leaned her hip

against the railing so she could see him. "You said God used me to help you believe you'd done the right thing." She angled her head, studying him. "You didn't give me details." She touched her hand to his cheek lightly. "Tell me."

"It won't be easy." He hadn't told anyone this. "But I want you to know. I planned on telling you sometime."

He took hold of her hands as he drew a full breath. "You know the beginning, how I felt about my parents before I moved to LA."

"Yes." Her eyes were kind, compassionate. The way they'd been that first day at Lake Monroe Beach. "You must've felt very alone."

"I did. I mean, the success happened so quickly and I was pulled toward things I never would've dreamed of doing."

Slowly, with a sort of relaxed inevitability, he told her about the one particular party. "I did things I wasn't proud of. It was a low moment in my life." He smiled, but he felt the sadness in his face. "I knew right from wrong. And after that night, I wasn't sure I'd ever feel good about myself again."

He told her how he'd come home and stared at the sleeping pills, and how he'd poured half the bottle into the open palm of his hand, and how the doorbell had stopped him. "That delivery from my uncle . . . it was the only reason I stopped long enough to think about what I was doing." He stared out at the water, letting the reality settle. When he looked back at her, she had tears in her eyes.

"I'm sorry. That's terrible."

Brandon nodded. "I figured someone must've been praying for me. Not my uncle, because he wasn't a Christian back then. But someone, somewhere. Because without the miracle of that doorbell, I wouldn't be here."

"Baby, that scares me." She hugged him for a long time and when she slipped back to her spot against the railing, she shivered a little. "How long ago was it? Four years?"

"Longer now." He didn't hesitate. "I know the date. I'll never forget it. February sixth of 2007. The day God saved my life."

Her reaction started in her eyes. They grew wide, almost fearful, and her expression became a picture of disbelief. "When?"

"Bailey, what's wrong?" He took a step closer and put his arms around her waist, steadying her. "You look like you just saw a ghost."

"Did you say . . . February sixth . . . 2007?" She searched his face, her shock getting even stronger.

"Yeah. Bailey . . . what?" He hadn't expected the date to stop her cold like this. The rest of the story was more compelling than the actual date. "Is that someone's birthday or something?"

"I can't tell you." She shook her head and moved toward the other sliding door, the one that led into the kitchen. "I have to show you. It's at my house."

Brandon had no idea what was going on. She'd never acted like this, but whatever she had to show him, it seemed vitally important.

She found her purse on the table and they returned to his Acura. On the drive home they listened to his playlist again, but Bailey didn't sing or say anything. But every few seconds she dabbed at a tear sliding down her cheek. Whatever it was, why that date held significance for her, the reasons were deeply emotional. Clearly.

At her house she told him she'd be right back, then she ran upstairs and returned a minute later. In her hand she held something that looked like a journal. "Come out back. I have to show you." Her face still looked serious, the moment obviously profound.

Brandon followed her out back to a glider

swing where they sat together. "I've never seen you so serious. This is about the date, right?"

She was flipping through pages almost frantically and then she stopped and held her spot. "Yes. It's about the date." She looked deep into his soul. "That same year, one particular night, I was feeling lonely and confused, not sure about the plans God had for me. I knew they were good plans." She smiled, the first time since he'd brought up the date of his near suicide attempt. "But I couldn't see proof in front of me. My dreams of dancing were up in the air, things weren't working out with Tim Reed, and Cody was away at war." She kept her pace even, her tone still more intense than usual. "My mom told me if I was doubting the plans God had for me in any way, and if I was feeling lonely, I should write a letter to my future husband." She smiled. "Which I did many times back then."

"Thank you." He kept his grin on the light side, allowing a little laughter into the moment.

But Bailey grew serious again right away. "But there was this one time when I felt compelled — absolutely driven — to pray for him. He was out there somewhere, and I felt God pressing it on my heart to pray as strongly as possible for him, because wherever he was, at that moment he was in grave danger. That's how I felt, and that's how I prayed."

A slight chill came over him and suddenly his attempts at humor fell away. "Go on."

"I'll always remember, because that day — I found out later — Cody Coleman was at war in a battle for his life. He should've died, but God gave him a miracle."

"That same day? When you felt God urging you to pray for your future husband?"

"Yes." She frowned a little. "I think that's why I held on to the idea of him for so long. Because when I found out about the battle and Cody's rescue, and how it all lined up on that day, I thought God was giving me a message."

Brandon didn't feel threatened by the news. "I get that."

"Even when I moved back here, I found this page in my journal and wondered about it. Like maybe I hadn't heard God right, or maybe I was supposed to pray for Cody just because. Nothing to do with him being my future husband."

"That could be it."

"No." She shook her head and the hint of a smile played in her eyes. "That's not it. This is completely crazy, Brandon. I mean it." She handed him the journal. "Here. See for yourself."

He didn't try to imagine what was on the page, because there was no telling. But he took the journal and it fell open to the spot where her thumb still marked the entry. She drew her hand back. "Read the date at the top of the page."

Brandon's eyes found the place and then, like a giant wave crashing in around him, the reality hit. No wonder Bailey had acted so strangely . . . no wonder she'd quietly cried the whole way home. Because the words at the top of her journal page were absolute proof that he'd been right. Someone had been praying for him, and that someone was Bailey Flanigan. She had been praying fervently for her future husband at the very hour of what could've been his death. Brandon knew all of this in an instant for one reason.

The date at the top of the journal page read February 6, 2007.

TWENTY-SEVEN

Bailey had never been so busy in her life. On top of the wedding plans, the deal had closed for her purchase of CKT. There had been time to add Brandon's name to the transaction, but he didn't think it was necessary. "It's your passion . . . you earned the money to buy it." He had told her that every time the subject came up. "It'll feel good to know you did it on your own. Just you and God."

He was right. She was able to put half the money down, and with her business plan, the payments on the balance would be very affordable. Yes, if she asked him, Brandon would've paid cash for the whole thing. The money he had in savings and investments from his films and endorsements over the last five years was more than they would spend in their lifetime.

But with God leading, work was supposed to be more than a way to make money.

She'd heard their pastor say that Christians should set out to be missionaries whatever their career choice. Missionaries on a bus or in a classroom or at a doctor's office. Bailey agreed fully. She couldn't wait to be a missionary with the kids from CKT. The way Katy Hart Matthews had been for Bailey and Connor and their friends so many years ago.

Between the purchase of the theater and the wedding plans, the holidays flew by and the New Year began with one of the most severe blizzards Indiana had ever seen. Their lake house was clean by then and ready for them to move their things in, but during the storm Brandon lived in the Flanigans' guest room over the garage. The drive out to the lake was impossible under the mountain of snow.

During that time and since then she and Brandon met with her parents to work through a Bible study for couples, a study called One-in-a-Million with a section devoted to guys and another for girls, and finally one that presented questions and scenarios every couple should look hard at before getting married.

The rough spots during the study were nothing that threatened their relationship, but when the conversation turned to his parents, Brandon grew quiet. "I still need to call them. It's worse now that Bailey made the first move."

"I wasn't trying to make things worse."

"I know, baby." He took her hand in his. "It's my fault. I need to contact them."

Bailey's dad had finally found a way to reach Brandon. "If your parents died in a car accident tomorrow, would you have regrets?" His voice was kind but firm, and Bailey admired him as she had so often over her lifetime. His direct and loving approach was what made him such a great coach.

Brandon had let the question settle and after several seconds his eyes filled with tears. "Yes. I'd regret that."

"Well, then . . ." Her dad gave a look that said there were no options here. "Looks like you need to call them."

Before the snowstorm let up, Brandon did just that. The conversation between them was brief and hesitant, but they made a plan for his parents to drive in for the weekend. They lived ten hours away, and they preferred the drive over flying. Bailey was with Brandon the day they arrived at the lake house.

Together they walked out onto the porch and watched his parents' car pull into the driveway. *Protect this moment, please, God.*

441

Bailey kept her prayers silent, willing the next few seconds to go well.

"I can't believe this," Brandon muttered. His teeth chattered, and he shivered beside her. "It's been so long."

His father was driving, and he parked not far from the porch. Already both their eyes were on Brandon. They stepped out of the car slowly and for a long time none of them made a move. Not Brandon or his parents, and certainly not Bailey.

Then, slowly at first, Brandon began to make his way to his mother. She held out her arms, tears streaming down her face. "Brandon . . ."

"Mom." He jogged the last few steps and wrapped her into a full hug, an embrace that lasted long enough to ease years of hurt.

Even from where she stood, wiping at her eyes, Bailey heard his mother's next words. She put her hand alongside Brandon's face and in a voice broken by years of regret she said, "Can you ever forgive me?"

Brandon was silently crying too hard to speak. His shoulders shook as he nodded and hugged her again.

By then his father had made his way around to that side of the car. The man's eyes were dry, but shame colored everything about him — the slow way he walked and the deep lines on his face. "Son." It was all he seemed to be able to say and then he, too, took Brandon in his arms and held on tight.

As if he might fall to his death if he let go.

Thank you, God . . . Bailey wiped away her tears. The moment, the weekend, all of it was exactly what Brandon and his parents needed to find forgiveness and the first steps toward healing.

By the end of January the wedding party was decided, and Bailey had found dresses for her bridesmaids. She had called Andi and asked her to be the maid of honor. Andi couldn't speak for several seconds, and when she did her voice held a mix of laughter and tears. "I can't believe this. I'm honored, Bailey. Really."

Andi and Cody were still dating — more seriously than before. Bailey and Brandon had talked about the fact that if Andi was her maid of honor, most likely Cody would be her date. But at this point they were both fine with that. For the most part, Bailey had been too busy to give the reality much thought.

The rest of the bridesmaids were four of Bailey's church friends and Katy Hart Matthews — whose little boy was already almost five months old. Brandon asked

Dayne to be his best man and Bailey's five brothers to be groomsmen. Ashley and Landon's son Devin would be their ring bearer, and Katy and Dayne's daughter, Sophie, would be the most adorable flower girl.

Eventually as things fell into place, the idea of Cody being at the wedding became the center of conversation for one of their premarital counseling studies. The question was one worth discussing. Could couples who had once dated be friends afterwards, and could they be guests at each other's weddings? Bailey's parents didn't have a strong opinion on the issue.

"Every situation is different. I could share a few guidelines according to the book, and from experience," Bailey's mom started the talk. "First, the former couple shouldn't talk about the past when they're together. Whether they were mostly friends or more than friends, the past was a time they shared exclusive to the new guy or girl in the picture. It can feel very divisive to sit around with an old girlfriend or boyfriend, even an old friend, and just reminisce about yesterday."

Bailey nodded. "That makes sense."

"I guess the issue is whether Cody should be at the wedding. Since invitations should go out in a couple weeks." Brandon leaned forward, his forearms on his knees, hands linked. His eyes were on Bailey's dad, whom he had come to trust in these conversations and counseling sessions. "I mean, is that sort of weird?"

"How do you feel about it?" Her dad's compassion was evident. "It's your wedding." He turned to Bailey. "And what about you, honey? Would it be weird?"

The question wasn't an easy one. Bailey felt like a different person from the girl she'd been back when she had feelings for Cody. "It makes sense, especially since he'd be Andi's date."

"Good point." Bailey's mom nodded. "That makes a difference."

"But what about you?" Her dad turned the conversation back to Brandon, who still hadn't answered.

"It really doesn't bother me." He straightened and caught Bailey's eyes. The love she saw there eased any concerns she might have had. He smiled at her parents. "Cody had his chance. He and Bailey weren't right together. And now he's happy with Andi. He'd be her date, like Bailey said."

"I'm okay with that. Really." Bailey gave a look that said she could make a case either way — including him or not having him at the wedding at all. "He's happy for me, that I'm getting married. It's not like he still texts me all the time or ever tries to come between me and Brandon." She shrugged one shoulder. "I mean, Cody was the one who told me to call Brandon after I left LA."

In the end they decided Cody would be invited. None of them saw any concerns that Cody's attention would be anywhere but on Andi, the girl he loved. Yes, Cody and Bailey had a past and there was something bittersweet about that. But even more, they had been friends. Family, practically. If everyone could handle the situation, and since he was so serious with Andi, it was fitting that Cody be at the wedding.

By the middle of February every detail for the big day was in place and Bailey's wedding dress had come in to the boutique. She and her mom went for a quick fitting, and other than a few adjustments, the gown was ready to go. They had finished arrangements with the florist and the DJ and the last-minute wedding planner, a friend of her mom's who worked weddings on the side. She'd come in for the final month to call vendors they had contracts with and oversee the execution of the various details.

Before she knew where the time had gone it was the third Saturday in February and

Bailey and her mom were driving back from the airport with Andi and headed to the bridal shower at Ashley Baxter Blake's house. The party was a more intimate gathering. The Baxter women — Ashley, of course, and her sisters Kari, Brooke, and Erin. Also Luke's wife, Reagan Baxter, and their step-mother, Elaine. Her bridesmaids would all be there, since Katy had flown in with Dayne a few days ago to direct the donation of furniture from the lake house garage. Brandon's mother had declined the invitation. Her husband had been sick lately, so she wanted to tend to him. But she called Bailey and said she'd be praying that the day was special. "God willing, we'll be at the wedding."

As they pulled into the driveway of the old Baxter farmhouse, Andi shivered. "I should've brought my coat. I forgot how cold Indiana winters are."

"You missed the storm." Bailey looked over her shoulder at the backseat where Andi was sitting. "Snow was halfway up our front door. Seriously."

Andi laughed. "I'll take LA."

"So you like it there? Enough to stay?" Bailey's mom hadn't caught up with Andi in a while. Bailey already knew her friend's answer.

"Yes. I love it, actually. It's warm every day and there's tons going on. The movie opportunities are everywhere and I can go to the beach whenever I want."

"Wow . . . you sound like you work for the tourism board." Bailey laughed. "I wonder if I would've felt different about it if it weren't so . . . well, you know."

"You mean if you weren't being hounded by paparazzi every minute." Andi sounded frustrated by the fact. "Uh, yes. You would feel a whole lot differently about it."

Bailey wondered. She loved Bloomington and at this moment she was sure she'd choose it with its snow and freezing Februarys, even if no tabloid in Los Angeles ever wanted her picture again.

They parked and Bailey's mom turned to Andi before opening her door. "Reagan will be here. She'll have little Johnny."

Andi's expression didn't change. "I know. I've been talking to Bailey about it, and Reagan and I talked yesterday. She's glad I'll have the chance to meet him again."

She sensed her friend's nervousness, so Bailey reached back and put her hand on Andi's knee. There wasn't time for a long conversation, but she felt for her friend. This would be the first time she'd seen the baby she gave up since he was born. Even so,

Andi had told her yesterday she wasn't worried about it or overly sad. She wanted to be at the party to celebrate Bailey's coming wedding. Seeing her birth son would only be God's way of showing her everything was okay, that she'd done the right thing. Andi had told Bailey she was convinced.

The other Baxters who would attend today felt the same way, from what Bailey had heard. There was nothing awkward about Andi being there. God would use the situation privately as He intended. Otherwise the day ahead was about Brandon and her, and the miracle of their love.

Bailey could hardly wait.

TWENTY-EIGHT

As they walked up the front steps Ashley opened the door. "Bailey! One month! Can you believe it?" She held her arms out and gave each of them big hugs as they walked in. "Help yourself to salad and bread. The food's on the table." Ashley walked inside with them. "I think we're waiting on a couple of your friends, Bailey. Otherwise we're all here."

Bailey hung back a little, chatting with Ashley as they entered the living room. She wanted to watch the moment play out with Reagan and Johnny without turning all the attention on Andi. Something that would make the moment more difficult than any of them wanted.

Erin and Brooke were in a conversation with Katy and Elaine near the salad table, and Reagan sat with Kari in the adjacent living room. Johnny was in her arms asleep, his long legs dangling off her lap. From here, the child's resemblance to Andi was even greater than it had been at the picnic. He was two now, sound asleep and looking like an angel.

Andi put her things down and walked tentatively toward the two women. Reagan spotted her first and smiled, motioning with her head. "Andi . . . you made it! Come sit with us."

She took the seat next to Reagan and stared at the boy. Bailey whispered to her mom. "I'll be back. I'm going to be with her. In case she needs me."

Her mom glanced across the room and then back at Bailey. "Good idea."

On her way to the seat beside Andi, Bailey said hello to the ladies by the salad table. Then she took the chair next to her friend and gave her a quick side hug. "Hi, Reagan . . . Kari."

Both of them said hello and congratulated her on the wedding. "A month from today, right?" Kari looked at ease.

"Yes. March 16. Four weeks." Bailey felt the thrill in a more real way. "I can't believe it's almost here."

Andi's eyes were still on little Johnny. "He's beautiful." She lifted her eyes to Reagan's. "Can I touch him?"

"Of course." Reagan also looked relaxed.

Their roles were clearly defined, and both of them were on board with that. This was merely a moment they knew would come one day, and probably again several times in the future. "He's a wonderful little boy. Full of light and adventure." She laughed. "A perfect match for Tommy."

Tommy — Luke and Reagan's older son — had always been known for his mischief. Bailey smiled as she pictured the two brothers.

Though Andi seemed to be listening, Bailey could tell that her entire attention was on the boy. As if he might break, Andi softly brushed her fingers along Johnny's arm. He stirred slightly and she drew back. "Sorry. I don't want to wake him."

"It's okay. He'll be hungry soon."

Bailey felt suddenly self-conscious. Like maybe she should leave her friend to this moment. She stood and motioned to Andi. "I'm going to get lunch."

Her words seemed to lift Andi out of the moment with Johnny and Reagan and back into the party. She grinned and nodded. "I'll join you."

The rest of the shower Andi visited with several of the women and Ashley led everyone through a trivia game to see how well they knew Bailey and Brandon and their love story. No one was surprised when Katy and Bailey's mom tied for the win.

Before the shower was over, Reagan took the floor. Johnny was asleep in his portable playpen in the den as she took her Bible from the diaper bag and looked at the faces that filled the room. "When I married Luke, my wonderful future sisters-in-law and Luke's mother threw me a shower in a New York hotel room." She smiled at Ashley. "My relationship with Luke didn't start out the way we hoped. Most of you know we had Tommy before we were married."

Bailey knew this, and she was pretty sure Andi did. Reagan's confession was proof that no one came to the room perfect.

She ran her hand over the Bible and continued, her eyes soft and full of meaning. "Everyone went around the room and shared a favorite Bible verse, something that would help Luke and me as we headed into marriage." She turned to Bailey. "That's what we want to do now, for you, Bailey."

Everyone used the moment to pull what looked like decorated index cards from their purses. Bailey had had no idea this was coming, and she was touched by the surprise and the meaning behind it.

"Since I know how much I needed this at my shower, I'll go first." Reagan pulled a card from the front of her Bible. "Mine is from Ephesians, chapter four." She read the verse slowly, each word speaking straight to Bailey's heart. Especially the last part: "Be kind and compassionate to one another, forgiving each other, just as in Christ, God forgave you."

Reagan talked about how she and Luke had struggled at times before and after their wedding, and always that verse would bring them back to the place of love, to the way they felt on their wedding day. "Just be kind to each other and forgive." Reagan met Bailey's eyes across the room. "You can get through anything if you have that."

"Thanks, Reagan." Bailey imagined a time years from now when she would look through these Bible verse cards and remember the importance of being kind and forgiving. It was a marriage manual all in itself. "I've read that verse a lot of times, but never in light of being married. I won't forget what you said."

A few chairs over, Kari Baxter Taylor smiled. "Funny how important forgiveness is. We didn't compare notes, but mine's almost like that. It's from Colossians, the third chapter." She looked at her card. "Bear with each other and forgive whatever grievances you may have against one another. Forgive as the Lord forgave you."

Bailey felt the familiar goose bumps, the way she reacted whenever she was certain God was speaking to her — in quiet ways from within or through people he brought into her path. Clearly God intended a personal message here, and Bailey was determined to remember it always. She could never let things get so bad or so distant with Brandon that she didn't stop to forgive or to apologize.

The rest of the verses had to do with clinging to each other and working together, loving in a way that was patient and not easily angered, and serving one another. Her mom went last. She smiled at Bailey and before she could speak tears filled her eyes. Bailey was sitting beside her, and she took hold of her hand. "It's okay." She spoke softly, encouraging her mom the way her mom had encouraged her so often over the years. They'd so enjoyed the season of wedding planning that emotional moments like this had been rare.

But Bailey understood. This was her wedding shower, and the insight her mom would pass on to her now had to culminate a lifetime of wisdom. Her mom struggled a moment longer and then found her voice. "I think you know the verse I chose for you.

Ever since you were a little girl I've told you to hold onto this Scripture, to believe it and live like it was absolutely true." Her eyes welled up a little more. "And you've done that." She looked at the card in her hand. "The verse is Jeremiah 29:11." Her eyes found Bailey's again. Reading wasn't necessary. They'd both known the verse by heart for years.

Her mom's tender voice spoke the words to a place in Bailey's soul where they would live forever. " 'For I know the plans I have for you,' declares the Lord, 'plans to prosper you and not to harm you, plans to give you hope and a future.' "

The two of them might as well have been the only ones in the room. Bailey leaned closer to her mom, wrapped both arms around her shoulders, and hugged her for a long time. "I always believed it."

"And it was always true." Her mom kissed her cheek and hugged her one more time. "Your life is an illustration of that, Bailey. God's promises are alive in you and Brandon. He's given you more than we could've asked or imagined."

Her words were more meaningful than anyone else in the room might've known. Because until that past summer, her mom had been certain that Cody Coleman was the guy who held Bailey's future. Here . . . she was telling Bailey a very specific truth: that in Brandon, Bailey had been given God's very best. More than her mom could've asked for or imagined during all those years when they talked about the plans God had for her.

Their hug lasted a few more seconds and then Bailey grabbed a tissue from the table and handed a second one to her mom. "You're the best. I wouldn't be who I am without you."

Her mother's smile said she felt the same way about Bailey.

As the shower wound down, Bailey collected her gifts — mostly beautiful lingerie and pretty lotions and soaps. Things that would make being married even more fun. The Baxter women all headed out about the same time, except Reagan. She had Johnny on her hip and she came up while Bailey was talking to Andi. Bailey noticed her, and she took a step back. Reagan smiled at her in thanks, and then directed her words to Andi. "I'd love it if you and I could share a few minutes."

"Do we have time?" Andi lifted hopeful eyes toward Bailey's mom, who was in the kitchen helping Ashley clean up.

"Absolutely." Bailey's mother motioned

for Andi to go. "Take your time."

Bailey took a few steps back. "Definitely. I'll help out too. We can leave whenever you're ready."

This was a moment Bailey had prayed for, that her friend would have the chance to hear from Reagan alone. Not only so they could talk privately about what a gift her decision had brought into the Baxter family, but also so God could use Reagan to speak peace and healing into Andi's heart.

Even while they did the dishes, Bailey thanked God that these days Andi believed the message of Jeremiah 29:11 as strongly as Bailey had always believed it. The two of them had talked about that recently, and how at this point Cody Coleman seemed to be part of God's plans for her. For Andi, God's plans didn't only include what He had given her. But in what He had led Andi to give away as well.

The great and precious gift of her son.

Andi followed Reagan into the den, the whole time wondering what she would say or how she would say it, and most of all how she would survive the next few minutes without breaking down. Johnny was fully awake now, and Reagan set him down as they reached the other room. Then she spread out a mat with the picture of a racetrack and handed him a toy car. "There you go, buddy."

"Johnny play?" He turned adoring blue eyes at her and pointed to the mat. Andi caught the fact that he didn't seem to notice her.

"Yes . . . you can play." Reagan smiled at him. "Stay in here, okay?"

"K, Mommy." He laughed and dropped to the floor and began racing the toy car around the pretend track.

"He doesn't stop moving." She sat in the nearest chair and Andi took the one beside her.

"I didn't realize he'd be talking." Andi was mesmerized by the child on the floor, the son she gave birth to.

"Our kids have all been big talkers." Reagan laughed. "He fits right in."

Our kids . . . Andi let the words rattle around in her heart until they felt comfortable. It was true. Johnny was Reagan's son. But he was Andi's son too. No question his lightly tanned skin was proof of his father's Middle Eastern roots. But otherwise he looked just like her. Right down to his pale-blond hair. She struggled to look away from him and back to Reagan. "Is he always this sweet?"

"Usually." She smiled at the boy. "He's been cutting new molars. That can make him pretty fussy."

"Hmm." Andi had her eyes fixed on Johnny again. "He seems so happy."

"He is." Reagan grew more serious. She turned kind eyes toward Andi. "He's a beautiful part of our family." She sighed, her look deeper than before. "I wanted to tell you something, before we said goodbye today." She reached over and put her hand on Andi's shoulder. "I wanted to thank you."

Andi felt the tears, felt them as surely as her next heartbeat. She nodded, unable to talk, and at the same time Johnny stood up and seemed to notice her for the first time. Still holding his toy car, he walked to her and put his hand on her knee. Then his eyes lit up and he grinned at her. "Hi."

"Hi, there." She looked at the little boy and their eyes met. *Does he remember me? My voice or my perfume?* She didn't ask the questions, but she couldn't help but think them.

"That's Andi." Reagan told him. She gave her a sideways grin. "He loves long hair." She flicked at her bobbed cut. "When we're out, he says hi to any girl with hair past her shoulders. Luke keeps saying we have to break him of that before he starts school."

Andi smiled, her eyes still on the boy. At the same time, he held out his arms. "Up?"

"It's okay." Reagan sat back, still relaxed. "You can pick him up."

This wasn't something Andi had counted on for today, but deep inside she'd hoped for it. She lifted Johnny onto her lap as he held his car out to her. "Johnny's car."

"Ohh." Andi took it and turned it several directions before handing it back. "I like it."

He raced it around in the air making engine sounds with his mouth. Then — just like that — the moment was over. He pointed to the mat again. "Johnny play."

"Okay." She eased him back to the floor. As they broke contact, the weight of the loss in her heart was so great she wondered if she could take it. "He's so beautiful."

"He is." Reagan smiled again. "He looks just like you."

"He does." She uttered a light laugh, one that was more disbelief. "I looked a lot like him when I was his age."

Once more from the mat, the boy who had grown inside her, the child who would always be her firstborn, looked at her and flashed a toothy grin. He held her gaze so long Andi had to wonder if it was possible. Did he know who she was? Tears filled her eyes despite her smile, and she had to blink to see him clearly.

About that time he did a half turn and ran to Reagan. "Mama!"

The word ripped at Andi's soul and made her rejoice at the same time. Because whether Johnny had a sense about who *she* was, he definitely knew who his mother was. And who she was not.

Andi watched him run to Reagan and the feel of watching him go was no less painful than it had been the first time she gave him up. Two hot tears splashed onto her cheeks and she brushed them away quickly. "Sorry." Her voice was strained, barely loud enough to hear. "I didn't think it'd be this hard."

Reagan put her hand on Andi's shoulder once more. "How do you feel now? More than two years after giving him up?" Reagan's concern was genuine. She clearly cared how Andi was doing. "I've wanted to ask, but I figured it'd be better in person."

Andi nodded, massaging her throat with her fingertips so the tightness would go away. "I'm fine. Really." She smiled at Reagan, grateful this was the woman God had brought along to adopt her son. "I'm dating Cody Coleman. You remember him?"

"I do. He was at a lot of get-togethers with

this group for many years. The two of you are serious?"

Andi thought about Cody and a warm feeling worked its way through her. "I feel like all my life has led to this, to the two of us being together."

"That's wonderful." Reagan hesitated, like she was waiting to hear more about how Andi felt. "He knows about Johnny?"

"He does. We knew each other in college, so he was aware of the situation." She couldn't help but stare as the boy put his chubby arms around Reagan's neck, completely comfortable in her embrace. The scene made Andi's empty arms ache, even as her heavy heart felt fuller than it had all day. Johnny scrambled down again and ran to the mat once more. Since he was not focused on them, Andi wanted to be honest. "You asked me how I feel." She looked at Reagan, her voice low. "I feel completely convinced that I did the right thing. I wasn't ready to be a mom. And I have nothing but terrible memories of the guy who . . . the birth dad." She smiled at the little boy. "It was the right thing. Definitely." She paused. "Even though I long for a time down the road when I'm married and ready to have my own baby."

"I understand." Reagan listened, her

expression full of peace. "God alone could've brought our families together, and He did it without either of us even knowing that we already had a connection through the Flanigans. You did the right thing, Andi."

"Thank you. I needed to hear that." Andi sniffed a little and once more she looked at the child playing on the floor. "And thanks for letting me have this time."

"We told you that when you chose us to be his parents. We'll raise him to know who you are and how your decision was rooted in the deepest love."

"I appreciate that."

Andi stood up. Their time together was over. Nothing left to say or do. But before they could head into the kitchen again, Reagan stood and prayed for Andi, that God would bless her relationship with Cody and that she would feel the Lord's divine peace whenever she thought about giving her son up for adoption.

Andi hugged her and Johnny at the same time and she thanked Reagan again. As she walked away, Johnny called out, "Bye!"

She stopped and turned around, and one final time, their eyes met and held. "Bye, Johnny. Be good for your mama."

He giggled and threw his arms around Reagan. At that, Andi met up with the others and as Bailey's mom drove away, Andi quietly thanked God for the very great chance she'd been given that day. She reminded herself that she was at peace with her decision. Absolutely. Still, with everything in her she knew she would remember two things from this day for the rest of her life. The way he had looked at her for that single sweet moment.

And the way it felt to have her baby boy in her arms one more time.

TWENTY-NINE

The days and weeks seemed to drag on, but only because Brandon could hardly wait. Not only for the wedding but for the honeymoon. He was surprising Bailey with a week at a South Pacific resort on Turtle Island in Fiji. The island was secluded and green and covered with low-lying mountains and stretches of white sand beaches. The water was shallow and warm and blue, and every day was paradise. Brandon had gone there once for a movie shoot a year before he met Bailey. The resort — the only one on Turtle Island — included residences for just fourteen couples. It was a famous spot even back in the 1980s when the movie *Blue Lagoon* was filmed there. They would fly to LAX and then to Fiji, and finally take a small seaplane into the harbor at Turtle Island.

For their honeymoon, Brandon rented out the whole place.

Dreams of their honeymoon fended off the chilly winter while Brandon and Bailey stayed busy painting several rooms in the lake house. They had constant help — not just with the paint but in finding new ways to keep from being alone. And in that way they survived February and rounded the corner into March. The new private life Bloomington afforded Brandon was something he still couldn't fully believe. Almost every day he told Bailey he had just one regret.

That he hadn't done this sooner.

The icy winter left in a hurry and starting the Friday before their wedding Indiana's March temperatures became the warmest in five years. Most of the rehearsal at Clear Creek Community Church was a blur. But Brandon would always remember bits and pieces. The way Bailey's parents looked at each other as the practice began, a beautiful look of love that had come full circle. Love that remembered standing in a church like this and being the couple all the fuss was about. And a love that had only become stronger on the way to watching their daughter make that same commitment.

Watching her find that same kind of love.

Brandon would remember that, and he would remember the way Bailey seemed to walk on air, flitting from one bridesmaid to the next making sure everyone had their dresses and shoes and the vintage necklaces she'd given them at a luncheon earlier that day. He watched her as often as he could. As long as no one was asking him anything his eyes were on her. She was a vision, a miracle, an answer to every prayer he'd ever said. Her prayers had helped save his life, after all. And he would remember the way her eyes danced as they held hands and stood in the same place they would stand tomorrow when it was the real thing.

"This is really happening!" she whispered as she leaned close to him, a soft squeal coming from her. "I'm so happy, Brandon."

He would remember that.

And he would remember his parents arriving at the church. They walked in through the back doors and stopped a few feet inside. Just stopped and stared at him as if they still couldn't believe he'd forgiven them or that they were privileged enough to be part of his life. He excused himself from the group of Bailey's brothers and walked down the aisle to meet them. This time their hugs came easier. His father wrapped him in the biggest, warmest embrace, a hug that said everything they hadn't said since Brandon was a teenager. And his mom put her arms around both of them, the tears on her face proof that they all still needed time to find true healing. Either way, as he watched his parents walk through the back door of the church during the wedding rehearsal, he felt like any other normal groom. He had parents.

A reality he would always connect to this day.

But most of all he would remember the way it felt after the rehearsal dinner when they left the church's fellowship hall and it was time to go their separate ways. When Brandon pulled Bailey around the corner of the church and kissed her goodbye. He would remember it because the next time he kissed her she would not be Bailey Flanigan.

She would be Bailey Paul.

Clearly she was thinking the same thing because she whispered to him as she looked straight through to his already full heart, to the heart that had belonged to her from the beginning, "After tonight, I never have to go home without you. Never again." She kissed him. "Isn't that the most amazing thing?"

"Not as amazing as your eyes tonight."

Her expression grew deeper, more sensual. "Not as amazing as *tomorrow* night. When the party's over."

"Mmmm." Brandon touched his lips to hers and the kiss grew until for the last time as long as he lived he did what he would never have to do again.

He took a step back.

And he realized he would also remember the look on her face in that moment as they said goodnight — the love and trust, the faith and hope, the intense and innocent passion . . . Without a doubt he would remember that.

He would remember all of it, and as he turned in that night he remembered one enormously important aspect of this, their wedding weekend.

The faithfulness of God, who alone had brought them to this point, and who would weave their hearts together from this day forward. So that one day when they had a precious daughter and she fell in love and found herself standing at the front of a church looking into the eyes of the man who was everything to her, Brandon and Bailey would be lost in their own moment, caught up in a look of love that had survived the decades.

Like Jim and Jenny Flanigan.

Bailey didn't want to be out too late the

night before her wedding. She'd had a plan since she was twelve years old about how she would spend this night. After saying goodnight to Brandon, she headed home with her parents and brothers. All of them, together in the family car, the way she doubted they would ever be all together again.

"It's sort of weird." Ricky sat behind Bailey. He put his hands on her shoulders and leaned close. "It's like the last night you're part of our family."

"Ricky!" Connor sat beside Bailey, and at that comment he turned, more surprised than outraged. "Don't say that."

"You know what I mean." Ricky allowed a little frustration into his tone at the possibility of being misunderstood. "Like after this she won't live here and she'll ride around with Brandon." He looked at their mom in the rearview mirror. "Right, Mom? You get it, don't you?"

Her eyes shifted to Bailey's, and in a handful of seconds a lifetime of memories flashed in her sad smile. She turned back to Ricky. "Yes, honey. I get it."

"Yeah, but she'll still be part of our family." Connor slipped his arm around her shoulders. "She'll be over all the time and nothing will change."

Bailey let the thought hang in the warm air that blew through the open Suburban windows. As she did, she slowly rested her head on Connor's shoulder. From the corner of her eyes she saw a single tear roll down Connor's cheek. She wasn't surprised. Her brother, the one who had been her best friend growing up, certainly knew that the truth was something they would all have to accept.

After tomorrow everything *would* change.

They pulled into the driveway just before nine, and as they climbed out of the SUV her dad turned to her and held up his hands, giving her a look that said the decision was hers. "Are we on?"

"Absolutely."

"Good." Her dad smiled even while his eyes glistened. "I've looked forward to this since the first time we saw it together." Her dad and mom joined hands. They walked a few steps ahead and her mom smiled back at her as they went. "I'll get it set up."

"I'll make popcorn." Justin held the door for their mom and then ran ahead of their parents. "Hot popcorn coming up!"

Shawn and BJ hurried in behind the others as Ricky came up and gave Bailey a side hug. "What I said . . . I didn't mean anything by it." He looked into her eyes.

"Okay?"

"Ricky." She put her arms around his waist and hugged him for a long time. "Of course not." Her eyes looked up and she gasped lightly. "What's happening here? When did you get so tall?"

He grinned. "Six-foot-four." With great relish he stuck his chin out. "Taller than any of the other Flanigan boys. Even dad. That's pretty good for fourteen years old."

"It is." She looked down at his feet. They were seriously the longest feet she'd ever seen this close up. "What about your shoes?"

"Size sixteen." Again he puffed out his chest. "Dad says it'll be a while before my age catches up to my shoe size."

Bailey wondered how she'd missed this. He was tall, of course. Always tall. But almost overnight he had changed. He didn't look like a kid anymore. Now he was a young man. "I promise this." She gave him a pointed look, enjoying the time with him. "I'll be around a lot. And the way I love you will never change." She kissed his cheek. "Okay, buddy?"

"Okay." The answer seemed enough for him. He bound inside after the others and as Bailey grabbed her purse from the seat and shut the door, Connor stepped out of the shadows. "Hey."

"Hey." She stopped and angled her head. "You okay?"

"Yeah. I guess." He dug his hands deep into his pockets. "I love Brandon. You two are perfect together." Tears welled in his eyes and he cleared his throat, trying to find his voice. "It's just . . . it's gonna be weird having you live somewhere else."

She could've told him that she'd already lived somewhere else for the year she danced on Broadway, or when she was in LA. But she understood what he meant. Those places were never home. And now her home would be at the lake house with Brandon. She waited long enough to acknowledge that he had a point. Then she linked arms with him. "You and I . . . we won't ever change. Our times at CKT, the growing up years . . . Christmas mornings."

"The movie lines and inside jokes." He chuckled, even though his cheeks were red from holding back his tears. "The dance parties in the kitchen."

"Right." She laughed too. "All that will always be here." She touched the place over her heart. "And here." She looked around the big garage and toward the back door. "Every time I'm home."

He nodded and coughed again. Then, in a move that she believed must've taken all his effort, he smiled big and nodded toward the house. "Let's go watch the movie."

By the time they walked inside their mom and dad had the movie on the big screen in the TV room paused and ready to play. The popcorn was made and BJ was handing out water bottles. "Definitely a chick flick," he raised his brow at Bailey. "But this once I guess it makes sense."

Everyone laughed and after Bailey poured herself and her mom a cup of tea, they sat around the room, all eight of them. One last night with the whole Flanigan family. The movie, of course, was Steve Martin's *Father of the Bride.* Bailey sat between her mom and dad, and Connor sat on the floor beside her, his back against the couch. From the opening line the movie was funnier and deeper, more emotional than any other time when Bailey had watched it. Same for the rest of them, she was pretty sure.

They laughed out loud when George Banks started the movie saying how he used to think weddings were a simple affair — until he threw one. And Bailey's dad exchanged a look with her at several points — when George gave Annie an espresso machine and when they were in the hallway of their house the night before Annie's wedding and her little brother told her goodnight and that he loved her. Because in that moment George knew what Bailey's dad knew at this very hour.

That tonight was here at last.

Through the hysterical planning Bailey laughed so hard she had tears. But her tears didn't start for real until the wedding scene when through voice-over George Banks realized that Annie was all grown up and leaving them, and something inside him began to hurt.

Bailey's dad reached over and took her hand. "I love you, honey." His voice was low so the others could still hear the movie.

"I love you too."

She fought her emotions through the beautiful wedding and even through the frustrating scenes when poor George couldn't get a minute alone with his daughter. Bailey didn't watch the movie so much as she lived in every scene. "Dad," she whispered. "If there's a problem tomorrow, don't get caught up in the details. Stay close so you don't miss anything!"

"Got it." He gave her a thumbs up. "You don't have to tell me twice."

When the movie was over, Bailey's dad turned off the TV and smiled at the group of them. "I love this. Having us all together."

He didn't add that it was for one last

night, but everyone felt the hours melting off the clock. Tomorrow would come and this moment would pass. But for now they all seemed to savor the look and feel, the familiarity and joy of having them all together in one place. Her dad pulled his Bible off a nearby table and opened it. "You all know this, but your mom and I have prayed for each of you kids, about your future spouses since you were born." He smiled at Bailey. "Which means we've prayed for Brandon Paul since we first brought Bailey home."

There were no funny remarks or silly laughs. Everyone in the room seemed to understand that God was among them, and that He was smiling at the wedding about to take place. Her dad read from 1 Corinthians 13 — The Love Chapter.

"Love is patient; love is kind. It does not envy, it does not boast, it is not proud."

The words resonated in Bailey's heart as she looked around the room. Her family wasn't perfect, but they were an illustration of the verses. Bailey looked at Connor and she remembered a thousand times when he had refused to take credit for one good thing or another. Same with her younger brothers. Her dad continued. "It does not dishonor others, it is not self-seeking, it is not easily angered; it keeps no record of wrongs."

A smile tugged at Bailey's lips. Weren't those the words her mom had always used whenever she and her brothers disagreed? Love kept no record of wrong, no list. It was something else she would take to her new life with Brandon.

"Love does not delight in evil but rejoices with the truth." Her dad turned to her, his eyes full of yesterday. "It always protects, always trusts, always hopes, always perseveres." He paused. "Love never fails."

"Amen." Ricky clapped his hands and looked around. "That's what I'm talking about. Love doesn't fail." He pointed at Bailey. "And it doesn't end."

Bailey laughed. "Definitely not."

They all said goodnights and I-love-yous, and as they shared hugs and headed for bed, Bailey spent a few more minutes with her mom. "You know what's strange?" Bailey sat at one of the kitchen counter barstools, one leg tucked beneath her.

"What?" Her mom finished heating up her tea and took the seat next to Bailey. "What's strange?"

"I thought I'd be sadder."

Her mother's expression was tender, understanding. "It's the happiest time of your life."

"I know, but all the lasts." She put her hand over her mom's. "Even this." She looked around slowly. "How many times have we sat here and talked?" Bailey folded her hands on the counter, still sorting through her feelings. "But I know I can still come home. We'll sit here and talk like this a thousand more times, at least. So I guess all I'm really thinking about is tomorrow." Her smile grew bigger, filling her face. She could feel it. "I can't wait to be married to him."

"Which —" her mom gently touched Bailey's arm and kissed her forehead, "— is exactly how it should be."

Bailey took her mom's words with her to bed, and even as she blinked back tears at the sight of her suitcase packed and standing along her bedroom wall, she knew what her mom said was true. God had brought Brandon into her life. Love had walked quietly through the back door of her heart and moved in before Bailey could do anything to stop it. Now, the night before her wedding, the reason was obvious.

God had created Brandon just for her.

March 16 dawned sunny with a cloudless sky, the perfect backdrop to the warmest day of the year so far. Bailey ate breakfast with her family and her bridesmaids, who met at the house at nine that morning. Then the group of them headed out to get their hair done. Bailey didn't plan to wear hers up or in a bun, the way some brides did. Instead she had the stylist pin up just a few strands, leaving the rest to fall in layers down her back and near her face.

Her bridesmaids followed her home and by one in the afternoon the photographer arrived. By then she and the girls were upstairs where her mom was about to help her into her dress. For the first few seconds Bailey and her mom could only laugh as they took the dress off the hanger and carefully lifted it over Bailey's head.

"We didn't snag my hair." Bailey allowed the giggles to pass. "That has to be a good sign."

But they both grew quiet the moment the dress was in place and Bailey's mom zipped it up. "Bailey, you've never been more beautiful." Her mom spoke softly as she fastened the faux silk buttons so they'd lay in a straight row down her back.

"Thank you, Mom. For everything." They stood side by side as Bailey looked at her reflection in the floor-length mirror. She hadn't seen it until now, but suddenly there was a resemblance that made her proud to be her mother's daughter. "I look a little like you did when you got married."

"You do." Her mom took a few steps back, studying her, the way the dress looked on her. "The gown . . . it's breathtaking. Everything about it." Her mom's eyes grew teary, and her voice trembled a little. "But I have to say . . . it's nothing to your eyes." She smiled, despite the very deep emotions between them. "The eyes are the windows to the soul. That's why yours are so full of light."

Bailey turned to her and took both her hands tenderly in hers. "You've always been the best mom. My best friend."

"Raising you has been one of my life's greatest gifts." She brushed at a few tears on her cheek and blinked. A sound more cry than laugh came from her. "Okay . . . I need to get a grip. I'm glad I haven't done my makeup."

Bailey laughed too, but she stepped closer and for a long while she hugged her mom. "I remember something." She eased back. "You told me I'd know he was the right guy if he couldn't leave the room when I was singing."

"Yes."

Throughout the wedding planning Bailey

hadn't thought about those long ago words of wisdom from her mom. But they were vivid in her mind now. She smiled. "And all I can see is Brandon in the front row at the theater watching me in *Hairspray* night after night after night. Nothing could've made him miss me sing."

Her mom's eyes were damp again. "He pursued you like a dying man in the desert goes after water."

"He did." Bailey thought of a hundred times when Brandon had done that, fought for her. Even at the end that past Fourth of July when he refused to believe they were broken up. A quiet laugh slipped from her happy heart. "I didn't make it easy."

Andi laughed as she walked out of the bathroom. "No, you definitely didn't make it easy." At that moment she caught the first look at Bailey in her wedding dress. As she did she drew in a sharp breath. "Bailey! You didn't tell me it was this pretty." For a long time she only stared in awe and then, blinking back her own tears, she simply looked at Bailey with a smile that covered years of friendship. "It's perfect. Like you and Brandon."

Before Bailey could respond, Katy Hart Matthews and the other bridesmaids returned to the room once more. They circled around her, remarking at the way she looked all over again, and agreeing with Bailey's mother that no dress could've fit better or been more stunning for her than this very one. Bailey was so glad they liked it and as she slipped into her shoes and her mom adjusted her veil she felt like she'd fallen into a fairytale where for this one most wonderful day, she wasn't just any girl making her way through life.

She was a princess.

THIRTY

Brandon arrived at the church an hour before the wedding and waited with Bailey's brothers and his parents in the church's hospitality room, just down the hall from the sanctuary. Security would remain stationed discretely around the church campus in case paparazzi discovered the location, but Brandon didn't think that would happen. They'd leaked a false date to the press in a release, so the public wasn't expecting the wedding until two weeks from now. Their guests knew not to say anything about the actual date, and so far the plan seemed to have worked.

Brandon paced the back wall of the small room and tried to grasp what he was feeling. Nothing in his life, no role he'd ever played or powerful business meeting at any studio had ever prepared him for the way he felt as he dressed in his black suit and white shirt and vest, and as his mom helped him fix the knot in his white tie.

The consuming sense had come over him when he woke up that morning and it had stayed strong with him up until this moment. He paced the room, glancing at the clock on the wall. It was a feeling that at any moment someone from some shadowy backstage or out-of-camera angle was going to yell "Cut!" and that would be that. Magical, unforgettable story over. Camera crews would pack up, the cast would say their goodbyes and the love story that was Brandon and Bailey would end the way it started.

Without warning.

Dayne knew him better than any of the guys in the room, and finally he was the one who pulled Brandon aside. "You okay, man?" His friend studied him, concerned. "You look out of it."

"Yeah, kind of." Brandon let loose a sigh that seemed to come from his Italian dress shoes. "It doesn't feel real."

An understanding smile lifted Dayne's expression. "We talked about this, remember?"

They had. When the bridesmaids got together for their luncheon yesterday afternoon, Dayne and Brandon had sat on the back deck of the lake house and talked about marriage, about honoring their wives and protecting them. Learning and lasting when everyone else might walk away.

But most of all they talked about loving.

What it meant to really love, to lay down their own needs and spend a lifetime consumed with those of their wives. And to bravely take a stand for lifelong marriage even in a world where people walked away far too often. How to live with that forever love Francesca Battistelli sang about in her song.

During their talk, Brandon hadn't felt frightened at all. He couldn't wait to love Bailey like that, to devote his life to loving her. He shook his head, puzzled by the unsettling mix of disbelief and thinly veiled fear. "It isn't that. I'm not afraid to take this step." He rubbed the back of his neck looking for the right words. His single laugh sounded as baffled as he felt. "I'm afraid to lose her. Like I couldn't handle that, you know? And like I'm not sure I can breathe right until she's standing in front of me saying, 'I do.' "

Dayne's expression relaxed and a smile filled his face. "That, my friend —" he took firm hold of Brandon's shoulder, "— is exactly how you're supposed to feel."

A looser bit of laughter came from Brandon and he remembered to exhale. "It's like it was one thing to win her love, but to have the gift of Bailey Flanigan all my life?" He looked over his shoulder and off to the corners of the room where the other guys and Brandon's parents were caught up in talk about the NFL draft. "Like I keep expecting a director to jump out and tell us it's a wrap. End scene. Roll credits."

"Brandon . . . what happens in the movies when the conflicts are worked out?"

A light began to dawn in Brandon's heart. His words came slowly. "They live happily ever after."

"Exactly. And when it's obvious that's where the story is headed, what happens then?"

"When they reach the happily ever after?" Brandon laughed. "Roll credits. Story over." He was suddenly aware of how crazy his feelings had been. "Maybe that's it, then."

"Yeah." Dayne patted his back and grinned. "You've lived in the conflict so long you don't recognize a happy ending when God's giving it to you. When it's rushing up to meet you."

Every uneasy feeling faded like darkness at dawn. "Or walking down the aisle to meet me." Brandon felt the peace of God for the first time that day. "Right?"

"Exactly."

Dayne's words stayed with him while the photographer entered the room and took a couple dozen shots — some serious, some fun — and while the wedding coordinator ushered the guys up the side aisle of the packed church minutes before the ceremony started. As an actor, of course the happily ever after taking place that day would give him a sense that the story was almost over. Now that he understood, he didn't have to fear what he was feeling.

He would hold onto this happy ending with Bailey for as many decades as God would give them.

They took their places at the front of the church and Brandon let the sight settle in around his soul — the view from where he stood, where he would only stand just this one time. Familiar faces looked at him from every section, friends and family and a few other actors and directors and producers. He spotted Cody Coleman near the back with Andi's parents and for a few seconds their eyes met.

Cody smiled politely and gave a slight nod, as if to thank Brandon for allowing him to be here, for understanding that he represented no threat. Not to Bailey and Brandon's love and not to this, their wedding day. Brandon smiled in return, at peace with Cody's presence here and how far they had all come to be in the same place this afternoon. Brandon shifted his gaze to the front row on his side of the church where his parents sat. Together they beamed at him, no longer burdened by the guilt of the past but only grateful to be part of this day.

He breathed in deeply. The church was beautiful, the weeks of careful decision making resulting in a gorgeous center aisle. The satin white bows and scalloped draping from one pew to the next framed the walkway and forced people to enter from the outer aisles. The air smelled of subtle cologne from the guys mixed with the sweetness of the spring flowers on either side of the stage. Their own hand-picked music played through the church speakers, filling Brandon's heart with the promise and depth and enormity of the moment.

The song finishing up now was an old one — a Bryan Adams ballad called "Everything I Do" that Dayne and Katy had used at their wedding. Next was Train's "Marry Me," and Brandon wasn't sure he would hold up, couldn't promise he would keep his composure. Especially when the artist reached the line about asking his girl to marry him today and every day. Brandon felt his throat tighten. That's how he felt, how he would always feel. That he would marry Bailey Flanigan every day for the rest of his life if he could.

He had never been more sure about anything.

As that song ended, another Francesca Battistelli song began to play. The pretty ballad was called "Hundred More Years," a song about wanting moments like this one to never end. It was the cue for the bridesmaids to walk one at a time down the aisle, starting with Bailey's high school friends, and then Katy Hart Matthews and Andi Ellison, one at a time.

Help me hold onto this, Lord . . . every moment.

Brandon felt his eyes well up. Everything seemed to skid into slow motion as the words of the song surrounded them — how the young couple had waited for love and how the decision had been worth it and how together they wanted to feel this same love for a hundred years.

Brandon stood straight, his heart pounding, more aware than ever in his life of the undeserved favor of their loving God.

A hundred more years. Father, that's how I feel. Help me treasure every second, every word, every detail today and over the weeks and months and years. And for the rest of our lives.

After Andi came little Sophie and Devin. Sophie held a small white wicker basket full of rose petals, and Devin carried a white satin pillow. They looked beyond adorable and the reaction from their guests only added to the fact. With his free hand, Devin worked to protect his little cousin, staying at her side, holding her hand and helping her keep balance as she threw flower petals along the runner. But in classic Devin Blake form he also managed to look up at the people watching him and blow a few dramatic kisses. As they reached the front of the church, Devin walked to the second row and left Sophie with John Baxter, as they had planned. Then Devin took his place at the front with the guys.

"Good job," Brandon leaned over and whispered, patting Devin's shoulder.

"Thanks." Devin held the pillow with both hands now. "Good luck on the wedding." His voice wasn't as quiet as Brandon's, and again a ripple of laughter flowed through the pews.

When the crowd settled down, a different song began to play, one Bailey and Brandon had decided on only a week ago for her walk down the aisle. The song Brandon had used to propose to her, the one Brandon had been singing and humming for the past six months: Forever Love.

The words were haunting and unforgettable, setting the mood that something special was about to happen. The audience stood and faced the center aisle. as the song began.

You are my forever love . . .

You are my forever love.

At that moment the church doors opened and from the back Bailey and her father stepped into the sanctuary. Brandon felt tears gather in his eyes, heard the way their family and friends softly gasped at the sight of her. She was a vision, more beautiful than any girl had ever looked on her wedding day or any day. Next to her, Jim Flanigan beamed even as tears slid down his cheeks. Bailey was his only daughter, and Brandon couldn't imagine how difficult this walk was for him. But Brandon barely noticed Bailey's father. As the song built and grew and filled the church, his attention was completely on the girl he was about to marry. The words from the song couldn't have been more fitting — she was truly an angel for him to love the rest of his life.

With everything inside I'll run to you.

'Cause all that I've become I owe to you.

No words could have been more true. She was everything he'd ever needed, far more than he had prayed for. And she was about to be his for all time. Bailey smiled at him and he did the same. She was absolutely stunning, and Brandon knew this was the way she would always look in his mind. Because no matter her appearance in the days and seasons and years to come, he would always see her the way she looked right now.

His one-in-a-million girl. His bride.

As pretty as her veil was, it couldn't hide her eyes, and for that Brandon was grateful. Because in her eyes he saw enough to set his mind at ease. They were filled with long- ing and loving and they were aware of only him as she came closer.

Like the two of them were the only ones in the church.

As she reached him, Brandon became aware of her father again, of what it must feel like in this moment to be finished with the job of raising a daughter. He looked at Jim and the answer came in the quiet tears still on the man's cheeks. He had raised Bailey from the time she was born. He had held her when she cried and read her bedtime stories at night and taught her to ride a bike. Brandon knew because Bailey had told him all of it, everything that made her relationship with her dad as special as the one she shared with her mom. He had bandaged her knees and tended to her broken heart more than a few times. He had cared for her and protected her and provided for her.

And now he would do the hardest thing of all: He would give her away.

Pastor Mark smiled at the congregation as the song finished. "Who gives this woman to be married to this man?"

Jim's eyes were dryer now. He smiled at Bailey and held her gaze for an extra few heartbeats. Then he looked up at the pastor and in a steady voice he said, "Her mother and I." With that, her dad carefully lifted her veil and shared one last look with her. A quick kiss on her cheek and he took her hand and placed it slowly, confidently in Brandon's. There was so much Brandon wanted to say, but this wasn't the time. He mouthed the words, *Thank you.* Jim smiled and gave him a quick wink. Then he turned and sat beside Bailey's mother in the front row. They leaned into each other, wiping at their tears and smiling at the same time, the significance of what had just happened clear in their eyes.

With that Brandon took a deep breath and

turned all his attention on Bailey, his most beautiful bride. He helped her up the few stairs while Andi tended to her train, straightening it so it fanned out behind her.

"You look gorgeous." Brandon's words could only be heard by her and maybe the pastor.

"We're getting married!" She whispered louder than him. Then she raised her brow and her face lit up in a way that brought another happy response from their guests.

Pastor Mark took his spot and smiled at the audience. "Welcome friends, family. I think everyone here knows what a special day this is, and what a rare and beautiful love Bailey and Brandon share."

He went on, talking about God's plan for marriage and the sanctity of the decision to commit to forever. He cited 1 Corinthians 13 and several verses Bailey and Brandon had chosen. Brandon let the words soak into his soul, the truth of God, the strength they would need so they could hold onto what they were feeling right now. Their lives would be built on the Word of God and on faith in Christ. The love they shared would last a lifetime that way.

Their attention was on Pastor Mark, but Brandon caught another glimpse of Bailey and he couldn't believe that in just a few minutes she would be his wife.

While he watched her, while he let himself get lost in her heart and soul and her loving blue eyes, he remembered their love story, every wonderful detail. The way he felt the first time he saw her and how he hadn't known girls like Bailey Flanigan existed. He blinked and she was driving him to the Starbucks near the university and being the kindest friend ever as they ran their scenes for *Unlocked.* And she was sitting beside him at Lake Monroe Beach listening to him as he told her things no one else knew.

No one in all the world.

Pastor Mark kept talking but Brandon stayed wrapped up in Bailey. He could see her opening the door of her house, her shock because he had flown in to help her pack before her move to New York City. And she was flying across the stage in *Hairspray,* lighting up the whole theater with her dancing and singing. She was in his arms at the only prom ever staged on a New York City rooftop and she was kissing him at the top of the Empire State Building. He saw the look on her face when he told her he wasn't leaving, that he would fight for her and wait for her all his life if that's what it took. And when she walked with him along the beach and when she told him yes near a lit-up fire pit last summer.

He blinked again and he saw her as she was here, stunning in the most unbelievable white gown, her face glowing, ready to trust him and love him for life.

The time had come for the vows. Andi held Bailey's bouquet so Brandon could take her hands. The feel of her skin against his only intensified the way he felt, the joy filling everything inside him. They had written the words they would say, and Brandon felt strong and determined as he began. Like there had never been anything in all his life that mattered as much as this moment, that he'd never been as sure about what he was going to say.

"I, Brandon Paul, take you, Bailey Flanigan, to be my wife. I promise to love you and cherish you all the days of my life. When the whole world crashes in and you're sick or afraid or discouraged, I promise to stay beside you and pray for you and remind you of the truth. I promise to lead you, the way God intended."

Bailey's eyes filled with tears. She was clearly struggling not to break down. She sniffed and nodded as a tear slid down her pretty face.

Brandon felt his own eyes blur, felt the tears gather there too. But he didn't cry, didn't let his voice break. The words meant too much to let anything stop him from finishing his promise. His voice rang strong with passion and sincerity as he continued. "I will hold you up when you cannot go another step, and I will remind you what love means when you're tempted to forget. Where you are, I will be, and that place will be our home. Bailey, I consider you God's greatest gift. And so I promise to be faithful to our love and careful with your heart. Until I draw my final breath."

Pastor Mark seemed deeply moved by the emotion of Brandon's words. He looked right at him. "Do you, Brandon, take Bailey as your wife, to love in the power of Jesus Christ for as long as you both shall live?"

"I do." A smile filled Brandon's face as he finished.

Because in all his life he had never meant any words more.

Bailey was trembling, the emotion of the moment almost more than she could take. They both knew each other's vows, but now it was like she was hearing them for the first time. Her turn had come and she felt herself gain control of her heart. She would say these words with strength and conviction, the way Brandon had said them. The way he deserved to hear them.

Holding tight to his hands, she began. "I, Bailey Flanigan, take you, Brandon Paul, to be my husband." She grinned, overcome by the amazing way it felt to say that. "I promise to love you and cherish you all the days of my life. When the whole world crashes in and you're sick or afraid or discouraged, I promise to stay beside you and pray for you and remind you of the truth. I promise to trust you to lead me, the way God intended."

With everything in her, she wanted to hug him before finishing. Because his look of love was beyond what she had ever imagined when she thought about this moment. Instead she drew a steadying breath and continued. "I will hold you up when you cannot go another step, and I will remind you what love means when you're tempted to forget. Where you are, I will be, and that place will be our home." She angled her head slightly, and smiled because she was ready now. If God called them to Los Angeles or to the Philippines or to the moon, she would go. Wherever he was, that's all that mattered. "Brandon, I consider you God's greatest gift. And so I promise to be faithful to our love and careful with your heart. Until I draw my final breath."

Pastor Mark hesitated, his eyes damp. "Okay, then." He looked at Bailey. "Do you, Bailey, take Brandon as your husband, to love in the power of Jesus Christ for as long as you both shall live?"

Bailey looked straight at Brandon, at the man he was and the man she knew he would be as they shared their life together. "I do."

The depth and meaning in the moment made them both lean in closer to each other, no longer aware of the people who filled the church. After a few seconds, Connor walked up to the side of the stage where a microphone was set up, and he sang a song he'd written for the day, a song that had been a surprise until this day. While he sang, Bailey and Brandon walked to a small table where they lit a unity candle and then took communion. Something they had both wanted to include in their ceremony.

Brandon prayed quietly over the moment. "Father, I commit my life to you and to Bailey, my forever love, my wife. Help me be the leader you want me to be, and help us to keep you at the center of our lives and actions and love. For now and always. In Jesus' name, amen."

Connor began to sing the second verse and every word spoke straight to Bailey's soul. The song was called "This Is What Love Looks Like," and Bailey could hear people sniffing and pulling out tissues across the church. It talked about how her parents and his had prayed about this moment all their lives. As the song ended, they returned to their spot at the center of the stage and Andi fluffed out Bailey's train once more. She barely noticed, so caught up in Brandon. God had done this, removed the mountains that once stood between them and He alone had brought them to this day. Brandon moved closer to her, running his thumbs along hers. She could read forever in his eyes and again it made her forget everything around her but him.

Only him.

Pastor Mark's announcement that it was time for the rings was the only thing that brought them back, ready to continue the ceremony. Dayne held Bailey's wedding band — since they'd put a fake ring on the pillow to keep the real one from getting lost. Now he handed it to Brandon while Pastor Mark looked at the congregation. "The ring is a symbol of forever, a symbol of unending love and promise. It has long been a sign of the covenant of marriage, and Bailey and Brandon have chosen to exchange rings as proof of the commitment they are making today."

Bailey held her hand out for Brandon, and she saw that she was no longer shaking. With all her heart, everything she was and would ever be, she wanted this ring, wanted the promise and love and commitment that came with it. She smiled at Brandon and their eyes held, the way they would for all time.

Repeating after the pastor, Brandon slid the ring onto her left finger. "With this ring . . ." he grinned at her, "I thee wed."

Bailey felt dizzy with a sort of joy and happiness she had never known before. It was her turn and she took the wedding band from Andi. Then she turned to Brandon and repeated the simple, traditional vow they'd decided on for this part of the ceremony. She felt her smile filling her face. The celebration was almost at hand. "With this ring, I thee wed."

She could hardly breathe, hardly wait to kiss him and know for now and ever more that she was Brandon Paul's wife.

"All right, then." In a voice full of rich enthusiasm, Pastor Mark looked from Bailey to Brandon and back again. "By the power vested in me by the State of Indiana, I now pronounce you husband and wife." He smiled. "Brandon, you may kiss your bride."

In a slow-motion moment Bailey would feel in her heart as long as she lived, Brandon took her face gently in his hands and kissed her — kissed her in a way that told everyone in the church and God Almighty that he would never let her go. Not as long as they lived. The kiss must've lasted a few seconds longer than usual, because the next thing Bailey heard was a wave of soft laughter from their guests.

They drew back and then hugged once more before turning to their friends and family, who were on their feet clapping and cheering and wiping away tears. Bailey and Brandon were married and ready for a lifetime together. And so they celebrated out loud because in that moment every single person in the church understood what Brandon and Bailey already knew, what Connor had sung about and Pastor Mark had talked about.

This was what love looked like.

THIRTY-ONE

In the limo on the way to the reception, when they were finally alone, Bailey leaned on her husband and tried to believe this wasn't a dream. "That was beautiful." She smiled at him. "Beyond what I imagined."

"It was perfect." Miraculously, they'd kept the paparazzi from crashing their wedding, thanks to Brandon's careful planning. Now he took her in his arms. "But not as perfect as you." He kissed her, tenderly and deeply without holding back. They were both breathless as he moved his lips lightly onto her cheekbone and whispered, "Have I mentioned," his lips found hers once more, "I can't wait for the honeymoon?"

The anticipation made her head spin and her body anxious for the time later that night when they could be together. Fully and completely together. "I can't wait. In fact," she returned his kiss, working her fingers along the side of his face and into his dark hair, "I have a feeling about to-night."

"Mmm, you do?" Brandon kissed her neck and then searched her eyes. "Tell me."

She could feel the passion in her eyes and she was grateful for the privacy glass that separated them from the driver. "I have a feeling it'll be worth the wait."

Brandon's expression told her he couldn't agree more. He sat back in his seat and closed his eyes for a few seconds. "Okay. Think about the reception. That's what I'm telling myself."

They fell onto each other laughing, and they were still lost in their own world when they arrived on the campus of Indiana University and headed into the Grand Ballroom. They saw Bailey's mom first, just inside the double doors. "The ceremony was so wonderful." She hugged Bailey and then Brandon. "Congratulations."

Bailey hugged her mom. "Thank you for this. It's a fairytale."

"It's what you deserve." She hesitated for a moment, their eyes holding. "Okay, so I'll let the emcee know you're here. Wait till he announces you before you come in." Her face looked like Christmas morning. "This is going to be amazing. I'll see you inside."

Brandon slipped his arm around Bailey's

waist and whispered to her, "We have to be serious now."

"Hmm." She gave him a flirty grin and brushed her face against his. "Not too serious."

As the emcee announced them to their guests, Brandon and Bailey held hands and walked inside. The bridal party had already been announced and they were seated at the head table. Bailey felt like she was walking onto a breathtaking movie set, because every detail of the ballroom looked beyond magical. Twinkling lights covered every post and railing, and the ceiling was draped with billowy white batiste cloth, underneath which additional rows of lights created a starry night sky effect.

Bailey made a point to savor the moments: the prayer by her dad before the meal and the music and conversation and laughter that played in the background while they ate with their guests. As dinner wound down, Andi and Dayne took turns toasting them. Andi went first. She faced the guests and for a long while she looked at Bailey.

"I've known Bailey since our days at Indiana University." That's as far as she got before her voice broke. For a moment she hung her head and put her hand to her mouth. She struggled for a few seconds and

Bailey fought the urge to go to her, hug her, and assure her that it was okay to feel, okay to cry. But before she could act on her thought, Andi looked up again and smiled through her tears. "Sorry." She paused. "No one has been a better friend to me than Bailey Flanigan. She's always been there for me," once more she turned to Bailey, "even when the situation was hard."

Bailey felt tears in her own eyes, and beside her Brandon slipped his arm around her shoulders. They all knew the hard times Andi was referring to, and how God had led them past that situation.

Andi turned to the front of the room again. "I've prayed for her and she's prayed for me more times than I can count. I can remember praying that God would bring her the perfect guy, the one He had created just for her." She gave a quick smile to Bailey and Brandon. "After watching the way Brandon loved her — right from the beginning — I was convinced he was that guy. And now, Bailey and Brandon . . . I wish you God's greatest blessings as you begin your life together."

Dayne's words for Brandon were shorter and with the depth and humor that marked their relationship. "Brandon, you are a changed man since you met Bailey. God used her to bring you closer to Him, and now God will use you to lead her and love her." He grinned at them. "I'm just glad you found her a real ring. That seaweed one wouldn't have lasted."

Everyone laughed and toasted sparkling cider — the way Bailey and Brandon had requested.

Their first dance was next, and Brandon carefully led her onto the floor as their song began to play. The song was Steven Curtis Chapman's "I Will Be Here," and it defined the promise and commitment that marked this day.

In Brandon's arms Bailey felt safe and sure, and once more her awareness of the people around them faded and there was only her and Brandon. Always her and Brandon. He was a good dancer, something she had learned the first time on the rooftop of the Keller's apartment building. Now, every step of their first dance as husband and wife felt etched on her heart, where it would stay as long as she lived. The moment was that beautiful.

The rest of the wedding party joined them on the floor, and for the next half hour the dancing changed from sentimental to celebration. The break that followed gave them time to cut the cake while their family and friends gathered around. Brandon had threatened to make the moment messy, but in the end they both took the gentle approach and shared a kiss afterward that led the ballroom to erupt in a round of whistles and applause.

After everyone ate dessert, Bailey joined the single girls on the dance floor and threw her bouquet, which was caught by Maddie — Brooke's daughter. As she left the dance floor Bailey walked alongside Andi. "It should've been you."

"Aww, thanks." Andi gave her a side hug.

And then — for the first time that day — it occurred to Bailey that Cody Coleman was here.

That somewhere in the room and, for that matter, somewhere back at the church, the guy she had cared for so deeply for so many years was actually here as Andi's date. The realization was both telling and freeing. Because if she'd thought about Cody before this moment she might've wondered at herself. Whether she had really moved on from the memory of him.

But the truth was she'd moved on a long time ago. She looked around the room and spotted him, making his way to the dance floor where Brandon was about to toss the garter to the sea of single guys. He looked older, more filled out, more confident. He wasn't watching her, didn't seem to notice her in that moment any more than she had noticed him the whole day to this point.

Andi was still beside her. "He wants to catch it," she laughed. Then she gave Bailey a more serious look. "Thanks for letting him come." She glanced from the head table back to Bailey. "Do you mind if I sit with him and my parents now?"

"Not at all." Joy filled her at the thought of Andi with Cody, how right it was and how happy they were. "We're finished at the head table anyway."

They watched as Brandon flung the garter and Connor snagged it before Cody or anyone else could. He held it up like a trophy and then smiled for the photographer while the other guys patted his back and teased him about being next.

The emcee announced that the next dance would be for the bride and her father. Bailey immediately looked across the room at her dad. Like he promised, he had stayed close by. Several times she had met his eyes from her place at the head table and always she was glad that this part of her special day wasn't like her favorite movie. She didn't want her dad to miss a thing.

Like every other detail, Bailey had this

part of her wedding planned long ago. The father-daughter dance was to Bob Carlisle's "Butterfly Kisses" and tears gathered in Bailey's eyes even before she and her dad met on the dance floor. He took her in his arms and for a long time, as the music spoke of a daddy's love for his daughter, he could only look at her, his own eyes full of unshed tears. The music told what felt like the story of her life with her father. The bedtime prayers and pony rides and funny moments. But always her hug every morning, and butterfly kisses at night.

Partway through the song, he seemed to compose himself. "I'm proud of you, Bailey."

The little girl she would in some ways always be could hardly believe this moment was here. "You've been the best daddy ever."

"I tried." He hugged her, the dance still playing out. As he drew back he smiled at her. "This part of the song . . . it always makes me cry."

"Me too."

The song talked about this being the day she would change her name, the day he would give her away, the feeling that as the wedding approached he was losing his little girl. And just like that their moment was over. Brandon and his mother joined them for the next song. With all the key events of the reception behind them, the band launched into a playlist of fast and slow songs that kept the party going. Brandon found her after his dance with his mother and he whispered close to her. "We need to go around and thank everyone for coming."

They had planned for this, and going from one table to another went smoothly and easily, faster than the old-fashioned receiving lines for sure. Not until they reached the Ellisons' table did Bailey remember once more that Cody was there. She and Brandon approached their table, hand in hand, and thanked everyone for coming. Some of the guests had stood and hugged them, while others had shook their hands or simply smiled and nodded in their direction.

Bailey held her breath waiting to see how this would go, and she was glad when Keith and Lisa Ellison took the lead, smiling and congratulating Brandon and Bailey from their seats. Bailey didn't look in Cody's direction until she had to, until the exchange with the Ellisons was clearly over. At that exact moment, one of the other bridesmaids called Andi over to another table, which left Cody by himself. Brandon looked his way first. "Hey, man, glad you could come." He held out his hand and Cody stood and shook it.

"Congratulations." Cody's smile was sincere. "Thanks for having me."

Bailey felt a sudden and deep sorrow, a sadness she couldn't put into words. Not because she still loved Cody or because she wished he were the one standing beside her. But because the moment felt distant. Different. But then Cody looked at her — and in the time it took for her heart to beat, the distance was gone. They couldn't have held that look for more than a couple seconds, but it was long enough for her to know how deeply Cody cared, how his love for her — though different now — would always remain.

"Congratulations, Bailey." He didn't look away, but his tone was proof of his absolute sincerity. "I'm happy for you."

"Thanks." Bailey's eyes were dry, her heart at peace with this new place they'd found. "You and Andi . . . we're happy for you too."

He smiled, and there was no question about his feelings for Andi Ellison. The look in his eyes at the thought of her was different than any look he'd ever had for Bailey. Further proof that these were the plans God had for each of them. Separate plans.

Brandon gave her hand a slight squeeze.

"Hey, well, thanks again. We're going to say hi to a few other folks."

"Yes," Bailey was easily pulled from the moment. "Thanks." And like that they moved on to the next table.

Through the rest of the night, Bailey only thought about Cody when he was on the dance floor with Andi, and then only to smile at the way they looked together. Like God was up to something wonderful with the two of them. The last hour of the party slipped away and their friends and family gathered around to see them off. Bailey and Brandon said goodbye to his parents and they found a quick moment with her parents, to thank them for the wedding.

"Your love is our example," Brandon told Bailey's dad. They shared hugs and then hurried out the door down a pathway through the guests, all of whom held lit sparklers. Tin cans and washable car paint decorated their getaway limo, and as Bailey and Brandon stepped inside and shut the door they both looked at each other.

"We're married." Brandon looked completely captivated, mesmerized by her. "You're my wife, Bailey."

"You're my husband."

"And we're headed to Fiji!"

They came together in a kiss that promised much about the coming days. "It's a dream, Brandon." She searched his eyes, knowing his heart and soul like they were her own. "All of it's a dream."

Before another moment went by Brandon prayed for them, thanking God for letting him film *Unlocked* and for giving them a friendship first and for the salvation that would guarantee them an eternity together. And finally he thanked God for the one thing they had waited a lifetime for.

Their very own happy ending.

READER LETTER

Dear Friends,

As a novelist, the Bailey Flanigan Series has taken me on the craziest journey of all. From the beginning, the character of Bailey Flanigan was inspired by my own daughter, Kelsey. Not so much her actual life, but her kind heart for others and her genuine love for God, her desire to remain pure and her belief that the Lord had great plans for her life. Also, Bailey shared Kelsey's determination to wait for a godly man before she truly fell in love. The man God had set apart for her.

Of course, for many of you, this resemblance between the fictional Bailey and the real-life Kelsey comes as no surprise. Because the entire Flanigan family was inspired by the real life that happens between our four walls every day. Nothing in all my life has ever or will ever compare with the sweet joy of writing about these fictional people and injecting real-life personalities, stories, and details along the way. From the beginning I could see those similarities and how they would play out in this series.

But I never could've seen the way real life would mirror the story lines in each book. As I wrote *Leaving,* the first book in the Bailey Flanigan Series, Kelsey was headed off to California for college. Something she hadn't planned to do. And here, as I finished writing *Loving,* we are planning Kelsey's wedding to Kyle, the young man we've been praying for since Kelsey was born. A year ago the two of them had only just met, and even as we shot the cover of this book, a wedding was the furthest thing from our minds. I love how God surprises us that way, and I can only say it made the emotional writing of this book very, very close to home.

Anyway, thanks for joining me on the journey of Bailey Flanigan . . . and yes, the journey of one more ride with the Baxter Family. As always, I look forward to your feedback. Take a minute and find me on Facebook! I'm there at least once a day — hanging out with you in my virtual living room, praying for you, and answering as many questions as possible. On Facebook, I have Latte Time, where I'll take a half hour or so, pour all of you a virtual latte, and take questions live and in person. A couple hundred thousand of us hang out and have a blast together. So come on over and "like" my Facebook Fan Page. You all are very special to me.

Also visit my website at www.KarenKings bury.com. There you can find my contact information and my guestbook. Remember, if you post something on my Facebook or my website, it may help another reader, so thanks for stopping by. In addition, I love to hear how God is using these books in your life. He puts a story on my heart, but He has your heart in mind.

Only He could do that.

Also on Facebook or my website, you can check out my upcoming events and find out about movies being made about my books. Post prayer requests on my website or read those already posted and pray for those in need. If you'd like, you may send in a photo of your loved one serving our country, or let us know about a fallen soldier we can honor on our Fallen Heroes page.

When you're finished with this book, pass it on to someone else. If you let me know, you will automatically be entered to win a signed novel through my "Shared a Book" contest. Email me at contest@KarenKings bury.com and tell me the first name of the person you shared with! In addition, everyone who is signed up for my monthly newsletter through my website is automatically entered into an ongoing once-a-month drawing for a free, signed copy of my latest novel.

There are links on my website that will help you with matters that are important to you — faith and family, adoption and redemption. Of course, on my site you can also find out a little more about me, my faith and family, the writing process, and the wonderful world of Life-Changing Fiction™.

Also follow me on Twitter, where I have an ongoing "Tweet a KK Quote" contest. You tweet a quote from one of my books and include my Twitter name — @Karen Kingsbury — and the book title. I retweet many of these throughout the week, and will give away a signed book to a winner every Monday.

Finally, if you gave your life over to God during the reading of this book, or if you found your way back to faith in Him, please know I'm praying for you. Tell me about your life-change by sending me a letter to office@KarenKingsbury.com. Write "New Life" in the subject line. If this is your situation, I encourage you to connect with a Bible-believing church in your area, pray for God's leading, and start reading the Bible. But if you can't afford one and don't already have one, write "Bible" in the subject line. Tell me how God used this novel to change your life, and then include your address in your email. If you are financially unable to find a Bible any other way, I will send you one.

One last thing. I will donate a book to any high school or middle school librarian who makes a request. Check out my website for details.

Again, thanks for journeying with me through the pages of this book. I can't wait to hear your feedback on *Loving!* Oh, and look for my biggest Baxter Family book to date later this year: The Baxter Family — *Coming Home.*

Until then, keep your eyes on the cross.

In His light and love,
Karen Kingsbury
www.KarenKingsbury.com

DISCUSSION QUESTIONS

1. Did you hope Bailey would end up marrying Brandon or Cody? Explain your feelings.

2. Why do you think Bailey ended up deciding Cody wasn't the right guy for her?

3. Why do you think Cody ended up deciding Bailey wasn't the right girl for him?

4. How do you feel about Cody finding a relationship with Andi?

5. Andi has a broken past, same as Cody. Why is their story so important for people reading this story? Explain what you know about God's grace and forgiveness in your own life?

6. Did you have a Cody or Bailey type character in your teenage years? What hap-

pened to that person?

7. How has God led you to the place where you are today?

8. True love makes sacrifices for each other. How did Bailey and Brandon sacrifice for each other?

9. How did Bailey sacrifice for her friendship with Andi?

10. Talk about a time in your life when someone hurt you, and when forgiveness brought healing to the situation.

11. What did you think about the reconciliation between Brandon and his parents? Have you ever seen something like that in your own life or the lives of one of your friends or family members? Discuss that situation and how it turned out.

12. Read Colossians 3:13. Jesus tells us to bear with each other and forgive each other. When have you seen this truth work in your life or the lives of others? Discuss this.

13. People refer to 1 Corinthians 13 in the

Bible as the "love chapter." Read it now. What stands out to you about the idea of loving the people in your life?

14. How have you seen the idea that love always hopes at work in your life?

15. How about the idea that love always perseveres? Give specific examples.

16. And finally, talk about how love never fails and how you have seen that at work in your life or the lives of those around you.

17. The song "Forever Love" speaks of the love God has for us, but also the love we might have for our spouse. What does the idea of Forever Love mean to you?

18. How would you have written the ending to Bailey Flanigan's story? What do you think the future will look like for Bailey and Brandon?

19. Tell about a special wedding in your life. What were the details you remember and why were they special?

20. If you could give Bailey any advice

about married life, what would you tell
her? Be specific.

ABOUT THE AUTHOR

New York Times bestselling author **Karen Kingsbury** is America' favorite inspirational novelist, with over fifteen million books in print. Her Life-Changing Fiction™ has produced multiple bestsellers, including *Learning, Leaving, Take One, Between Sundays, Even Now, One Tuesday Morning, Beyond Tuesday Morning,* and *Ever After,* which was named the 2007 Christian Book of the Year. An award-winning author and newly published songwriter, Karen has several movies optioned for production, and her novel *Like Dandelion Dust* was made into a major motion picture and is now available on DVD. Karen is also a nationally known speaker with several women's groups. She lives in Nashville with her husband, Don, and together they have six children, three of whom were adopted from Haiti. You can find out more about Karen, her books, and her appearance schedule at www.Karen Kingsbury.com.

The employees of Thorndike Press hope you have enjoyed this Large Print book. All our Thorndike, Wheeler, and Kennebec Large Print titles are designed for easy reading, and all our books are made to last. Other Thorndike Press Large Print books are available at your library, through selected bookstores, or directly from us.

For information about titles, please call:
  (800) 223-1244

or visit our Web site at:
  http://gale.cengage.com/thorndike

To share your comments, please write:
  Publisher
  Thorndike Press
  10 Water St., Suite 310
  Waterville, ME 04901